Early praise for *We Are Not in the World*

'Haunting, mesmerising, and so deeply intelligent about the interwoven strengths and frailties of the human heart.'
Kamila Shamsie

'Wonderful, wrenching . . . full of enormous feelings very precisely rendered.'
Sara Baume

'Beautifully drawn in its observation of relationships, intimacy, love and the fragility of family. Unusual, utterly original and mysterious, O'Callaghan is a stunningly good writer.'
Elaine Feeney

'Shot through with poetry, a sad and stunning meditation on love and grief.'
Jan Carson

'A whirlpool of memories, regrets and hopes.'
Tim Pears

We Are Not in the World

CONOR O'CALLAGHAN

doubleday

TRANSWORLD PUBLISHERS
61–63 Uxbridge Road, London W5 5SA
www.penguin.co.uk

Transworld is part of the Penguin Random House group of companies
whose addresses can be found at global.penguinrandomhouse.com

First published in Great Britain in 2020 by Doubleday
an imprint of Transworld Publishers

A CIP catalogue record for this book is available from
the British Library

ISBNs
9780857526854 (hb)
9781781620533 (tpb)

Typeset in 10/16pt Haarlemmer MT Pro
by Integra Software Services Pvt. Ltd, Pondicherry.

Printed and bound in Great Britain by Clays Ltd, Elcograf S.p.A.

Penguin Random House is committed to a sustainable future for
our business, our readers and our planet. This book is made from
Forest Stewardship Council® certified paper.

1 3 5 7 9 10 8 6 4 2

We Are Not in the World

Wednesday

This is it, she says.

No less.

Clearance to enter cockpit?

Clearance pending.

Paddy . . .

She is: behind me on the other side of the bunk's shut curtain, twentysomething, not supposed to be here. I am: in the driver's seat, officially alone, on the lam.

It's a disgrace, she says.

Is it?

Big time.

Hold fire, there's a good girl.

Some of us are dying in here, she says. She adds nothing for a bit. Then: Is this really necessary?

Please.

If you must, she says.

S'il vous plaît.

No less.

Vær så snill.

I can hear her laughing in on her bunk.

The latter being?

Norwegian.

Aren't you the dark horse, she says.

Smattering of the old Norske.

Les Miserables!

Who dat? she says.

Nobody.

Time does then what time always does. It passes. After time has passed, she resumes.

And do you know what else it is?

I don't.

It's like the confessional, she says.

What is?

This. This me this side, this you that side and this thin veil between.

She says those final three words like objects being handled with care, someone else's property.

Bless me, Father, for I have!

Sinned? I have.

You sure have, she says. And how long has it been?

Since my last confession?

Give it a shot, ballpark figure.

Oh thirty years.

Jesus!

Thirty years. Thirty years and then some.

Now that really is a disgrace, she says.

It is.

An act of contrition is sorely required.

You have all the lingo, petal.

Amn't I blue in the face saying it?

Chocks away.

For real?

Movement ahead.

Thank crap for that, she says.

Then when we're clear and hit open country.

I can slip through?

I see no reason.

The relief, she says.

But until such eventuality, I need to request.

I sit tight and keep schtum?

Vær så snill.

Remind me.

The cargo door opens. It opens incrementally. It falls forward, away from us, into foreign day. There are men down there, stevedores in hi-viz and hardhats shouting to one another. I rotate the ignition to halfway, to check for evidence of light. The instrument panel flashes and falls still. There are chains. There is shrieking of iron like gates of hell. Then this fluorescence gradually floods the floor between rows and creeps towards us and feels warm.

We've been in black this past half hour. We've been blathering the glossolalia that she and I have been wont to blather years now. Lovely, hollow soap bubbles blown in one another's faces. Me up front, her in the bunk at my back. We've come this far without anyone knowing that she's in here, with me. Now this: this square of extravagant light at the far end of the hold and people shouting and distant semaphore and hundreds of engines revving at once. I love this.

You always say that, she says.

Did I say that? Increasingly, I can't tell the difference between what I think and what I say. And she has spent so long with me alone that she has a hard time not responding to those things I think I think only.

You always say you love this, she says, this moment when.

She remembers right. American high school holidays gave us two uninterrupted months back in Ireland. A few of those summers, weary of extended rain and family, we rented a campervan and toured the continent. Of every ferry crossing, when she and I and her mom were still an item, this was my favourite bit. The cargo hold opening and men bellowing above the roar, all the vehicles starting up and sidling out in lines and separating into a whole continent of heat the way blown dandelion seed scatters in hundreds and thousands on the wind.

I do. I love this.

Me too, she says. Will it take forever?

Will what take?

This. This disembarkation. This pretending not to be here.

Last on, love.

Last off? she says.

Last to embark at Dover we were. We were in good time. We missed the traffic and checked in with hours to spare. But we were flagged to one side out of the line. She asked from within what was happening and I made explaining look like I was talking to myself or mumbling a song. We were made to wait while all other haulage disappeared into the hull. A guy with clipboard and walkie-talkie instructed me to climb down. What's the problem? I couldn't hear a word. I was signalled towards a prefab cabin on the water's edge.

An obese supervisor sat in a fold-out camping chair under an orange skylight, the glow of several screens in front of him. His feet scarcely reached ground. I wasn't sure if he realized that I was there and I almost said something before he spoke without looking up. I was taking on Howard's Volvo, was I? Only till Howard got back on his feet. He shook his head. He had a bag of sunflower seeds on the side. He kept typing with one hand and eating with the other and glancing back and forth between screens. All very sad, he said. When he added nothing to that and typed more with one finger and seemed to forget that I was there, I said Carl would be taking care of me. He looked up then.

I assumed that he knew Carl as well. I assumed that, did I? He said 'assumed' like he'd run a magic marker through the word. Did I know what 'assumed' made? Of you, of me . . . I did, but acted like I didn't. He referred to Carl as Mr O'Neill. He knew Mr O'Neill however many years. He inspected my paperwork, my tachographs. He looked peeved that everything was in order. And I was travelling solo? An icicle trickled down my side ribs. All alone. And it would be just the six days? Very wise. The key was to do as few miles as possible with an empty load. Far less control with an empty load. He handed back my papers.

No pressure, she says.

We're still waiting to be flagged into motion. It can't be soon. The real hauliers are standing down, doors hanging open, signing to one another over the roar. Sitting in gear, with the ignition to halfway and the instrument panel flashing, is for amateurs. Real hauliers hold off until the very last, slip all at once out of sight like stagehands, are in motion within seconds.

No pressure!

Fuck. Off.

The trucks, in lines, start inching into the glare. Our row moves too. I check for the umpteenth time. Drive. Thumb on the handbrake's release button. The brake lights in front go dark and edge away. Handbrake released. Nothing. We get honked. I rest my head on the wheel.

Wakey wakey, she says. Year please?

Two thousand and fifteen.

There you go, she says. Day and month?

I look up. Second Wednesday of August. I say that too. I mumble the training litany from memory. Neutral, back to Drive, release handbrake.

We move. Very gingerly, but move we do. There's that moment when the cab, after its rest in a stationary position, reconnects with its load. Like memory and forgetting. There are a couple of millimetres of slack, when the truck's cab is moving and the truck's load isn't, before the engine is forced to remember the weight it's here to tow. And then the weight moves with us. Every time we stop for some minor bottleneck ahead, the load bumps minutely against the cab. The welded threshold, where vessel gives onto solid ground, necessitates an extra push of juice. The light without, after all this black, is blinding.

Wow!

She must be peering through a slight partition. I bark 'Stay put!' louder than I mean to.

Much more like it, she says.

The douaniers are shooting the breeze in the shadow of an inspection awning. They don't seem especially bothered. Carl said that the haulage line usually crawls. Weighing stations and what have you. Today seems brisker than I expected. We are at least moving. Traffic departing north across the Channel is at a standstill. The tailback goes as far as the eye can see. The undercarriage of every seabound artic is having several torches shone into it. The authorities don't seem interested in us. I let down the driver's window. Air enters, but the din is overwhelming and all about us. Only a handful of disembarking trucks get searched. It takes a while, but even we slip through and with the bare minimum of inspection.

The road is lined with wire fencing, fingers pushed through, faces pressed against. Behind them, waves of tents and shacks. The fence is staring at us. And we're trying not to make eye contact, with the fence. A truck with an Irish reg gets pulled out of the contraflow. Live bodies, one by one, are prised from its chassis.

Not far beyond the clearance area we park in a layby. No familiar trucks in the immediate vicinity. Carl was on an earlier crossing. The coast is clear. I say so. Nothing back. The coast is clear, I tell her, she can come through.

The nylon of her sleeping bag rustles. I hear my daughter groan. The curtains part. She peers through like one woken from sleep decades-long. She was in there the whole crossing and is now complaining that her legs no longer work. And still she manages to drag herself through the slit, footling, rotating as she re-enters the world backwards. Black hair shaved to bristle. Tartan jeans, magenta mohair jumper off one shoulder, aquamarine bra strap, a tatt of barbed wire and rose thorns around her upper arm, green Docs. She never changes and lately smells not great. She seems more amused than anyone by her Lazarus routine. She rubs one eye with her knuckle and, as if it's me making her smirk in spite of her best efforts not to, whines:

What?

Quite the performance.

Oh really, she says.

She remembers that she said the same phrase to me. She remembers when. I know she does by the way she glances up and dark clouds materialize on her horizon. I have mentioned the thing, her thing, we never mention.

She went through her difficult teens with a mane of purest black down her spine. She got it all cut off a couple of years ago and now never lets it longer than a tennis ball. I miss her hair – its gloss, its black so black it bordered blue – yet love the duller suede of her buzz cut. My little refugee, I called her once. No way was she having that. My petite hooligan. Me? I have a hard time not running my hand over her head.

Would someone like me to carry her?

You're grand, she says. She grins a little and insincerely. Thanks all the same.

She kneels on the passenger seat and scrolls her window down and asks where all the noise is coming from. She pulls the catch. She jumps down onto the layby's patch of grass. She yawns theatrically, shades her eyes from the sun. Twenty yards up the layby, a campervan is taking its poodle for a pee in the grass. She's way past carrying. We both know that. Must be ten years since I picked her up. I don't remember when. If I'd known, I would have told myself then never to forget. She effects, down there on the verge, these daft stretches that she calls her tai chi.

Quit.

What?

Making a scene.

This? She keeps doing it. Nobody can see me.

She grabs the mink that she found in my mother's armoire at home and now wears pretty constantly. She throws that over her shoulders. Its pelt gleams like polythene in this light. We take a footbridge across the main dual carriageway out of town. We pause halfway. The nearest horizon resembles a mass dump, a mound of gulls and tatters. Beyond that is the ferry terminal. Beyond that the Channel's azure speckled with yachts.

This is mad, she says.

Good mad?

Good mad.

There's a German discount supermarket the other side. The cool within is delicious. I pick for both of us. I find body mist when she's in a parallel aisle. The only item that she has chosen for herself is a pack of mints. Between us we fill a basket, mostly of non-perishables for the road, water for the icebox under the bunks. She says what a novelty standing in line and paying is. I pretend to ignore. We carry armfuls out to the nearest wall. I eat. She prises apart and peers inside the half-sandwich that I've forced upon her and places a mint on her tongue as if it were communion wafer.

What's going on? she says.

Refugees? Some such.

All these people.

Families drift around, all worldly goods in tow. Children bare-foot and crying, parents carrying everything. They all seem part of this floor of noise that's everywhere and nowhere in particular. For me, I say. She looks askance. I nod towards her sandwich. At least eat a little, I mean, for my sake if not your own. She does an elaborate swallow. She flattens the sandwich hard between palms. She begins.

Whither the plan, big guy?

She knows I hate her calling me that. I won't rise to her bait.

Short term? We wend our merry way out of this particular circle of hell, ideally without being stopped. Thereafter we hit the northern rim of Paris before sundown, check in with Carl in some pre-ordained routier. Thereafter egg, chips, bed. Long term? The two of us on the road, with only the occasional incoming or out-going text to maintain radio contact and to stave off all search parties.

Roger Wilco, she says. Six days?

Six days minimum.

Meaning?

We may investigate the possibility of stringing it out. Not a dicky bird.

Seriously? she says. She stares bewildered into middle distance. Who am I gonna tell?

Your mom?

You really worry me, she says quietly. You know that?

I know nothing.

We get approached. A desperate creature, one hand extended towards us. He's very slight and dark. Torn beige slacks and shirt-sleeves that together must once have formed a suit. He mumbles language that we don't exactly understand. We do what we always do: we say back language that he doesn't understand, we shrug to indicate that we have no money either. And yet we have in our hands sandwiches bought not twenty minutes ago and he can see that. He pleads once more. We shake our heads once more.

The world coming to an end? she says.

So it would appear.

Why didn't you just?

Give him something?

Yeah.

This hurts, this being seen by her lying to a man with no money. Why didn't *she* just?

I have no need of money, she says, and therefore have none.

Very zen, I'm sure.

Nada, zero, diddly squat.

The once I do feel into my pocket for loose change – part response to her guilt-tripping and part horror at the degree of desperation before us – other desperate souls flock around. She looks scared. A boy of two or about, vest and disposable nappy and beautiful black eyes, barnacles himself to my lower leg. He has done this before. He knows how and what works. He will surely many times again. I can feel his tiny bones clamped around my shin and calf. He's screaming for mercy. Mine. A crowd gathers until a bulletproof vest pushes through and prises the boy unceremoniously from me. The bulletproof vest turns on us and snaps rapid fire of which *naïf* is the only scrap I catch. My mother would have understood him. I want to say that. Speak to her, she'll follow. Instead, I hold hands aloft. He moves on, locked firearm cradled diagonally across vest, spitting double Dutch.

Shall we, darling?

Oh yes, she says. Let's.

We don't take the footbridge back. All ferry-bound traffic is at a standstill and can be drifted among at will. It resembles the carpark of some festival, the windows lowered and the music up loud and the banter between lanes. The far side, the outbound current, is moving more freely. Fast enough that we have to pause on a triangular island of grass, in the cool shade of the footbridge, before taking our chances and dashing across. Our cab's inside is stifling. She can stay up front. I tell her that she can. We're beyond anybody's caring now. We keep windows down until the aircon kicks in.

I miss something? she says. Is the world actually ending?

Where have you been?

The hard shoulder is lined with families straggling the opposite direction, to heaven knows where. Their arms are full. Some pushing supermarket trolleys. It's like we're drifting through one of the reports on the evening news. It takes the guts of an hour to get clear and accelerate into open road. Still they keep coming, from all angles, dribs and drabs on the margins of three-lane autoroute. We're silent mostly, lost in the same thought that she thought first. Has there been an apocalypse they're fleeing from? Are we, unwittingly, driving towards the eye of some hurricane that made landfall while we slept?

How are you feeling?

Grand, she says, not a bother.

Pas-de-Calais is pretty nondescript. Like one long industrial estate. Only occasionally does land rise and give way enough to something closer to what we might have expected: village, river, plane trees.

Banjaxed?

Am I?

Tired?

I didn't do that on purpose. The word that I used is one from home. She was born in Ireland, during a two-year jobless spell when we were living in the summer house of her mom's family, but she spent most of her childhood across the Atlantic. Now she thinks that I occasionally slip in certain picayune phrases to exclude her. And maybe sometimes I do. I just didn't do it now.

Bit all right, she says.

Bound to be.

Stop fretting.

She's filming the passing countryside, such that it is, as she speaks. She holds her phone to the windscreen and records in thirty-second snippets and reviews each and discards most.

It won't work if you fret all the time, she says.

I can see that.

My locked screen lights on our dash and displays a text in its entirety.

> Left a few voicemails.
> Be good to talk. All in
> your own etcetera. A

My brother. I never listen to voicemails. All in my own what? Time, is my guess. The locked screen darks out.

Who are these for?

These?

Little films you keeping filming.

Just me, she says. And this person we're meeting is who when he's at home?

I'm meeting.

You're meeting, she says.

Carl.

And Carl being?

Our guardian, chum of Howard.

And Howard being?

The man who owns the wagon in which you are presently and clandestinely riding shotgun.

Fair play, she says. And we know Howard how?

Howard how?

Her phone shakes. She shouts at me to stop making her laugh. She calls me Paddy. I prefer Paddy to big guy. She aborts filming.

She presses the red square and scrolls backwards with her middle finger and swears at me.

We know Howard through darts league.

Did she hear me say that last bit? She recommences filming. Darts was the community of sorts that I stumbled upon in an English city in which I knew nobody. It passed a few northern winters. I pretended to belong more than I did, to be something that I really wasn't.

A month ago I sat in the front room of Howard's thirties semi in Salford. This was a meeting arranged weeks in advance, so that Howard could act as broker between me and Carl. A month ago this was.

I walked the handful of miles out from my apartment downtown. Pauline answered. Howard was in the front room by himself. Howard said that it was best not to talk specifics until Carl got there. I was in no rush. Did I know Carl? Carl wasn't much of a darts player, Howard said, just liked the company. Carl was more spiritual.

The TV was on, but the light of evening flooding through their west-facing bay made seeing difficult. Howard asked about my season. I missed half of it. He said sorry for not making a prizegiving night that I hadn't attended either. I asked Howard about his treatment. He was just knackered most of the time. He turned up the volume on the news to hear people in rafts within screaming distance of some luxury beach resort on the Adriatic. Howard muttered 'Christ alive . . .' and hit standby.

Carl let himself in. We could hear him in the hall. That'll be Carlos, Howard said. Then we could hear Pauline's voice greeting Carl from the kitchen, and the pair of them discussing the patient. Howard smiled tiredly. When Carl slipped through, he was softly spoken in a way that felt second-hand. Like Carl had once seen someone else speak softly in the company of a person who was poorly and had decided that he would do likewise whenever he found himself in a similar situation. Carl seemed to fill the room. Pauline flicked on the overhead light and said that she would leave us to it.

Carl wore a leather jacket of shiny chestnut brown. Its cuffs were unbuttoned and turned up and lined with cotton print of forget-me-not blue. Early sixties at a guess. A miniature mohawk and reading specs on a string. Carl hugged and sort of fell on top of Howard at once and stayed there on the sofa. They were leaning against one another, speaking news, football gossip that meant zilch to me. One United, the other City. Then Howard nodded across the room, at me. Then Howard spoke to Carl, of me.

Since Howard's trusty Volvo was lying idle, and since I had the licence, we had agreed that I would take his wagon on the road and that we'd split all proceeds. See how that worked. But we had also agreed, due to my lack of experience, that I'd need some chaperoning to begin with.

Carl looked at me, appraised me, while Howard spoke. Carl possibly knew me, Howard said, from darts. I'd seen Carl a few times and was about to say so when Carl shook his head and said that he hadn't made as many league rounds last season as he would've liked. Carl didn't recognize me from Adam.

Howard said that Carlos was his oldest pal. I would be in good hands.

So you'll be answerable to Carl, Howard said by way of conclusion. At all times. On the road.

When Howard tapered off, out of a fatigue that was almost tangible, Carl sniffed the stale air between us and folded arms so that the leather of his jacket squeaked. Carl appeared not to like what he beheld.

This scheme of Howard's was clearly out of the regular run. Where to begin? Carl addressed me. Not my usual game, this? You could say. What was then, my usual game? This and that, desk work, bits of supply teaching. I was hardly going to tell the truth. And how had I come by the licence? Employment scheme in the early nineties, back in Ireland, before the boom. And the crash, Carl said with some satisfaction, and the crash . . . We had each to choose a supplementary training course. I did truck-driving and warmed to it more than I expected. I passed a test and had Class 1, rigid, on my licence ever since. The qualification automatically transferred over. Had I ever used it, the qualification? Not as such. I'd done a refresher in Urmston, passed the next level and got upgraded to Class 2, HGV, made a couple of monitored runs up the Lancashire coast. That was all.

And why now, Pat?

Carl addressed me as 'Pat' and has done since. I wanted to correct him, but couldn't before Carl fired ahead with his third degree. I didn't correct him then, nor ever have. What would have been the point? Carl knew my name. Carl wanted to be wrong, to be corrected and to continue getting it wrong after the correction.

Why now, Pat, if I didn't mind Carl asking? Life gone pear-shaped, I told him. This remains the one truth I've told Carl. Divorce that left me by myself in a strange town. A dead end I mistook for new love.

Carl sniffed once more. Carl seemed pleased. With himself, with me. I'd shown him my weakness, deliberately bared my belly. The inquisition stopped.

Often the way, Carl said. Lads who go through turmoil.

Carl looked especially chuffed with that last word. Carl had savoured it, given it an extra syllable. Like Carl had happened upon it in the quick crossword (fifteen down, a state of upheaval, seven letters, ends in L) and taken a shine to it and filed it away for future usage among discerning listeners. Something the matter, Pat? The word in Carl's burr. Lads who have been through, Carl said glaring me down, turmoil and need the road to clear their heads and come to old Carlos. Carl did that. Carl referred to Carl in the third person, like Carl was his own second cousin and not in the room and forever out of earshot. It's something that Carl does.

Carl gave his little rehearsed oration. No fannying around and certainly no passengers of any description. Insurance will not cover.

I have you, I said.

There was confusion then, a moment of, in which Carl just glared again in my direction. I had him, did I? Carl asked me what that meant. I said it meant only that I understand. I follow. Je comprends.

That last variant was a mistake. I knew it was even before I had it said. And yet I couldn't hit the brakes. When he resumed speaking, after yet more suspicious silence, Carl told me repeatedly to calm down. I was to calm down and take nothing personally and heed his counsel. All right? Fine. He kept saying it. To Howard as well, though Howard was out for the count.

We would be there yet – me speechless, Howard asleep, Carl squealing at both of us to calm the fuck down – had Pauline not entered with a tray of mugs and custard creams. She shook Howard awake for his medicine. Carl took a call into the street. Pauline, at Howard's pained bidding, fetched the Volvo keys from a ceramic pineapple on the mantelpiece and passed them to me and wished me luck. I said that it would be a month yet and parking in town was tricky and if it was all the same with them the truck was best left where it was in a lockup in Stretford. Carl laid his cuppa on the outside window ledge and tapped the double-glazing with his Claddagh ring and twiddled this soundless valediction.

I tell her this. Most of, a gist that she might have listened to for all I know. She's still filming her little films. After I finish, I wait for her to speak. It takes a bit, but speak she does.

And the guy whose lorry this is?

Howard?

Is Howard, like, on the spectrum?

No, love, he's dying.

Ah, she says. It's a fine line.

Between?

Dying and being on the.

Being on the spectrum is her hobbyhorse. She thinks everyone is on the spectrum.

Not true, she says. And Carl is waiting on us?

For us.

Same difference, she says. And this Carl and Howard, are they?

What?

You know . . . She sucks her cheeks hard inwards. Her lips pucker like those of some cartoon tropical fish. She releases the suction with a gradual rasp. *Luvvers.*

Good Christ! I glance over at her squinting off into yet more distance. Precisely what has you ask such a thing?

Oh just, she says, bits you couldn't help yourself.

Namely?

That detail about the cuffs, par example.

Carl's cuffs?

The floral print, she says. So very delicate.

They were genuinely forget-me-not blue.

You see? There you go again. You didn't have to leave that detail in.

I see.

But you did, she says. Is it even true or just another you-ism?

I see.

Wake me when we're there.

She sleeps then, a couple of hours, who doubts her old man's every utterance. She curls away. She bunches the mink against her window and rests her head. Are there me-isms? I say scraps, a little heartsore, and get nothing. The dash lights again. Number only, no name.

You anywhere near?
Call me whether you
are or not. Pleasexxx

I deleted you from my contacts. Yesterday. You trained it north to my flat and let yourself in. I found you in kimono in my kitchen. After I'd seen you back onto the London train and we'd said our so-longs, I deleted your number. Yesterday this was. I'd still know your number anywhere. I won't. Not tonight, nor tomorrow.

The radio autotunes to some local talkshow. We flit through several tolls. The télépéage subscription has been reactivated in Howard's name. It will come out of my cut. We slow, blip, pass through. I love this too, this free space just the other side of tolls, the clearing before we get separated back into lanes.

The radio is discussing refugees. That much I gather. My mother – *our mother* – would be ashamed of my gathering little else. She came here in the early fifties. Somewhere in the south. Just turned seventeen. She loved French at school. Her coming here, once, was one of the rare details from her girlhood that my brother and I prised out of her. Usually dismissive of nostalgia, this was the one memory to which she returned voluntarily in our company. Three weeks with the daughter of an acquaintance of her father, a shoebox of undeveloped black-and-white negatives like a fresh mackerel catch.

We start getting lights and speed limits. I can see Paris before we get there. I've memorized the road numbers to get us where we need to be. I prefer this to satnav. We never get there exactly, to Paris. We graze the magenta light pollution and pull in, in near dark, to a lot full of trucks under a flyover. My shoulders, feet, ache.

Hey.

She doesn't budge. And again. What if she were dead? What if she had died in her sleep on the road between here and when she last spoke? I would try reviving her, cradle her head in my arms. Carl would know what to do. Whooping and violet and paramedics speaking in fragments of two tongues and a sympathetic shot of something puissant on the house. What would I tell her mom and her godfather? All hell to pay.

Come on, funny girl. Please.

She groans, finally, without stirring. She emits a low internal hum of dissatisfaction.

We're here.

We're always here, she says.

Deep.

She turns further from me. She buries her face in the mink's ox-blood silk lining.

Leave me alone.

Precisely what I have to do.

Meaning? she says half turning.

We've reached our primary destination. I have to go and check in with Carl. Assure him that all is well. She tells me to pop the locks from without. I'll keep it short, plead fatigue, bring takeout back. She is, she says, going nowhere.

The restaurant is heaving, lit like a supermarket. A stew of voices and nationalities, windows steamed with condensation. Carl is in the far corner, holding court among half a dozen younger hauliers. Carl is telling a story that has Howard's name at its centre. I breathe. I edge towards. The truck's dozen or so split gears, the load's tonnage at my back, the ferry's roll-on-roll-off, the switch of lanes, I can handle. This? This charade of belonging, of being a man among men, is what comes between me and peace.

Thank God for that!

Carl has copped me across the room and has risen to his feet and is shouting. All the faces at his table turn. Other tables turn as well. Carl's getting up looks laboured.

And there was us starting to fret about our new baby!

The lads laugh. Carl performs the intros. Pat. I should say my real name, but it's too late. The nearest pushes his chair back and offers his hand for shaking the way that you're supposed to among real people and tells me his. I go around and shake and don't catch any, the names.

Did you lose your way or something?

No fuckin fear.

Nobody says anything. I'm trying too hard. I'm still standing.

Grab a pew, Carl says. Never stand on ceremony here.

There are no empty seats. I beg a chair off the next table. A couple in matching maroon fleeces. There's no room at our table. I sit in the fringes, back to the wall. Will I have a beer?

I'm fairly fuckin bushed, my voice says. Perhaps best not.

Someone asks if I usually swear this much. A spare bottle is passed back to me, uncapped and room temperature. Just the one so, to mark my maiden voyage.

Speaking of which, Carl says. The lads give a little cheer. We've had a bit of a whiparound, Carl says, and we've only gone and bought you.

Carl places a paper bag on the table. I mumble thanks and stand.

Don't get too excited.

The lads laugh. The lads always laugh. I feel the bag before opening. I feel a peak's hard crescent and act mystified. There was no whiparound is my bet. Carl paid for it. Inside is an emerald baseball cap. Its forehead reads 'King of the Road' in gold comic font. There's even an exclamation mark. Carl insists that I give them a twirl. It doesn't fit. I have to leave open the tab at the back to get it partly down.

There's a time when nobody speaks. I leave on the cap, though the joke has ceased being one. My beer is lukewarm. The fleeces at the next table are staring at me. How was my crossing? I say something off-colour about Calais. The table returns to whatever was under discussion before I landed, as if I never had. I leave it as long as decency permits and give Carl the signal and thank them collectively and say that I'll see all in the morning. I won't see them, any more than they'll see me. They know that. This is the get-out clause we agree to. I'm halfway to the counter when the table behind falls asunder.

I order to take away. The woman looks at my cap. King of the Road! Carl materializes beside while I wait. Carl's using a crutch.

You okay, my lovely?

Grand. I sound less angry than I am. I bump the base of his crutch with my toe. You?

This? Carl says and winks. Carl's a great winker. Old wound from Dunkirk!

Very good.

I tell Carl that I'm going to take some food back to the cab and have an early night. Carl knows that I don't belong. But Carl prefers to have it look like not belonging is my choice, my mistake. Carl doesn't want me at his table, any more than I want to be there, but Carl is keen to look the host. Carl wants my not being there to be my doing, not his. And I'm happy to oblige.

Carl says they're great lads. I pay. Can Carl drop over before lights-out, go through a few details? Carl could pick Howard's Volvo out of hundreds.

Can it wait till morning?

Carl squeezes my forearm with his free hand. Carl seems gentler than when we first met. Of course it can. Carl likens himself to an old hen. Forever clucking around.

Someone has to.

You done well today, kid, Carl says.

Carl lets go of me and faces back towards his lads and walks without using the crutch and sits where he belongs.

We eat, curtains pulled around the windows and windscreen, doors locked. I still have the cap on. She asks if it's meant to be witty. What does she reckon? She reckons it is, wit of some description. She tries it on. It half covers her eyes. I laugh.

So it is witty, she says peering up from under. That's something.

Otherwise we're speechless with hunger. I don't even have to ask her to eat. She salts a box of fries with a sachet and eats with her hands. I'd like a few, but don't dare ask for fear that she'll tell me to have the rest.

in tent avec petit garcon
- too sad to sleep trust
you got there xxx

I blank it before she can see. She asks why everything is a secret with me. Not secret, just private. Subtle difference. She drains a juice carton with one suck of its straw.

Speaking as one of your myriad secrets, she says breathlessly, the distinction between privacy and secrecy can begin to seem like splitting hairs for convenience's sake.

Leave it.

She wipes her hands finger-by-finger with one of the paper serviettes I took from the café. Her fingers are stick thin and so long there might be a fourth phalanx in each. She works so hard to sound Irish, to be. I see it in her. I hear her and it hurts to hear. I hear, too, how much the effort exhausts her. Sometimes she appears to lay down tools, to accept that she will never fully belong either side of the ocean. She scrunches the serviette into a fist that she eventually opens. She considers its white ball in her palm.

I have to go, she says.

Go where precisely?

I never want her to leave my side. After she quit college in Dublin, there was talk that she might move back across the Atlantic to her mom. But that talk appears to have dissipated. I never want her to go. She rolls her eyes.

Go, she says. I have to *go*.

Gotcha. The sanitary facilities. Just inside the front on the left.

Jesus.

She pulls her door's catch.

Low profile.

Relax, she says. Nobody's gonna see me, are they? Even if they do, they'll not get who I am or who I'm with.

Whom.

You're a super travelling companion, she says and takes a bag of trash.

I watch as she drifts across the unlit parking lot, mink around her elbows. All front she is, more lost than she cares to admit. On her bunk is the aquamarine plastic sack that she has brought as luggage and her weird entourage of objects spilled onto the nylon of her sleeping bag: inhaler, a Love Hearts dispenser, iPhone and white buds, passport complete with embossed harp and washed-out mugshot of her fifteen-year-old self, lip balm, an unopened tin of Fisherman's Friends, a pair of sawn-off woollen mittens, an ounce bar of solid gold . . . I place the body mist among them. She can take a hint.

I check the undercarriage. Nothing. We're headed the wrong direction for any stowaways. The load is sealed for the night, the night air fragrant with overheated rubber. I face into the hedge and take pleasure in my waters plashing among leathery magnolia petals.

Our mother did graduate in French, and trained as a teacher and taught in a convent. Just when she might've been happier on the shelf, she met our father at a function in some rugby

27

club. Any career stopped there. The French stayed with her. It became, all through our boyhood, this private realm that none of us dared trespass. She read *À la recherche du temps perdu*, painstakingly, all seven volumes, in the original. It took her most of the eighties to read. She died three years ago. On her bedside locker in the hospice we found, among other things, the large-print edition of a life of Rimbaud that I have somewhere in the back.

All history now.

In a few days, going to plan, we'll be within sniffing distance of the Med. I've half a mind to find the house in the Camargue where the girl that our mother was once stayed. Not the happiest of stays, from what I gathered, but I've carried it decades in my head. I've half a mind to go there and knock and ask inside.

I wander around the front of the truck just as she's slouching back across the darkling lot. I go to meet her. It's only then I realize that she wore the bloody cap there and back.

What the hell's wrong with you?

The cap is a one-off and seven people in there would recognize it even if they didn't recognize her. She hears me and raises the peak an inch and sees me and lets it drop. With this on? She says the loos were just inside like I said. She didn't, she assures me, venture any further. She had the ladies to her lonesome. She calls me a bag of weasels.

You're a bag of weasels, she says, what are you?

She says that she's not feeling great. I let her link my arm and walk her the rest of the way. She honks of mothballs. In our respective sleeping bags we undress. She has the upper bunk, me the lower. We are rustling. We are breathing. The dash vibrates one last time. The cab's inside lights up, is briefly silver.

You, she says.

Positive?

I've mine with me.

Sound as a pound.

Not bothering to get it? she says.

Fair idea who it is.

Her?

She has a name. And I've a fair idea what it says without looking at it.

Some boyfriend you are.

This is her reminding her old man that he too has a thing all his own that she can reference whenever it pleases.

I'm not.

Not what?

Her boyfriend. Anymore, that is.

Sad that, she says after the longest pause.

This once does sound like she means it. She never wanted to meet you, to hear tell of you and, now that you're past tense to our present, it sounds like she's grieving the loss of you.

Need to download?

Not specially.

I want to be there, she says.

She's only saying what they all say. They want to be there. I'm never certain where that there is.

Where, darling? Where exactly is it that you suddenly want to be?

29

My saying this is cruel. I know what she means. And that she means only good things: kindness, love, forgiveness . . . But I, as she rightly tells me, just can't help myself.

There, she says. For you, with you.

Since when?

Be like that.

Night so.

Fine then.

Years since I heard her say those last two words. They are what she said when she was small and wanted something and I was not inclined. She was cross, determined to do it anyway. She was, her phrase always meant, going to show me. And once more.

Fine then, she says.

Night night.

Her breath thickens above me within minutes. I'll hardly sleep. The dash glows again. Just the locked screen's reminder of a message unopened. Nor will I respond. I'll rise before anyone and get us on the road. I can already see us pulling out of here in grey banlieue light.

I hear our mother's voice. Am I there? Her shadow is on the wall of my room at home. She's speaking from the landing. If she enters, she'll find me sitting on the end of the bed. Come in, I want to say, come in and find me as I am. When she repeats 'Are you in there?' I wake in the same truck and the same dark in which I drifted off. I can't have gone under long. There are the valedictions of English hauliers out in the night and doors thudding and sirens flitting in the distance overhead.

Sorry We Ever Met
August 2015

You trained it from Euston up to his, just after the morning rush had subsided. You had left some fib at home about an away day that you couldn't miss. Second Tuesday of August. You powered off for the journey north.

You had said your goodbyes the day before. In the canteen at your work. The sale of his flat was happening. He had volunteered for a redundancy scheme advertised via his staff listserv. He had signed all legal documents and come down to London on a whim to mark his final day. A late lunch and just the pair of you. He was clean-shaven. He had come in sports jacket and sleeveless pullover and open neck. He looked like the person you met six years ago. The shutters were being lowered on the serving area. He said that he had some false sense, dressing, that respect was due. He walked you to the ring road. He had even offered a farewell bow at the lights and taken your hand and kissed it. For old times' sake. Then he had disappeared back into central August.

An elderly man opposite you on the train was raised in the north and asked what had you going up there for the day. Visiting your Irish lover. You heard it out loud in your voice before you thought better of saying it. The man gazed out at cooling towers. You wanted to have it said once while it was still true. Nothing the whole rest of the journey. When the train came to an incremental standstill and everybody stood, the man said:

I'll bid you good day.

You powered back up on the walk across Piccadilly Gardens. No missed calls. Not from him, not from home. He must have been still in bed. His place was in the Northern Quarter, between a casino and a strip club. You knew the code to the entrance of his block. You still had the spare key to his unit. You entered onto the upstairs living area. The blinds all drawn. But for his shabbychic chesterfield dragged to the centre of the floor and a few boxes, the place was empty. Tuesday, he always said, was lie-in day. Below stairs, the basement where he slept, looked dark as well.

His kimono hung off the rail on the back of the apartment's door. You slipped out of your cotton dress, the one with brown and orange floral print, there in his entrance passage. A surprise for him. You kept on your knickers, boots. For modesty and because screwing in footwear, you knew, somehow moved him. You would ring him and stand in his kitchen against his stainless steel worktop and wait.

The kitchen was empty too. You hadn't noticed at first. Nothing in the cupboards. Even the kettle was gone. Where the plywood shelving had been, to the left of the sink, was now just a grid of grey dust squares on white silk vinyl. All its trinkets, its curiosities, were wrapped in newspaper and layered with care into a wooden wine box that had belonged to his mother. Château Something. There was a single mug only, unwashed, and a coffee pot on the ceramic hob.

No answer, no sound of ringing or vibrating even. Maybe he wasn't down there. You had just assumed that he was. But the chain wasn't on when you arrived. Maybe he was gone. And maybe you were naked but for boots and knickers and third-hand kimono in a deserted apartment, waiting for one who had left without so much as a by-your-leave or sayonara.

The kimono had been a gift from a woman in Kyoto. To him. Long before your paths crossed. Petrol blue. The property of a famous kabuki actor in the thirties. The woman had bought it in a flea market for a lover who never returned. You were always exercised by that, the gift of it from her to him. She was just somebody, he insisted, whose name he couldn't remember.

Its silk felt cold on your skin. There were goosepimples on your breasts. You could see yourself there, alone on the stage of some kabuki theatre between the wars. The auditorium unlit. The only sound that of men and women alike all looking at you. Some-one coughs. You turn the ring on your middle finger backwards, so its stone doesn't get in the way. You dribble saliva onto your knuckle and begin. Closer and closer to the edge. They are all watching. Even the lover, the one who never returned, is out there in the dark.

Don't stop, he said. On my account.

He was standing in the archway to the kitchen. You hadn't heard him arrive. He was leaning on the doorframe in T-shirt and

33

shorts, a bunch of keys on a lanyard around his neck, smelling of outside. Without saying hello, you asked him to enter you.

Prefer to watch, he said, if it's all the same.

He watched and cleaned out the coffee pot while he watched and refilled it and stood with his back to the hob staring at your rotating hand. You held yourself apart with two fingers so that he could see properly. The coffee rose.

I have to get milk, he said.

The fridge was under the counter that you were perched on. He opened its door between your legs and, leaning into the light, kissed your hand. You came and shuddered against his breast-bone. He stood holding a pint of semi-skimmed, the freckles of his forearms illuminated by the fridge's internal bulb, until you stopped shuddering.

You said sorry. Sorry. You had let yourself in. You pulled the kimono's lapels tight around.

You're grand, he said. A dame in kimono for breakfast. Mustn't grumble.

Would he like to? Enter you? Not sure. Please. He did try, but seemed half-mast, distracted. He said that he felt too sad possibly, but kept trying. He removed the lanyard and laid its keys on the countertop. He laid the milk on the countertop as well, his palms on steel either side of your thighs. When were you leaving? That was the other thing that moved him besides footwear, chit-chatting during fucking. Pack tonight, you told him, off at dawn, morning ferry out of Plymouth. You wrapped around his head, kissed his temple. He loved you and you knew he did and he said that he could smell fish. You'd had plaice for supper the previous

34

night, had even eaten the skins. You giggled against one another and he withdrew.

I can't anymore, he said.

Can't?

Come, he said.

He pulled his underpants and shorts back in place. He pulled his kimono's lapels around you once more. How did coffee sound? There was sourdough for toast and a pool of butter melted at the bottom of the sugar bowl and the dregs of lemon curd. It was the antidepressants. He said that waiting for the bread to toast. What was? One of its side effects, of serotonin, was a loss of sensitivity.

In certain areas, he said.

He looked beyond towards the communal courtyard. He was looking out of his own embarrassment it seemed. How long had he been taking them? Initially, he acted like he was sure that he must have mentioned it. He hadn't ever mentioned it and he knew you knew he hadn't. Since earlier this year, he said vaguely, after that bad time off the rails. Just to keep the head above water.

Then he carried up the coffee and toast on a board, and you ate on his wreck of a sofa in a patch of hot sun at the centre of what had once been his dining room. He was really going through with it? He was. He smiled his first smile of the morning. His sale was going through at three that day. He was getting nearly twice what he'd paid for it at the bottom of the crash. He had flogged his car to a woman from Cameroon. All negotiations conducted in French of sorts.

Mother, he said, would've been quite proud.

And the other thing?

That too, he said. Just fetched Howard's truck. That's where I was. It's parked above. There's room for a few boxes. Otherwise leave the place spotless, bomb down the M6, sleep in some service area, pick up the first load at a depot north of London and plough south for the late afternoon sailing.

You had assumed all along that this was just another of his fantasies for your benefit, the way that turf-cutting or fishing for mackerel by moonlight had once been. It was really happening. Your voices echoed when you spoke. Why this sudden emptiness? You had never loved his flat. He bought it at the lowest ebb. A blind auction. He had decorated, made a lovely job, but you could never shake the memory of the dump it had been. Now that it was going out of his hands, there was this grief you couldn't articulate. Nor needed to.

He spoke of Howard and Carl. Yet more faceless names. Did these people really exist, or were they figments of his imagination? Six days, east down the Rhône valley, west along the south coast, north again towards Brittany. And when he got back?

There's no back, he said.

He seemed troubled that there might have been some misunderstanding. He looked around the room.

What you see here is the last of me.

You kissed then. More you him, if truth be. You laid the mug and board to one side. You straddled his lap. It was the kissing you loved most. Kissing was active, convex, the closest you ever got. You forced hard inside and heard his pain. An internal squeak. His breath tasted of Colombian and citrus. You bit the hard muscle of his tongue's stub. He groaned 'fuck'. You tasted blood, his, like battery acid on the tip of yours.

It was akin to swimming. A rhythmic coming up for air and breathing through your nose and burrowing back under. He was thrashing for dear life beneath. He had never learned to swim. You had always known that about him. Somewhere the run-off from your lungs was drifting in bubbles across his black pool.

You could keep pushing and smother him with love and leave him lifeless and trust that there was nobody in the world, not really, to find him. You dropped your mug in his lap and covered his eyes with your fingers and locked harder still and felt his left fist club your cheekbone. Some force behind. You fell sideways. He pushed you further from, and struggled upright.

A lot of blood in his mouth. In yours too, though not as much, and the blood in your mouth was his.

This is destroying me, he said.

This?

This is fucking killing me.

You gathered your things from the floor of the entrance passage. You could hear him gargling while you dressed, and spitting and muttering to himself. You had a four-year-old to think of. Your boy came first.

Boy. Every utterance of that word seemed overshadowed by inconsolable transience. Your boy was starting school in a month. His father was a good man with no family in England, who had taken early retirement to househusband. Tomorrow you were heading to the Pyrenees again, with boy and caravan and Self.

Self, he said stepping back up. Gets me every time!

He must have been listening. Six years and still he found your husband's surname hilarious, the way you referred to him by it. It was just his name. It wasn't funny any longer. You couldn't do that to Self, to either of them. You couldn't leave. You said it quietly. Your cheekbone already swelling.

Don't, he said. You're in a bind, he said, with a husband now and a son together. I get that. I just have to do, at long last, the decent thing.

You had been expecting this. It was why you came. You had come up to get the big valediction over with, and maybe still hoping to discover you were wrong. He handed you a coarse lump of ice wrapped in a barista serviette. He apologized for the punch. You had it coming, you said. You were sorry too. For? Biting his tongue, hurting him. The ice was agony. He wrapped his arms around your neck and laid his forehead very gently against yours.

Won't ever not love you, he said.

You didn't want this. You wanted to ask him not to. You wanted to promise him that you would make a clean break. He shushed you before you said anything, as if he could hear the same old phrases lining themselves up. Once more would have been an unkindness. The only kindness left was letting him go.

How many times?

You hoped it sounded jolly. A valedictory inventory. Did you screw? Yes. How many times did you screw, give or take? He

38

flopped back into the chesterfield. Jesus! He seemed prepared to jolly along.

Oh in the hundreds, he said clearing his throat. Easily in the hundreds, if not.

Yes.

There was once parked in the viewing gallery at Gatwick. Sort of. He emailed to say he would be in town and drove. It was only you who came. Once in the Travelodge at Gatwick. Was that the first time? First time proper. It was you who propositioned him. The woman at the desk said 'Enjoy!' handing over the keycard.

There was that once on the back stairs of his office building, between levels three and four. Once? There was a period when those back stairs honked of nothing but us. You had to listen for door magnets releasing and footsteps. How were you never caught?

All lovers, he said, believe they're invisible.

Is that so?

It is.

Somebody had said that to him at the photocopying machine. Back then. She was marking your card, telling you plural that you could be seen far more than either of you realized. And she had just declared this like some eternal truth? She had. All lovers believe they're invisible . . . She hummed it to herself while he was on the next machine and she was waiting for her handout on *Troilus and Cressida*.

It's true, he said. It's a huge part of love.

Once in the disabled toilet in an Odeon. The hand dryer kept coming on. The door knocked. Was somebody in there? Once on your father's picnic rug in a field out in the valley near your house. Directly under a flightpath. What you thought was a hidden suntrap turned out to be a hikers' track. A breathless group ascended minutes after. This is a designated right-of-way! How were you never caught?

It's possible we were, love, he said, but just too blind to notice how caught we were.

Once in his childhood home, the first summer following his mother's death. He was acting like some fugitive from the law. He wasn't supposed to be there. You guessed where he had gone and booked the ferry and appeared out of the blue. You slept on an old mattress dragged downstairs to his mother's fire. And smoked and sipped some whiskey that had a suggestive name. More than once? He looked at the ceiling as if trying to calculate from memory. Two and a half times? He was gone in the morning.

Twice earlier this year, he said, in the caravan at the end of your garden.

That was naughty. The big snow came and you convinced yourself that he was still down there in the caravan in the snow all that week.

Not likely, he said.

Your son still begged for the bedtime story about the Bookle, the name given to the giant in the caravan, that means 'boy' in Irish.

Once on this sofa, he said, me on top of you.

Many many times on this sofa, but you remembered the once that he was thinking of. A couple watching down from a flat on the other side of the courtyard. You could see them over his shoulder and closed your eyes while he bolted inside. Then you knelt up and made yourself come in seconds.

Once more? Now? He looked hollowed out.

I can't, he said.

Can't?

Couldn't, he said. I'm not able.

If you caught the mid-afternoon, the chances of either of you bumping into anyone you knew and having to explain would be minimal. He disappeared to the lower floor. You refolded the kimono neatly according to its creases and laid it in one of his boxes. One day, far south of here, he might happen upon it and find your scent intact within its silk.

On the walk to the station, amid an acre of parked vehicles and a budget hotel with a royalist name, he said that you wouldn't be hearing from him any time soon. There was no need him saying that. Was he pushing it? He did like his valedictions to be violent. You wouldn't have put this past him, to push it, forcing it in the hope that you might snap.

The tram tracks past the courthouse. The footbridge. Your step quickening. Him trailing. The station's esplanade.

Have I said something?

The Virgin express to Euston was running late. He would sit with you until. You dearly wished he wouldn't. He queued for coffee and brought it to a table within view of your platform. He had a muffin for himself, one moist strawberry at its centre that he scooped out with his index finger. He offered the rest's wreckage in a napkin.

No thanks.

Your dad rang. Your dad's face comes clearly onto your screen when he rings. Weren't you going to take it? Not at the moment. You said that your dad was sure to text if it was urgent. In block caps? Your dad had only recently learned to insert spaces between words. Every text still arrived in block caps. Decline.

And do we know, he said, this year's Christmas production?

Your parents had used early retirement to branch into amateur musical theatre, an annual show that opened after Boxing Day and ran into the first week of the following year. He always teased about that. Not so much lately, not since your own mum's death. You did know which show had been chosen, but you weren't inclined to tell him. You would, you promised, message him to say.

Lately you had been daydreaming his beautiful suicide. You told him there in the station café. Charming! He goes off the radar a few days. Countless texts and nothing back. His body gets washed up by the Irish Sea. You sip brandy for shock. You're heartbroken, though in a way that feels manageable. More than anything, secretly, you're relieved it's over. There is peace of mind knowing that if he's not with you then he's not anywhere, nor with someone else.

I have been seeing someone else, he said. So to speak.

The first you heard. There at the table. Had he? It was true. You knew it was because he didn't look up when he told you. How long was this? Couple of years, on and off. The news hurt like hell, but explained a lot. The tannoy said your destination.

That's you, he said.

You laid his key on the table and walked ahead to the platform, unsure if he was following. There was an issue with the train's doors. They took several seconds to part. He rested his cheek sideways on your neck's nape.

So long, he said. Sorry we ever.

You were too. Really sorry.

And then? Then you stepped forward without turning. You could still remember the feel of him, his cheek on your skin, his arms behind yours, his belt buckle against your lower spine. There seemed to be an impression of him palpable for hours, weeks. After it stopped, you could at least remember thinking, as you stepped away from him, that this would be the last time that you felt him against you. You were at least sufficiently aware then to tell yourself to remember. You stepped forward and this feeling, him against you, transitioned from feeling into memory and somebody blew a whistle.

You bought a couple of shots off the trolley on your credit card. A teenager with a rucksack asked if anything was the matter. A group of folk minstrels wandering up and down the carriages. 'All Around My Hat'. 'Wild Mountain Thyme'. 'Scarborough Fucking Fair'. Everyone joining in. You texted him from the last viaduct before re-entering the Midlands. You lost coverage and got a missed call notification when you came back into range. You asked the minstrels nicely to put a sock in it please. He went straight to voicemail.

Was she beautiful, this someone else? Was she younger than you? What did 'seeing' mean? He had been seeing someone else on and off for. For six years it was you and you alone in the vivid sunlight of his gaze. Now clouds had rolled across. Now his gaze was elsewhere.

Before you knew it, London was doing what London does, happening long before you get there. Park-and-ride signage and stadiums and walkways over fast-moving traffic and undulating rows of rooftops becoming ever more densely packed. Self was barbecuing ribs out the back. How was your day? Self's big brother and sister-in-law, in town from Minnesota, were coming to the Pyrenees. If anyone asked about your bruise, you were going to say that you'd had an affray with a train door and came off second best. Nobody asked. Chat all about Syria, this jungle in Calais, no onus on you to contribute. An episode of something with your son, the night as sweltering as ever. The Green Man on the corner had an extension on its serving hours and let out just as you were dropping off.

Nothing in your locked screen when you woke at dawn. You tried again from the kitchen. It went to voicemail. Nothing the other side when the continent's mainland edged into view and your phone picked up Orange. Nothing from the toilet of the terminal in Saint-Malo. You tried one last time from the campsite in the Limousin where your journey was being broken.

There had been many separations in the past. But this nothing felt different. You could see the pair of them, your son and your husband down there in the campsite communal area, rolling pizza slices. It didn't even ring.

He's dead.

You said that out loud. A group within earshot turned towards you. They belonged to another language. They all glanced in your direction, like you had declared the evening glorious, and nodded assent. He's dead, you said again and folded arms and rested your sore cheekbone onto one cupped hand to hide the bruising and powered off. He was dead to you and, if that was what he wanted to be, you could be to him.

Thursday

Can I ask you something?

Prefer if you'd just fire ahead and ask me.

Rather than?

Rather than ask me if you can ask me.

Fine then, she says. I'll just fire ahead and ask.

She is: full of beans this morning, twisting the plastic tag that has remained on her wrist these past two years, inclined to over-share. I am: an even speed on the inside lane, in want of sleep, rehearsing what I'll say to my brother.

Why were you there?

Why was I where?

Oh you know, she says and clicks her tongue. In Grandma's house that time.

When's this?

You know.

Pretty sure we've been over this, sweetie.

Pretty sure we have not, she says. She's enjoying this too much. Honey!

When?

That time.

Why was I in the house in Ireland that time when you had your thing?

Yes, she says quickly to bypass my point and return to hers. That time, she says.

When you had your thing?

And they were all up the wall, she says. And yes, I had my.

Why do you ask?

Always wondered.

Is that so?

And then there you were, she says, out of absolutely nowhere like you'd been in the next room all that time.

I was.

With the big sad head on you.

We both laugh when she says that.

And even as I was lying there, and you were holding my hand and talking the shite you always talk, even then I kept wondering where you'd come out of.

She says this in open country. We're in a slow ascending lane somewhere west of Dijon.

It's a disgrace, she says.

What is?

This, she says.

Enlighten me.

This driving around anywhere and nowhere, she says. This sunny ephemera tossed between you and me. This aimless remembering.

This.

Is this not on the old spectrum?

This again. You think everything and everyone is on the old.

And are they not?

Well riddle me this, darling girl.

Go on.

What's the difference between this all-consuming spectrum of yours and being an awkward bugger of la vieille école?

Of la?

Old school.

Right, she says. It's merely a matter of nomenclature.

Excuse me?

Don't do that.

Do what?

That, she says. Always pretending you don't understand.

I do that?

Big time. You do that, even when you do.

Even when I do . . .

There you go again, she says. Pretending you don't understand, even when you do. Understand?

I do. I do that.

My brother wants a word. I've been in receipt of several texts. One yesterday, three more today between the early hours in which we ground off and now. We've put daylight between ourselves and the dawn smog of Paris and Carl. This is the mid-morning's rolling boil. My brother's latest has just lit the screen. Nothing specific as yet, merely that he feels we should converse in the near future. Chasing, I shouldn't wonder, his goddaughter's whereabouts. Have I seen her? She's my care, not his. I should tell him that, and where to get off.

Well ain't you Mr Popular this morning, she says. Not responding?

Kinda busy at the moment.

Want me to?

No.

And who, pray tell, have we now?

Your uncle. Family stuff.

Right, she says.

She says it as if she knew already who it was, not a flicker of surprise in her syllable. Am I reading too much into this? She says it all blank emphasis, like one who has been detailed by my brother to get me to return his calls or reply to his texts.

I'm family last I checked, she says. Am I not still family?

You are, pet. House stuff.

Right.

She's quite close to her only uncle, to an extent I often forget. She has her own direct line to him. They've always texted. Mostly sarcastic emojis, so far as I can tell, at one another's expense. Have they been texting since we came on the road? She always seems well informed. About the particulars of his life, about his concerns for me. Does she inform on me to my little brother? I prefer to think not. How else might he hear the stuff that I never tell him and yet he somehow seems wise to? Not that she willingly offers gossip about her old man, I prefer to imagine, more that he whittles it from her piecemeal when she stays. She's stayed a lot.

I had reason to be grateful to him for their closeness. I may not have been grateful when I had reason to be. I never thanked him. I never indulge her speaking well of her uncle. Their closeness has survived its necessity. I play the indifference game. To it, to them, to myself.

Time passes. She's fierce quiet.

I love the road. I knew I would. Twenty plus years I've had the licence. We were living in her mom's family's holiday home on the Shannon, expecting, on the dole. I was obliged to do a scheme and chose this as the lesser of several evils. I never used it, until now. The possibility of this has been simmering in my hip pocket ever since. I would pull out my wallet and make sure the X had not worn away, was still crossed next to the little line drawing of a truck in profile. Someday, I told myself, someday . . . This anonymous thread between names and drop-off points. This poplars and folds and shimmering frequencies. This anywhere and nowhere.

Grenoble, she says.

What about it?

Will we be passing anywhere near Grenoble?

Could be.

Monsieur Mangetout has a grave there, she says.

You say it like he has a chain of graves all over the country.

He's buried there. Okay? We might pay our respects is all.

Her fascination with France's celebrity metal-eating freak always troubled us. She had a poster of him taking a bite out of a propeller on her bedroom wall. In middle school, she did an independent project entitled 'My Hero: The Man Who Eats

Everything'. After an image-heavy presentation of her project, which several of her classmates found distressing, her mom and I were invited to chat informally with a ponytailed vice principal. Was everything cool at home? We said that everything was hunky dory at home. We didn't talk on the drive back.

Can I ask again? she says.

The asking if she can ask me, before asking, inevitably lands as a warning. It's the same question that her mom asked in the bad time, when I had too much to hide and occasionally let myself get cornered into the question that I couldn't reasonably refuse.

Why? she says. Not where, *why*.

We're hiding in the shade of pine tree now, in a service area, when she returns to this. Already stifling. We've done four hours. The law says an hour's break before another four on the road become possible. That will take us to late lunch. We're sucking icepops.

Why was I in Grandma's when you had your thing?

We've never spoken of this. I know we haven't. Nor even close. I've assumed, ever since I brought her from hospital to our mother's unsold house, that not discussing was her preference. I've taken my cues from her. She cuts off any slight allusion, as if knowing asking about my movements would open up discussion. This is the first time I've heard her initiate it.

When I had my, she says. Why were you there?

Is it me? Sometimes I wonder if it's me who cuts away. Or wonder if she thinks it's me. Maybe she wants to get closer to what happened, and she thinks our not doing so is because I don't want to. Maybe she's steering clear for my benefit.

51

She points at her chin to tell me there's lemon juice dribbling down mine. She hands me a serviette with a filling station logo.

I disappeared two summers ago. I was holed up at home in Ireland. I was playing hide-and-seek, not supposed to be there, getting a rush out of feeling on the run. I got phoned around dawn. The afterwards, where I might normally have had to explain my prolonged absence and sudden presence by her side, got swamped by a flurry of events in no particular sequence that we now reference remotely as her 'thing'.

I went to your grandma's to help with the clearout. Satisfied?

I shouldn't have been there. The place is no longer mine. There was no clearout to do. I read thrillers and cooked off a gas cylinder and tippled whiskey and tramped the dunes and burned driftwood. In the middle of one of those nights her mom rang. In a right state. I left immediately. That was how I got bedside within hours of her thing. And I took her home with me.

Time does what time does best. We're back on the road. Time slips underneath and gets sucked into a pinhole of past in a rear-view's middle distance. And the foreseeable future? A long down-hill between service areas and Benedictine monasteries, several channels funnelling into a single-carriageway tunnel and brakes that don't work as well as they once did.

And how is she?

How is whom?

Dear old Grandmamma, she says. How is the old stick?

My daughter and mother were never close. There was scant overlap between one's new world and the other's old. More likely, our mother saw in my daughter a duplication of the sentimental nuisance that her elder son had long since become.

She died. You did a reading at her funeral. Ring any bells?

Oh. Yeah. She says that like a bulb has just come on. Saint Paul to the Chrysanthemums.

Corinthians.

The very man.

You could remember reading at her funeral, but not that she had popped her clogs?

I really miss her, she says.

She possesses her generation's declarative emotionalism. She tells me, with all the joie de vivre of a stoned hippopotamus, how moved or excited she is.

You miss your grandmother?

Is that, like, so unimaginable?

You thought she was still with us and still the frosty old stick she always was. Have you been stricken with grief in the past minute?

You are such an A-hole, she says.

And she was never your biggest fan, was she?

Being this much of an A-hole, she says, is not actually obligatory you know.

I reckon you met her about five times max.

Last time she said my accent made me, her only granddaughter, sound like a minor character from a Trollope novel.

Her cuffed fist covers the lovely partial overbite that she inherited from her mom's side. She always does that when she giggles and feels guilty for giggling.

She was two when we moved west across the Atlantic and got solvent. Sixteen years in suburban Long Island and she never once approximated a native's nasal drawl. If anything, her accent went the other direction. She affected drab consonants as to the manor born. She adopted this adolescent punk shtick that she has never shaken off entirely. Her classmates thought her British. She got a kick out of that, but feigned offence.

Being from elsewhere was her original thing, before the thing that we never mention. Then those times I took her home, my teenage daughter realized how equally foreign she sounded in the elsewhere that she was supposed to be from. That killed her. Even the stagey phatic crap that she and I waffle didn't cut it there. Not really. It dawned on her that she had erected this whole identity around an elsewhere where she didn't belong either. I could see that killing her.

And was she?

Was she what?

On the old spectrum.

Ah here.

Well, she says.

Maybe just don't.

Our mother was, it's true, detached from any world not hers. For most of her adult life her only attachment to workaday reality was through our father. Once he expired, thanks to a coronary embolism at temporary traffic lights on the coast road, she seemed happy to be cut adrift. We were – her two sons had late – left largely to our own devices, to locate for ourselves whatever outside world there was. Her youngest found his via the boarding school that he chose to attend. I stayed at home, with her, longer than anyone. Not that she was grateful or noticed. I got for myself. I kept out of her path, for fear that she might ask me to explain my enduring presence. I was to her, mostly, the peripheral hanger-on who banged doors in the background and for whom she left a gigot chop on low under the grill. Otherwise, she smoked and completed cryptic crosswords and dozed fully dressed upstairs in the afternoon and read to all hours and slept late. If our mother was indeed on any spectrum, it was one of her own making.

So you were there to clean around after Grandma died?

I was. And I took you back there.

You did, she says. Though if I recall correctly, you didn't have much cleaning done.

She has her bare feet up on the dash. She's painting her toe-nails gold. Taking the utmost care with every stroke.

And you okayed this little holiday with The Godfather?

Staying in the house?

The Godfather is my brother. She will even capitalize in texts to get the point across. He is hers, so the soubriquet comes naturally and shouldn't be a problem. I'm probably making too much.

Staying in the house, she says. Little bro greenlight that, did he? Or was this one?

This one what?

Clandestine.

Lovely word.

Clandestine, she says again, a ring of smoke in her voice. Is, isn't it?

My brother is a good godfather. He has always asked after her welfare, sent bank drafts for significant birthdays. For years she lodged the cheques into a post office account and sought his advice regarding investment. I found her, odd moments, perusing the financial pages. I eavesdropped on her once, discussing with him the short-to-long-term outlook for gold. On the strength of whatever he advised, she cashed her grand-and-a-half of post office savings and had just enough for that ounce bar that she now totes everywhere like some medieval accessory.

Even when she speaks of him, I hear implicit caps. The Godfather. He became head of the family in the dim and recent past, and I seem to have become a running joke between them ever since. Once, I saw a partial text from him in her locked screen. Regards to Fredo! The joke was his instigation, I told myself, and she was playing along to feel included. Does she get it? Fredo to his Michael I am, the flaky elder sibling who got stepped over. She has never, I know for a fact, seen any of the movies.

House was up for sale and needed clearing out. That's why I was there.

And it's sold, she says.

Is it?

No question mark audible after what she said. This hurts too, that she might know before me that my family home is gone.

You tell me, she says with a cotton bud dangling from her lips. Busted, embarrassed, she shakes her head. Jesus . . .

My brother has three sons she's close to. She has holidayed with them. They have a group on some messaging app. There have been parties in her cousins' house in south Dublin to which she has been invited. There was a time when she was seeing this grungy, affluent kid from among her cousins' friends.

He know you're here?

Who? she says.

You know.

My Godfather?

She wants me to say it. She wants me, for her pleasure, to refer to my little brother by the nickname for him that she retains at my expense. I sing dumb. We go miles thus. Eventually she mumbles: 'I don't think so.' She means more that there is no way my brother could know this. I whistle the movie's theme. *Speak softly, love . . .*

I really wouldn't read too much into it, big guy.

My girl among my brother's family. Such intimacies arrive to me like rumbling on the horizon. I look away. I keep doing whatever was at hand.

After ground zero, her term for the gradual meltdown of our little family that was all her father's doing, my brother took her under his wing. She was sixteen and sounded foreign everywhere. She was flailing for some buoyant debris to cling to, in need of rescuing. Her father was too fogbound in desire to recognize that. My brother stepped in, called her long-distance daily, renamed their spare room her room during the summers, insisted she stay over once a week when she came to college and made her keep down solid food. Hard thing is, she seems still under his wing. These past few years, while I was looking the other way, a circle that includes my daughter closed in the distance behind my back.

It's how I always imagine your old age, she says.

How you?

Always imagine you old.

57

This is news. She has fantasized my winter years. But for the mere matter of time, she has me there already. This news is natural. The way it should be. Where I can't ever conceive of her non-existence, mine has already begun forming in her gorgeous shaven head.

Go on.

Living back there, she says. Back where you guys grew up. In the same house Grandma lived. By the sea. Living pretty much the same day-to-day. Alone and unapproachable.

Not fussed on that last bit.

But way more doting on your grandkids, she says. No Trollope jokes.

On my?

She already has me in our mother's living room somewhere north of the biblical three-score-and-ten, all paperbacks and drams of single malt, bluster without from the night's onrushing tide, tolerably loveless but for visits from her, and doting on the offspring that she in turn will naturally find impossible to imagine not existing.

Grandkids, she says. I bring them to see you and you spoil them.

I'd do that.

She has both feet up, drying her nails on the south-facing dash. Ten gold coins in a row, two big sovereigns in the middle, two little pennies at the edges. I will spoil my grandkids, happily, and their mother. But I leave the thought of my old age, the thought of thinking it, to her. My end-of-days will reach me in due course. Nothing surer. No sense my meeting it halfway.

There was a time there I wasn't myself.

And that time, she says, was when you went AWOL over the water and stayed in Grandma's house?

I was off the planet.

Come back, she says.

I will if you will.

We've figured that if we do four early hours and make an hour-long pitstop around ten, then we can drive through lunch and dine mid-afternoon together. No lads. The lads dine around noon as a rule and use the post-lunch lull to make time. We've figured that if we leave lunch to after two at least, we'll find a routier that's still serving and is devoid of hauliers, where she might join me. And if we hit the road before anyone, like this morning, our pitstop will be a couple of hundred kilometres further along. A few extra hours of early evening on the road and we can make an overnight of some remote service area, minimal belonging to be simulated.

Cock.

Language, she says.

Carl's Scania is parked at the routier we pull into. Carl has traced us to here. Carl's is the only other familiar truck at this peculiar hour.

He's onto us.

This mean I can't come in again?

She sighs heavily and slides down her passenger seat.

Getting pretty cheesed off here, she says, and bursting to go as it happens.

Go?

A urination?

Right.

I'll do what I did last night: show my face, shoot the breeze as best I can, buy takeout. My daughter is wiser. She tells her father to sit with this Carl, for once try to fit in. The loos are as you enter, most likely. They are always. Once I'm in situ, she can slip in and back to the lorry with all due discretion. I leave her the fob. I tell her not to wear the cap this time.

Carl and I meet at the entrance. Me in my father's vintage golf windcheater, Carl in Hawaiian shirt. Like travellers in some folk allegory we are, in different places at different times of the year when their paths cross.

Carl asks what had me in such a hurry this morning. Carl heard us pulling off. Carl says that there are lads who keep to themselves. If I'm one of them, then well and good. I just can't, given our arrangement, be a stranger to Carl. I say that I know that as well. I say that I have no wish to be a stranger to Carl of all people. There are items to discuss. Carl has eaten, but can come in and sit with me while I do.

Carl sits opposite and talks. I order in English.

Café for Carl, love, Carl says.

Carl speaks French. At least Carl thinks Carl speaks French. There was me suppressing my schoolboy smattering in front of Carl, so as not to look too up myself. Now Carl is translating my order for our waitress into pretty much the same words that I used.

He wants frîtes, Carl says, avec a couple of slices of jambon on the side.

Carl winks at me. She writes and drifts away. Carl says:

You'll learn scraps as you go along.

Good show.

Simple drop-off and pick-up. We agreed to keep it basic for a first outing. Get the load to its destination. Couple more picks, drops. Back north, stopping at some distribution depot on the way to fetch a load of condiment sachets bound for Wolverhampton. Carl will assist with all import papers once we reconnoitre (Carl's word) in Calais. Calais, as I must be well aware by now, is a bit of a minefield. I'd never seen the like of it in my life. Carl winces. How will it ever end?

Carl's 'we' is troubling. It seems to waft between us. Carl means, most likely, nothing by it.

We?

Me, Howard, you.

How is he?

Howard? Carl stirs his coffee with a black straw. As well as, I imagine.

Then I ask. I bide my time, pick my pause, say my piece about stopping on the road longer than six days. Carl doesn't look all that shocked. He did wonder, Carl says after a fashion, if six days would prove sufficient. Most lads, especially after their maiden voyage, can't wait to get back. The good lady, the sprung mattress, the home cooking. But there will always be the occasional . . . Carl snorts. Rogue trader! No home to speak of, no special person to get back for.

Is that our Pat?

You could say.

Thought it might, Carl says.

Carl has four rings. Three on one hand, one on the other. The lone ring is Claddagh, heart offered outwards. Carl has a gold wrist chain with 'Carl' engraved in script on a plate. Carl can see my embarrassment.

Don't worry about it, Carl says. Carl seems kinder than before. A bit like that myself, Carl says. Must be the Irish in me.

O'Neill.

Always ways round, Carl says.

Go on.

The regs are there to ensure you drive within drivers' working hours, Carl says, and take the required rest period in every fortnight. Yes?

Yes.

Doesn't matter where you rest up, Carl says. You can stay out here as long as you like.

I like.

And if you care to push the proverbial envelope . . .

Go on.

Howard's Volvo's so ancient it predates the digicard. Whereas all info goes straight from your digicard to the system in HQ, tachograph is analogue and gets logged manually every month or so and is therefore more open to.

To?

Flexibility, Carl says.

I see.

There's always fresh loads that want shipping and always some, as we say, who may not be under any company umbrella or who may not be unionized as such, and who may want to be.

Be?

Taken for a ride, Carl says.

Carl has given this speech before. Something about its fluency of delivery. Now is my turn. Carl wants me to speak. Does Carl know that I'm not in any union? Carl wants to hear me say that I'm one of those who's only too happy to be.

In which case, Carl says when I fill my mouth avec frîtes to buy more silence.

In which case, Carl says, there's a little switch down the steering column that makes the tach read 'rest' even when you're on the road. That's the beauty of it. So you're getting ahead even when the system thinks you're snoozing. Few enough walks of life we get the chance to do that. Happily, Pat, this is one. As long as we take care of one another, me and thee, the way me and Howard used to.

I have you.

I'm not sure that I do, or do correctly. But I say that I do. That option, to return to zero and keep returning, is what I want.

I want to stop out here, as long as . . .

As long as, Carl says, we can get away with it. No longer. And don't ever get caught on the road with the tach disabled.

Of course.

Very serious, Carl says. You'd do time for that. And when I call ship to shore . . .

Understood.

Carl drains his cup. Carl picks his keys and lighter off the table.

Know the rules so you can break them effectively, Carl says. Dalai Lama.

Very good.

Miss him, Carl says.

The Dalai Lama?

Howard.

Of course.

Miss the chuckles, Carl says rising to his feet. The seeing him at the end of the day, Carl says, the two amigos aspect if you like.

I'm sure.

Carl insists on taking the bill. There'll be no end of opportunities to get Carl back. We step together into the glare. The air is breathless. I tie the old man's windcheater around my waist. Carl makes his shades fall from his forehead down onto the bridge of his nose with one flick of his middle finger. We will, Carl assures me, maintain radio contact and see one another further along the trail. Leave the tach and all other relevant details to him. We shake. This is a first. I don't remember us shaking in Howard's. Carl's hand feels huge and cracked with calluses. Carl even rests his left over my knuckles, so that mine is cupped whole in both of his.

She has left the door unlocked. Her aquamarine sack is in the passenger seat. The key and fob are on top of that. There's breathing behind. There's a while, too, when Carl's truck doesn't move. I want him to leave first. Carl prefers, it would appear, to ride with us for a bit. To keep an eye. I faff around with the glove compartment. I hold my phone horizontal to my face as if on speaker and mouth words, looking around me and leaving long convincing gaps that a person at the other end could be filling for all Carl knows.

> who you on to carl!

Carl does this too. Carl signs his every text on the assumption that I haven't him saved in my contacts, and inserts an exclamation mark where an X might otherwise occur. He's watching me.

> mais mon frère!

This is what I do in return. I respond in the cod patois that Carl finds a scream. I hold the phone back up, like a tray of drinks, and resume pretending to speak.

> i'm watching u carl!

Those words slide down the top of my screen and slide back up. I continue speaking. I want Carl to see me not opening his latest billet-doux. Keep talking. The idea of Carl in our slipstream the rest of the afternoon does not appeal. I want Carl to lose patience, until he does.

> c u l8r carl!

In my peripheral vision Carl grinds away, around the side of the filling station, towards the exit ramp and, with one blast from his horn, out onto southbound autoroute. She asks from her bunk what all that was about, the mumbling gibberish into a dead phone, the cat and mouse. She asks how it went. Fine if slightly odd. Odd how? Another day, I tell her. She asks what I brought foodwise, is mildly stroppy when I say that I forgot, begs me to go back. We move. I promise another stop within the hour.

The road does what the road does this time of the afternoon. Starts clear, piles up at exits for cities and sites of historical interest, thins out. The déjeuner hiatus. We get the benefit of it. We're permitted two lanes only, inner for driving, middle for passing. The outer third is fast-moving cars. Let them at it. Water towers flit by, the undulating lines of vines in season, billboards and graffiti on footbridges about immigrants, handpainted signs for fresh oranges and eggs. We hold the inside, go ages behind an empty car transporter. Let others make the running.

We can keep moving and reset once time comes close to the edge. Is she right about Carl and Howard? Maybe they've been lovers all these years. We're within sight of Lyon skyline. Have they had Pauline's blessing so long as they confined it to the road? Very soon my brother and I will have to speak. And then? We insert a new tachograph and go back to zero and recommence.

Maybe we could let Carl have his way, if that's all freedom costs. How would that work? Me leaving the door unlocked and hearing Carl enter Howard's Volvo. Carl's abdominal flab like empty chamois luggage, his tobacco breath in my ear. Not a dicky bird. Carl persuading Howard to bequeath his truck to Pat.

Something to be said for that, being young in an old man's eyes, the object of another's autumnal longing. So much of love is this. You said that once. So much of love is not love of the other but love of the other's longing for us.

And then? Carl's enduring terms of endearment. Carl's exclamation marks becoming kisses. The lads' running gag about Carl's taciturn Mick, who hailed from old money and watched his life wreck on the rocks of some ghost, that Carl strings out on the road for his exclusive edification.

Are we not, she says, getting a little ahead of ourselves here?

Come again.

In one day, she says, you've jumped from the floral-print cuffs of a leather jacket to some pensioner's toy-boy.

This is the next service area that I promised her. She has her passenger door hanging open. She was about to climb down before she said that.

Don't even think about it, she says.

Okay!

I say that as if she's in a world of her own and I have no clue. She's not buying. She spins away and continues descending.

You know, she says.

She wends across the forecourt of the filling station, amid lorries and campervans, arms folded, sleeves of the mink bunched around her fists. She inhabits her own season of perpetual winter. Before she's gone from sight, I pop on the dumb King of the Road cap and jump down and shout after.

Yo!

Yes?

She stops and swivels on the same spot. She's shading her eyes and smiling through whatever glare is behind me. She gets a kick out of the fact that I couldn't just let her go.

Get me something!

Any something in particular, big guy?

She knows I hate that. What she appears not to know is how much it means to me that she should want to get under my skin.

Surprise me! And do please pay for this.

She rolls her black eyes and turns her back again.

On second thoughts . . .

Yes . . . She calls that wearily. She has paused mid-step, tip of her left boot on the heat-softened tar. No way is she turning a second time. She's calling towards the sky. Yes?

What I say I know, even as I say it, I'll regret. And yet I can't help myself saying it. I can't stop.

Get me a bar of something! Get me a Freddo!

She turns then, face gone ashen. I'm telling her that I know. That I know what? I know she's been in cahoots, albeit passively, with my brother and that harmless joke of his at her father's expense. And she knows that she has been snared in a minor renunciation of me. She looks like she might cry. She never cries.

One Freddo coming up, she says through a minor quaver. She really looks like she might. You are one serious freak!

She waits there, gazing at me. Say something. I should say that I've known for ages. I should say that I thought it was funny and no big deal. I should throw my daughter the lifeline she's waiting for. I've never been good with those things that I should do. She shakes her head when I fail to fill the void between us. She twists away from me again. She diminishes with distance. She vanishes through automatic doors. Her uncle rings.

The photo beneath my brother's saved number is of him, his wife, his three boys and his goddaughter even. They all look sunkissed. The kids in front, his arms enveloping them.

I took the photo. They came over as a family one August. They stayed a week with us and a week in Manhattan. The image is from one scorching afternoon when we bathed together off Long Island's shingly north shore. I gave the original as a gift to our mother. It lived on her landing windowsill, next to a black-and-white of our father as a young man on the links.

The image in my screen is a photo that I took of that photo last time I was home. That time she was asking me about. You can see the edges of a walnut frame that I bought en route through JFK. You can even see the outline of my reflection. Their faces are partially obscured by the daylight behind me when I took it. The windowsill on the landing was our mother's private shrine: the old man in his heyday, my brother and his family and my eight-year-old daughter among them . . . My only image of my brother is a copy of our mother's favourite image of him, and I'm present only by my shadow.

My brother doesn't expect me to answer. I never do. It just occurs to me that there's still time. To? Catch us both off guard, be unselfconsciously brothers again. I hit Accept's green circle.

Well.

Well! he says.

How's tricks?

My brother has long ago shed the words that we said as kids. He seems perennially amused when I say them to him. I say them to remind him of where we're from, and maybe also that the place was more mine than it was ever his.

You're a hard man to pin down, he says.

Sorry. Did see I'd missed some.

And this finds us where?

Us?

You, he says. The editorial.

A service station above the Rhône valley. Does the editorial 'we' require precise coordinates?

No, he says. He sounds not thrown by my whereabouts. Nor by my tone. That won't be necessary. You okay?

As well as.

Me too, he says though I haven't asked.

When did he start being this pleasant to me? I don't get that. Used be I sniped and he sniped back, the way competing male heirs are wont. Nowadays I get all this bewildering, patronizing kindness from him that I pointedly won't reciprocate.

We have an offer, he says.

On?

Maman's, he says.

On?

Tír na nÓg, he says. Home.

Years since I heard anyone say the name that our mother insisted we call her, since I heard the words that our father chose to christen the house. The words flummox me when he says them.

Sounds like saying them flummoxes my brother too. He hadn't planned on saying them and, now that he has, their cavities have winded him.

Maman's?

Kitty's, he says.

No less.

Come on, he says. He's trying extra hard. To be nice. To me. Don't be a dick, he says.

It was me who took to using 'Kitty'. Until he said it there, I'd forgotten that Kitty was my name for her. In my ironic teens this was, aware how cringing 'Maman' sounded where we lived. For the fun of it. I remember how perplexed my brother was, on rare weekend forays from his boarding school to our provinces. Apple of her eye he undoubtedly remained, the more so for being mostly absent. And yet there had blossomed, in that absence, an intimacy between his older sibling and his maman that centred around my teenage tongue-in-cheek fondling of her given name. She liked it. He could see how much she liked it. And I liked how troubled and on the outside my calling our mother Kitty made my brother feel.

An offer on home?

That I'm going for, he says.

He's on speaker. Odd hearing his groomed voice, as if from within a matchbox, echo in Howard's cab.

And do we know?

Third party, my brother says, via solicitor. Local.

I once told his little sons that their father and I shared many a bed. I said it that time they came and stayed with us. 2001 it was. I remember now. A handful of weeks before the World Trade

Center. They thought it was hilarious, the idea of me and their father in one bed. My brother was inclined to blow it off, to pretend to forget. He told his sons that their uncle, godfather to none of them, likes to make stuff up. I sure do. But I can equally, I know better than anyone, make cast-iron truths ring apocryphal. It's a special gift I have.

My brother is wary of me. I'm the last person living who knew the boy that my brother was, before he became this man of means and some renown that he now is.

Hello? he says.

Je suis là.

And you're cool with that?

My brother was the executor of our late mother's estate. He was also, coincidentally, its primary beneficiary. I got her car. What can I say? I say that. My brother, wherever this finds him, sighs.

I bought your share of the house, he says, so you could procure your lovenest. Remember?

He has never said that before, at least not to me. My lovenest stops us, momentarily, in our tracks. This is how he sees my life. Did he and Kitty speak of it? My sleazy periphery to his responsible centre.

And you got everything else.

This is a courtesy, he says, I didn't need to pay.

Aren't you very good.

Fuck. Sake.

He's right. He paid me adequately while Kitty was alive. He bought my half of a house that we had yet to inherit. I was sufficiently on the skids to let my little brother bail me out.

Sorry. You're right. When?

Soon as, he says. No chain either end.

It's true, what I told his sons. There was an age when their father and I shared the occasional bed. We were boys together, on holidays or staying with Kitty's people in Kildare. Before he was suited and booted and groomed for a family business that ultimately got subsumed into an international corporation, he and I straggled every morning to the same roadside national school. He was a sprat with big brown eyes and wisps of golden hair.

Is there anything you want? he says. From the house.

Can I have a think?

I was summoned out of the line, his very first day at school. Was I his big brother? I was to go down and help. He was backed into the corner of the infants' cloakroom. All elbows and knees, a turquoise T-shirt with chrome zip. He was sniffling. He was begging me to take him home. I coaxed him to his room, his desk. I was allowed to sit with him until milktime. He found an abacus and didn't notice me leaving.

There's nothing.

Nothing? he says.

In the house I want. Leave it.

Honest injun?

I say that I'm willing to return a portion of the half he gave me, if the offer is nowhere near the estimation that we were working on. He says the offer is exactly what was estimated.

Hey . . .

Yes?

Remember the place Kitty told us about? In France.

73

No, he says.

Where she did this exchange thing?

Vaguely.

Maybe it was me alone she told, when it was just ourselves, me with whom she shared the negatives. Somehow I can still see my brother's hand sifting into the box. Maybe I've included him retrospectively. Usually, I'm proprietorial around my memories of our mother.

I'll be passing near there in a day or two.

Very good, he says obviously humouring me.

You don't remember, do you?

Not really, he says. Just yours that one. Yours and hers, he says.

I'll go there and get digital updates of her negatives. I'll ask if I can look inside. I'll message pictures to my brother when I return. I even promise that I will.

Do that, he says. You do that.

There was a period, after their holiday with us and 9/11, when my brother rang a lot. Were we all safe? Could we see the dust cloud? He continued phoning between then and Christmas. I remember telling our mother, that he had been to stay and we were talking lots. I thought that she would be more pleased. She told me how they had raved to her about their week in Manhattan.

He mentions madam. 'Madam' is how he refers to his niece. Every time he does, I want to remind him that madam has a name and that he was there at the font when we christened madam by her name. He says that he texted the other day with madam's mom. I climb down from the cab while I'm listening. He says that madam's mom seems in a good place, relatively, has even met someone. I stand some way ahead of the lorry to see if I can see madam inside. I'm madam's dad, I want to say, not him. Enquiring after madam's whereabouts is my job. There's maybe a toilet in the back of the shop that she's using. If I'm not bothered, then my brother has no cause to be. Instead of saying what I want to say, I say:

That's fine.

Meaning that my brother can chew the fat all he wants with madam's mom. Meaning that madam remains my care if madam is anyone's.

Fine? he says.

She's fine. Trust me.

Is everything okay?

Where madam is, out of nowhere, is right next to me. She wasn't visible inside. I never saw her queuing at the till. I never saw her coming across the parking lot. Now she's next to me and I'm pressing one finger to my lips and she's shrugging as if to ask why on earth she would bother speaking.

You there? my brother says. You gone?

She fishes into a silk-lined sleeve of the mink. She holds aloft a Freddo and presses it against my eyes and keeps pointing at it, as if somehow I might not have seen. I tell my brother that I am, I'm still here, but the line is dead.

A Story at Bedtime
January 2015

Once upon a time there was a giant. The giant lived in the caravan at the bottom of the garden. How the giant got there, when or where the giant went, nobody can be certain. The giant had a huge coat and heaps of hair and a beard of orange and brown that looked like a tabby cat on his face. The giant ate beans cold from the can and drank liquid honey from an oblong bottle and slept loads. When he spoke, white clouds billowed out of his black mouth. His voice was funny. He was from somewhere else. A very far away to where he would eventually return.

The giant had a name. The Bookle. There was a small boy who lived in the house of the garden that had the caravan where the giant lived. It was the small boy who found the giant down in the caravan one afternoon when snow was coming. It was the small boy who gave the giant his name. The Bookle. This is how the small boy thought of the name for the giant.

The caravan lives at the bottom of the garden all through the winter. In summer, the caravan lives in the drive at the front. But it is too cold to go anywhere in the winter. So the caravan stays at the bottom of the garden under a tent of tarpaulin that the boy's father calls 'tarp'. In summer, the tarp sits folded on a shelf in the shed. Every Halloween, the boy's father tows the caravan around the back, shakes out the tarp and bangs it to the ground with heavy iron pins. Then the boy's father pats the side of the caravan and says to the caravan the same words every year: 'Winter well, old son!'

But one winter, in the first weeks of the New Year, the boy woke too early from his afternoon nap and padded around the empty house and couldn't find his mother and saw tracks to the caravan in the dusting of snow and went down in his wellies and opened the door of the caravan without knocking. His mother was curled under a duvet in her clothes. In the middle of the floor, there was a giant with a beard and a funny voice. The boy's mother sat up and said 'Hello chicken!' the way she always says it, except this time she sounded frightened and she looked frightened as well. The giant put his hands on the hips of his greatcoat.

Well! the giant said to the small boy. You're some bookle!

Bookle means boy. His mother told him this later, when the Bookle was no longer down in the caravan and nobody could be certain if he had ever been there. The boy didn't know what it means when he gave the giant that name. The Bookle was a secret between the boy and his mother. The boy's father never knew about the Bookle. Not really. The boy and the boy's mother decided during bathtime that the boy's father wouldn't believe them, or worse might chase the Bookle away. So they agreed, the small boy and his mother, that the Bookle would remain their secret. When the boy's father was out, they agreed, they would bring food and hot water bottles down to the caravan. It would be an adventure. They would never be sure if the Bookle would still be there when they opened the door.

The one time that the boy said 'Bookle' at the table, his father stopped speaking. The what? The boy stopped speaking too and looked at his mother. The boy's mother explained to the boy's father that the Bookle was the giant from the bedtime story that she told him every night. That was all. Often the boy's mother fell asleep on his bed and stayed there until morning. How very strange, the boy's father said then started speaking again. The boy's mother shook her head when his father wasn't looking, and put her finger to her lips.

Then the snow came as promised. Proper snow. It lasted weeks and weeks. The whole world wrapped in it. Everybody stayed at home. The small boy, his mother, his father. Even the boy's grandfather came on the train and was very sad and had to stay longer than they had planned. Weeks of that. The boy and his mother couldn't go down to the caravan anymore because then his father would know about the Bookle. Even when his father wasn't at home, they couldn't go down. Going down to the caravan at the bottom of the garden would make tracks in the snow and the tracks in the snow would be seen.

Was the Bookle still down in the caravan? The boy asked his mother that, when nobody else was in the room. His mother lifted up the boy and stood him on the windowsill and stared out at the darkness of the garden in the middle of the night. I have no idea, she said. There was no light, no sounds anymore. For all she knew, the boy's mother said, the Bookle could have flown away on the time machine that he was making. For all she knew, the Bookle could have been just a dream between them, the small boy and his mother, one they shared happily ever after.

Your son was asleep. He was often asleep before the story ended, his eyelids only half shut and a constellation of freckles across the bridge of his nose and his little fleshy arms raised either side of his head as if in never-ending surrender to sleep. Some nights he was asleep before the story was halfway through, but you preferred to finish the story anyway. The story was as much for your sake as for your son's. Other nights you couldn't be sure if you had reached the end before you had drifted off yourself and woke fully dressed on your son's bed and went to the window of your son's bedroom. Was he still down there?

Before any of this, before he showed up at yours just as snow was coming, you hadn't seen him in a year. He was living up a mountain then, having imported his mother's hatchback. His decree absolute had come. He was renting his place in the city. He had taken a lease on a three-roomed cottage for half of what he was getting. He needed, he had claimed, the extra cash. The spec online was a sofabed, a woodstove with a flue that came up through the floor of the only bedroom and disappeared into the ceiling. Visiting would have meant three trains, two changes. But you were never sure where exactly, and you weren't allowed to anyway.

His number would skip straight to voicemail. It wasn't even his voice. The voice was a woman's, southern informal, an automated green-belt breeziness. When had he deleted his personalized voicemail message? You were, you realized, dialling to hear the space from which he had deleted himself. Few things he loved more than receding, making himself scarce. You could just see him doing it, the pleasure taken in wiping his own voice off his memory card. He adored backing away. He alone savoured the crunch of empty supermarkets, the rows upon rows of real estate signs, the foreclosures and clearance sales and chains in receivership. He had become, he once said, an epicurean of recession.

He had opted out of all pension schemes except those that were mandatory. He had cancelled his union direct debit and was rumoured to have scabbed a strike. He didn't cross the picket, just slipped through the facilities entrance on a lower floor. Someone told you, someone who knew people up there. He had been spotted. He wanted to be. You knew him enough to know that he was getting high on this. He was eradicating himself piecemeal, retreating ecstatically into oblivion.

In November your own mum had died in her sleep. You called him once more and got his voicemail and did something that you never do: you left him a message. Your mum had just. Please. There was an echo on the line. You said other stuff, but please was the most of it. You could hear your pleading rebound even before you had stopped.

The funeral took a further four weeks up to Christmas. There had been industrial action in the funeral sector. A settlement had been reached, but there was a month's backlog of bodies to be processed before they got to your mum. In that lag – between the first flush of mourning and finger food in the function room of a roadhouse past the crematorium – he never responded or returned yours.

This was the end. You told Self after all of you had driven back from your father's opening night as Tevye. This was the end. Self laid one hand on top of your head. He would never leave. Nor would he ever let you go. Your stomach fell. You felt shit for not being more grateful, for having a stomach that fell every time your phone flashed your husband's name, for feeling nothing but disappointment.

Once in the early hours of the first Tuesday of the New Year. He buzzed on your pillow. You had fallen asleep in the room with your son. You found him in the back lane. You stepped out still wearing the dress that you had worn the previous night and had fallen asleep in on your son's bed. He looked rough, like he hadn't shaved or slept in weeks. You scarcely recognized him. He was in a black woollen greatcoat that was soaked through.

You told him to wait in the back lane and went indoors very quietly. You came back with a padlock key and spare duvet and led him into your caravan on breezeblocks under tarp for the winter. It was perishing inside. You peeled off his wet clothes. Not a peep or there'll be war. He lay above you under the cold duvet, propped on his elbows. You told him to let himself go. You wanted to take his full weight. Over a year since last time. He said sorry into your. You shushed him. Sorry. His skin smelt ancient. His breath tasted of some syrupy spirit, like that of a mercenary returned from overseas. Fatigue made him swell inside. It was painful and quick. He trembled so infinitesimally in your arms that you weren't sure if he had.

You changed into a dressing gown for breakfast. Self would be chairing an arbitration session all day until late, would be gone when you got back from the crèche run. Gave you a little hug. Between two worlds you felt. One's avuncular unrequited squeeze, another's semen dribbling down your inner thigh.

Once after the coast cleared. You parked on the street and went directly down. He was still out of it, on his back. You crouched above and coaxed him barely awake and made him bite your nipples. You came from that alone. All that day you lay together. Was this doable? It was fine. You meant for that afternoon only. The coast would remain clear until one, when crèche let out. He seemed not to hear the rest. He would have to leave. There would be too much risk, too much to get done. Work and the boy and none of them his.

You described for him your mum's funeral. The strike, the service, the spread. Seeing him would have helped. He hadn't known what to do or think. Your parents had refused to acknowledge his existence, so why should he acknowledge your mum's death? You told him how bitter that sounded. He rolled onto his side facing away. On another level, he wanted nothing more than to. What? Mind you, he said. But he knew that he would never get near even if he tried. He would have to watch you mourn from a distance, from your secret.

You know he wrote to me, he said.

Who?

Your dad, he said. I got a letter. That's why I came.

He had written to your dad. A long time ago this was. You did vaguely remember him mentioning ages back that he was going to write to your dad. The second bit, the reply, was news.

Go on.

His letter to your father had begged forgiveness for all hardship caused. Please accept his presence in your life. Please let us just be sweethearts in silence, and that would be enough. You found yourself crying, the idea of him begging that of your dad. He wrote it by hand, on duck-egg blue Basildon Bond stolen from his mother's bureau. He had even used, he said, the lined underlay for tracing. You could have taken a spirit level to his handwriting. Two double-sided pages folded into a square envelope meant for a birthday card.

Over a year and nothing until yesterday when one paragraph typed onto white multicopy got delivered up his mountain by a minivan. Yesterday? Yes. He had stood with the stable door's top half open. He saw the postmark and knew. It felt flimsy. Hardly worthwhile coming all the way, he had said to the postman. He leant over and reached into his jeans and held this torn envelope in his hand. He pulled the page from its envelope and unfolded. About six lines only. You could see the shape of it against the light of the window. You could see the bumps of full stops piercing the underside of the paper.

The plummy accent he did for your dad was all wrong. The letter said that Self had phoned your dad to say that it was finally over. Let this be an end, the letter said, to the whole sorry. The last word was 'affair', complete with speech marks. He scrunched the letter into a ball and pitched it across the caravan's solitary room. You heard it land on the lino's vinyl.

Affair, he said. Subtle.

Once lying face-to-face where you had talked. Heads on one cushion. You felt self-conscious and shut your eyes during it. You opened them only after he had come and fallen into fathomless sleep. Sleep was the thing of his that you loved the most. The word didn't go deep enough. This suddenness and depth must have been what they meant when they spoke of slumber. You never loved him more than watching him slumber. Funny that. Was he really there? He looked there and felt there, but even then it felt possible too that he might not be. You pushed him away and pulled on his hoodie, jeans.

One of the women at the crèche teased you about what you were wearing, about the lovebite on your neck. You said how complicated life is. I bet! Your son was wiped. You sat together at the kitchen table and shared a tin of ravioli for lunch. Your son couldn't finish his half and dozed beneath a blanket on the sofa with the TV running.

He was still down there in the caravan, in the dark of the afternoon and the tarp. You shouldn't have gone back. The inside had warmed some, but there was condensation and the smell of mould. He was barefoot, in underpants and greatcoat only, pacing the floor. You asked him to lie with you. He was immensely hot. A vast furnace you spooned yourself into. He was moving back into the city. He was going to test the market's buoyancy, put his place up for sale.

You woke sleeved in sweat in that pewter light before nightfall. You wedged open a window and he asked what was happening. You were boiling! He got that, he said, a lot. It had been your understanding that he was promised to you alone when you were not there. Was he? You had no right to ask and, for fear of what truth he might tell you, you hid behind the fact that you had no right asking.

He spoke about his daughter, eyes shut, mouth half muffled by the cushion, from some semi-conscious place. The closest he came to telling you. She had been doing a line with this pup she met through his brother's sons, who was not very nice. Picked her up and dumped her several times.

They're gone, he said.

They're?

All gone.

What are?

The pictures, he said, all deleted.

Everyone in her year had seen them. She stopped going out. Stayed with a friend, bingeing on this fantasy series and wine gums. He hadn't known any of the particulars until it was too late. Too? Late to stop her attempting what she. Of course. That night he legged it from his mother's house.

Dandy, he mumbled several times. Everything's dandy now.

He had said the same word the very first day you met. You could almost visualize the remote crevice of dream from which such an odd recherché stone had unloosed itself. Everything's dandy! He said it again and laughed his sleep-clagged laugh into the cushion's crushed velour and opened his eyes wide and looked beyond you and jumped into the centre of the room.

Your son had appeared in the doorway, had put on wellies and followed you down to where he had seen you disappearing earlier. Now your son was standing at the door of the caravan. Now your son was staring upwards at your clandestine lover and asking him what he was.

A giant! he said.

That your son could see him was at least proof that he had to have been real. He couldn't have been in both of your heads at once. Your son smiled around the edges of a wet fist and stepped up into the caravan's room. Did you plan on doing the introductions? They shook hands. A weirdness too far this was. Your three-year-old shaking hands with an Irishman in greatcoat and underpants in your caravan.

This is Oscar.

Well! he said. You're some bookle!

Dada's friend, Oscar said.

In a sense . . .

He's fierce cute, he said. It's not from the wind he gets it.

There was your own dad to be fetched off his train. You told him that. Your husband was liable to return. And there was a bath to be had before any of that. It wasn't safe, for him as much as you. Did he understand? You rose from under the duvet and gathered the boy into your arms. He had to leave. You heard 'So long!' from the other side of the door that you closed behind you.

It was during that bath, the two of you up to your necks in it together, that your son first christened him the Bookle. Your son asked you, rinsing conditioner from his hair with a glass jug, if the Bookle was there on holidays. Silly goose, you said. Before you could of him, your son asked of you not to mention the Bookle. You saw then how it could work. You could harbour a lover indefinitely at the end of the garden, so long as it was your son's secret and not yours. You could hide your lover behind your son's name for him, as if your lover were just another of your son's imaginary cast of characters and the end of your garden this other realm where benign giants wait in shadow.

Dark when you reached the station's set-down area. Your dad was unrecognizable to begin with. He had to knock the passenger window and said that you looked in a world of your own. He seemed worn out, adrift. *Fiddler on the Roof* had been a triumph, he said in gridlock. Everyone told him it was. The show must go on. Jacket potatoes for supper, the radio forecasting a big freeze and swan's feathers already visible against the floodlights of the five-a-side pitches. Would crèche be cancelled tonight or would they wait until first thing? Your father questioned the wisdom of his coming into the city. What with all this weather in the offing.

You're being more than usually quiet.

Excuse me?

They had stopped speaking. Self was addressing you, had rested one of his hands on one of yours.

Is everything?

Fine . . .

It was then that your dad told you something. After your son had gone down, after Self had retired to watch a documentary about wild swimming, you sat with your dad in the kitchen and he asked about your special friend. He had never asked before and, now that he had, you weren't sure where to look. Did you still see him? Not as such. Part of you felt certain, for a second, that your dad knew that your special friend was at the bottom of your garden and somehow knew as well that you had seen the letter.

Your dad told you that your mum had often made reference to your other life. Must be nice, she once declared, having a special friend to go to and come back from without any of the bother. It was never, you said, as simple as it looked. He said he thought that your mum was jealous of you. He knew how daft that sounded, but it was true. Your dad wasn't sure how to take your mum's jealousy, any more than you were. The two lives she saw you having left her thinking less of the one life she shared with him. You were cross with your mum for saying that, with your dad for snitching after she was gone.

Snow fell as promised. In spades. All that week. All the next. The whole world frozen. Public services in lockdown. No going anywhere. No cars on the road. Even those lone souls out walking trekked up the centre of the road. And certainly no going down to the bottom of the garden, no leaving tracks between this reality and the other.

The more your son babbled of the Bookle, the more he sounded in that realm all his own. Just the story that you had started telling him at bedtime. It was hilarious. His very own little magic realism. Everyone said. Mostly you were too stressed to hear exactly. And all the while he could have been down there still.

There were lots of noises: soft thuds, dull remote slams, oblique creaks. Just snow sliding off, Self said. Your dad dozing in the armchair opposite. But the noises could have been anything. There were times those noises without resembled, to you, him constructing a time machine at the bottom of your garden. In the living room, watching TV, you blathered above any noises you thought you could hear. You hadn't prattled that much in years.

It was then, among those weird weeks, that you began fanta-sizing his passing. After the thaw, you find him lifeless and make calls and sit that evening with your family. Nobody to witness. An inquest returns natural causes. The body gets shipped over. You take a ferry and stand at the back of the church. You see his family receiving communion and condolences away up at the front. You queue with all the others. His ex glances askance in your direc-tion. She looks the way she looked in the photos of her he showed you. Darker maybe. You place on his coffin on the altar a single lily. Not once spoken to. A letter arrives several months later. Items plus a modest sum bequeathed in his last.

Will I pause it? Self said.

Pause?

This is ridiculous.

What is?

You're not even watching, Self said. If you're wiped, just go to.

So you did. You went to bed and recounted to your son for the umpteenth night in succession the story of a giant called the Bookle in the caravan at the bottom of the garden. Snow kept coming down. You woke in your clothes on your son's bed and stood at the window looking down into night snow-covered as if lit from within. Violet with snow it was. No thaw in sight. Stu-dents whooping out on the main road, high on snow. Was any of this really happening? It felt reminiscent of that myth he loved. The lovers, the land of eternal youth. Where you stood was within time's pale. Where he lay was a timeless beyond and you wanted to join him there.

There were silences between noises. With each silence you breathed a sigh of. The relief! Then, just when you had decided that he was gone, it started again. A faint adumbration. God moving furniture. How your mum described thunder. She was terrified of electrical storms. As kids you would sit with her on the floor of your hall at home, no windows and all internal doors drawn, until the storm had passed into a neighbouring county. You remembered that. The sonic echo of lightning in cloud was God rearranging furniture.

If you stayed away long enough, he would get the message. Movement and silence and movement again. With each silence you held your breath. And each time the silence ended, you felt disappointment. Finally, there was a silence that didn't end. Days of silence. The snow stopped. A warmer front moved up from the Bay of Biscay and roads became passable again. Your dad seen onto the train. The crèche reopened. You got back from dropping your son to find the iron pins of the tarp pulled up, the wheels refixed, the door hanging open, your husband sweeping inside.

We left it in a real mess, Self said.

There was an empty bottle and bedclothes strewn around. There was, as well, a single ball of white paper on the fold-out table. The letter. It was the letter that your dad had sent him, that he had read aloud with his lip curled around 'affair' and rolled into a ball and tossed away. Now it had been retrieved and not binned like the other rubbish, but rather placed carefully on the table for someone to see.

You pocketed the letter and loosened all windows and wedged all doors so they wouldn't slam with the through-draught. You waited until Self had gone above, before taking the letter from your pocket and flattening it on the table. Nothing. No words either side. No full stops piercing through. Absolute white only, blank both sides, except for creases and those tiny shadows that creases create in paper.

Friday

This, she says staring straight ahead.

This?

These more like.

I'm gonna need a few specifics, darling, please.

There you go again.

These what are a bit what?

Carparks, she says.

Ah.

They're a bit samey.

She is: bored in her reclined passenger seat, in shades and King of the Road cap, rambling aimlessly. I am: about to go indoors to check that it's safe for her to join me, working overtime to humour her along, inclined to lose track of days that we've been here.

They are, I suppose.

They are, aren't they?

They are.

It's not just me, she says.

Not just you, love.

Same nothing spaces, she says. Same caffs, same staff, same drab grub. Same sun even, same dome of unblemished friggin azure over our heads.

You poor thing.

Same graveyard slot, she says, when nobody's about except me and you talking the same nothing crap. Same post-lunch lull we have to wait until, that makes me want to strip down to my birthday suit and run buck naked over the nearest friggin vineyard doing objectionable Arapaho wah-wah noises.

Jesus.

Well, she says.

I had no idea you felt so.

Strongly?

I had no idea.

Well, she says.

Some time passes. We let it. We let time pass.

I love this.

Love *what*? she says.

Everything you said.

You love this?

I do.

Precisely what do you love?

This.

Specifics, she says, as you'd say yourself.

Us, this, the interminable twaddle we spout at one another. I love it. It's ours. They can't take it from us. And yes I love these provincial spaces where time warps. And yes I love this moment specifically when everybody has drifted back to work and nobody's about and there's a particular nothing to be listened to this closely.

Jesus, she says.

Ennui in these here parts.

As in?

Boredom. The blues. The flat terrain between.

And this is what you?

Love? It is. This is what I love.

Jesus, she says.

It's exquisite.

This?

Ennui.

You kidding? she says.

The given moment's exquisite ennui.

You've lost me.

I know that, love.

I don't mean.

I know that too.

And is that not, she says, on the old?

You could open your very own pub.

Could I?

Ye Olde Spectrum.

Good one, she says. Is though, isn't it?

Probably is.

More than.

Than what?

Probably, she says. It more than probably is on the spectrum. I'll go first.

If you must.

A business park in the hinterland of. Somewhere. Saint-Étienne? Most of the tables inside are empty. The major lunchtime traffic has been and gone. Two members of the kitchen staff are sitting opposite one another, in grease-spattered jackets, eating their own leftovers and swiping phones rather than speaking. Are they still serving? The woman who looks in charge, who approaches me from behind the counter, seems to suggest that we'll have to giddy up. I point to outside. I mean that I will, we will, be back.

While the world piles indoors, or is on the road wordlessly, she and I dine together in some out-of-the-way dive where nobody will see us, where we can be ourselves knowing that we'll never dine here again. I've promised Carl a rendezvous later this evening, some similar backwater a handful of hours away. I owe Carl that. I keep Carl sweet.

Halfway across the tarmac I see her face among the wind-screen's clouds. The letters on her forehead glitter. King of the Road! I stop walking and signal. She thumbs a cheesy okay and removes the cap. I want her to eat. She labours out. I want her to enjoy herself. She drifts towards.

Always adored this time of day, ever since I was a teenager. The numinous doldrums. Kitty napped away the afternoons. In summer, nothing else doing, I sat in the reading chair that was hers the rest of the day. I watched test matches or wartime black-and-whites. My brother, as I like to remember it, was mostly not with us. Thanks to his boarding school, he had access to more worldly others and moved effortlessly among them. I had our mother to myself. Odd times, sitting alone at this hour of mid-afternoon, I nicked one of her Silk Cut. She never had them counted and the living room reeked of her fumes anyway. I smoked and felt as high as I felt nauseous and listened to the house. Something of day reinventing itself. A front moving out to sea across the dunes and a second, less settled front arriving from the inland west. The light's waiting room.

So starving, she says.

I'm glad to hear that, but have learned to feign indifference to her eating. I pop the central locking from where I'm waiting for her to reach me. I'm tempted, now and then, to offer to let her do the popping. The way she used want to. She still wants to, nothing surer, but would feel obliged to be withering. So I do the popping and she links me and we go in together arm-in-arm. I love when she does that. When she links me, lets me mind her.

My legs, she says, they're still asleep.

Only a couple of tables are occupied. The dining space is L-shaped. We choose around the corner. We sit at right angles to one another, at those two sides of our table facing in towards the wall.

Paddy . . . She's whispering. We must look like such skulkers.

Is skulking a vibe people pick up on?

You shitting me? Like we're having some sleazy affair.

Could anybody think that of us? It's true that she has her mom's complexion, her dark eyes and jet hair and sallow skin.

She doesn't look remotely like my side. It's only when she opens her daft mouth that those within earshot are left in no doubt that she's mine. She wishes she could swallow back her own words. I do what I always do in these situations. I rescue her by speaking quickly and proofreading the menu with Union Jacks in the corners and generally treating her accidental allusion to my thing as one might treat a bump a mile ago that's now forgotten.

I know what I'm having.

Sorry, she says.

I'm having an omelette and chips and a classic fully-leaded Coke.

I'm good, she says. She seems grateful, shattered too from mentioning the sleazy affair. Not very.

Hungry? That's such bullshit, love.

She pushes her lips into an exaggerated pout. She seems not bothered. Does she want me to beg her? Sometimes I think she does, and sometimes I do. Such as now. Skin and bone she is. I tell her that. This can't go on, I tell her. She has even started smoking. I know that she has and she knows I know, even though I've never seen her doing it. Smoking is just another place we never go. At odd moments, she honks of the inhaled fumes off burned tobacco. I've seen a glossy navy ten-pack among the things spilled onto her bunk.

None of your beeswax, she says.

What is?

My playing dumb is a constant rib-tickler. I didn't say a word of that. Or did I? The skin thins. Increasingly what I think was internal has happened so close to the surface as to be audible. If only to her.

It's my business, she says, and I'm a big girl.

You are.

We'll leave it there, she says. Okay?

Fair's fair.

She has this trick. She holds her wrist out and swivels it furiously and the plastic tag remains completely still. She does it now. Her name on card within has lost all definition with the moisture of years. A blur of black faded to purple. I turn to face the room. I raise my eyebrows a fraction, the way you learn to do with age, that makes you feel old and powerful in equal measure. Our waiter approaches.

Let me, she says under her breath. Une omelette et frîtes et Coca, s'il vous plaît.

He's her age, give or take.

Monsieur?

Le même.

Le même que?

Une omelette et frîtes et Coca, s'il vous plaît.

Très bien! she says patronizingly, as if it's me copying her and I'm doing way better than she expected.

He writes, thanks in English, disappears into the kitchen. When he's out of earshot, she comes over all giddy.

A very impressive young man!

If you insist. I liked him up until you did.

Did what?

Insist. Now Basem's tip is plummeting.

Basem being? she says.

Arabic, I'd say. Her stare at me is blank. Our waiter? His nametag says 'Basem'.

She repeats it with such quiet wonderment:

Basem!

I thought you weren't terribly peckish.

Basem, she says, has restored my appetite.

Jesus.

You do realize what a trad pop you've become?

A?

A trad . . .

She can't finish her own dumb phrase without covering her overbite.

A trad pop . . . I finish the phrase for her. How is it, someone please explain, that I raised such a knobhead?

Stop!

Basem glides between the tables behind our backs, floor-length apron tied at the waist. Basem fears a joke at his expense. Basem seems worried that he might have done or said something wrong. His worry is only touching. She keeps swooning at him over her shoulder.

We must be, she says, fierce exotic.

You're some girl.

Basem comes back empty-handed. She points at his nametag and says his name. *Basem.* Is everything very fine? His English is good enough to be useful, imperfect enough to be attractive. He has perfect skin and teeth. I assure Basem that everything is fine. We're just hungry. Is there something he can get? She says that we want our mangetout. We haven't ordered mangetout. I possess just enough French to explain to Basem that she has decided 'mangetout' is the French for food. I don't possess enough to tell Basem that she was once, as a kid, obsessed with a French light-entertainer who ate everything including a two-seater plane. So I leave it altogether. Basem says it comes soon.

Algerian at a guess, from the name, second or third generation. I have Marseille in my head. A big family. A matriarch, and a father who drives a taxi and tipples to excess to drown the sorrow of irreversible displacement. Lost in the middle of half a dozen offspring, Basem is the good boy who ploughs his own furrow and wires money home.

What was it The Godfather wanted?

The?

This is how it goes. I worry about her eating, her perilous weight. She deflects from that by asking about her uncle. We move forward thus. She applies to him the moniker of power and watches clouds roll in over my head. She gets a tiny electrical buzz, I don't doubt, from the hurt it causes. It must hurt too, seeing her old man squirm at the very mention of his younger sibling.

Oh stuff. Your grandmother's place.

What's going down?

Something about the way she says it. A carefree intonation that feels practised. She shrugs. She never shrugs. Like she knows the answer to her question already, and is asking only to look as much in the dark as I was until my brother and I spoke. Was that really only yesterday?

He has a low-ball offer for Tír na nÓg. As you suspected might be the case. Though what that has to do with me is anybody's guess.

Meaning?

Just leave it.

We've been through this, she and I. She'll never just leave it. How my brother bought me out. How he was the executor of our dying mother's will and had power of attorney and could make that happen. The number we agreed upon was based on the evaluation of a local auctioneer. The auctioneer was someone I had sat beside at school. The number was unrealistic, given the state of the house and the low times that were in it. I knew that. My brother paid me the entire sum in one instalment to be a gentleman. Was charity in there as well? Charity might well have been in there, and I took it.

Not what I mean, she says. Not what I was asking.

What then?

Tír na nÓg, she says. She tries to say it in the original. It comes out all wrong, all narrowed vowels and misplaced emphasis. What's it mean? Remind me.

Call yourself Irish!

This is also how it goes. We fret over her eating, she fights back with digs about her infinitely more successful uncle, and I tease her about her impoverished nationality.

It's your doing, she says. She's looking out the double doors towards the café's terrace of sorts. By all means drag me halfway around the planet at your whim, she says, but don't expect me to cling to the native friggin patois as well.

Fair enough.

We did drag her around. We never accounted for her preference. Not really. She lived the life we chose for her, but was always looking the other way. Then I looked the other way as well. I forgot that she was there and needed me more than ever, until it was too late and it seemed possible that she might not be there and might not need me.

Tír na nÓg, she says.

I don't correct or tease, and yet she believes that she sees me wincing and seems furious. With herself, with me.

Just translate, she says. Whatever the fuck.

Land of Youth. I have told her this before. That's what it means.

So you grew up in the Land of Youth?

We did.

Was that like a sick joke? Irony Irish-style?

Our food arrives. We each have to lean backwards to let Basem serve. Will there be anything else? If we think of anything, we will be sure to give him a shout. His English doesn't extend that far.

Breakfast to these late lunches can be a long haul. Usually, we stop mid-morning for a mandatory hour of caffeine and sugar. That buys the extra four hours of road. She sips Coke from a translucent straw and takes a mint from her pocket.

Hit the spot? she says.

It's lovely.

What the doctor ordered?

You know you want to.

Her gaze at my plate is out of focus. I can all but feel the saliva accumulating beneath her greying tongue. I clink my knife on the plate's edge and she starts eating. She does so with a desperation that's truly troubling. She goes at it with bare hands. She tears the omelette's lukewarm rubber into several large slabs. She forces everything in at once and is close to gagging and sucks long gulps from her straw and belches so loudly that it feels as if the rest of the room has fallen silent.

Atta girl.

Satisfied?

Thank you.

She rubs grease from her hands into the pelt of her grandmother's mink. She ignores my horror at her doing that. She knows that she has done the favour I wanted of her. She pushes the plate away towards the corner.

You all right?

Right as rain, she says in dazed monotone.

Did I ever tell you the story?

The story?

About Oisín in Tír na nÓg.

Only a gazillion times.

I can't have. If you didn't know what the name means.

Oh you have, she says. Trust me. I just forget everything. The dude and his fair maiden in the land of eternal whatsitsname.

Youth.

There you go, she says. Dude goes home to his beloved Ireland and can't touch the ground or else he'll croak, and the old neighbourhood's a ghost town, and guess what, dude falls off his magical donkey and . . .

She spits the story, her version, at me.

Talk about dystopian, she says.

I finish the story for her. She pushes her tag further up her forearm than it should go and closes her eyes and shakes her head. The end she finds particularly grisly.

Oh lord, she says.

Funnily enough, those were Oisín's very words.

She doubles into her lap and buries her face in her hands. There's nothing funny about it. And yet, I keep telling her the story long after the story has effectively ended.

It's not funny, she says. She means it. Way too close to the bone, she says, like me.

She pulls a long line of toilet paper from one sleeve, much as end-of-pier illusionists do with scarves, and tears a piece and blows her nose into it.

Like you?

Am I not too close to the bone as well? she says. You're the one who's always telling me I am.

I am.

Stepping out, she says.

This is what she says when she plans to smoke. Her chosen euphemism. Stepping outside, getting some air. She rises. She uses the fire exit next to our table. She stands on the terrace. She holds a blue box and lighter in one hand, lapels closed with the other. She vanishes around the near corner of the building. Within seconds, threads of frail smoke shift sideways across the terrace.

I have told her. She's right. And many times. What the words of the name of our house mean. Of Oisín and three hundred years in the Land of Youth and the magic horse that the fairy Niamh gives him to go back to visit his old friends. The promise Niamh makes Oisín swear, never to touch the ground. The man on the road and Oisín leaning over to help, the saddle snapping and sliding off. I've known that I have told her every time that I've asked her if I have. I just like repeating the story. And she has been indulgent enough to pretend that she was never certain if I'd told her the story, to let me tell her it again. And again.

The name is still on the left-hand gatepost as you approach the house. It was done by someone our father knew, one of the golf club's greenstaff who carved woodcrafts in spare time. Its letters are charred into a slice of ash and varnished over. To this day, I'll drift off to the thought of navigating the track along the perimeter of the links that leads to ours. Conifers one side, estuary opposite. I'll hear wind and sea somewhere beyond the immediate field of vision. I'll stop at the name's three words, their gloss long since worn off, the wood's grain raised by salt wind and silverfish. I'll wake in whatever murk it was I drifted off. I'll take a lifetime to get back.

So an offer's been made on the Land of Youth?

She's next to me again. How long has she been standing there? She smells of smoke and sick.

Long and the short of it.

And you don't give a monkey's?

I don't have any say in what happens to it. I relinquished that five years ago. I don't stand to benefit from its sale, so I don't really see the point of my brother telling me.

Point of courtesy, she says.

Remarkably, my dear, that's exactly what your beloved God-father said.

She slumps into her seat, mink bunched around her brittle frame. I nibble bits of our leavings. Point of courtesy indeed . . . I can feel, without looking up, the heat of her embarrassment.

She's doing this only to be impartial, I tell myself, not to side with her old man's predilection for self-pity. That I can forgive. I look up. She's staring right at me. She sighs and seems perplexed and looks away. My very own double agent. No greater treason, my gorgeous girl, than being more indulgent of another man's self-pity than your father's.

So tired, she says without looking back. You not tired?

Basem clears our things. He's not sure what to do with the food only half consumed. He's worried. No good? I ask Basem to put the rest into a small takeout box. It was excellent. I ask for espresso. She doesn't acknowledge him. Basem backs away again. I thank him as he does.

Not exactly bessies, she says, you and the bro?

No.

And that would be because?

Ask your uncle.

I did. He said ask you.

Just leave it, will you?

Your answer to everything, she says. *Leave it* . . . She even mimics a deep voice that must approximate mine. No doubt that'll be your attitude to me as well, when the time comes. Leave it, she says. Only the 'it' will be me.

We never spent any time together, after the age of twelve or so. My brother went to the boarding school that our father had gone to. I was less inclined.

That's what I don't get, she says. He did and you didn't.

I didn't get along with it. Okay? I did go for a term.

You never said that part.

Too homesick.

You're not Oisín, she says. Her pronunciation this once is spot on. You know that?

Blubbing every night for a home that probably vanished the second I departed. Making a right show of myself. Refusing to go back after the first Christmas. Being frogmarched in the New Year down to the local tech and left there to fend for myself.

The Godfather took to it?

Duck to water.

Just to slight you, she says.

We barely see one another now. The only contact we have is legal stuff. And mostly that's a matter of courtesy, him to me, as she rightly argues in the very same terms that her uncle used.

Our table buzzes. My phone lights up and vibrates sideways over the formica. There's a square of dense text visible at the centre. She tells me to go ahead. I enter the day and month of her birth as passcode. She says someone seems desperate to hear from me.

That's one humdinger, she says. Would quills and vellum and carrier pigeon not be the simpler option?

You'd think.

> KINDLY HAVE THE
> COURTESY TO LEAVE HER
> ALONE. SHE IS MARRIED
> NOW. SHE HAS A SON + A
> HUSBAND NOW. THAT
> SHOULD BE ENOUGH OF
> A MESSAGE FOR YOU. STOP
> HARASSING HER WITH
> CALLS AND MESSAGES, OR
> WE WILL HAVE TO GET
> AUTHORITIES INVOLVED

The unsaved number is not yours. Nor can it be your other half's. Someone who treats texts like formal letters and hasn't yet mastered the case settings on their phone. Someone close enough to care, but not close enough to be aware of my radio silence.

I produce a fresh twenty and tell her to settle up. I've something that needs doing. She doesn't understand, seems stricken with fear.

What now? she says.

Settle up. Pay. I'll see you out there.

You okay?

I don't answer that. My heart is hammering. Do I look okay?

See you outside. Tip Basem. Take your time. I've a couple of calls to make before we hit the highway.

She looks very small. She lifts the note off the table and gazes at it wide-eyed, as if she has never seen such riches before in her small life.

Paddy, she says, is everything okay?

It's fine.

None of this is her fault. The fault is all mine. I don't blame her. And yet she thinks I do and I let her go on thinking it.

The glare outside is immense. There's good heat in it as well. I have to lower my driver's window to get some air in the cab. I activate the handset legend beside your number and wait for it to start ringing. Even before it connects, I can see it going off in a room somewhere in the same country. I can see my name pulsing among your family and nobody knowing what to do.

Next thing is voices the other end. English, vaguely estuary, together. Children yelping in the background. I say something. Nothing back. Gone half past three. The carpark four-fifths deserted. Is anybody there?

For a few years, before I left home, I had our mother to myself. Between my refusal of his alma mater and my brother's expedient embrace of it, our father had died. His funeral was cursory. The evening of the burial the three of us, his survivors, ate a regular weekday tea. When my brother first tried on his uniform's blazer, Kitty said how smart he looked and how proud our father would have been. We shook hands one Sunday, he and I. Then he and she drove away. I didn't miss my brother, nor the father he was named after. For several years I bussed it to and from the local third-rate secondary. Kitty would be in lamplight in the living room every afternoon I got home. Lost in Proust she was, an English version open on an armrest for reference, and seldom bothered to look up.

Our Oedipal years. My brother receded into his own hinterland of friends from school and weekends in the leafy streets of well-heeled Dublin. We saw less and less of him. Alone with her, I slipped piecemeal into the role that our father had vacated. I wore his seersucker robe after baths. I watched TV from his recliner and commandeered the remote. I caught her peering over her book at me. She thought me ridiculous, but seemed tickled all the same. She shook her head and pursed a tight-lipped smirk. One Friday I pushed it further. I stretched upwards in the centre of the living room and asked the question Dad asked at the end of every working week:

Shall I fix you a drink, Kitty dear?

It could have gone badly wrong. But she laughed. She never laughed.

Go on so, she said and spoke fondly for once of the past's grey unshifting expanse.

How her father bred horses in the Curragh. One year her father arranged for his youngest, his only daughter, to go to the Camargue with the family of a man from whom he had bought a cream-grey yearling. Kitty was only seventeen. How she planned on doing an M.A. after her degree until her mother insisted that she get an M.A.N. first. How she met Dad and his family made its fortune running cigarettes across the border during rationing and he shared a first name with Rimbaud. How they lived in a wooden rail carriage while they were waiting for our house to be completed. How, in her thirties, all hope tacitly relinquished, they discovered that she was expecting a first child. Me.

A weekly ritual that had been theirs became ours. Hers and mine. I fixed both of us a whiskey and red lemonade and ice, and convinced her that mine was lemonade only. She reminisced and I listened. I was, I think, waiting to be put back in my place. It never happened. I had grown flirtatious and lanky. And I think my mother liked it: my use of her name, my adoption of the old man's part that must have been a joke, but a gentle one and agreeable enough to bring us closer.

I had won. I remember thinking that in his robe and chair while Kitty spoke. The unpromising elder son that our father often referred to sarcastically as 'himself', often to his promising younger son and often within earshot of me deliberately, was last man standing.

There was one summer in particular, in the eighties. My brother was en vacances with school chums. She wore dresses with her arms bare. We bathed lots. There's a track from our garden down through dunes to a beach of shingle. We changed in our rooms and, towels in hand, trekked barefoot. Mine were old football shorts with stripes and aertex lining, hers a one-piece patterned white and black that sagged at the abdomen. I let Kitty lead the way. She was stick-thin, long-limbed, like Popeye's Olive Oyl. But she was pretty to me. She seemed to know that, to take pleasure in it.

We walked out for miles, until the water was up to our knees. Sensing it would never deepen, we made do where we were. Kitty insisted on swimming, however shallow it might have been. A common-or-garden breaststroke, head tilted out as if the tide were a bad smell to be waded through on sufferance. I'd never learned to swim. I usually sat and picked up fistfuls of muck that sieved through my fingers. Our house became indistinguishable from the dunes and tufts of marram.

Back at the towels, it was my job to pat her shoulders dry. Her skin was papery, constellated with freckles. Her arms were bony, her legs ghostly white, her nipples visible under her swimsuit. Once I extended the drying to her neck, her hairline. It lasted longer than was essential. She sat perfectly still. I paused. She held her posture and said 'That's nice' and I began again. She would wrap her bob in a turban and make off towards our garden hedge. I became aware, as never before, of my mother possessing a body. There were days when I stayed on where I was, knees hunkered to my chest, while she walked back up. Nights when I woke in the silvery light before sunrise and didn't understand how the thought of my mother's wet bathing costume matted to her body could hurt so much.

She had always seemed incalculably ancient. But she would have been still only in her mid-to-late forties then. Pretty much the age that I am now. Still a young woman. I think she realized. She realized that she had committed prematurely to seniority and roused herself from it. A sky blue A-line sleeveless number, last spotted in the early seventies, made a comeback. A yellow butterfly hairclip, a gift from our father back in the day, held her bob to one side. She draped a cardy over her shoulders out of doors or after seven. At odd times, her lips turned a French rouge.

One of Dad's old boys, or some codger from the bridge club, must have been making overtures in those daytime midweeks when I was off the radar. But nobody visited and she never slipped a name into our chats to see how I would react. Was I in the way? She got a telephone installed. It idled in the hall. Sometimes, in passing, I lifted the big bakelite receiver and listened to its dialtone humming the blank wall of an indifferent world. Or had I become the way?

We should be getting on. Still four good hours of road to make up, before another mandatory rest period. Carl has given me the name of a café that I'm to be at later. I disable the satnav. Instead, I memorize the map, tape all road and exit numbers to the dash. The numbers are surprisingly few and my memory is too good by half.

She has one hand tucked inside the mink, a pink styrofoam box in the other. She's making a meal of crossing the carpark. She has seen me watching her. She looks down and keeps coming. She wants not to look like she knows that I'm watching her. She's become painfully thin. In spite of her best efforts not to, she smiles at me looking at her.

Are we set?

What? she says.

She clambers over her seat into the bunks. Her torso rummages in there, legs flailing across the parking brake.

Are we ready?

For?

The open highway.

Not as such, she says from within. Change of plan.

She drags herself back out, King of the Road cap, aquamarine sack in her lap. She's flushed, out of breath, wired with excitement. Have I seen her inhaler? I ask her to tell me what's going on. She says that Basem has invited her to a party. It's Friday. Is it? Basem lives in the nearest satellite town. Two days off, starting tomorrow. They're hitching together to the sea.

What about this?

This?

This.

Bro, she says, I can never tell when you're being for real.

She does this. She reverts to American when overcome with guilt. Whenever she suspects that she's not behaving well, she rediscovers the identity that she had never really warmed to when we lived there, and is suddenly all dude for real whatever what's the big deal.

I thought this was me and you, one last voyage.

Before?

You go off into the world.

Before I go off! she says all callous hilarity. Into the world!

We'll be hitting Grenoble fairly soon. I thought we were going to pay our respects at your man's grave.

Whose?

Monsieur Mangetout.

That was a joke, she says. Dude . . . You being for real? I can't tell!

Fuck you.

Beautiful.

You don't even know this kid.

He's cute. And if it helps, he has met you and seems suitably terrified.

I feel desperately foolish. I honestly thought that this was going to be just us, together again. My daughter next to me and me getting her back.

Oh no, she says then. Really? You're doing this?

I am. I'm doing the thing that I've not done in four years, not since the first of many goodbyes in an Econo Lodge in the middle of a working week. The memory of that, coupled with the idea of her being somewhere else with someone else, comes in on top of me. She's mortified, impatient, just about kind enough not to abandon her father in this state.

Basem appears at the service door. He loafs around like one who should be doing something to justify coming out. He should be smoking, realizes how silly being there not smoking looks, slips back inside. Maybe he received, out of my line of sight, a not-yet signal.

Care for a snotrag?

Yes please.

She passes me a sealed pack from the glove compartment.

I have to head, she says.

You have to?

Big time. And I'm sorry I do.

Piss off then.

This might be enough for you, she says. I need more.

And Basem will be the more you need?

Maybe, maybe not. Only one way to find out. If you think about it.

I won't think about it.

Very well, she says.

Where guilt brings out her inner skater kid, contrition makes her some Edwardian comedy of manners.

My apologies once again, she says filling the pockets of her jeans with essentials and fixing my King of the Road cap on her head.

What?

My sincere and heartfelt . . .

Oh piss off. Run away to sea with Basem or whoever the fuck. Knock yourself out. No doubt you'll find me when you need a shoulder to sob on.

Her door slams. She's left the mink and aquamarine sack in the passenger footwell. Her seat still bears her warmth when I lay my hand on it. Somehow, doing just that means I miss her re-crossing the carpark and re-entering the restaurant. Maybe I should follow, make a scene, lay down whatever law is left to me. Before I can think again, she's gone and I'm taking the ramp onto the autoroute without remembering how I got from there to here.

Everything they say is correct. A wrecking ball I am. I weave in and out of the fast lane. I shouldn't be here. Will she tell my brother of this? She's mine, my responsibility, not his. I get flashed by the inner lanes. I'm well over the limit. You're out there with the father of your son, doubtless having a blast with your family and the families with whom you travel in convoy every year, and doubtless by now sharing a jolly titter at that rather peculiar tinkle received some time back. She's my responsibility, my care, and I let her go.

*

That summer would be my last at home. I cadged fags from Kitty's handbag and drank cider on the prom of the nearest village in the weekend darks and slept to all hours. The last week of August, last of summer, turned dirty. A succession of squalid skies renewed themselves from the western side of the links. The temperature dipped ten degrees. Seas turned high and choppy. I mooched around the arcades. I caddied in the rain and blew the couple of quid I made on Silk Cut, ostensibly for our mother.

There was one evening in particular. We had tea. Pickled beetroot and cut meats and bread pre-buttered. Kitty suggested a dip. I thought she was joking. She wasn't joking. Go on so, I said. We ran all the way. The tide was right up against the dunes. It was churning peat brown, like ale. A few yellow pinhead lights along the coast. We raced into the breakers and screamed and felt freer and wilder than either of us probably had before then or did after.

Out of the water, I asked: Want me to dry?

Too cold for that, she said. We'll catch our deaths.

She threaded the black straps under her arms, knotted the towel across her, and let her swimsuit bundle at her feet. She lifted it off the shingle with one hand, towel held in place with the other, and started towards the house. I took off my togs. I followed her through the dunes. Her towel drooped to her lower back. The slow rise to our garden, the shells underfoot, the gap in our hedge. As she approached the French windows to the living room that we had left open, and dissolved from the last of the light into the interior's absolute black, she let her towel fall altogether onto the patio's pebbled concrete.

There were no lamps lit downstairs. No answer when I called her name. Kitty? I went up with my own towel held against me. I could hear the hairdryer humming in her room across the landing. I went into my bedroom and left the door ajar. I spread the towel on the end of my bed and sat back on its damp. Of her skin I was thinking, of those dark hollows, the inkling of bristle.

The hairdryer stopped. I could hear her carpet dragging, her handful of footsteps.

Are you there?

I could see the shadow of her profile on the wall just inside my door. Nose, throat, the pouch of her slight breast. I wanted her to come in. I wanted her to see how I had grown.

I said nothing. I could hear a gale getting up. I could hear her held breath at the centre of that.

Are you there?

Three times she asked and three times I couldn't respond.

Are you in there?

There was nothing I could say, however much I wanted to.

Her shadow backed off, leaving only the straight line of the door's edge on my wall's barely differentiated grey. Her carpet dragged once more, and again some minutes later. Next thing was the kitchen singing its kettle's song, the wireless beeping its nine o'clock bulletin.

All history now. I power up at the far end and immediately get a text of welcome from the signal provider, as if I have forever just arrived. And then another.

Sorry sweetheart. Really couldn't take that. Meant to hang up and hit wrong button. Took few seconds to realize you were still on the line. Home to cold and wet. Speak soon? xxx

The internal twilight of the drinks cooler is the only bulb lit. Doors locked. The deli counter is empty. Food has been removed to a refrigerated antechamber. Chairs on tables. A bucket at the centre of the floor. Carl's text of instructions contains the name of the establishment as a hyperlink that releases a virtual map. It takes ages to load all pixels. I zoom in, out, in again, until every crevice has a legible name. This is definitely it. I walk back to the truck and pause halfway.

La vraie vie est absente.

Where's that from? I recite it aloud without remembering. The true life is absent. Yes.

This is the fringes of a zone commerciale. Over the wall is a roundabout and the neon of various chains. Pizza posts and a multi-screen cinema and two discount leisure warehouses and a three-star hotel advertising vacancies. There's a twenty-four-hour self-service carwash. There's a fruit-and-veg shack on the verge of the roundabout's most westerly exit.

Here, this café, feels like it predated those chains. This was the original hub. Families came in for Fridays just like this, a week's travails behind, to see faces and exchange news. Then planning shifted the centre a hundred yards from here and now here feels achingly marginal, all the more so for being so near the new centre. The warm amorphous drone of the weekend commencing is at once invisible and within earshot. Existence is elsewhere and you can hear it.

In the grounds of the hotel, a local covers band is doing a sound check. A twenty-first or the afters of a wedding. They say 'One two three' here as well. I listen from midway between Howard's truck and the café's locked doors. Singer and band start in unison. I recognize the air before the words in English, such as she makes of them. How is that? Like music is fast-moving light to meaning's sluggish sound. I'm humming before registering what I'm humming to.

The singer struggles to enunciate. The words mean nothing to her. I can all but feel her trying to shape her lips and teeth and tongue around each hard consonant. The harder she tries, the clearer it is that she has no idea what is being said. *Is someone getting the best the best the best the best of you?* The song is about love, I would love to tell her. It's about, more specifically, that love that's nine-tenths the heartache of torturing yourself with thoughts of what another might be in receipt of in your stead.

It breaks down, the song does, in their version of it. She mutters a handful of regional expletives over the PA. One two three. The same song from the top. The lyrics seem to detach themselves miraculously from any meaning and acquire, in fragrant humidity, all the sheen and substance of bubbles blown by a child in a suburban garden. Vowels funnel out in clusters, chimerical flurries, and rise sideways and separate and cross walls roofs street-furniture trees and ascend the azure and glimmer infinitesimally and are not there.

Nous ne sommes pas au monde.

I like that too. I recite it too. From the same thing it is, the same source I can't recall.

This is it all right. This is the place Carl said to be. This is the correct hour and the correct day. It's just that I am, I realize only now, a fortnight late.

We have lived in the Land of Youth. We've lost all track of. Time? Time passes. Or rather, this is what passes for time.

We are not in the world exactly. This is more the future we return to, its municipal spaces derelict or in some limbo of sublime incompletion. Nobody remembers us. There's nobody to remember. All old comrades, the ancient order, have fallen from memory into myth. The saddle is sliding off. We're sliding off with it and can't stop time happening.

The Country of Winter
July 2013

You changed at Crewe. A pub lunch in Holyhead. You were among
the foot passengers allowed to embark first. From the deck's
fluorescence you watched solid earth, its gantries and arable rect-
angles and mountain silhouette, slide off. A Tuesday in July. The
slow afternoon crossing. You had left Self a note on the kitchen
table. Home tomorrow. You were strung out, back smoking, desperate to locate signal.

Ireland looked more similar than you expected. There were
gulls everywhere, even on land. The train was packed with home-
bound commuters and stopped at umpteen coastal stations, each
with two names. You had a screenshot of the satellite view of the
nearest village to his house. Another passenger told you which
stop. The woman driving your taxi seemed to recognize the general address. The taxi slipped under a viaduct, through a dilapi-
dated river port, and veered out to face the same sea that you had
just crossed.

Where was she from? Estonia, she said. A long way. Yes. She
had come over when the going was good. It sounded funny in her

accent. And now? Now everything was gone to pot. Gone to pot, she said again, and times very terrible. She would go home but she had two Irish kids by different fathers. And you? She looked in the rearview. You could see the sides of her eyes crinkle. It was, you said, not uncomplicated. Tell me, she said. Strangers were good to tell. So you did. You told her everything – the son, the husband, the lover who was from where you were headed – and telling her did feel good. So you had a father for your boy and this lover you were going to surprise? Fair play to you, she said. She said that she often thought. What did she often think? That everyone should agree. A person for the family and a love to surprise.

She pulled into the carpark of a shut shorefront pub. The Nineteenth Hole. You offered plastic between the front seats. Cash only, sorry. Might there, you asked, be an ATM in a supermarket nearby?

Hole in the wall?

Very possibly. Was there a supermarket nearby? There was nothing. She said that it was her fault for not telling you back in town.

Lookit, she said, I get you next time.

You told her that you would be returning tomorrow. She gave you a business card, and wrote her mobile on the blank back and her name. Marta. Marta left you then, deposited you there more like: an evening turned enamel, squalls off a tide on the turn, no life about.

The TV was on in the pub, but there was nobody serving and no drinkers. The one street, such as it was, dead-ended at the

Members Only sign of a golf club. A grey Edwardian manse among conifers and palm trees. Many times he had shown you the map and satellite images. To the right of its entrance pillars, a car track along a fence of rusting wire. You walked that until you reached the only house. The further the track went, the more shells and mica underfoot. The track led to a private gate with a cattlegrid, a For Sale sign discoloured and lurching sideways, a name in three Gaelic parts carved into a slice of wood that had lost its varnish. The hedge had run wild. The drive was S-shaped and spongy with moss. At the far end of the S, concealed behind more conifers, the house came into relief: two storeys of sixties pebbledash and teak window frames in want of treating, a detached garage with flakes of magenta gloss peeling off a flap of mottled aluminium.

The bell made no sound within. The postbox was chest high. You peered through. Shadows mostly: bannisters and parquet and a brown frosted partition with daylight behind. You shouted his name into it. The indoor air too dead for echo.

Down the side, the privet almost up against the exterior wall. It was all you could do not to panic. What if he wasn't? There were French windows: original, wrought iron, single pane. Through them, through the reflection of rainclouds at sea, you could make stuff out. A table with gingham oilcloth and condiments arranged neatly on a tray. A lacquered fireguard and red-brick hearth. A pair of armchairs dragged to either end of the room. A huge outmoded TV in the far left corner. A dining table pushed up against the French windows.

You dialled his number. He wouldn't answer. You knew that. It started ringing your end. You could hear it minutely, speaker off.

Nobody knew where you were exactly. He had mentioned something about this place last time you saw him, something about hiring a skip for all the crap, but here could have been anywhere and there was no skip. Maybe your dad had been more right than you wanted to admit. Who this chap really was, how he could have been a complete fantasist for all any of you knew and this just another of the hoaxes that he played at regular intervals on hapless Quixotes in search of abandon.

His indoor murk pulsed. It was at the centre, his phone, down out of sight. It was like one of those little votive flames that you saw in grottoes in the south. Sacred heart. Its glow caught the edges of objects: a mirror's ebony oval, the frame of a portrait of a boy not him, the bronze of fire dogs. You hit End. The light fell away. You counted to ten, hit Call again and again the light within. You could even hear a vague vibrating hum. Still nobody entered the room.

He was near. You laid your bag on the patio and walked to the end of the garden. There was a gap in the privet where a gate must have been. Across the gap someone had propped a wooden pallet that you had to pull away. Its grain was pronounced and shiny from the sea air. You stood on a loose breezeblock positioned as a step. There were a hundred or so yards of dune. Beyond the dunes looked like beach of sorts. Beyond that a horizontal blade of stainless Irish Sea and a lot of sky. Here, from any angle, seemed two-thirds sky.

You had said nothing to him about this, this coming. You always preferred zero contact in those hours leading up to, zero contact in those hours immediately after. You wanted him to feel you without knowing. Feel you getting nearer. Feel you moving further away. Only when separation had plateaued into whole days apart would you talk. He was bound to have noticed, wherever he was, your radio silence. He would have felt you getting ever closer. You were sure of that. It was like the way a mobile somewhere can be heard to burble with static seconds before it bursts into ringtone. That agonizing pleasure of expectation that you half want never to end.

He appeared as a tiny silhouette in that fissure where track gives onto shore. He was trekking this way. He was black at first. Gradually, the colours of him neared into view. Something in his arms. He was chatting to himself, or possibly singing. He was already three-quarters the way when he looked up, when he stopped.

He looked down and started walking again. Driftwood. The something in his arms. It was driftwood.

You stayed on the breezeblock. His mother had died the previous summer. There was stuff as well, you knew, going on with his daughter. He had been over and back several times. She was dating some boy from a suburb of Dublin that had remained affluent after the crash. He was unshaven, in jeans and that brown golf jacket that had been his father's. Without looking up or laying down his driftwood, he rested against you, forehead on breastbone.

Are you really here? he said.

You were. You were really there.

But how?

Ferry.

No, *how?*

You had just left without saying.

You could feel his sticks and elbows pressing against your tummy. You unzipped your raincoat halfway and he kissed the square inch of skin between your breasts. You wrapped your arms around his head and squeezed. You held like that until he couldn't breathe and struggled free.

Come in, he said. We'll catch our deaths.

With one free hand he repositioned the pallet across the gap. You got your bag from the patio. He led you into an unlocked entry through the rear of the garage. There was a cream Renault coated in dust, a pushmower, tins on shelves with paint drips dried down their sides like candlewax.

He didn't have a key. He had bought a screwdriver on the way and unscrewed the lock on the internal door that went straight from garage into kitchen. It had given in seconds. In the kitchen, a gas cylinder tubed to a rusted two-ring hob. Boxes of marrowfat peas on the table and sachets of packet soup. He walked through without stopping to the same living room that you had peered into. The room's cleared centre turned out to be a horsehair mattress dragged from upstairs, strewn winceyette sheets and an antique flesh-coloured quilt.

Maman's eiderdown, he said.

He lowered the driftwood onto the hearth. He fetched his phone from among the bedding.

I seem, he said, to have missed a couple from you.

Once on the floor of the living room of his late mother's house. He still had on his jacket, you your raincoat. You removed your boots, your tights, lay on the mattress, dress bunched above your waist. He pushed his face between your legs and you clenched quickly on his tongue. He lay on top and covered your eyes with one hand and guided himself inside with the other. How long since last time? He grazed your upper lip with his lower. You could smell mothballs off his jacket. He wasn't sure if you were really there. You were. My love . . . He said your name twice and lay still and knelt upright.

You asked him who the pretty boy on the mantelpiece was. The boy in soft-focus with blond hair combed sideways. Had he heard?

Brother, he said after long silence.

Younger or older?

Younger, he said. Golden boy.

His brother was news. He had mentioned his mother in the past. That was the first you heard of a sibling. Were there others?

No others, he said, just ourselves. And then mostly only me.

He used the driftwood to start a fire. Miles away again. He banged the hearth to shake sand from it, and still it hissed and steamed. There had been a bag of Texan coal in the garage. It must have lain there since his mother's day. Had it not gone off? The coal? He called you silly without looking round. After millennia in the earth's bedrock, he said, a handful of winters in his old doll's garage was hardly going to knock a feather out of it. Then he moved about, not speaking, while you lay on the mattress and watched him. He seemed to accumulate darkness as he moved.

You lit one candle that was red and patterned on the outside with tinsel. It felt as if you had departed high summer that morning and arrived the same evening in deepest winter. You said that when he came back into the room with a pot of beans that he had heated on the hob. You were, he said, in good company thinking that. You weren't sure what he meant. Hibernia? Winter country. The Imperial Roman Army must have thought better of invading unremitting winter.

You ate on armchairs either end of the mattress. Or rather, he ate and you watched. There was some buffalo jerky in the kitchen if you preferred that. No thank you! Did the TV have signal? No signal. He had knocked off the mains fuse for fear that power usage would get traced. It was clear that he wasn't supposed to be.

Here?

He looked hurt.

The house is my brother's, he said, but it was my home far more than it was ever his.

The wind was big against the French windows. He dragged away the dining table, drew drapes of mustard velvet and returned to his place. Out in what was fast becoming night, a remote rumble like gravel spillage.

The house belonged to his little brother. He said this staring into firelight. Little brother had been appointed executor of their mother's will. Little brother had bought his share of the inheritance, three years ago, so that he could buy the apartment. Their mother never knew that this had happened. Her will had to be altered so that her youngest would be sole heir. Little brother had power of attorney. Little brother had changed the locks with immediate effect and put the house on the market within a month of their mother's final breath.

So essentially he was breaking and entering?

Essentially, he said. Breaking and entering is what you and I do, my dear.

His mother had never known about you. That hurt. Little brother had long since taken control of all family finances, which were not inconsiderable. Little brother alone had a direct line to their mother and could therefore edit. What she knew, what she didn't need to.

Used be I'd call her, he said, and then little brother would call me within twenty-four hours, asking me to go through him. So I just stopped. I was fucked if I was calling him to speak to her.

No.

Moments in the past when you thought that you had seen this bitterness, like lightning flicker miles off. You had seldom witnessed it at such close quarters. Why no mention of his brother before now? You stepped across the mattress and knelt at his knees. You asked him to unfold. Come on. You did it for him, unfolded his arms when he wouldn't. You pulled yourself up into his lap and crouched there and felt his arms relent around your shoulders.

You told him about Marta. He said that he had stocked up in town with non-perishables, a fresh gas cylinder, and got a taxi right to the gate. His driver was Ghanaian and would have had no idea that he wasn't supposed to be there. He knew that the door at the rear of the garage was swollen and secured with nothing more than an iron weight. The lock of the internal door from garage to kitchen, his father had always said, would keep out only an honest man.

We already know, he said, I'm not that.

Not what?

An honest man.

He had no reason to go up the street. There were never any viewers. The house was far enough off the beaten track that lights or smoke wouldn't be noticed.

Thank you, he said.

For?

Coming, he said, here.

You were heading back tomorrow. He had guessed as much. You undressed to your slip and lay on your side on the mattress. You watched him place pebbles of coal one by one, with tongs, onto a low flame. The night without inclined to storm. He snuffed your Christmas candle and stood above. You told him to take his clothes off. You watched the contours of his body in what minuscule glow the embers gave.

Everything?

Everything.

Can I leave the vest on?

He was such a bumpkin!

In these environs, he said, we prefer 'culchie'.

Very well.

Once when you plural lay under his mother's eiderdown. It weighed a tonne. You crouched on top of him and removed your bra without taking off your slip. He always liked that. He bit

131

your nipples through the slip. It lasted longer than the first time. You rested your palms either side of his head, so that your hair covered his face. You thought that you could hear a voice speaking elsewhere in the.

Listen!

You rested your mouth gently on top of his mouth.

The difference. This not being able to get near enough. This room he left for you to enter, you to want in. Quest to his lost you were. He was only to your many. You were echo to his cave. He was in there in darkness and freefall and agony. And this once you were.

Hear that?

That? he said.

That voice.

Describing everything we?

Yes! You were uttering into him uttering back. There it is again!

Yes, he said.

Yes?

Yes.

You stayed a while staring up at where the ceiling must have been. You could hear, behind your own breath heaving, his. Behind that, the rain's arrhythmic dabbing on glass and big gusts and the sea's underlying traffic.

Your phone buzzed in your bag. You ignored it. And again.

Do you need to get that?

You knew who it was and what it would mean. And things were how in general?

Every togetherness would arrive at this point, him asking you where things stood. He tried to play it cool, but his pain was palpable with every asking. You knew before you arrived that your visit would get to this. You had even caught yourself rehearsing lines in the terminal earlier. There was no sign of him divorcing, you were going to say. He never asked you about your ceremony, the registry office. Your son needed the security.

Sometime around then he stood in his vest and disappeared into the house. He came back with a bottle half full of amber and a pair of gilt-rimmed tumblers, relics from the seventies.

Black Bush, he said.

Not quite. He actually giggled. That was nice. A while since you had seen him giggling. He held the label up to you and let you read. It was the name of the whiskey. Kitty's favourite. His father wouldn't have it in the house. Presbyterian dram that it was. Only after his father's heart attack did Kitty splash out. And even then she blessed herself and asked forgiveness before every thimbleful.

He threw on more driftwood. This burned better. You knelt up beside him against the blaze. Being there, the house he grew up in, felt more familiar than you imagined. Was he ashamed? He did seem ashamed. He even asked:

Think less of me?

Because of the house?

There was one point, it was true, when you pictured mountains that gave onto ocean, turf smoke possibly, sometimes even thatch for heaven's sake. It was true also that you never imagined this nondescript nowhere of filling stations and palm trees and

B&B signs in the tiered gardens of dormer bungalows and golf umbrellas and dog-eared airport blockbusters on mahogany dining tables and the dull shine off mudflats where sea should have been.

Well, he said. Not very romantic, is it? He drained his tumbler. Nor terribly Irish, I suppose.

Silly.

It was still early. Scarcely ten. They could have been small hours, the way that you were acting. You laid your right hand to rest on the lukewarm inside of his naked thigh and held your tumbler in the left. He inspected your wedding band. He praised its vintage purity. You took birdlike sips and swilled the Black Bush in your mouth and cradled the tumbler in your lap. He helped himself to another. A capful that overspilled its edges. He held his tumbler to the light of the fire and asked if you were aware that gold had peaked historically on global markets in the past few years.

My daughter, he said, has converted all her post office savings into gold. So I'm informed. Me? She hasn't spoken to me since our mother's funeral.

This mind full of currency, this fluency with commodities, was news too. You glimpsed more clearly the world he came from. You had assumed, when you first met, that he was dyed-in-the-wool like yourself. Now you could see the posh boy he actually was.

Irish in England, he said quietly. They hear the accent and guess salt-of-the-earth. And – after *one's* initial horror – you realize how expedient it might be to let them go on thinking that. The plight of Paddy in Blighty.

One's initial horror! He was funny. Would smoking be all right?

I'll not ask you to take it into the garden, he said. Kitty must've smoked thousands in this room. What did for her in the end.

You broke off a fine parched splint and held it in flame and lit up. When had he started calling his mother by her name? Your phone again in your bag, somewhere in the dark part of the room. His mother became Kitty when they lived alone together during his teens.

And they were?

We were, he said.

You had meant were they very close. Was he saying something else?

Intimate, he said. It was, we were. Unusually intimate, he said.

He described how they were alone together in the house after his brother started boarding at a school the far side of Dublin, and how they bathed lots in the sea and he called her by her name. There was a phase, he said, when his newly widowed mother seemed to confuse him with his father. But that passed without anything. Happening? Nothing he could recall.

Then all these photos of her started popping up. Online. Of his mother? Selfies at the bathroom mirror that she had texted this boy. Was this his daughter he meant? Somehow talking about Kitty had become talking about his daughter. Months it had been going on. She was too mortified to tell anyone. Had he seen them? Sort of. He wanted law involved. Her mom had told him where to find them. One of those grimy low-res ex-shaming accounts. He had opened a page of thumbnail images and hit Close the second he recognized the outline of something familiar, someone, to one side.

I can't think about it.

Did he need to? He said that she hadn't been, since. Hadn't been what? Herself, he said. You came so close to telling him then, that you had once seen her. If not now, you thought, then never. He said that she hadn't been herself for a couple of years, if truth be told.

The water was still on and not metred. You could pee before bedding in for the night. He led you by the hand into the hall, up the stairs, by the torch on his phone. How did he keep his phone charged? A hokey resort up the coast. Once or twice a week, depending on the times, he could walk there at low tide and soak discreetly in the corner of a known Republican establishment where nobody knew him or the family, where he could charge to his heart's content and check messages and make it home before dusk cut off the shore's mid-section.

You squatted on the bowl in darkness and he excused himself. After all that you had done together! He was always prudish that way and you always teased him for it. You called him from the landing. No answer. You wouldn't have put it past him. To leave you alone in the powerless house of his late mother.

In here, he said from the master bedroom at the top of the landing. I'm in here.

The only light was the light through open curtains. He was at the centre. Everything seemed as you imagined it would have been, but for the stripped bed base.

Kitty's room, he said.

There was a dressing table and mirror just inside the door. There was a fireplace: a cold grate and a hearth of cream tile. On that a translucent Virgin Mary filled with holy water. Books still bedside, their places marked. There was a free-standing armoire with one of its doors hanging open. You could see inside, even in that light or lack of, the sheen of real mink.

The page wouldn't close, he said.

The page?

The page of thumbnails. It kept popping back up. He covered his face with his hands. Come back down. The no-coverage of his mother's place, he said, had come as such relief. The only means of exit had been to hold the power button until the whole machine shut off.

He lay curled away from you on the mattress in the living room. You dragged his mother's eiderdown up around and spooned in behind. The fire on its last legs, the night without full of its own noise.

He said something with his back to you. He said that he went directly to your house from his mother's funeral. Really? Last year. He climbed your back gate and, from the humid dark of your garden under London's semi-tropical din, watched the life you lived inside with the kid and the kid's father. You had wandered several times into the light and departed again with arms full. Laundry night or something of the like. And he just sat there watching? He did. You looked, he said, very content.

What did the name mean?

The name?

The name in three words on the piece of wood at the gate. He mumbled the words so quickly that they sounded like one. You tried saying them. Your pronunciations were all wrong.

Tír na nÓg, he said in three slow parts. Tír as in 'fear'. Na. NÓg as in 'brogue'. Tír na nÓg.

What did it mean?

Land of Youth, he said.

And it came from where?

His father's favourite story. A warrior named Oisín who falls in love with a fairy named Niamh of the Golden Hair. Niamh takes Oisín home to Tír na nÓg, where they'll stay young forever but from where Oisín can never return. They bear a son. Oscar.

He paused then. You smiled to his turned back.

Stop me, he said, if any of this starts sounding familiar.

After three years, Oisín is homesick and wants to see his friends. Niamh tells him it has been three hundred years, not three. Oisín doesn't believe her. He wants to go home. Niamh finally agrees and gives him a white magic horse that Oisín must stay on. Oisín rides back to Ireland and finds the country gone to ruin, his comrades long forgotten. Your phone vibrated again in your bag. You could see the inner lining pulsing. On his way back to Niamh, Oisín meets an old man who has heard of Oisín's father. Moved by the old man, Oisín bends over to shift a rock and slips to the ground and withers in an instant.

Was that the end? You waited for the longest time, to be sure, in case it was still not over and he had more story to tell. Even when you told him about the debacle of last Christmas's production of *My Fair Lady*, he didn't tease or respond even. Which wasn't like him. You said something about time that flitters away more quickly than you feel. Something about your son, how you had craved a child for years and how your son came when you had almost stopped hoping. Going back to work had been one of the toughest things you had ever done.

You would come home and Self would tell you every new development and you felt awful. You wanted it to be him telling you those things about your child. You didn't give the sex a second thought when it wasn't happening. So much time got squandered fantasizing that it was him there to meet you at the end of the working day, him ringing from the supermarket, him listening to records in the next room.

Sometimes your phone would vibrate and you didn't dare look at it for fear that it was not who you wanted to hear from. Sometimes you would turn your key and find the house silent. You would sit in the kitchen, coat still on. Possibly minutes only, but it felt like hours. And there were moments when you convinced yourself that more time had elapsed than you realized, and the movement in the next room and the footsteps approaching belonged to him.

I want to be with you.

You said that to his back in the dark of his mother's living room. Had he heard? The siege had gone on long enough. Four years since you first met. You were sorry, for the years, the burden of them he bore mostly. Tomorrow you would tell Self. The truth. Enough was enough. No secrecy anymore. Now it was time.

Next thing was dawn and the space where he had lain. He wasn't in the kitchen. He wasn't in his mother's room. His clothes and phone were gone. He had walked to the sea. That was what you figured. He had walked to the sea to fetch more wood. The bedclothes vibrated.

On train. Got called all hours. walked to town speak soon x

This was so him.

wtf mister?x

You dressed, pulled stuff together. Marta's card was still in your wallet. You tried him. Miraculously, he did answer. The line was very broken. Something about his daughter. You asked him to repeat and he started to say what his daughter's mother had said, when your phone died and you swore out loud.

The door from kitchen to garage. The rear exit and the metal weight in place. Still hours to opening, but a lorry was delivering bright steel kegs to The Nineteenth Hole and the lounge's side entrance was lying open. No lights on. A man appeared behind the bar. You needed to get a cab. But your phone had. It could happen to a bishop, the man said. Find a pew, a socket. The kettle was on. You plugged in under a bench seat. A radio behind the counter, tuned to a local station, was chanting some weekly litany of bereavement notices. *The death has occurred of . . .* You thanked the man twice when he passed through the room. *The death has occurred of . . .* Thank you, you said, thank you. No bother at all. *May their souls and all the souls of the faithful departed . . .* The table hummed and there shone on your screen's black plasma a white apple.

Saturday

I'm parked on hard shoulder, the middle of nowhere. Dozens of us lined along the road. I've a mandatory rest period of eleven hours to see out. Here since six. I travelled in convoy with Carl and a couple of others. Back on the autoroute shortly after five tomorrow morning, with a load of disposable nappies bound for the Middle East. I go out for one goodnight slash among the pines and there are lit cabs as far as is visible in either direction. Not a sinner coming or going. My breath plumes ghosts.

The centre of every country, I've come to learn, has a place like this. A warehouse complex accessed via feeder roads through forest. A windowless principality. There was never anything here until online shopping became a reality. Imports are shipped to here and from here they get distributed internally. Exports too. Here exports are pooled before they get disseminated outwards.

I have cheese and wafers. I have a CD of Breton shanties that our mother listened to on vinyl. My screen on the dash is silent and dark. Curtains closed. No word. And for darks such as these, when it feels as if the world has receded like cumulus across a bay, I keep a thermos of Black Bush under the driver's seat. Our father won a bottle in the Saint Stephen's Day shotgun scramble and made a great show of leaving it on the table of prizes in the club-house. Black Bush was the drink that I fixed Kitty.

A capful, she said.

In time, I would let her capful plash over its edges.

All Hallows' Eve. My girl is . . . Who knows? South of here, most likely, with the waiter who served us. Basem is a nice boy and she's the big girl that she likes to remind me she is. I keep telling myself this. She hasn't sent a solitary word since taking off, nor has she a solitary word of any of Basem's languages. Basem can't know the rough time that she's had these past years. It suits me to have her meeting Basem's family. Good people in a tower block of some sketchy graffitied suburb, a big table and sharing plates and brothers cracking jokes over her eternally shaven head.

I promised that I might see Carl tonight. Carl parked closer to the depot and I meandered further along. Carl is bound to text. This is something I do, promise Carl that I might see him. Carl has yet to twig that I promise to see him in lieu of seeing him. I have a stack of used daily tachographs. I'll give them monthly to Carl, the plan is, who will in turn hand me a fresh month's worth and log all readings into the system on my behalf. Who knew time's cup could be so easily refilled?

When I moved from the States, where such refills are com-monplace, my teenage daughter would visit me and ask at coun-ters if her drink were bottomless. The ladies of England hadn't the foggiest. I had to explain. To her, to them. Not only no refills ad infinitum, no refills period. Asking made her feel dumb and look out of place. She wanted fitting in way more than everlasting soda. She hammed up the accent and stopped asking.

This deal I have with Carl means that time comes with no end of refills. It drains to the dregs. The gods catch your eye and stop what they're doing and come down with a flask full of time off the hotplate and ask how your day is going. Thus my cup of time is forever full. Brimming with the stuff. Alas, bottomless means also forever lukewarm and without particular flavour. Time suddenly all feels and tastes the same. Its texture is grit and synthetic creamer.

> Free bit later. Self taking boy trick or treating. First time! Maybe speak then? Answer please. You feel very far away xxx

I lost you. That night two years ago. I was in Kitty's house alone. The house was my brother's, up for sale. I wasn't supposed to be there. Nobody knew that I was there except you and you were only guessing. You appeared unannounced. I saw you standing in the gap between the dunes and our garden. We spoke lots on the mattress in front of a fire of steaming driftwood. We did lots to one another. We sipped whiskey, kneeling at the hearth. In excruciating love.

Our daughter had gone silent. I'd thought little of it. She often went silent and resurfaced wondering what the big deal was. Her mom vibrated next to my head. I took it into the hall. Dawn or as near as made no difference. Where on earth was I? I whispered not to worry about that. They had phoned her. Who had? Some hospital in Dublin. Just tell me, I said. She had taken, had been admitted, was still at that point. I dressed in the hall, desperate not to wake you.

It was then and there that I lost you. I lost you in sleep in the dark on a mattress on the floor of the living room of the house that I grew up in, before a fire long gone out. And I found her at the other end.

I caught a taxi from the station, said who I was to the first clipboard I met at reception. Whoever it was that I spoke to, who gave me directions, must have called ahead. They were all standing around. Like tailors' dummies in the disinfected corridor of an IC unit. Like they knew that I was coming. It had only just. They were all staring at me with. What? Pity? Few things irritate more than this. This simpering self-congratulatory pity. Directed at me. Someone even rested a hand on my forearm and seemed shocked when I recoiled as I did.

It was, I am, too late.

One white coat took the lead. Had I ID? Excuse me? I wasn't trying to buy a fucking drink. He smiled. Not meanly. He was just embarrassed. He needed to be certain that I was who I said I was. This wasn't a situation one was liable to gatecrash, was it? He folded his arms. Would I prefer to wait until her mom got there? Her mom was in a summer house out the west. She wouldn't make it till lunchtime earliest. They glanced at one another. Was I entirely? Certain? I was. I would be fine, thanks all the same. They handed me a sack. Of what had been on her. Her person.

Standard-issue aquamarine plastic, its neck tied and tagged with her name. Almost nothing solid in there by the feel. Her denim jacket and bits of hard crap that had been in her pockets and her green boots and one small heavy object at the bottom. Did I want to go in then? I did. I said so blankly. I wanted to go in, thank you very much.

She looked so beautiful. She was flat out on her back against the far wall. There was an upturn on her lips, like this was a massive pantomime and she was bound to crack. The machines were many and without light. Could we get a pillow for her head? I requested a pillow and got yet more pity. One sheet folded across her midriff, arms at her side. A plastic wrist tag, her name and some numbers handwritten within. A gown of pale sickly pink. Face pure white, lips blue. But she was always wan. A daft mistake all this, I remember thinking. She looked no different now to how she always.

Would you like some time alone?

The white coat asked me that. I'd forgotten that he was still with us.

Alone?

I mean with your, the white coat said. He rubbed the seam of his forehead with the nail of one thumb. He apologized.

I mean time alone, he said, with your thoughts.

With my thoughts!

He backed away. As much time as I liked. And if there was anything. Pillows? He was little more than a boy himself. He would see what they could rustle up. He pulled the door behind him.

Her fringe was damp and dragged to one side. It looked like someone had brushed her hair. It was sleek. It was gathered around the back of her neck and over one shoulder. The ink of the tattoo on her upper arm had faded a purple that blurred at the edges. Her hands were cold. She was forever whingeing about her hands being freezing. Normally, I said that she was just being a baby. But this time they were, freezing that is. I punctured the sack. Her mittens were in either pocket of her jacket. I knew they would be, among strips of toilet paper and loose matches. They were charcoal, lambswool, fingerless. I smoothed them out and fixed them carefully one at a time onto each and laid them, her mittened hands, back by her side.

Now, I said.

I sat for heaven knows how long, knuckles of her left hand cupped under the palm of my own left hand. She was always expert with the silent treatment. Given whatever petty grievance. Days it could go on. This seemed different. This was the silent treatment writ large. I felt self-conscious. Of all the things . . . She was my best friend. I'd never felt self-conscious in her company. I pulled away and did a turn of the room. I even checked my phone. A flurry of cryptic messages from her several hours ago, that must have landed only after I'd entered the hospital's open network. I sat down again. I took her hand again. And I started speaking to her.

Just the same old meaningless guff that she and I had been saying to one another ever since she was a kid. Sure quit and this is it and what harm as the fella says. Etcetera. Nothing back. We would be, I told her, out of this daft cul-de-sac in seconds. I flattened out her sheet, though it needed no flattening. She looked longer than I'd ever noticed, and willowy with it. She had, it struck me only then, the bearing of the grandmother whom she'd barely known and after whom she was named.

Kitty, I said. For God's sake.

She was skin and bone, all protruding jawline and clavicles and elbows. Her flesh seemed almost translucent in places. Her throat, her inner arm, that hairless crescent behind the ear.

Would you ever cut this out like a good girl?

Her skin was completely unblemished. I remember being put in mind of lemon sorbet, even then, left long enough at room temperature for its yellow to come to the fore. Her shut eyelids were naturally a darker shade than anywhere else on her body. Her tattoo was barbed wire. I'd never looked at it that closely before. I'd assumed that it was some generic Celtic design chosen to signify her difference, her origins. It wasn't that. It was a braid of barbed wire interlaced with rose thorns and I'd never looked closely enough.

Come on, Kitty, I said, cut the old man some slack.

She was born in a different wing of the same building, twenty years before. I could hear a breakfast trolley doing its routine in the corridor. Same time of the morning she was born, between dawn and first rounds. Then I hitched, the morning of her delivery, up the coast. I was picked up by a van driven by someone from the golf club. I arrived in our kitchen and announced the family's first grandchild.

Kitty, I said. For me.

You never call me that.

She had started smiling where she was lying flat, eyes still shut, even before she spoke. She had been planning on playing possum indefinitely in her hospital bed and finally couldn't help herself. I squeezed her knuckles and she squeezed weakly back.

Call you what?

Kitty, she said. You never call me Kitty.

What is it I call you then?

Daughter.

And is that not what you are?

Needn't have bothered christening me, she said. Her breast heaved once beneath her gown. And after your poor mammy and all.

Is now really a good moment to make cracks about my late mother?

Her gown quivered, properly this time. But her eyes never opened.

Bro, stop, she said. I've got my whole mortality vibe going on over here. Seriously?

It's a good look for you. Suits.

The white coat leaned diagonally around the door. Was everything as it should be? Did I need more? Time? I was good for time. It was completely commonplace, the white coat said, to want a few words for one's own sake and closure and what have you. Sure thing. There were some people waiting in the corridor. For me? Only when I was ready. No rush. None at all. The white coat slid backwards again and the door closed again.

New friend? she said.

Best friend.

That not someone else?

You?

Nice one, she said. Just can't help yourself. Encroaching on my ontological space.

Oh fuck off.

There you go again! She lifted her free hand to her eyes. This was hysterical, to her only. I read that last word in a book, she said. Ontological!

This was showboating. This mortality malarkey was precisely the class of showboating that she and I identified regularly and with impunity. Noticebox! It was her favourite word. She would yell it at whatever reality junk was on. Now here she was. She had whatever attention she sought. She had made her point.

Darling, I said, this is showboating of the highest order. This is, indeed, being the very noticebox you despise in others.

Fair cop, she said. What do we propose?

That your dear old da goes out to have a quiet word, explains that you and I have our very own exit strategy.

Do we?

Assure them that your pater can take it from here, persuade them to discharge.

Look at you, she said, all the lingo.

And then we'll slip away, the pair of us.

We will, she said.

And then it'll be just us, the old team.

It will, she said.

And then? Then I stood out of my bedside chair and leant across my daughter and kissed each of her shut eyelids. Kitty. Her lids didn't flinch, nor did their lashes flutter. Just you wait and see. Her skin had the texture of wax. Not real at all. Like kissing that stuff they wrap hard cheese in. Light of my life.

I left her things where they were in the plastic sack on sterilized tiles. I blew my nose, cleared my throat. I had the handle of the door in my hand when she asked me not to take long. Don't be long. She sounded in pain. Like a spasm had gone through her. Please. I didn't look around. I said 'No fear' where I was and pushed down the handle and pulled the door towards me and stepped into the corridor.

The dash again. Leave me be. Nobody hears when I say that. My phone's opal rectangle is reflected in the underside of the windscreen of Howard's truck.

> where u ur missing
> action carl!

That Carl has my number and can text me at all hours is part of the deal. This is their way, his and Howard's, of keeping me at the end of a leash. Nowadays Carl texts stuff other than business. Hand-me-down jokes. Gifs of jungle animals being innocently obscene. What now? Some singalong around a lit barrel between cabs. The Nuneaton crowd that Carl is forever banging on about and I have no desire to join.

> mais quelle action?

I pour a measure into the cap of my thermos. I bless myself and ask forgiveness. I'm going nowhere.

> opposite main gate –
> path in woods – ur
> missing it carl!

Carl is near. Where I can't be sure, nor care that much. Carl always knows exactly where I am. Carl's action is probably negligible. I don't want to go there. But part of me knows that I should put in ten minutes, press the flesh, plead the earliest start of the lot and be back within half an hour. For once not be the stranger that Carl insists I've become.

What the hell . . . I say that to myself. I say it out loud in the dead air of Howard's cab. Saturday night after all. Carl's action would surely beat remembering all those details that happy pills once helped me to forget. I half fill a hipflask of our father's that was a gift from our mother, that I took with me from home. It's teeming. There's thunder, remote and hollow, out there as well.

Carl's path is where he said. Opposite the main entrance. I navigate with the light off my phone. The depot's salmon glow recedes. The only noise at first is that of my boots treading a floor of damp twigs and leaves. Hearing my own footfalls has always made me nervous. A quarter-mile of forest and still nothing. Inclined to give up, turn back, I stop. It's only in stopping, in my footfalls fallen silent, that a din rises like the congregation of some obscure sect or lynch mob in old south.

Caravan all tarped up for the winter. Pair gone out. Oz wrapped in toilet roll as a mummy! Said I'd stay put, fix supper. Now? Please xxx

The din, the nearer it gets, separates into parts. I go towards it. The further I go, the more its parts acquire distance from one another. Soon it's no longer one thing. It's several: shouting and whooping and cheers.

I could ring you from here. There's signal. I could ring you and say sorry. I would love to hear your voice. I would love to start again. And then? We hang up and I wait for something to happen and nothing does and I tilt off the rails again? Pass.

In a small clearing there are about thirty hauliers. From all over and all huddled into a solitary inward-gazing circle. A fight I'm thinking. A grudge so old that nobody can be sure how it started. There are phones held overhead and pointed down. There are flashes. I'm thinking bare knuckles, blood. My breath has quickened. There are dull waves. I lean up against plaid and fleece and denim that I can almost see beyond. I can hear, from the circle's centre, calmer voices. One of the voices belongs to a woman.

My pocket vibrates again. Your unsaved number fills my cracked screen. My heart balloons and blows away. I choose Decline again.

There he is! Carl is shouting towards me. Whip out yer old chap, there's a good lad!

What the holy fuck?

I say that for Carl's ears only. There's the crackle of leaves being trodden. There's an overpowering stench like disinfectant. There's this staggered groaning beyond the row of heads.

Just a bit of a jerk is all, Carl says, nothin nasty.

Jesus Christ! What have you in there? Livestock?

No! Up close Carl's face is puckered puce and beaded with rain or sweat or both. That's the best bit!

That so?

Toff lass! Carl says. Carl's still shouting, even though he's right up against me. Lectures in the local college! Loves it!

You'd hope she'd find more than that to love.

You what?

I didn't mean to say that, but it seems I have. Now Carl has his face on. Who does Pat think Pat is? Carl's not having it. Carl could bawl me out, send me packing. But that, ultimately, would be unsatisfactory. Carl won't let me go that easily. Carl won't release me until I belong on Carl's terms.

Don't be such a fuckin mardy arse!

Carl grabs me in this playful headlock. Carl's shirt is clammy. I can feel the folds of Carl's flesh undulating against my ear and temple. Am I going to behave? Am I? Carl locks tighter. I can hear up close the internal draining of Carl's digestive tract. Close to retching, I submit. I am, I say, I am! I'm going to behave! Carl releases me, withdraws from. Carl looks dazed, post-coital. When Carl speaks again, Carl is out of puff. I'm to behave, stop my bloody moaning, get myself in there and my champagne cork popped all over mademoiselle's Marie-Antoinettes.

Others have gathered behind. I've begun being pushed in without noticing. Carl drifts, a running commentary, sniggering and pointing. The place honks testosterone and blow. Men push out the opposite direction. Belts being buckled, they brush shoulders. They're spectral, spent. Back out in clearing, they shake spume from their hands and smoke and exchange language and disperse.

I slip the hipflask from my windcheater. Further in a foetid stink like reheated flesh. I can see one bare leg suspended in air, the belt buckle of a designer rain mac. More gather behind. I want gone. They're pressing up against. Carl is nowhere now. I mumble God forgive me and swig and hold the fire water under my tongue. I'm being forced, incrementally, to the core of this nothing that I increasingly feel.

Don't be long, she said. Please.

There were, that morning, two guys in suits in the hospital corridor. The white coat said their names that I either didn't recognize or deliberately didn't catch. The white coat said that he would leave us to it and disappeared down the corridor.

We shook hands. Me and the two suits. One gangly and learning the ropes and speechless, one my own age and shorter and greying goatee. I did what I always do when backed against a wall. I acquired Maman's distracted hauteur. What could I possibly do for them? The older goatee did all the talking. They were very sorry. He started with that and I almost guffawed. He said more after. It went over my head, most of it, or took a shortcut through me. He kept referring to my trouble. My? Trouble, he said, we're all very sorry for it. I said that we'd covered the sorry bit. Could we crack on? Could we perhaps come to the? The point? Please.

He was peering at me, the older one. He asked me something. Had we, he and I, been to school together?

School, I said.

My voice juggled that syllable, as if dandling some obsolete nugget of antiquity. He thought he recognized the head. My head. I said the name of the private boarding school where I lasted one term. Lording it over him on false pretences. If he had gone there, I said, then it was entirely possible that he and I had indeed. Had he? I said so gambling that he could never have gone there, nor could have known that I was bluffing. His head bowed.

Sorry, he said.

There was one word that got stuck. He spoke it somewhere in there. The word, adjacent to something else, was peculiar to where we were. It was early days, they understood, but if I had any preferences for the. So that they might push ahead with arrangements for the.

I said nothing. Not for want of trying. It was just that it felt as if the word – that word they had used – had entered me. The word had disappeared into me. I put my hand under my father's jacket and placed it flat on my abdomen, like I had a twinge or stitch. I was expecting to find a patch of blood sticking my shirt's cotton to my skin.

Have a think about it.

About the?

Removal, he said with a minor rising terminal.

Had I heard the first time? I gathered myself. I assured him that I would. I would certainly have a good think about the.

The word had lodged in me. There was never any exit wound that I could find.

You're very good, the older said.

I'm?

Very good.

Am I?

Nonsense, all of it. I dearly wanted to scream that, what risible braindead nonsense it was, into their generic provincial faces. But pity is best met with pity. Theirs for me, mine for them. I yawned and stretched and squinted the other direction, like they were Jehovah's Witnesses on my doorstep and I was too in the middle of a delicate situation to pay any attention to their folie à deux, their delusional well-meaning prattle.

Can you just give me a sec?

Course.

I walked backwards from them, simpering thanks as I did. I let them believe that I was a sound man just like them and worthy of their trust. I left them in their suits in dawn's corridor.

The door to the ward office was ajar. I tapped on its frosted pane with my wedding ring. The white coat was sitting on the edge of a desk. Could I possibly have a quiet? Certainly. There was a handful of nurses in there as well. They had all, every one of them, their arms folded. They looked up when I. Come in, they said. I said that there had been some sort of. Yes? They faced towards me with yet more pity. Some misunderstanding. I just wanted to take my. Yes? She had tried this before, on several occasions. They really needed to know that. Would I care for something? To calm yourself, the white coat said. I was perfectly calm, thank you very. Some mild sedative? Listen. This was horseshit. I said that. There were raised voices, my own among them. Pathetic fucking horseshit. One placatory hand reached towards me. It was perfectly natural, in the circumstances. Home with me, I was insisting, out of that godawful morgue, to where I could, in which she might.

I remember a tumbling backwards and his actual white coat billowing with the updraught and paperwork cascading and two overweight uniforms and the emerald rubber flooring that my cheek was restrained against. A new voice somewhere out in the corridor, polished and rounded off at the corners, pronounced my name. My little brother. He was out there, the other side of the door. I remember the shading of nicotine on fingers holding me down, a rectangle of dust beneath the consultant's desk.

I have arrived at the heart of Carl's clearing. I've arrived without even trying to. More rows behind me. Before me, flashing in and out of various lights, white goosepimpled flesh on the bonnet of a car and a paper witch's hat and a triangular tuft of auburn crisscrossed with cuckoospit. Feet with expensive orthotic sandals. Heels that are cracked. I feel nothing. Rien. Only sadness at the orthotic sandals, the cracked heels. My turn has.

Come.

It's our mother's voice says that. She turns to face me. A foreign hand shoves my shoulderblade.

Come, she says, come down.

Fuck this.

I back off, push out. No parting of the waves of those awaiting theirs. Just jeering. Just calling after. A faggot I am. Pat! Carl is calling a name that echoes in the forest and is barely mine.

I run past men beyond the circle. They're chatting and swigging off the neck and taken aback by my running. When did I last run? Possibly decades. Fly like the wind, our mother would urge when we were late for something or it was raining, fly like the wind. I mislay Carl's path back and all bearings. I thrash through leaves and branches and, after what feels too long, emerge at a roundabout at the far end of the same feeder road that we came in on. I trudge half a mile along the hard shoulder. The line of trucks looms back into view. My windcheater is saturated, pocket buzzing. I pop the lock from several hundred yards. The hazards of Howard's cab flash. Its internal bulb fades up. I check around the back, the chassis, as we're told to do every time. No self-respecting asylum seeker would be anywhere near here.

> Never going to speak to me again? For someone who talked so much about kindness, this is not kind mister . . .

I lock the cab from inside, power off. I'm not here. Nor is the hipflask here, in my pocket. I must have dropped it. Sterling silver, engraved. My one keepsake from home. It could be anywhere now. In that clearing underfoot among Carl's circle of jerks. In the undergrowth of the path I came back on that turned out to be not a path. On the sodden margin between the roundabout and here. I find the thermos. I pour a mouthful into its cap. The rain is really coming down. I find, as well, under the passenger seat, a melted Freddo that I unpeel and lick from the wrapper's underside. I raise the capful of whiskey and toast my own reflection.

God forgive me!

It's now that I decide. To what? It's now, in this blanked-out glorified sardine tin of Howard's, that I decide to cut loose. Give Carl and his darkness the slip, communicate via text and then only business, drop off the given month's tachographs in a jiffy bag at agreed pick-up locations, be back on the road before anybody comes. How long have I been out here? Longer than I realize. Days turn out to be months. I've enough darkness to be going on with. It's now that I decide to get away with absence inasmuch as I can. Answer Carl less, and less still. In time stop responding altogether. Drift on sans load.

Tonight's plan is to leave the jiffy bag under one of Carl's wipers. I have to hold onto the tachographs of the past three days. That's the law. If the law pulls me over, I have to be able to produce discs for the last three days. Everything before then can go.

We've been exchanging the same jiffy. It's getting worn, marked black from handling, the stuffing leaking out of one of its cracked corners. It's decorated with ornate doodles and dates and little back-and-forth notes. In my inscrutable print, in Carl's loopy cursive.

What should tonight's note say? That I'm sorry for coming to the clearing in the first place? Fact. That I'm sorry for leaving unceremoniously? Less so. Tell Carl that I haven't experienced anything in the ballpark of arousal most of this year and was unlikely to then? True to form, I choose nothing. I write nothing, except those dates covered by this latest dispatch. I replace the cap on my pen before its felt tip runs dry.

I did one night in a cell. Twenty-four hours in a station in Dublin's inner city. How I got from the hospital to there is anyone's guess. All I remember is one afternoon of fluorescent tube and the imprint of lino swelling my cheekbone. The light of high summer resembled winter. And her mom appeared.

Not for very long. Nor was I ever certain whether or not I'd dreamt it. The wrong end of the afternoon. Looked different. Younger somehow, taller. We were still married then. We hugged for the first time in ages. That was strange. My brother had offered his spare room. Would I like to get bailed out of there? I said no. No thank you. That was the one prison that I wanted never to be released from. Came directly from the hospital, from seeing our daughter. We agreed how beautiful she had looked. Beyond that, neither of us could speak enough to say goodbye.

The duty officer was this lovely kid. He was doing a line with a nurse who made soup for him when he was on nights. Would I like it?

There would be no question, he said, of anyone pressing.

Thank you.

His accent was far west. Where exactly? Clew Bay. He possessed that earthy oversized gentleness. He was one of those in whose company I pretend to be Irish even though I am. Some long word overlooking Clew Bay that I'd never heard of. I handed him back his empty bowl and spoon. My daughter and I, on the east-bound red-eye across the Atlantic, adored the beginning of the descent at first light when the cabin crew served smoked salmon bagels and orange juice and all the islands of Clew Bay were visible below like loose change scattered on a floor of sapphire.

It was just precautionary, he said.

I'm with you.

The one night only, he said, for your own.

Course.

If it was down to me, he said, I'd let you go now, but your brother was adamant.

My brother?

He was here, he said, do you not?

My brother?

He was, he said, he was very good about it.

The young duty officer was sorry for my. That word again. He had bits to get done and would leave me to it. To my trouble. One horrendous night, my season in hell, head in hands and souls more desperate than my own echoing further along. I dreamt that I was running around Tír na nÓg in pitch black. Up the stairs, in and out of several bedrooms, down again, into the kitchen and the living room with its French windows banging open. I woke to pure night. Kitty! I shouted her name and others shouted back to shut the fuck up and I shouted her name with even greater force. Kitty! The officer called down several times. I was to keep a lid on it. Kitty! Drunk on grief I was, bellowing her name over and over. Kitty! Kitty!

Last warning now, the corridor said.

The same officer returned around dawn, more wary of me, my few belongings rattling around a sealed see-through tub. He gave me her things in a fresh aquamarine plastic sack not punctured. We shook hands. I told him that I was sorry. I was. I was sorry for being such a.

Forget it, man, he said.

I'll hardly manage that!

We shook a second time. He had rung my brother. Just now? Just there. My brother had said to keep a hold of me. And my brother was on his way? He was. I said that I'd stand and wait for my brother out the front. The officer bought it. No acting the maggot? No . . . I promised and said he was a decent man. The station steps were granite, gleaming from rainfall.

Quite the performance!

She was leaning against the blue gloss railings. She spoke without looking up from her lit screen. She was still wearing the fingerless mittens that I'd put on her. Somehow her head had been shaven since. She was still wearing, as well, the plastic wrist tag that bore her name.

Gotta hand it to you, she said, I give you one job.

Go screw yourself.

Beautiful! Now that definitely is a bit.

Good to see you so.

So what?

Back to yourself.

I shouted that over my shoulder. Even I was surprised by the fury of my shouting without stopping or looking back.

You cross with me? she said.

What do you think?

Paddy! It was then that she started following me. She started then and has been ever since. You not speaking to me?

No, nor ever will again.

It was then that she started and stopped all at once. When she next spoke, she sounded further behind. It was that, that sounding further behind, that made me stop as well.

If you won't speak to me, I'll have nobody to speak to.

I turned then. She looked utterly. Crushed? I pointed dumbly at her sack of things and tried to humour her along and went back when she didn't move. She was shivering.

Bloody eejit.

Nobody, she said.

I untied the sack carefully and took out her jacket and put it on her. I knelt and got her to push her feet into boots that I laced for her. I removed my father's windcheater and got her to slip her cold arms into its sleeves and zipped its zip and wrapped its lapels around her throat. Now. I wrapped my own arms around her and pulled her buzz cut into me. We had to get out of there before anyone came. She never asked who might come. I planted several arid kisses on her shaven hairline. Even then she tasted stale, an hour beyond her sell-by date.

My bloody eejit.

For all, she said.

I shushed her. All what? I was making light of.

Eternity, she said. For all.

Ssshhh. I have you now.

*

A soft knock on my door. This was always going to come to pass. There was no bolting from the forest clearing, I do understand, without the forest clearing coming after. Through the gap in the curtain, Carl is waiting in the rain. Carl has knocked with the rubber finial of his crutch. I say 'Just a sec' to outside. I have to straighten myself, square the recent past with Carl. I unlock and jump breezily into Carl's rain.

All right, my lovely? Carl says. Carl says it with some trepidation, at what he has stumbled upon and the state he might find me in.

Yeah grand.

You look like you've seen a.

Do I?

Carl does something that flummoxes me. Carl asks after my brother.

Who's this Art? Carl says.

Excuse me?

Has my brother been onto Carl? Asked Carl to keep tabs on me on his behalf? Stranger things have happened. Carl can see my amazement. Pleased with himself Carl is. Carl can see it dawning on me that Carl knows more than I'd have ever guessed or ever wanted him to.

Who's this Art when he's at home?

Little brother.

Give him this next time you see him, Carl says.

Carls unfurls and holds aloft my lost shop-soiled hipflask. Carl shakes open his reading specs with his free hand and painfully mispronounces the inscription engraved on its convex unpolished front.

À Art
de Kitty
pour toujours

Answers on a postcard please, Carl says passing it over.

To Art from Kitty for always. The old doll's gift to the old man for his fiftieth.

But you said Art was your kid brother?

Named after the father.

How come the little brother, Carl says, was named after the dad and not the big brother?

Search me.

Carl does just that. Carl searches me like there has been subsidence in my surface and now Carl can glimpse into caverns hitherto submerged.

I was due to be named after my father. But Kitty's father died shortly before I was born and I got named after him instead. Dad and Kitty's father were never close. Did my bearing our mother's father's name come between me and our father? Art was held back for my brother.

Funny one that, Carl says.

You could say.

I hand Carl the jiffy bag of tachographs. All present and correct? All present and. Carl wedges the jiffy under the arm with the crutch. Carl glances backwards in the general direction of the forest, the track, the clearing.

Bit of fun, Carl says, bit of fun is all.

If you say so. I raise two hands in surrender. Not my bag.

Thought as much. Howard the same.

Come again?

Howard, Carl says, same as you.

You don't say.

Carl is smiling. Carl has Pat cornered, assuming himself a cut above, when the world and its wife knows that even Pat's daddy stepped Pat over.

You're no different from the rest of us, Carl says.

Carl has come for his due, for what Carl feels that Carl has owing to him. Carl has come to play the heavy. Carl has done this before. Carl studies it on all those boxsets stashed beneath his bunk, the sympathetic yet emphatic lean. Carl recognizes the codes.

It's just that, when push comes to shove, Carl comes off unexpectedly vulnerable. This means too much to Carl, to come the heavy. Even with me and all the airs and graces that I've fallen from. Carl looks up at my lit cab.

Join you? Carl says.

Actually got company.

I'm half mouthing when I say that. I don't want us, my way of whispering says, to be overheard by the person who isn't up there.

Ah, Carl says. Carl is whispering too. Gotcha.

Carl knows that I'm fobbing him off with my phantom other. There's nothing Carl can reasonably do. I feel oddly touched. By

Carl. I even touch him. I rest my hand on Carl's upper arm. I say maybe some other time. Carl has been indulgent. Carl deserves repaying. I see that.

Promise? Carl says.

Promise. My fingers are crossed in my pocket. Scout's honour, not a dicky bird for now, Carlos.

Meaning from me about him, this. Nobody else need know that Carl approached me tonight. Carl possibly takes my promise differently.

Good lad, Carl says. Rallying himself, trying to. Of what denomination? If you don't mind my.

As in Catholic or Prod! I know what Carl is driving at. My lame jokes are just my way of holding Carl at bay a little longer. Pounds or euros!

Girl or boy, Carl says in no humour for lame jokes.

Girl.

A?

He looks crestfallen. Carl does. Carl looks crestfallen.

It's a girl.

Those three words. I realize, in saying them, where they come from. They come from a six a.m. twenty-plus years ago. I think this in the flicker while Carl watches. A Saturday during Easter and an anaesthetist in scrubs handing me my newborn swaddled in the same three words.

It's a girl.

A Punnet of Loganberries
September 2009–August 2011

Once in November in a viewing area near Gatwick. He had emailed early autumn. He would be in town. Wasn't sure if you remembered him, and completely understood. You took five weeks to reply. You suggested he come for supper with you and Self. He preferred to get on the road before rush hour. Lunch? You met in a pub on the edge of campus. He was there before you. He even wore a tie and stood when you approached the table.

This is bold, he said.

He was down in an external capacity. Meetings all morning. And you? You had taken half-day leave. You hadn't planned on telling him about taking leave, and when you did there in the pub he actually blushed. Don't flatter yourself! He had eaten. You weren't remotely hungry. His car was on a meter around the corner and if you fancied a spin. Had he ever been to Brighton? Was Brighton not ages away? About fifty minutes that hour of the afternoon.

Go on so, he said.

You never got that far. You parked in a layby off Gatwick's inner perimeter and watched international landings and spoke of your lives. You had been Self's grad student, longer ago than you cared to remember. You felt huge loyalty to Self, to what you had been through together.

He told you how he had almost drowned earlier that year, a week after he was over for the interview and met you. The pool of a friend's house. Old-fashioned, kidney-shaped, a twelve-foot drop in the middle. He had gone down alone on a full stomach. Attempted a dead-man's float and hit the bottom and panicked. His feet touched the pool's floor. He was rescued only by his daughter, in the screened porch, hearing his screams.

Did his life flash before!

It did, he said. Underwater. My whole life. And you were in it.

He asked if he could hold hands. You acted scandalized but let him. He held your hand to his face. Early winter, very damp, no plane-spotters around.

Does this count as once? You did kiss. It was chaste, closed-mouthed, to begin with. It was you who initiated tongues. Sheep as a lamb, you thought. He tasted of coriander. He undid the button of your jeans, the zip, and slid his right hand between. You kept kissing until the last seconds. You came on his middle finger, in his passenger seat, and rested your head on his tie and held tight against for ages after.

Are you okay? He asked that several times. Are you okay?

You spoke every week on the phone from then to the following February. Same time every week. That was the deal. It was your idea, all you could cope with. It was him called you. He went back to America for a month over Christmas and still called at the same hour of every week. He even rang from a filling station in a place called Shawnee, in the Pocono Mountains. Where? Indeed. You realized then how much you loved his voice and said so. They had been given the loan of a lakehouse. He had come out to buy logs for the stove. You could hear him shivering, topping up with quarters.

If I perish out here it's your fault, he said, and nobody will be any the wiser.

Once in February in a Travelodge just down from the same layby. First time proper. He collected you from the top of your road and drove out to where you had parked last time. Neither spoke the whole journey there. It was you who suggested getting a room. You had steeled yourself to do it and you felt lost when he seemed as hesitant as he did. Would just sitting here not be enough? This might be the one chance we get. He drove over to the terminal and withdrew cash so it wouldn't appear on either of your statements. You stood at the centre of the room. I don't know what to do. He said he didn't either. You undressed in the en suite and when you stepped out, clothes held against, he was undressed too. You lay side-by-side on the duvet, both a little embarrassed. You told him to go on top.

I thought you'd never arrive, he said. Like I've been waiting years.

Yes.

That once was once for hours as opposed to many. You never stopped entirely. He rolled onto his back and said he wanted a good look. He counted the veins in your breasts. You came three times, twice by his hand and once by your own. He couldn't at all. The only time you paused was when you lay under the linen, him on his back and you half on top with his hand pressed into the concave at the base of your spine. You should be getting home. He asked you to kneel on all fours on the mattress. You did without answering. He passed under, above, through. You could feel him. He said he wanted to look at, to sniff, to burn every inch of your skin onto his hard-drive.

He dropped you in the carpark of a supermarket. Self left the entrance with shopping just as you were about to.

What?

You flipped down the sun visor.

So that's my opposition, he said.

Don't.

Self asked that night, or maybe the night after. Would you ever be lovers again? Last summer was the most recent, and even then you were thinking of someone else. You said that in the dark, in the small hours. Someone else who had given you a lift in May and phoned the same evening? Yes.

You're no poker player, Self said.

The house went up for sale the same week. It was Self who approached the agents, discussed realistic prices given the market, cleaned rooms furiously for brochure pics.

Once in March. A Wednesday. You trained north and surprised him at his office with a picnic for Saint Patrick's Day. It was an Irish bank holiday after all. Nobody knew who you were. There was freedom in that. He introduced you to the admin staff as his dear friend. That was nice. He took you to a derelict park with a cholera monument, hands held there and back. Nobody around. You sat entwined among ragwort as if the ragwort were a field of sunflowers. You left teeth-marks on his chin. He described how many of his waking hours were devoted to onanism and thoughts of you. You snogged on the platform, like teenagers with nothing in the world to worry for.

Once in the ladies of a darts league alehouse in Stockport. He had no clue you were coming. You drifted through the rear room and said 'Gentlemen' in passing to the assembled blokes. He followed you in. You were undressed completely, shoulderblades against the brick wall's yellow gloss. For most of it his name was being summoned to the oche. He was mid-match and didn't acknowledge your leaving.

Once in April in a halfway house in the Midlands. Sheets of rain. He was seated on your platform when you got there and seemed spooked. The hotel was one-star two streets from the station. There was a rumpus down the corridor for most it, some pig begging some Lorraine and kicking her door. The bedding wasn't fresh. You sat on the edge in your mac, him on the chair under the TV. You felt numb. He did too. No signs forbidding you from smoking.

Never say, he said, that I didn't show you a good time.

You took off everything except the mac and sat on his lap and blew rings in his face. You like that? He shook his head and laughed despite his best efforts not to. He called you a dirty English tramp, you him a thick Irish prick. You wrapped the coat around and he inhaled the inside dark.

Once mid-morning at the end of May, in the kitchen of your house. He rang from Hertfordshire because he was passing near your parents' village. There were, he said, millions of buttercups. You told him that you would leave a day permit that had date/month/year already scratched under a rock just inside the gate, your door on the latch. Let yourself in.

Hello?

You were standing in your kitchen, the same black one-piece and green sandals that you wore at his interview. Was this safe? You said it was, but felt as scared as he looked. This day one year ago. Oh yeah . . . Your first anniversary. Let's get out. Not yet. You wanted one memory of him in the place where you had pictured him so often. Here? Yes. There on the table's edge. You lay back. He removed your knickers and walked his fingertips, carefully, up your bare inside leg from ankle to arse. The breakfast bowls clinked around your head.

Once the same afternoon in a valley directly under the Heathrow flightpath. The weather was warm. You had a rug that you had confiscated from home and a wicker basket with a lid. You both lay naked in long grass and got mild burn in parts not ordinarily exposed to sun. You had brought tapenade and oatcakes and the leftovers of Mateus rosé from your fridge. You smoked. He ate.

You were saying?

You exhaled towards the skyline. It was not uncomplicated and not remotely funny. You were ten years with a man a generation older, nearly your father's age. You were never sure if it was him that you needed or if it was how he saw you? So much of love is how another sees you. Your partner was a good man who deserved better. Self was completely without family in England and was, after the initial fury, now prepared to sit it out.

It would be so much easier if you were married. Self had asked you years ago and now you wondered if you should have said yes. Being married would at least give you something legal to dissolve. The house was up for sale, but nothing was selling. There had been a feature in the weekend supplement of one of the nationals, couples who couldn't afford to split, whom the financial crash was keeping together. And now this.

This?

This screwing in suburban wilderness.

At the narrow bridge over the spate culvert that marked the borough's historic boundary, you confessed that you had couples' counselling that evening. You owed Self that much. He dropped you on the street parallel to the one you lived on. That was safest. That way no neighbours, nobody who knew you, saw you being dropped by him. He was flying home to see his mother. She lived alone out on the coast. Was she okay? She was having trouble swallowing and had a doctor's referral. It hadn't been your idea. What hadn't? The counselling.

Anything to add?

The counsellor was looking at you. Already five to the hour. You had been silent for most of it. The counsellor was pleading with you to say something. There was zero breathing room. Even this hour . . . You didn't say that, just wished you had. All the air had been sucked out of the room. And now the quartz numberless clock on the wall behind the counsellor seemed to suggest that your hour was almost up.

No, you said, nothing to add.

Once on the phone. He was close to his mother's house in a field full of rusting agricultural hardware that he likened to Coney Island or some such antiquated theme park between the wars. You were in the pantry of your parents' at home, ostensibly fetching a pot of homemade plum preserve. You turned the key from within and shushed him down the line. You pretended to have knelt. You were, you said, guiding him into your mouth. He went quiet and choked and asked if you had as well.

In Clapham, in June, out of rain under the awning of an artisanal bakery, you got a withheld number and his voice said to be outside the tube station of Chalk Farm in two hours. He was on a payphone in Stansted. Really? He said that he didn't know which freaked him more, being in Stansted or speaking on a payphone. When you emerged from the tube, he positively hollered across the street.

I feel like Crocodile Dundee!

He was decked out in flipflops and some antique windcheater that you had never seen before. Comically out of his realm and relishing it. He had borrowed his mother's Clio and flown via Belfast. Not a sinner in the universe knew that he was there. He seemed wired, to see himself as this film noir fugitive. He had blagged a basement for one afternoon from some American connection, a dorm of metal bunks with a hotplate and a sheltered yard.

Once on one of the lower bunks. You had your period and laid out a bath towel. Your head kept hitting the slats of the top bunk. So in love with you, he said, so in love with. You showered together and held under the faucet until the hot ran cold. You walked up the hill to a chichi gastropub on England's Lane. It was far enough away from your patch to be safe, but you were still terrified of bumping into someone and wouldn't let him hold your hand and felt shit for not letting him. He spoke to all and sundry. His accent seemed hammed. He asked if he embarrassed you. Did he want you to be embarrassed by him? You assumed that that was the point.

How you find me, he said, is how I am.

You bought rocket pesto on Primrose Hill and tossed it in linguini and shavings of Parmesan. You ate in the yard on white patio furniture. Your phone humming at intervals indoors. The purchase had gone through on his grainstore conversion repo. He had still to tell his daughter the truth.

Twice on a pair of bunk mattresses formed into a square on that floor. Once was on all fours. You wore your chocolate slip. You couldn't sleep for the lemon tang of adrenalin under your tongue. The other was when you mounted him without his waking or knowing. You were still nervous of him then, wary of his capricious off-the-planet swings, scared that you would jump and find mid-air that he had gone. You said this to him before he woke and seemed surprised to be there. His flight was eightish. His mother wouldn't have noticed. He would park and go straight through from garage to kitchen to his old room. The only light downstairs that of his mother's anglepoise through frosted glass.

Once on the foundations of demolished flats, in wasteland that backed onto his office block. July. You took a day's leave on the sly and trained up and got covered in bites. A community police officer, hi-viz and mountain bike, appeared in the offing of sunlit midges just as he was unbuttoning your blouse. She questioned, from that distance, what you thought you were doing. You were, he called back, partaking of an extramarital tryst and that was an issue of ethics rather than legality and therefore beyond her jurisdiction.

Once twenty-four hours later when he appeared out of nowhere at your office door with takeaway sushi and bottles of craft ale, trained down on a whim that felt of hysteria, and dragged you to a bench in Bushy Park and said sorry. For what? He had promised his wife the night before to try again. His daughter was in bits. He was meeting them in Ireland. You felt relieved as well as sad. That was a shock, the intense relief you felt around the sadness that you expected to feel.

The welcome interregnum. Him out of the picture, trying again with his family somewhere in Ireland. You sipping cranberry juice to stave off cystitis, content to sit in one place even if that place was where your secret seemed no longer kept.

Men approached you as if a tiny bulb, newly connected, were lit above your head. Some held your elbow and spoke confidentially and were, to a man, on the brink of a separation of their own. Women left spaces in which to offload. Others texted advice and expletives. You trained it down to Whitstable to see the mother of your girlhood sweetheart, with whom you had stayed in touch. You had missed her husband's funeral. She hugged you on her steps. Even she seemed in the know. She offered Noilly Prat and ginger nuts and remembered late thirties being a perilous juncture. Ice? You told her about the expletives, how grateful for them you were. She said she understood. It was a sight better than all the bloody tact. She forced on you the keys to their holiday home that would be lying dormant.

Your phone vibrated in a bedroom in the Pyrenees. It lit the inside of your bag on the dressing table under the window, blanched the shutters. All your strewn things flickered and retreated. You tiptoed around the dark. You didn't open the message, for fear of waking Self. You saw most of it in locked screen anyway.

> So much for trying again! Fishing mackerel by moonlight, thinking about biting the tip of your ...

A horseman rode up on your second to last day. The horseman was in tan safari wear, a kerchief knotted at his throat. His horse was huge and the same shade. You recognized *pèlerin* as pilgrim. The horseman, without dismounting, requested a cup of water in formal address. Self was more preoccupied with the dialect that the horseman was speaking than with the horseman. Catalan, possibly Occitan. You let the tap run until the water was cold and filled the enamel mug that was cream with a lip of royal blue. Then horseman and horse rode on towards the troglodyte church. He had said something about you while you were inside. What had he said? Self couldn't be certain.

Once at the end of August on the floor of the master bedroom of his new apartment. The ruse was a lunch date with an old friend. You boarded the train an hour before the train you'd pre-booked and got away with it.

He was in painting clothes. Cargo shorts and a varsity basketball T-shirt spattered with paint. You hadn't long. His daughter was in town. Over visiting. He had told her everything, that he and her mother were thinking of trialling parallel lives, even about you and your coming today. She preferred to make herself scarce. She would be starting college in Dublin next year and said she really didn't give a crap. He had forced upon her keys to his place. She wouldn't ever use them. But still. He had told her this would be her home as well and spread his arms into the empty room.

You described your hols, the horseman, the counselling. The latter remained ongoing. You were worried about Self, who was drinking like a fish and veered daily from marriage proposals to retiring to a ranch back home, wherever 'home' was. Your dad had written you a letter. Your mum just reiterated what a good provider you had and you never knew how lucky you were.

His apartment was a state. It had belonged to a couple who had declared for bankruptcy on their PR consultancy and had, by the look, left in a hurry. They had sprayed a cock-and-balls in luminous orange on the big wall of the main room, a swastika of sorts across the kitchen units. There were clothes still in the walk-in wardrobe. There were coloured hangers lying around the place and wires spooling out of holes and loose peas in the icebox. There was even a discoball on the mezzanine, with a corona of miniature mirror panels on the floor around it as if it lay where it had been dropped.

His bed was a mattress on cement. Do you even want to? You said you did. All very wordless and very sad. Neither of you undressed fully. Him on top and you kissing his temple. I need you. He had never said that before and kept saying it then. I need you . . . Just as he clenched and skipped a breath, this face appeared in the doorframe over his shoulder. Piercingly pretty. Eyes shocked wide and sleek black hair and an old-fashioned nightshirt worn as a dress and a single key in the hand raised to her open mouth. He rolled off just as the door upstairs could be heard to click. What was that? He walked you out to the street. The afternoon was golden. Should you say something? Your phone went. You had to take it. You were saying 'I'm here, I'm here' when his glass door closed automatically.

You got home the third Monday of September to men removing the For Sale sign from your hedge. What the hell? Change of plan, the men said. First you heard. Ask the boss, the men said. They meant Self. On the kitchen table there was a small square box and 'Will you?' handwritten in blue biro on a page torn from a refill pad.

You took the hybrid, the guts of two hours for rush hour and roadworks around Hemel Hempstead. Your parents sitting to the leftovers of yesterday's roast when you barged into their kitchen. Your dad all of a fluster.

What's this?

Impromptu visit. That all right?

You asked your mum if you could borrow ten for chips. Had you come out without your purse? There was no sense wasting money when there was plenty in the pot. You had already taken twenty. You had a craving for haddock and chips. You told them to fire ahead. Eat. Don't wait on my account.

The takeaway was at the top of their hill. You kept the order to a minimum and went next door. Vodka and Coke. A double. The lady behind the bar asked if everything was. Dandy, you said before she could finish. Just the drink please. You stood at the bar. Even asked her to top you up. The regulars watching on. And again please. One of those nights? The lady looked worried for you. You thanked her. Yeah, one of those. You even drained the ice and ate it. A treble, a double, two Cokes and you found yourself short seventy pence for the haddock and chips. You thought that you had tallied it down to the last. You slapped the pile of silver and coppers on the chippy counter. It's all fucking there. Swearing won't help, the apron said. You had started crying. Queue out the door and you start crying.

It was then that you became the person. That person everyone watches from a safe distance, all self-satisfied pity, glad they're not them. The public meltdown. The walking cautionary tale. There was no way of telling them that you had the money. The money wasn't the problem. You had seen this person yourself, many times you had been one of the pitying onlookers. Now was your turn to be the pitied one, and you were crying and publicly strapped for cash.

Seventy pence, the apron said, is seventy pence.

For pity's sake!

Some big bloke had stepped from the queue and was already counting change. Seventy pence! He was muttering angrily, though not in your direction. Now pet, the big bloke said to you and pushed more change into your pile. We'll not fall out, he said, not over seventy flamin pence we won't.

In those couple of minutes, on the steep downhill to your parents', you felt so full of hope. Like being on speed. You felt as if you had broken through some invisible barrier and had emerged the other side in an acre of unfenced pasture and were overcome with this huge rush of. What? Freedom? Maybe this was what freedom felt like. Like amphetamines crushed and inhaled and hurtling through your bloodstream. You even started running and fairly burst back into the kitchen.

The professor had phoned. The? Professor. You hated how your dad always referred to Self. Your partner was supposed to be cowed by your father, not the other way round. You poured your haddock and chips onto a small plate. Shouldn't you call back? Your dad was speaking as you left the room. Didn't say a word by way of response. Sat in the back glued to *Deal or No Deal*.

You bunked in your old room at the top. You made the bed and returned below to say a cursory goodnight. Your mum was washing up. Your father was in the family room and would be grateful for a moment of your precious.

This sort of thing happens in all marriages, he said.

We're not.

Not what?

Married.

Their concern was for your peace of mind. They were a bit worried about you. And that poor chap. He meant Self. How senior Self had become, how well Self took care of you. Your mum came through and sat in an upright chair in the far corner. They had been wondering. Your dad said that and nodded at your mum to pitch in. Hadn't they, been wondering? You mum said that they

183

had. What had they been wondering? They had just had their vote on the Christmas show. *Calamity Jane* was the unanimous winner. It was all you could do not to snigger. Ten years since they had staged it, your dad said, and the last person to play the lead . . .

Your dad splayed his palms outwards in your direction. It stood to reason. You knew all the words. Still had your voice, your looks. He started tapping his foot, like he thought that he was getting places. A few proper show tunes would clear your head and lift you to the other side of this daft pickle. His leading lady. Years since he called you that. Your eyes brimmed when he did then. Daddy! He even started humming and mumbling your favourite number. *We'll be home tonight by the light of the silvery moon* . . . The doorbell went and Self called through.

It was that night that your son's gestation got dated from. Self was circumspect, shamefaced possibly, had trained and taxied it. Sipped a sherry in his raincoat and indulged for once your dad's harmless am-dram anecdotes and went up with you to your old room and offered the apology he felt he owed you. Even buried his face in your lap.

You flicked off all lights and undressed. First time in almost a year, reverse cowgirl on your old bed. No going back. The market was dead. Zero viewers in six months. You needed fifty per cent out of the house to make leaving an option. You released your pelvic floor, tightened, released again. Something had happened, a month back, on the mattress on the floor of the master bedroom of his repo. Some upstream spawning, some purchase tangible almost immediately. Your breasts already ached. Now these minute thrusts in dark were just the motions you needed to go through. To explain later. You tightened, released, tightened. Calamity Jane indeed.

Once the following August in the Econo Lodge of a business park. Booked by him months in advance, one of those half-nothing specials that go on offer in low periods. He dialled your work landline and met you behind the station. He had a bottle of white plonk in a knapsack. He said about the hotel booking. You didn't want to. You hadn't with anyone since the previous September. You'd had a child since. He as good as begged. Please, he said, please . . . This would be the last.

He had a punnet of loganberries brought from home. He ate them, one at a time, off your clitoris. The riots on mute in the corner. His mother rang. Each call he let go to voicemail. Her throat cancer had returned. There was one voicemail that he played on speaker. His mother sounded almost English, but for some colour around the edges of certain phrases. She addressed him by the full version of his name. He winced when she referred to herself by a French word. You felt like hiding while she spoke. He said that she couldn't see you there naked in the bed beside her wayward son.

And everything had gone okay? This was his first reference, however oblique, to the birth. Everything had gone fine. Few weeks premature, but fine. And what name had you picked? No less, he said when you told him. It was a big name in the Self family.

He suckled the last of your colostrum. It tasted, he said, of sugar. Had his daughter said anything about that time in his flat? No evidence that she had. She was just starting her first year of college then, something to do with behavioural psychology. He climaxed in your excrement and wept on the nape of your neck and said being promised to you alone made him safe.

You thought of your own son then. His cradled head when they handed you him. Tenderness of such fathoms it hurt. His eyes closed not so much out of sleep as out of not having surfaced fully in this world. How, when you kissed his lids, his skin was sheathed in the same warm reek.

You prised yourself from under him. You dressed and let the door click as quietly as. You had your sandals in your hands. To this day you can still remember the coarse thread of the corridor's industrial carpet on your bare feet, the bell of the lift, the glare of outside. The gridlock that evening was something else. An English Defence League demo, mounted police, hundreds bussed in from all over. There was an incident at the tram stop, a circle of onlookers on tracks. You stopped off at Spar for tobacco, formula, and walked the rest of the road.

Sunday

> wtf r u mate come too
> far to cock up

I stay eating, phone propped against vinaigrette beside my plate. More is forthcoming. The three bubbles on Carl's side of the screen are pulsing. We had a deal, and for a while I was good on it. Now? Now I'm the worry that Carl feared I might become.

> narbonne load never
> fetched wtfs going on

Carl's bubbles keep pulsing. Every text hitherto has had Carl's signature on it. This lack is a first. Carl brands everything with his name. His fingers, chains, texts. Even his conversation. Maybe it's a memory issue, and branding everything is Carl's only means of remembering. Is there a semi in Fallowfield with a plate on the door that reads 'Carl's House'? Carl's bubbles vanish.

I select Home. I feed 'Kitty' into the search bar. The only active dialogue is one-sided, me to her, and mostly sleeved in dust. For someone who spends so many of her waking hours on her phone, she's not particularly assiduous at messaging her old man. Since she hightailed it with Basem? Nada, as she'd say herself, zero, diddly squat . . . To reach the last from her in my direction, I have to scroll back and back again and leave it load. From two years ago.

> what happened? where
> did everyone go xo

And one before.

> they've all seen them
> everyone

And one before.

> Wish you didn't leave.
> This is too much

All three from the same night. All landed at once via free hospital wifi. Only one before those, and that from way before and in a context that I can't for the life of me remember.

> traffic so crap don't go without me!!!!!!!!!!!

Thereafter the cliff's edge.

Everything my side of the screen is stuff of painful nonsense, two years of news scraps and hollow teases and lower case kisses. All unanswered. The most recent is a week-old selfie of yours truly crouched over Monsieur Mangetout's headstone. The light is not great. The granite looks bleached by the flash. So do I. The rest of Saint Roch Cemetery is completely obscured.

I try a new tack.

> It's a disgrace!

What is? I can all but feel her thumb twitching, Basem looking on and wondering what she's smiling at.

> Sure this is what I'm saying!!! It's an absolute complete and utter . . .

Funny girl, come out and play.

> what's that word again?!

Not a flicker. I leave it, lock screen and, after a couple of minutes, press Home again. Nothing. Maybe the more parental approach.

> Let me know yr
> movements. Please…
> need to hear yr safe xx

She'll go straight to voicemail if I ring. She always does. Her recording is her voice saying 'hello' repeatedly, long gaps in between. Like it's really her and she can't hear. It gets me every time. I keep saying her name. I keep asking if she can hear me. Then I realize the trick that she thinks is a hoot and all the more so because her old man falls for it. I tried not messaging her for a while, give space for her to come to me, but that didn't work either. The silence, hers matched by mine, was unbearable. So I text into an abyss for my own sake.

> Be sure to tell Basem
> your darling father
> hopes he's behaving
> himself!!!

My brother dropped into the top of my screen, just there, while I was typing, and slid back up.

> Can you speak? Just
> found out! Hope yr ok. A

When did my brother start being so nice? More house stuff, doubtless. That the house at home is sold is good news. It had become a source of grief. The news of its sale will prove a fresh grief to return to.

No mention was ever made of that evening swim. Our mother and I avoided one another for weeks. I was embarrassed. She, her old dismissive self, regressed to 'Maman'. I assumed my father's mantle with ever-diminishing certainty. One by one, the trappings of her last tilt at glamour faded as gradually as they had appeared. Her lips rediscovered their shade of chapped magenta. The sky blue A-line was washed, ironed and folded into a supermarket carrier bag for the charity shop. The yellow butterfly presumably had perished in autumnal fog.

I got an offer from a university that was my third choice and returned every weekend of my first term. She was there in her armchair with her books and her ashtray and her smoke-filled anglepoise. I was homesick, in a double bedsit with the son of one of our late father's golf cronies. My flatmate was doing engineering, had oodles of friends who were intimidatingly normal, and brought food from home. I missed my mother. I missed our mutual littoral solitude. One weekend, sitting watching her in our living room, I felt sufficiently sentimental to tell her. That I had missed her. She peered over her reading glasses, muttered witheringly 'For goodness' sake' and resumed her place. After Christmas my weekends fell away. Once a month, and eventually not even that.

The summer between first and second year, I whiled away the humid tedium with paperbacks devoured up in my room and fags pilfered from her bedside and the occasional nine holes played against myself with two luminous balls – lime versus orange – in dwindling blustery light. The summer between second and third, I was promptly informed that I couldn't realistically expect to kick my heels around the joint like some corner boy ('corner boys' being Kitty's phobia de choix) and have her wait on me hand and foot. As if. So I went to Cape Cod on a student visa, and I met someone with a Portuguese mother and a father who grew up on the banks of the Shannon. She was in college over there. I went back after my finals. We were engaged by graduation, expecting within the year.

> come on mate more
> than just yourself to
> think about

Too true. The young woman in hijab at the counter stops tallying her till and smiles over at me and goes back to where she was. I must have said that out loud.

I've been homesick ever since I left in my late teens. After two years of failing to make a go of Ireland, during which our daughter was born, we moved an ocean away. We came back most summers. Even then it was mostly to the more populous other half of the family. My side was pretty vacant and increasingly a chore to which none of us looked forward. She didn't want us there. Her greeting would be to ask us when we were leaving. Eventually, my girls found reasons to stay across the country. I visited and made apologies on their behalf. The Dublin coach, a change at Moate and the local stopping service northeast. I could have picked up a rental. Too expensive, I said. The truth was more bitter than thrift. I didn't want to get there any quicker. I wanted the journey to go slowly, and slower still. I wanted it to take as long as it conceivably could. I preferred the verdant malaise of Midlands Sundays glimpsed in passing through tinted glass, truth is, to our mother's ticking clock.

Art joined us. Initially with his wife and boys. They brought roast dinner in disposable aluminium tubs and news of a world that seemed more real, even to me. They scolded our mother for smoking in spite of her diagnosis. They washed up, misplaced delft and disappeared down the motorway for the city's coming week. My brother's wife and boys would find excuses of their own for not travelling north. He came alone as well.

We had nothing to say to one another. He had effectively left home at twelve. There was almost nothing we both remembered. Our father's industrious elsewhere, our mother's oblivious presence. Couple of those dutiful Sundays, at her urging, he and I walked up to The Nineteenth Hole. I knew a few faces. My brother the actuary looked like a fish out of water. We sat at a bar and made conversation, mostly about our offspring. His boys were into lacrosse. He would ask after madam. He seemed to feel there was something proprietorial about christening my daughter after our mother and couldn't bear to say her name.

But even then there was this intimacy between my daughter and my brother. She stayed on and off with them during their summer hols. He asked my permission for her to join them on a jaunt to the Black Forest. Once, there at the counter of the bar half a mile from our family home, my brother received a text. He grinned and left it close enough between us that I could see. From her. My daughter was already gravitating towards her uncle's relative solidity.

In that dearth of mutual past, we usually got around to our father's estate. Or rather, Art did. I listened. Bonds, annuities, what was tied up long term, what surplus interest might reasonably be skimmed off the top for Maman's care, what equity could be released quickly in the event of. The subtext being mortality. Hers. I kept thinking of cream risen to the surface of a churn and taking a teaspoon to it and tasting its room-temperature sweetness.

We both wished her dead. It sounds cruel put that bluntly. It was not a cruel impulse. One of those drab Sundays, at the bar with my brother and his internal calculator, I saw clearly how daydreaming the previous generation's passing is a natural animal process. Someday my own girl, in whose head my old age is happening already, will start imagining mine. Our elders are the buffer between us and our own mortality. Once they're gone, we're next. And yet in spite of that, perhaps because of, we're hardwired to daydream their non-existence into being.

That's everything.

Everything?

That I can think of, my brother would say along the counter. Are we in agreement?

We are.

Trips home grew less frequent. Our mother whittled herself down to a handful of rooms and the mobile library once a fortnight. A woman from the village cooked extra and brought a hot plate. It was an informal arrangement, for which Art dropped in a cheque each Christmas and pretended it was a gift and chauffeured our mother back to his place in Sandycove. She stayed longer with him into New Year, and longer still. They spoke of me, I felt sure, as some hopeless adolescent. I moved to England on the ruse of caring for her and went off whatever rails they clung to for dear life.

All history now.

The Sunday front pages are consumed with attacks in Paris. Eagles of Death Metal. Out on the forecourt I refuel. With no account to syphon off, I'm on my own cash, my maxed-out plastic. Already plenty dark. Word of black ice on higher roads.

I've lived my adult life with this floor of underlying homesickness. Not for our mother, nor the seascape in which we grew up, nor any mythical golden age. It's more a homesickness born of absence, of having had no home to yearn to revisit from our Tír na nÓg of health plans and malls and resident alien paperwork. It feels the way certain illnesses or functional syndromes must feel. A walking low-wattage virus you live with for decades and stop noticing, like the hungover whirr of a fridge in small hours.

Just before the uphill ramp onto secondary dual carriageway, my headlights catch a flicker of gold among lemon trees. The gold gathers into letters, words on the forehead of an emerald cap. A lit screen illuminates her features. She hears an engine and peers from under the cap's peak and holds aloft one arm and keeps gazing into her phone's infinity pool.

You look like shit, she says.

She smells of mould, of damp. She plants green boots up against the glove compartment and tightens the mink around herself and buries her face into its pelt.

Don't start.

What have you been doing? she says.

Her voice is muffled, her emphasis heavily on the 'have'. Does she know about the clearing with Carl and the libertine academic? I think this. I don't say. But I don't care to have her hear me thinking it, however mad that sounds. How did she know where to find me?

What?

Her answer, this monosyllabic near-shout, comes after the longest time. She seems upset. She's wiping her nose, her eyes, with the mink's cuffs. She goes away for how long, and I hear nothing, and then she appears out of nowhere and my wondering how she found me seems the daftest question imaginable.

You really want me to tell you?

She's livid. With me. She is effectively shouting now.

Everybody knows except you, she says, and you're just kidding yourself. I paired our phones. Let's just say. For your sad sake. Okay?

After a dozen or so kilometres of silence, she coughs and, trying to compose herself, says:

My apologies once again. Just figured you could use a bit of stalking.

There was one night, when she was three or thereabouts and a freakish wind outside and weathercasters issuing tornado warnings. I often think of it. Her mom asleep, our girl in pyjamas in darkness on the landing and me reassuring that everything would be in the morning exactly as we left it.

And you've been well?

A-okay, she says.

And Basem was?

Basem?

The boy from the caff. Was that not who you were with?

Jesus, she says like some remote memory has been stirred. Forgot about that kid. That was weird.

He didn't try anything?

He was lovely. It's not always.

We're seabound, not that she knows it. I'm guessing our route, following the gradient. We're headed downhill towards the unlit horizon where coast must be.

What then?

We went down to his, she says. Southwest. Miles of beach and pine forest right up against.

Did you swim?

You know me, she says.

I know her. She did love to swim as a girl. It was the one thing for us to do in summer visits to her paternal grandmother's. Now she's painfully thin. I've glimpsed her ribs. The backside of her jeans is baggy on her pelvic bone. When she doubles over and her jumper falls off her shoulder, sunken ridges become visible up to her throat. Wrapped in vintage duds, she inhabits the world by hiding from it.

They swam, she says, I watched.

Probably best.

There were friends and a chalet in the forest. Basic but cool enough.

And?

It got weird, she says.

Weird how?

She says that she couldn't understand a word anyone was saying. Nobody spoke much English apart from Basem. She went on long walks. She says that she sat at the campfire every night and listened and clapped when they did.

Our full lamps are lit. The gloaming of early winter. There's a warning, orange for medium, of floods on lower roads in the early hours of tomorrow.

But he was all right, the lad?

He was lovely. Stop, she says. It's like you'd be more comfortable if I said they were all rapists. Like that way you'd know how to react. He was a total gent. Okay? Can you handle that?

Good lad.

I was gonna say that if anything he was too much of a total gent for my.

Ah now here.

That I might have preferred, she says, if he was a little more.

I don't need to hear this.

Forward was all I was gonna say.

Thank you.

Dude, she says, what the fuck goes on in your head?

You?

So it would appear.

They all had this past she didn't share, and they shared it in a language that she doesn't speak. She sniffles again, tissue unfurled, chin knitted into itself. It was that, that feeling of inhabiting a foreign movie with no option for subtitles, that became unbearable.

It was like I was this imaginary friend of his, she says, one they were all used to indulging. Always wondered what that must be like.

What was like?

Being an imaginary friend, she says. Now I know.

We reach the autoroute. Just before, there's a slip lane signed with two legends: sea's horizontal squiggle and a parasol. We pick that slip. We pass under six lanes with a gap between. We veer into land so flat that it's hard to say where land falls away and sea begins. The first stars rendered lemon by the windscreen's aquamarine visor strip.

Another detour? she says.

If you like.

You know what your problem is?

Oh do tell. This'll be good.

You can't forgive people for caring about you, she says. It's what mom says.

About me?

Mom says you can't ever forgive people for caring about you.

What the hell? A few days here or there won't make much difference.

Months, she says. You do realize it's been months now?

*

An épicerie is taking in its fresh produce for the night. We park in the bus layby on the opposite side of the street. No buses this hour. We're greeted by a lady with mop and goggle eyes. She sings 'Bonsoir how are you very fine today' in a single uninterrupted flow. We could go to some auberge with wagon wheels on the walls and a DJ with a mullet and a fondue special. But tonight feels different. I choose food that needs no cooking. Cheeses, pâté, crackers. I choose red by the carton.

I'm waiting for whatever change is owing to me when she sidles to my shoulder. I feel her, the bulge of her mink against my bare arm. The lady, handing me coins in the nest of a single note, smiles and asks when the baby is due. At least, I think that's what. I turn. My daughter is cradling a full round tummy under the mink and staring blankly back.

She wants to know when you're due.

Tell her very soon, she says.

Very soon?

It can't be very. I haven't enough French to tell the woman that this is something that even I don't understand. And even if I did, I couldn't explain.

À très bientôt, Madame.

The lady is desperately sweet. She wishes luck. She surely knows I'm her father rather than the child's father. There's no child.

We three stand looking at one another across the counter of the épicerie. I must look mortified. The lady frowns like she heard a joke that she fully went along with at first, and then on second glance suspects that she might not have completely got. My daughter acknowledges with the weary satisfaction of an expect-ant mother. Maybe this is real and she really is pregnant and I, thanks to our mother's stolen mink and the gloaming, didn't notice. She has returned to tell me that she's carrying the love child of a waiter who served us lunch much longer ago than I realized.

She says 'Merci beaucoup' for both of us in an exaggerated Irish accent. She does her nativity routine from counter to door. She links my arm and waits for me to hold the door and smiles back tiredly one last time and steps gingerly into early winter. She ignores my 'What the fuck? What the fuck?' She asks me to take it easy. She even requests a push upwards into the cab. This is for real, is really happening. I go around to the driver's side. This changes everything. We're being watched. I climb in next to her. I start the engine. Is she okay? She emits this protracted natal groan. Does she need a doctor? She opens the mink's lower half and spreads her legs apart. An avalanche of crap spills into the footwell of the passenger side. Chocolate bars, nachos, lollipops, fruit juice in pouches, a box of discount-brand madeleines. They pile in drifts around her green boots.

Oops, she says, looks like the old waters broke.

What the fuck? I'm growling quietly. You even want fucking lollipops?

Not a question I've asked myself!

She's smiling, albeit bitterly.

Buzz of the chase, she says. You of all folks must get that.

She says this to do damage. It does. Her eyes directly at mine, her pupils that black that glitters, irises a scarcely lighter grey. She has developed this tiny squint I find heartbreaking. We move into gear before seatbelts are even buckled. The instrument panel starts beeping.

Sorry, she says.

Fucking shoplifting.

I mean the other thing, she says. Sorry for saying that.

Ask me anything you want. Just drop the asides.

The épicerie lady has come out under her awning. Hands on hips, watching us. What just happened? An apron, a headscarf over thinning black hair, boxes all inside. I wave. I set us grinding forward.

Leave it, she says, for the whatsitsname.

Time being.

Leave it for the time being, she says. It's fab having a man to finish my sentences for me.

The land gets flat and featureless. Sea level. Night air seasoned with salt. The road narrows. We cross countless little canals and tributaries. We shouldn't be on this. We take up the width of the road. Several max tonnage signs that I ignore and she points at limply. Being here would require some explaining. I haven't inserted a tach in a couple of weeks and for that could, as Carl says, do time. We take our chances. Nothing the other way.

We travel in parallel silence. Mine is horror at her. Hers looks like a dazed delight at my horror and a sliver of shoplifter's remorse. A while of that and she starts eating. She performs a theatrical rustling of wrappers. She nibbles several bars and parks them on the dash. She sucks peach-and-mango concentrate in one long drag of a straw until the pouch implodes in her hand. She yanks a red lollipop from its see-through square and sucks on it for ages. A coin of strawberry, a poppy in her mouth. Against her east-facing passenger window, she's silhouette with a stick protruding from its lips. We pass a few houses. We enter the edge of something. She removes the lollipop and looks my way and pokes out a long vermilion tongue.

I'm not laughing.

Ah you are, she says.

I'm not.

I glance again. She does it again. The same bold red tongue.

I'm really not.

Ah you are a bit, she says.

Great to see you so.

Back to myself?

She's reminding me. She's reminding me of something that I said to her before. The last time that I said it to her is just another thing we never mention.

I pronounce the name aloud, flitting by the sign of welcome. Twinned, as it happens, with a port in Donegal. We're really crawling now. Not a sinner. I knew this morning that I'd be passing close. I was, back there, in two minds. Then, when I saw her waiting under the lemon trees by the service area, for some reason best known to myself my first thought was coming here.

What is this?

What's it look like?

Some bargain-basement seaside place, she says, after everyone went home.

Bingo.

There are shut moules cabines. The pirate-themed minigolf has pools of standing water. All roadside arcades are boarded up. We can drift straight over each flat roundabout without fear of cross-traffic. One official notice says that the holiday village has been designated an asylum camp. And yet there is zero evidence of life. Have rafts like those on Howard's TV washed up here? Probably too far west. Another sign warns of submergence on certain byways that have manual booms at the entrance.

Dude, what does 'inondation' mean when it's at home?

That would be flooding, and it does seem to be close enough to home.

No fear in this big boy, she says.

Still.

The further we creep forward, the more tar and markings taper off under wet sand and puddles. The apartment complexes give way to pines. Very soon our tyres are sloshing through it. We stall at a max height barrier. In the immediate distance a lake where parking is meant to be. Beyond that, through gaps in the dunes, an angry tide is rising towards us.

Don't like this, she says.

We manoeuvre about-facing with a dozen patient points and the leeway provided by a bridle track. We take some blossomless bougainvillea branches with us and slosh back up what appears to be the main drag.

Look at you, she says.

What about me?

You really get this shit.

I do. My daughter is not a million miles wide of the mark. It feels so similar to what I grew up with.

Such a nostalgia freak, she says.

Something else as well.

There's always something else!

There is. There's always something else. There has to be.

Namely? she says.

Where indulging my past is usually a chore for her, and usually a chore performed half-heartedly at best, this time she does appear to be listening. We're in first gear. Barely moving. She even pursues when I leave it.

What's the something else? She squints at me across the pause. On this occasion?

Her grandmother spent three weeks here, on an informal exchange, somewhere in the early fifties. I tell her this, the bones of it. The stud farm in the Curragh and the trader of yearlings and the maison de vacances hereabouts and the shoebox of negatives that never got developed. She spilled the shoebox onto our dining table once, raised the negatives to the light, mumbled names that meant nothing to us and passed each on. Faces outside houses. The dark of bright sky and white sand, the glare of black dresses.

Hence her French obsession? she says.

It must have been in her, partially in place, when she went on the exchange. Her grammar and accent were strong. It was more that those weeks, their singular unhappiness, took root.

So if she'd had a whale of a time?

She wasn't capable of that.

But if she did, she says, if she'd had a mega blast?

Then our mother might have got over it. That's what I think. Her French obsession might have exited her system before she ever left for home. Happiness comes and goes. It tends not to hang around. Unhappiness has a habit of outstaying its welcome.

You're gas craic.

She spoke about it, one of those Fridays that I mixed her a whiskey and red lemonade. She spoke of it without any bidding from me. Her counterpart, the horse trader's daughter, had a life that our teenage mother could never slip into. She had a boyfriend who fetched her every night on an upcycled military scooter. Instead of minding her, she abandoned Kitty to parents on the cusp of a fairly dirty divorce. The woman had confined herself to upstairs quarters. The man came, went, and bunked in the front room downstairs on a bed settee that he didn't bother to fold back during daylight hours.

Evenings were toughest. The family ate in silence or grilled her with questions that she struggled to answer or gossiped over her head. There would come a honk from the road. The daughter gathered stuff and quarrelled with her parents about their guest and vanished down the coast in a dust cloud. Raised voices at the top of the house paused when Kitty, at the foot of the stairs, sang up 'À plus tard!'

And did she go back with Grandma?

Who?

The daughter of the horse guy, my daughter says. Did she go back to Ireland?

She did not. It was an exchange in name only. It was one-sided.

There's a lot of that about.

We take the first right in from the shore. Immediately, the habitation looks temporary. We bump over a discontinued level crossing. The map says that if we see this road to its logical conclusion, a T-junction, we would rejoin the tertiary road that we came in on. That tertiary road leads naturally back to the autoroute.

These past years I've studied the online maps so often. When I squatted at home on my own that one time, after our mother had died, I took several of her belongings with me. Among them were two postcards, in her young hand, which our mother in turn must have found among her own late parents' things. On each she had printed, carefully, the return address and begged them to write. I typed in that return address to examine satellite images of the very landscape we're now drifting through.

We don't see the road to the junction. We're guided, instead, into a right-hand dirt track in the general direction of the sea. The track dead-ends at an empty space, a rectangle of concrete foundations enclosed by a copse of bamboo.

Dear God, she says, this is it?

Indeed.

A plot where some class of chalet once stood?

I expected more. A house. A wreck at least. The satellite view does have a roof, but the image was five years old when I took the screenshot, and that wasn't today or yesterday.

I promised him I'd send a pic.

Who? she says. The Godfather?

Your uncle. Yes.

Of?

Well, indeed.

We leave the engine running, headlamps casting our shadows over the concrete. There are straight uneven lines where walls once stood. There are intact patches of tile. Red, or red and black. There are gulls overhead. There's the staggered hush of waves dissolving.

This has to have been the kitchen. This has to have been the front room. These are the remains of the chimney. We're saying this to one another from either end of the plot. This is where the front door was. And this was the entrance hall. We meet at the centre, in a box open at one end and pivoting into nowhere.

Not much of a room, she says.

It was most likely the casement of the stairs. We stand then, looking up into watery stars as if gazing into a whole other level. I tell her that her grandma slept up there, once in another world, above where our heads are now.

Deep, she says, something verging on wonderment even in her small voice. Very deep.

I steer up into the far corner, back on a hard right lock. She stays standing down in the dark, issuing directions through the open passenger window. In the end we're lengthways on the plot, facing the lights inland where we came from.

We eat by dim internal light. Me mostly. She unwraps stuff, sniffs, nibbles edges. She guzzles wine from the cap of my thermos. It tastes initially of whiskey. After a while, she says, the whiskey taste has worn off. I say to go easy. She raises her wine to me, black eyes swimming, teeth and lips stained damson.

Here's to you, she says.

I thank her. I return the compliment. This is her night. She looks confused. Why is tonight her night? Tell me what happened. I'm working overtime to hold my voice. She never told me.

You never asked, she says.

I'm asking now.

Do I have to?

It happened very gradually. People started not speaking. She was bunking for the summer with a friend that she had made in the True Crime society and couldn't be sure what was going down. Just knew something was. She deactivated all accounts. It went on months. Pictures of her online and getting deleted. People not speaking. I know that much. Then one night, a Tuesday, the friend stayed out and messaged. Couldn't say it to her face. The pictures, taken by herself in a bathroom at halls and sent to the boy, had gone live again. Big time. She says that she remembered the cache of heavy-duty over-the-counter painkillers that she had been shoplifting. Loads of them, from several different pharmacies. She swallowed the lot in an hour with a mix of sickly Finnish vodka and a can of rock shandy. Next thing was a bed down in the dark. She says that she remembers wishing it hadn't happened, none of it, and feeling desperately sad. Next thing was a roomful of pissed people screaming and this incredible blue revolving in the street.

I could see myself, she says.

My wee pet.

Then you appeared.

I did.

You came, she says, and put gloves on my hands.

I did.

That was a bit . . . She laughs snottily. You kept talking to me.

And then you talked back.

I did, she says. It broke my.

What did?

You, she says. You down there like some hobo, she says. You talking to me the auld crap you always talk to me.

You were always my best buddy.

Best!

Only.

And you calling me that, she says.

Kitty?

You never called me it, she says, and when you did I realized how much I love it when you do.

Kitty. From now on.

She's been with me ever since. I found her outside the station with shaven head. We spent a few nights back in Tír na nÓg. We even bathed a bit. But it wasn't safe. She took a shine to my mother's mink. I let her bring it with us on condition that she returned over the water with me. I signed a lease on a damp stone cottage halfway up a moor. I slept on a latex mattress on the floor of the only bed-room. The fold-out sofabed at the woodstove downstairs was all hers. She was on it every morning that I left for work. She watched *Game of Thrones* religiously, several times over. When I came back and it was night, she had the bed folded in and the sofa dragged over to a fire lit with hawthorn that she had foraged off the moor and dried. I released myself piecemeal from all contact, inbound and out, with the rest of the world. I wanted it to be just us. Ourselves alone.

It's you! A

She asks who. Her uncle. She mumbles that she has to go.
Go where?
Nature, she says. The call thereof. Relax!
She jumps out and leaves the door hanging open for light. Her uncle, I tell her again. Her precious Godfather. What now? The same stuff, I tell her, house stuff.
It's pitch black, she says.
I keep speaking to reassure. Did she get my pic of Monsieur Mangetout's grave? Possibly the worst photo ever taken. She says that I look like a corpse in it. I tell her his real name. Michel Lotito.
Mikael originally, she says out of breath. Nobody fucks with me when it comes to Monsieur Mangetout.
She asks from the night what my something is.
My?
Story, she says.
I can hear her zip zipping shut.
What's your story? It definitely over?
She climbs back in and, shivering, pulls her passenger door.
It is.
Too sad, she says, after all that.

What she said earlier, about feeling like someone else's imaginary friend. I knew something of that.

Really?

Six years I went, a wind-up toy in someone else's wardrobe, waiting to be taken out and played with. It was my own fault. I put myself there, or at least allowed myself to be put there. I started doubting that I existed, like I was invisible to everyone but one person.

I get that, she says.

Nature calls me too. Use my disappearance to change and turn in, I tell her. The hemisphere peppered with planets. The ground underfoot squelches slightly. Are the lights ahead mountains or constellations? Hard to tell.

Look what I found! she says. Do you mind?

She has on your kimono. I mind. I say that I don't. She found it in my box of chattels. Just be careful. She wears it to bed. Later, above me in dark, she asks again what the deal is.

I wanted to come to where she was.

Grandma?

And part of me thought I might find her here.

Your mom?

I did.

In the morning we'll pull away in a foot of muddy seawater. I'll hang out my side and take a snap that will fail to send to my brother. For the time being she's breathing heavily above.

The dash lights again. My brother again.

It was you! It was you all along...

212

I reach over and lock the screen. There are certain thoughts I can't think now, for fear of being overheard.

If I listen hard enough, I can hear the diminishing footsteps of our mother before she was, before our father, before us. On one of her evening promenades. The early fifties. Seventeen, painfully out of place, an old soul in ankle-length floral dress and cardy over bare shoulders. A film of sweat on her upper lip. Her good shoes scuffed with the chalk of whatever cinder path she's on. I have her pause there, where path rounds back towards enclosed bay. There's faint music. There are lights pulsing down along the shore. There are too, among the soft plosives of surf, pockets of cheering that she would give anything to be among.

She hesitates. She doesn't trust herself. I feel such tenderness at that thought of Maman, a girl dithering on the outskirts of young womanhood. She pulls the two halves of her cardy tightly around and hugs herself. She faces back the opposite direction then and walks slowly, killing a little more of what should be the time of her life.

Have a Nice Life
May 2009

There were interviews. They needed someone neutral to monitor morning presentations. Your name got put forward. You had been on leave since last November. It would be, you said, a way of easing back. You felt poured into that slate black Vivienne Westwood number, brown as a berry. You bought a takeout flat white and walked in shades downhill through broadleafs. Last Tuesday of May. Glad to be back in the world. The year still on the rise. Evenings longer with every one and shallow darks and light flooding the bedroom by four.

Presentations were open to all-comers. Interviews would be in the afternoon, in reverse order, and for the few. People were very friendly, but you didn't belong as such. It was just nice to be there, to observe. It would be your job to ensure that procedure was followed. There were pastries. There was talk of the pub after. Someone who grew up in California said that a candidate was being flown in from the States especially. A large gang, demob happy, using this as a last hurrah before summer's languid hiatus.

Candidates came and presented and thanked the room. Half a dozen suits. You sat in the back corner. When each candidate had one minute of their presentation remaining, you caught their eye and mouthed, 'One minute, please . . .' You were miles away for most of it.

Someone did bullet points that included the sound of a bullet with each point, which was grating. One minute, please. Someone who resembled Quentin Bell mislaid one of his pages and mumbled 'Balls!' and begged a moment to compose himself. One minute, please. Someone passed around a lucky dip of acceptable questions handwritten on cue cards and had answers rehearsed, which had charm. One minute, please. The person from the States was second to last. All freckles, a cocktail of shyness and arrogance you found weirdly familiar. When he spoke, the colleague from California yelped: 'You're not American!' That was the first thing, how he responded to being yelped across.

I'm not, he said, as if he were returning her grammar gift-wrapped, in inverse form.

He began with a story from folklore. Eternal youth and the passage of centuries. He linked that to coverage of Libyan asylum seekers who had just been turned back from the shores of Sicily. He talked for a bit about the qualifications implicit within certain locutions, such as contentment. That was another thing. And then occasionally his accent and his own locutions seemed at odds. One smacked of turf smoke, the other of strip malls. He cracked a joke about believing until recently that pedagogy had something to do with feet. He looked relieved when people got it.

How am I for time?

He was looking at you. His time was up, but you hadn't said one minute. I was promised a warning! He thanked the assembled faces and invited questions.

Would the candidate care to lick your throat?

The room exploded. You had a split second of panic where it seemed as if you actually might have blurted that out loud. It was, in the end, something funny someone else said. Another candidate came after. You didn't hear a word of that. One minute, please.

Lunch was a buffet in one of the adjoining meeting rooms. Sandwiches and fruit and mini pork pies. You sat on a table in one corner and chatted with lots and watched him being buttonholed. The room thinned out. Those not on the interview panel thanked you and drifted off. You should have left. The afternoon's running order meant that the person from the States was slated to go second and would be done early. You tidied things around. It wasn't your job to tidy, but you made it look as if it might have been. Last group standing said that lunch was very pleasant and left you feeling like the cleaner in a room of paper plates and half-eaten pineapple segments.

You were there when he emerged from interview and found you and shook your hand and said his name. You couldn't help yourself. Was his name not? What? A cliché. He looked like one who had long since grown used to being asked that. He told you not to overthink it. He glanced at the empty room, the see-through bag.

Is this your brief?

Not as such. You just thought.

Can I give you a ride?

He had a hire car. He had done another interview somewhere in the northwest the day before. He had a deluxe in an airport hotel, a return first thing out of Heathrow. Did he plan on celebrating tonight? Nothing as yet to celebrate. You said come now. Just like that. Oh come now . . . He was being unnecessarily modest was all you meant.

The carpark was good and warm. He made this show of feeling the cold. He was telling you that he was used to better. This was real summer, you assured him, of an order that he was going to have to come to terms with. You had to wait in sun while he cleared maps and shades off his passenger seat. His radio went straight to Rock FM with the ignition. Foo Fighters. 'Best of You'. He took several stabs at powering off. He swore. You quite liked that song. Were you one of those musos?

Ish.

Ish? he said.

Your partner mostly. Self was a good bit older. Self? Everyone referred to him by his second name. Self was from, as it happened, Minnesota. The family from Derbyshire, way back. Self had a German turntable and a collection of nineteenth-century chamber on vinyl.

Groovy, he said.

He was as interested in Self's provenance, or not, as you knew Self would be in his. What he seemed to hear, there in his rental, was that you were spoken for. It sounded, even to yourself, like that was what you were telling him, marking territory. You wanted to respond to what he had spoken about in his presentation in relation to contentment. How you were working overtime to inhabit those implicit qualifications.

Did he have kids?

A girl just, he said. Sixteen.

Won't she find this hard?

This?

Coming back?

I've never been here before, he said. He shifted gears, clicked his tongue. We've never been before. Nor anywhere near.

You hadn't meant it like that, but it was what you said. You said sorry. He told you not to worry about it. He got crossed wires like that all the time. His daughter wasn't moving with him. They, his daughter and her mother, would be staying put for the time being. So his partner wouldn't be moving at all?

My wife, he said pointedly. That remains to be seen.

He said that he was coming over to be nearer an ageing mother. There were no vacancies in Ireland in his field. Here was the closest he could get. You told him that your mother always claimed to have descended from the High Kings of Connaught. The? High Kings of Connaught.

No less, he said.

Those words were so familiar to you for as long as you could remember, that you had just said them without thinking how they might come over when said out loud. The High Kings of Connaught. It was only there, in the car next to him, that you heard how daft the words sounded in the real world.

Don't, he said. It's cute.

There were roadworks on Hampton Court Way. Traffic at a standstill. The afternoon was hot. He didn't seem bothered. The driver's window was open. His forearm, releasing the handbrake when the traffic ahead started forward, brushed your thigh. Budge, he said. You liked that. The brush and what he said and how he did. You asked again about his daughter. Her mother, his wife, was American but had lived a bit in Ireland. Their daughter was born in Dublin and was planning on going to college there.

And you? he said. Any kids?

The question you dreaded. You had just come back from leave that was two parts compassionate to one part sick. Meaning? You had miscarried at Christmas. Five months gone. There was a car accident and you miscarried as a result. You said then the phrase that you and Self had agreed upon for when people asked: a grey area between miscarriage and stillbirth. The traffic had stalled again. He didn't say what everyone else said. They always said sorry, how terribly sorry they were, and you always wanted to scream in their stupid faces that it wasn't their fault, that it had fuck all to do with them. He didn't say sorry and you liked him for that. He said nothing to start with, and then:

It'll happen.

He could drop you wherever, you told him, if he needed to get his things from the hotel. Everything was in the trunk. The? Trunk. You smiled and looked at him and he smiled too, looking straight ahead. The trunk. He said that he had stayed the previous night in a B&B out near campus. HR had offered to put him up in one of the big chains more in towards the city, but he preferred something less corporate and found this number online. He described the proprietor as an elegant French dame. A throwback to la belle époque if ever there was one.

You knew immediately who he meant. She was actually Russian. You said so looking the other direction. That was the first time that your fascination with his life felt requited. You knew the lady? You did, still looking the other way. An old acquaintance. Had she an oval portrait of Pushkin in the entrance hall? She had, but grew up in Paris. White Russian. Stalin-era émigrés. Nadia was a baby when her parents fled west.

So how come you knew this broad? You laughed out loud. Was he not overplaying the Yank? Nadia had been married to a colleague of Self's back in the day. She moved here to be with him. Then he promptly died within a couple of years of her moving. She had been here ever since. Nadia inhabited three storeys on a leafy dead end that backed onto the golf course at Strawberry Hill. Time was you had her to the house every New Year. She arrived like some exotic maiden aunt with Turkish delight talced in icing sugar and was intimidatingly tall in a floor-length yellow leather overcoat. She would sit into the early hours of the following year gorging on caviar and political philosophy.

He said that he seemed to have been her only guest. Nadia had served him fried plantains for breakfast. Fried plantains with clotted cream. He had told her that he didn't want the beans with his full English and got this withering look. You knew the look he meant. He did her voice. He held his Rs in the back of his throat and let them go piecemeal like miniature gravel loads.

We don't go there, darling.

You laughed. Plural.

It had been years, a decade, since another man. And that was still the case. Nothing happened, on the lift he gave you, to undo that. The rest of the journey went quickly beyond the roundabout. But as long as it lasted, you felt this tinge that you didn't recognize at first. It was like the way a cube of sugar gets placed on a teaspoon of hot coffee and the one absorbs the other. It was guilt. Guilt rose through you, gradually, like coffee through a sugar cube.

He had pulled over, at your instruction, on the uphill shortcut towards the M25. You let his passenger door swing naturally on its hinges down towards the pavement. Before you could leave it at that, he said there was something else as well. You suspected that there was always something else with him.

Go on!

He had arrived mid p.m. Nadia had brought him up to his room. A lot of tassels. Then he went for a walk. Early evening. He got back nineish. A radio playing off in the house, something resembling a polonaise. The landing in darkness. He pushed into his room and found the switch in the neck of the bedside lamp. There, on the back of this linen-covered armchair in his room, was a pair of lady's undergarments. Knickers? Panties. Yes. And he was sure they hadn't been? When he checked in? As sure as sure could be. And he didn't bring them to her?

I did in my hat!

Can he have been as innocent as he made himself seem? Surely even he could recognize the knickers as a sign.

The woman's my mother's age if she's a day, he said.

It was then that you said an aside you couldn't bear to remember the rest of the summer. Maybe he had missed his chance. Of? A casual fuck.

I don't go there, darling, he said in Nadia's voice. He wasn't being judgemental. And then, in his own voice: I like love.

Was he offended? Not a bit. The way that Nadia had gone about it, the gesture. It was, he said, beautifully delicate. That wasn't what you had meant. You meant was he offended by what you had said rather than by what Nadia had done. You told him that you looked forward to seeing him again in September. Did you? It was just a way of saying thank you, so long and getting out of there before there was another something else.

He said that you hardly would. Would what? You would hardly see him again.

I got the impression, he said, that you belonged elsewhere in the institution.

It was true.

Our paths, he said, are unlikely to cross.

Too true.

Have a nice life, he said, as we say over the herring pond.

He didn't pull away. Not that you looked back, more that there was no engine revving behind. You could feel him watching you walk down into your evening and your nice life.

You masturbated in the toilet under your stairs. Seagulls in the street. First time in how long and very quick. The door knocked just as you. The husband of next door leaving off a textbook bought online that they had taken delivery of. You could hear 'Hello! Hello!' in the hall. He had let himself into the kitchen. Was everything all right? You ran your fingers under the kitchen tap. You had to get tea going. That seemed the most polite tack, rather than bluntly asking him to leave. He touched your arm with his hand. It was like he knew something about you before you did, and that knowledge made him concerned enough to lay one hand on your shoulder and ask if he should pull the door behind.

You rang your parents. It was your mum answered. She rested aside the receiver, to muffle her beckoning your father from the garden. You could hear the static of her cardy. You wanted to tell her that you had met someone. Today. She said that your dad was in his shed, had finally got around to dismantling *Jesus Christ Superstar*. Not himself. She said that by way of gentle warning.

Your mum had taken care of you, after your grey area between miscarriage and stillbirth. Three months you were bedbound and stopped with them in your old room. Self came weekends and rang from work and otherwise buried himself in projects. Three months of celery soup and Dostoevsky's letters from prison. You hadn't wanted to leave when the time came. It was still recent enough for you to want back.

An Irishman had driven you into the city. You were dying to tell someone, to have someone to tell, but your mum was not the person. She sounded older, more frail, with every call. Next thing was your dad chuntering through the kitchen and Self getting home and you saying tea was ready by way of valediction.

Patio doors wide into the evening, you lay stretched on the sofa and pretended to watch *Friends*. He was near. In an airport hotel, not ten miles away from where you lay stretched. You could see him, checking in and taking the lift and leaving his luggage unopened on the bed and seating himself on a high stool at the counter of the bar downstairs. You could see yourself being there on some flimsy ruse, recognizing him from earlier and saying the breezy 'You again!' that you had practised in the car.

Will I turn it off? Self said.

No.

You could hear, out there, sirens and the tidal traffic of the bypass and the rhythmic thump of some club mix from a garden in exam fever. How were seagulls so far inland? You could hear his voice repeating your name and offering you a seat.

The landline rang beneath the TV. It rang a second time and wouldn't go away. Self crawled over on all fours and laid the receiver on the small table and shrugged in your direction. There was a person with a lilt. With a? A lilt. Asking for you.

It was him, who had interviewed earlier that day and dropped you off at the top of the road. You had left your sunglasses on his dash. His voice was how you remembered it. He hadn't found them until it was too late. Meaning not until he had arrived the other end. Meaning not until he was too far gone to turn back.

You could think of nothing to say, except make it seem that you were unsure who this was.

Who is this, please?

Paddy, he said.

Someone had left a pair of sunglasses on the dash of his rental. It could only have been you really. He hadn't seen them, the glasses, until he got there. He had them in his hand as he spoke. He had blagged your number off . . . He said a name you couldn't put a face to. You saw your shades on the dash of his rental, melted minutely by the sun of early summer. You felt again the brush of his forearm against your thigh when he moved up through the gears. He said that they had offered him the job. He had asked them for your number. He hoped that was okay.

Did he plan on accepting?

I don't, he said. I've an offer up north. That I'm taking.

Really?

Closer home, he said. And . . .

And what?

Probably for the best.

Yes.

He said that he could mail them from the airport first thing. You spelt out your address and postcode and thanked him. Even to yourself you sounded softer than you knew yourself to be. And for the lift again. The lift would take some explaining. You wished him happy moving. You even heard your voice telling him to have a nice life. The phrase was from earlier, his.

Dandy, he said.

Self appeared in the kitchen while you were emptying the dishwasher. Still light out. You hadn't heard him come in. Self was standing behind you several seconds before you realized that he was in the room. Self asked about the day, the presentations, the person who had given you the lift back into town and whose voice he had just listened to in miniature in your living room, to whom you had wished a nice life. You didn't want to be looked at while you answered, so said what you said without stopping or turning around.

Do you still love me? Self said.

You stood and faced Self and hugged then. Of course you did! You found some ancient tobacco, skins, at the bottom of the bag that Nadia used to refer to as *un bordel de sac*. You lit up in the covered passage between front and back so nobody would see. It was like you were sixteen again and ashamed of the desire to smoke and in need of hiding from your parents' disapproval. How long since you last smoked? Long enough for a tiny hit.

You held your breath.

Official summer in six days' time. The whole green belt seemed to brim with it, with chlorophyll and petrol fumes and what felt possible.

You exhaled.

You liked love too. That was the truth you wished, bitterly, that you had uttered earlier. Casual fucking was not your proclivity either. You pulled one strand of tobacco off your lip and curled it in a ball and tossed it towards the rear garden's overgrown grass.

Ten years you had been faithful. For the first time you wondered if your fidelity had been as much to love, the idea of, the hope of love one day showing up, as it had been to any one person. What you said earlier in the rental, you just said that to sound worldly, to appear adequate to a world that the other might have inhabited for all you knew. Turned out he didn't belong there any more than you did, and now you dearly wished you had made that clear when the chance was yours.

Any future out there was immediate. There would be an open-air festival in your park that weekend. There would be floods within a fortnight, three months' precipitation in two apocalyptic hours, power outages, a dog on a floating door on early evening news. Your specs would wash up with your name in his hand on a jiffy bag that you would keep hidden all summer, that you would take out and run your finger along when it was just you.

No way that you could have known any of that then.

Coming in?

Self had opened the side door, had spoken around the corner of the house. You begged a second more and took one last long drag and held your breath again and, eyes tight shut, waited for the latch to click.

As for the other person? Out there too, on the same landmass until tomorrow morning. Not that that made any difference, though it did seem as if it might. At that very moment, he was finishing himself off in the en suite of a deluxe double in an airport hotel, recalling the collarbones of the woman who had sat in the bottom left corner of the room and twisted coloured wooden beads on her breastbone, the hint of her sweat from the passenger seat of his rental.

You couldn't have known that either.

I don't go there, darling, you said out loud to nobody in particular and exhaled once more. I like love.

This must have been what they meant when they wrote of immanence. This tingling. This stillness happening as if in an adjoining room. This static frisson. This something-of-nothing that feels so very nearly within reach. You stubbed the embers under your green sandal and went indoors.

Monday

I feel great, she says.

That's great.

I do, she says, I feel great.

Great.

She is: barefoot, poker-faced, still there. I am: backed into a mass of dripping alder, without load, perpetually on the home straight.

Tip top, she says.

Be the hokey.

Hundred and ten per cent.

And what, if you don't mind my asking, has you in such?

Sparkling fettle?

Exactly.

It would have to be, she says, this jaunt in foreign parts with your good self at the wheel.

Though it's not ages and ages since.

Since I was less enamoured? It's not, she says.

Whither the change?

Swings and roundabouts.

Profits and losses.

Fair means and foul, she says.

Very good.

Oh the power of good.

These things are never without.

Never, she says.

And as the saying goes, you can't take sixty lads to Cork and ask each and every one of them to pay their fares down and back. Can you?

I guess!

And each man on the team has to pony out for burgers and chips? Sure that'll never wash.

You've finally lost me, she says.

I should go in.

This again, she says.

Yeah.

Your man again?

Carlos.

He majorly into you?

May well be.

Meaning?

Meaning his preferred bet may well be a pound each way.

I won't be, she says.

Won't be what?

Daddy.

Ages since she called me that.

You won't be?

She clambers into the back. Her clambering reveals sores and welts around the knuckles of her spine. She straightens out her bunk and draws the curtains and completely blanks my third time of asking.

What won't you be, my love?

This morning finds us in grounds of a disused train station where Carl has told me to meet him. The Cévennes foothills, couple of hours inland of where our mother holidayed as a girl. The roads closed in and moved more sideways as we ascended. There was mist and the smoke of lit woodstoves. We came across several chasseurs with rifle and hound. Our satnav lost its way and had to be overridden with Carl's directions texted yesterday. They led us to this gravel dead end among pines in need of pollarding.

A couple from Reading bought this complex off the local authority. Carl mentioned them before. Carl has been coming here since here existed. One of hundreds of similar stations that have lain derelict since the autoroute bonanza of the sixties and seventies. One triple-barrel hyphenate in the litany of a local-stopping line long since discontinued. The couple run a caff from what was once the waiting room. They trucked together. Years they were doing that. Then they stumbled across this place and set their married heart on it and scraped all savings and got it for a song.

End of the road.

Does feel that way.

I'm scared, she says.

It'll be grand.

Just a bit scared.

The platform eastbound has been recommissioned as terrace. There's a natural extension to it from the indoor area. The tracks are ochre rust, overgrown with ragwort. The platform opposite, what would have been westbound, remains swamped by bramble and fern. The brambles are bare of leaf or berry. The ferns are copper.

The past hour has rained. All parasols on the eastbound platform are folded down. We're watching them, the folded-down parasols and the rain falling, from the far end of the parking lot. Our empty chassis is backed in under the berryless alder. The tar between us and the station building is blistered with weeds.

> I can see you

Carl can see me. Carl, not for the first time, wants me to know that. On the platform opposite, among the wet westbound briars, is a sign with the station's name still in place. The paint has completely eroded away. The sign is now an ornate oblong of sable pig iron with a series of raised ridges that are legible as letters only from an oblique angle. The hyphens are more pronounced than anything. Can Carl see us both?

You're all about the buzzing, she says.

Look who's talking.

Bro, have you seen me receive a single message out here?

She's been so wedded to her phone that I just assumed. That she's been sending and receiving with the best of us. Now that she says it, I realize it's me and me alone who's been buzzing.

I have not.

And who, she says, have we now?

232

Carl is looking across the carpark from a window trimmed with frosting and festive lights. Least I assume that the silhouette among reflected cloud and branch, against the interior's back-light, is Carl's. It's so long since I last saw Carl in the flesh. Far longer than the day before yesterday. I've survived thus far in the wager that Carl would be slow to take my off-the-radar shenanigans to the authorities. Carl would be implicated as much as me. But now I've dragged this out as far as I could. Carl's most recent texts have implied that law, regardless of the consequences for himself, will have to be his next port of call.

Carl. Monsieur O'Neill and a riot act he wishes to read your old man.

Scared, she says.

Don't be.

Can't help it.

The man's bark's worse than his bite.

Carl instructed me to meet him here. His white Scania was in situ when we arrived. Has Carl passed the night here? The Face-book page advertises a handful of B&B rooms, for those who prefer creature comforts to a bunk. Carl is acting for Howard, calling my number to shore for the umpteenth time, as he promised would be the case. This time I answered. This time I made a promise of my own that I intend to keep.

I should do it so.

Do what so? she says.

That thing it is we came to do.

We're where we started. Me at the wheel, gazing blindly into time travelling faster than I experience it. Her behind, curled facing away in her sleeping bag on her fold-out bunk, curtains drawn between.

This is where she was in Calais. Had to be. Nobody knew that she was with me. For days, weeks, she rode shotgun. Since returning from her months southwest with Basem and heaven knows where else, like one undoing their coming into life, she has regressed into the crypt where she started. Now she barely ever leaves the cab. Not to pee nor wash nor stretch her skeletal limbs. Certainly not to eat. Full circle we've come. Now she's little more than a smell as warm as it is rancid, a mink and kimono sleeved into one another in a heap on a travel mattress, a plethora of questions that I would sooner not have to answer.

Oh by the way, she says all brightness of a sudden and rolls audibly towards me. I've been doing research of my own.

Have you now?

This Oisín dude had a kid with his mother.

Excuse me?

So the annals tell us, she says.

Jesus.

His mom was turned into a deer, she says, and Oisín nearly killed her while he was out doing a spot of hunting, but at the last second Oisín realized that the deer he was about to shoot was actually his mom and him recognizing her meant she turned back into human form and then they went and had a kid together.

And how, pray tell, did Oisín know the deer was his mother?

Must have been something, she says, about the look in her eye before he pulled the trigger.

Oh that look? The look that says 'Don't shoot, son, it's your mom'?

Kinda thing.

She has picked her moment to add relief to a story that I've been telling her since she was a kid. And the detail gleaned from hours on her phone is news and macabre as all hell. And we're pissing ourselves so hard that I hit the horn by accident, and its echo across the empty parking lot of a station on a discontinued regional line in foothills in the Languedoc brings us to our senses. And more time passes.

Tell me the story.

The story?

Tír na nÓg, she says. Tell me the story of Oisín and Tír na nÓg.

I thought certain persons were sick to the back teeth of hearing certain stories.

I was.

And now?

I want to have it right, she says, the bare bones at least. To take with me.

Take with you?

Into the next world.

So I tell her. Oisín returns to Ireland on the magic steed that Niamh gave him. And Carl comes to the window. And someone leaves via the eastbound terrace and hollers foreign farewells to inside. And I already know that this telling will be an end. And an old man on the road recalls Oisín's ancient order. And the person who hollered goodbye gets into a small delivery van across from us and 'Fairytale of New York' comes to life mid-stream on his radio and his reverse light shines like the last star of morning.

So sad, she says.

Yeah.

And he never sees Niamh again?

That song diminishes downhill too, amid a pocket of rainfall caused by fresh shifting among pine needles. We sit then. How long? I no longer trust myself to tell. We sit watching milky sun and counting drops off the alder onto the tin roof above our heads.

What are you going to do? she says.

Some point, my angel, you'll have to stop asking me that.

If you gave me a straight answer, she says, I wouldn't have to keep asking.

I am going to go in there and talk to Carl. Carl is going to tell me, in no uncertain terms, to quit fannying around and get his mate's truck back to Salford pronto. Or else.

Else what?

Oh law I imagine, taking matters further.

That phrase is Carl's, from last night's text. It came in the dark. One of those threatening platitudes in which Carl specializes lately. I pronounce Carl's words as if they were italicized and quoted from the warning implicit in some solicitor's letter.

Sounds fair enough.

You don't say.

You promised you'd bring his friend's truck back, she says, and you haven't yet and now your friend is cross at you.

When she says these things this simply to me, I find it hard to work out if the simplicity is real or feigned, innately hers or put on for my benefit. She speaks carefully. She leaves spaces for the weight of each word to soak in before carrying on. Do? I? Follow? Is this, this way she has of speaking to me, a residual childishness on her part or just that childishness you adopt when addressing a child?

> there you still are carl!

Carl has started enjoying this. His name and exclamation mark have even made a comeback. Carl has me where he wants, at the end of his line of sight and ready to be reeled in. This is Carl's preferred dynamic. Carl prefers having me squirm than having me. Carl prefers, to me, the prospect of.

That's the immediate future sorted, she says. And are you sorry?

What does my girl suppose I should be sorry for? For messing Howard and Carl around? It was always my intention to renege, for as long as I could get away with, on the deal that I made with them. What then? For the way I allowed the latter believe that I might be a plaything of his, were he in turn to indulge my need for being out here and never turning back? Possibly, though only for the way that Carl has had with me.

I don't give a fuck about Carl or Howard, and won't apologize to either. Nor will I be sorry to get this jalopy back to the dump it came from.

Oh Daddy, she says all despair.

I've reverted to this again. Hers again. Years since she. This must be serious. More rain is hitting the roof of the cab. Big drops by the sound, gathered in leaves and falling to us at irregular intervals. For the guts of a decade, in which I misplaced hers, she called me by my name, like I was a hopeless older sibling of hers as well and in need of her minding. I never cared much for inhabiting that role with my little brother. But I never had a sister and I liked how her treating me that way felt. This morning I'm her father again.

I must have dropped a load at some point, but where and when I can't remember. There must have been no pick-up. Now we're just a cab. Now we're doing what the super in the container at Dover said not to, heavy mileage without a load. A load is family. I see that. The load's ballast gravitates you to a steady keel. Without it, I have felt all over the shop, buffeted by cross-winds, headlong and not enough to fix me to the ground.

Daddy?

Yes, love.

What will you do? she says.

Go in, say sorry just to keep the peace.

After that? After this?

Stop, will you.

You can't keep doing this, she says. You can't keep pretending you don't know what I mean.

Can't I?

Carl has materialized at ten o'clock to us on the near end of the platform. Carl is in shirtsleeves. Carl shrugs in our direction, leans into his phone, takes an age over it. Carl is scrolling with his right hand and smoking with his left. Carl's thumb twitches on the screen. This is for me. I can feel it. I mumble that and we watch Carl until Send is hit and Carl looks in our direction for evidence of arrival. Strange this, watching another in the act of messaging you.

This is going to be a whopper, she says peering through the curtains. Look at them thumbs go.

Ssshhh. He'll see us mocking him.

War and Peace bejasus.

Our dash lights. I don't need to open it. The message's entirety is available in locked screen. The murk is such that Carl can see himself lighting up the inside of Howard's cab. He sees me, too, lean forward and read his words aloud.

> stop mucking round
> carl!

That's it? she says. The sum total?

It is.

I give the top lamps of Howard's Volvo a solitary jab. I do that to inform Carl that I've received him loud and clear, that I'm finally coming. Carl looks dazed. I do it again. Again the head-light's blue square flashes in the instrument panel. Finally, to acknowledge my signal and its gist, Carl clicks his heels together. Carl salutes marine-style. Carl backs out of the rain.

Maybe she's asking me if I'm sorry for leaving her, for going off to live an ocean away and waiting for someone to spare five minutes in her week to ring me. Is that the thing I'm to be sorry for?

I'm sorry for going away. Yes. I'm sorry for leaving her half alone in a place where we were always already strangers. I'm sorry for all those Tuesdays when I was too in the fog of desire, balls-deep in long grass with the woman of another man, to take or return my daughter's calls. I'm sorry for all the lies that that desire necessitated, the cock-and-bull stories about meetings overrunning and roadworks on the motorway. I'm sorry for all those years in which I couldn't see her and she arrived home some afternoons to a house that was empty. Yes. I'm sorry for her that she's more like me than anyone else. I'm sorry for forcing her to watch her father thus, among second-hand furniture, on a beanbag on the manky carpet of a mezzanine in the centre of a city that was never anything but foreign, subsisting on strong store-brand cider and reduced-to-clear sandwiches. I'm sorry that I hurt so much to be around. I'm sorry for disappearing. Yes. There are whole years there somewhere still, when she was more of a girl and more in need than I could see or she would have allowed herself to admit, that her old man would have again and do over and make better. Alas, not even Carl and his everlasting supply of tachographs can grant me that.

I almost say this. Instead, I say:

Right so.

I have to go, she says.

This again. Can your bladder not wait for once?

Not that. I have to *go*. I won't be.

What won't you be, my petal?

Here, she says.

You don't say.

When you get back, she says.

The rain is getting harder. It's clattering the roof of our cab. Nice life here, I'd say. Do they get home? Chances are they have cashed all chips at home and blown the lot on this and live daily with the manageable loss of knowing that there is now no home to return to. They have rooms above the station. Past the opposite platform is all mountain. I could see myself being them. A village a mile downhill, a crossroads with tabac and boulangerie, a market in the playground of the école maternelle every Saturday. I could see myself here.

You're not listening, she says.

Yes, love.

They can't want for company, the couple from Reading whose place this is. For all their burned bridges, there has to be at least one truck in their lot most nights of the week, even out of season. News from the past, the occasional special delivery. Carl says that this place is a secret guarded closely among 'our lads'. There would be, Carl insists, an avalanche of passing trade if word got out.

> ffs this is taking the
> Michael

There's a sticker of a George's cross in a gable window. There are probably a few legendary nights here in high season: a dozen lit cabs in the dusk, a mélange of accents, crates of beer and hands of cards, old faces that haven't seen one another since last time and won't till next.

I won't be here, she says.

Stop saying that.

I'm tired, she says. It's been four months now.

Please don't.

I should make tracks. Carl needs to give Howard a positive result. Howard will be sitting in a living room strung with red tinsel, waiting for his own screen to light up. Carl needs to be able to report, once and for all, that this is happening. Carl needs Pat to repent and mend his ways. I can all but hear Carl bitching to the couple from Reading about Pat stonewalling out here in the rain, all but feel the end of Carl's tether wearing down to its final threads.

I should head.

Me too, she says.

You stay put. Keep an eye on Howard's wagon like a good girl.

I didn't make it, she says. Tell me you know that.

Know what?

That I didn't make it, she says. I need you to let me go.

Carl's waiting.

Dad.

You pick your times.

Daddy.

Can this not keep?

I didn't make it, she says. You know I didn't.

I'm asking nicely.

I've been in your head. I was in Mom's head too.

Is that so?

It is, she says. I said goodbye to Mom ages ago. I stayed longer with you, she says. I wanted to mind you.

Sunlight, a dusting of, rather than any sharp definition, like the earliest version of new thought. And there was me thinking that it was me minding her! I lean across the steering wheel and peer upwards into the blue patches it appears to be raining out of.

Letting you think it was you minding me, she says, was every bit as exhausting as minding you.

You don't say.

I do say, she says. And now I'm really tired saying, she says, and I need to go away and I need to stay there.

Sunlight proper. There are even a few shadows surfacing as if from underground. The rain is at its hardest. The last of it. That golden cloudburst that releases just before clear skies.

I look over my left shoulder. Her index finger is hooked around the side hem of one curtain, holding it open. I can see the outline of her beautiful mouth in the slight parting. I see her, or as good as makes no difference. She resembles one of those shadows that have begun to surface with the sunlight. A diagonal line across her face. Upper half in dark, lower in light. When she speaks, she's just lips and teeth and tongue. She does seem there. There are even streaks, a handful, falling slantwise from shadow into light.

Go home, she says.

Hazardous territory this, for her as much as me. The last thing in the world I want to hear from her. She knows it. It sounds like she's been working up to saying this. And now she has brought herself, finally, to saying.

Home?

Do.

The auld sod?

You know you want to.

Forgive me, darling, but that's a crock of shit. I have to take deliberate even breaths to stop myself from shouting. Give me this Tír na Fucking nÓg any day of the week.

Daddy, she says.

Fat chance.

For me.

> whats the hold up? pat
> got more company?

I pull the phone from its holder on the dash. I stab down the power button and swipe to Off. I really should go in before Carl gives up on me and gets law involved.

Go home.

To Ireland? That seriously what you're asking of me?

For me?

I hate the place. I say this to her. I loathe it, love. You know this. I loathe its tinny folksy junk, the treacly export-only senti-mental piss, its shitty little sound-man consensus, the skin-deep liberalism the place wanks itself off with. It is, daughter dearest, the original fucking kip. For you? I absolutely loathe the fucking kip for what it did to you. I won't ever forgive the cunts. And I won't ever go back.

Carl is on the platform again. Carl has come out for a ciggie. Carl drags and leans back and gazes at, assesses more like, the foothills capped in raincloud. Not much north for three hundred miles. Uplands and holm oak and wolf howls. Carl is performing a state past caring. Mid-morning. Everyone long on the road. Except us and we're special cases. Just before finishing, Carl faces our direction and exhales hard and profanes soundlessly and shakes his head.

Whatever happened, they'll ask around a routier table ages hence, to that Paddy? This is going through Carl's head. I can hear it. What became of that sweary Irish bloke who leased Howard's wagon for a week and was never seen? Went native, Carl will tell them. The tale will be so old by then that telling can do no harm. Went all *Apocalypse Now*. They'll say how strange and up himself he was, how not entirely flabbergasted they are. Had to be brought to heel in no uncertain fashion. His own worst enemy, our Pat. Bit off more than he could chew with old Carlos. The lads will laugh. The lads will always laugh.

Carl wants this done today. But it's down to me to come to him. Carl has too much patience, dignity, to submit and meander this way. Carl flicks the firefly of his lit stub out across the tracks and disappears inside.

The second I do.

You do what?

The second I tell you what you want me to tell you.

Tell me, she says.

The second I tell you. That I know. The second I do, you'll vanish and that'll be an end to it.

But you have, she says.

Have I?

Just now. Daddy?

Yes, love.

I'm tired.

Please don't.

I'm so tired.

She says it exactly as she used do, when she was my pet and confused upset with tiredness and cried because of it and fell asleep in my lap, her face in my breast and her moth's heart palpable in my own.

I know.

Her finger slips inwards.

I know, love.

The curtain's opening closes minutely. With it, the last light on her face slides down.

Kitty?

I hear her roll away. I hear her breathing taper off. I sit then.

Kitty?

There were moments, decades ago, on our landing. A grey afternoon of summer, say, when I circumnavigated our mother's nap. I wanted money with which to make myself scarce. She had brought her bag up with her and I listened on the landing.

Kitty?

She left her door ajar. Her dressing table was just inside the door, at an angle to the room. If I heard her, her breathing, that meant sleep in which she was and from which she was not to be disturbed. Silence meant that she might still be in the land of the living, that she might yet still speak.

Kitty?

I might see her then, stretch out on her eiderdown and mark her place and, via the mirror of her dressing table, peer towards the void that her eldest was calling from and call back:

What is it?

Can I look in your purse?

When she did eventually answer, she did so in a manner peculiar to herself.

To what end?

She would ask that of my angled reflection. I might have smiled to myself. None of my classmates' mothers addressed them thus.

To get some change.

Her bag was on the dressing table. Her purse was in there. I was asking permission. I was letting her know that I wouldn't be there when she woke.

Go on so, she always said.

And then there was once when I couldn't hear her breathing and she didn't respond.

Kitty?

I said it several times from the landing. I paused at the threshold, hand on the handle of her door. I could see, in the undulating glass of her dressing table mirror, the curl of her in half-light under her eiderdown.

Kitty?

She was gone. That's what I thought. Our mother had drowned in the shallows of her afternoon nap and it would fall to me to settle all arrangements. My brother summoned via the office of his headmaster. The dining area of the clubhouse booked for family from the Curragh and those friends of our father who felt obliged.

Her room had louvre blinds: teak, in need of dusting, shuttered. On her dressing table: a music box that had played 'Isle of Capri', a compact full of old powder and pads gone black, brushes overspilling with grey hair. There was also, on the doily of a serving tray, Dad's outsized gold wedding band and the yellow butterfly hairclip that she once wore for me.

She was facing the wall towards the sea, the one with the window. I was behind her back. Her shoulders and arms were bare. Her dress was draped on a tub chair. Her underthings on her dress, in the order that she'd taken them off: slip, nylons, bra, pants.

Kitty?

She turned then. Or rather, I remember up to the point she started turning: the ball of one shoulder twisting backwards, the tissue of her breast dragging in the eiderdown's hem of ribbed satin.

Kitty? Can you hear me?

It's raining again. It's all I can do not to open the curtain between seats and bunk. And find what? Two halves of a blue nylon sleeping bag, mink and kimono, bottle green Docs and a King of the Road cap, inhaler, a phone with no charge, grey fingerless mittens, an ounce of solid gold, a severed nametag that was once on her wrist . . .

This is it.

I say that in Howard's loadless cab.

Sure quit.

I say that too. Playing both parts I am, one last time.

It's a disgrace.

It is that.

A total and utter.

Who are you telling?

Who indeed!

Maybe there's been nothing behind me all this while. There's surely next to nothing ahead. A mug of iffy French roast if I'm very good. A bollocking softly issued from a tattooed sexagenarian who wished to lie with me. The road north. A sorry of sorts to Howard in Salford. Some new life that awaits my imagining of it.

I jump down and feel suddenly ancient. The world depopulated, but for the scent of woodsmoke and a chainsaw intermittent down the hill. Where did everybody go? My daughter said that to me on the phone a few years back. There was nobody in the house and she had lost her key and she blew her data on a meltdown down the line to her father in exile. Where has everybody gone?

The till is unmanned. Only Capital FM on satellite on top of the drinks cooler. I pull a pew up to the table that bears Carl's things: ciggies, lighter, a newspaper from last week open at the puzzle page. I could call out. There's no point. They're back there somewhere. They're bound to appear eventually, without my summoning.

A new song begins. The same song that was on the radio of my rental the first day we met. The same song rehearsed in hotel grounds however long ago and God knows where. A loo flushes in the distance. Carl enters shortly after, through a Staff Only passageway down the side of the counter. Carl is singing along. Carl is halfway across the floor and still buckling his belt. Carl knows the song. Carl has all the words by heart. Carl is seated opposite me.

Some song, Carl says. You know it?

I do.

Sometimes not getting what you want, Carl says, is the greatest stroke of luck.

Dalai Lama?

The loo flushes a second time. This guy comes through. Slight, mid-fifties, a cashmere sweater tucked into jeans. His face flushed. He ties a fresh apron and goes to work behind the counter without acknowledging us.

Brian, Carl says.

Carl has reached the chorus. Carl is staring at me staring at Brian. Carl's version of singing is not a million miles above croaking. I won't meet Carl's eye. It's like Carl has learned the lyrics to say them to me, like he believes they mean something between this 'us' that Carl likes to speak of. Carl finds my innocence touching.

You okay, Pat?

Sorry for all the shit.

It's a start, Carl says.

A woman descends the metal steps outside, from the upstairs quarters to the platform, and slips through. She squeezes Brian's arm. She asks if everything is in order. She does her own thing when Brian doesn't answer or look up. Then Carl is at the counter. The woman leans over the till to hear the quiet word that Carl wants. She looks down my way and the red buttons of her red cardigan brush the till's keys and Carl is handing me a fistful of serviettes.

Wend, Carl says.

Wend?

Wendy. Brian's wife. Proper person.

No doubt.

Calais, Carl says. Tomorrow. Sail at twenty hundred hours. No more pissing about.

That's a haul and a half.

Are we complaining?

I'll be there.

Good boy.

Carl is being kind. As with everything of his, Carl's kindness comes with an air of self-satisfaction, but I'm glad of it. Carl passes me a handful of doctored tachographs, in case I get stopped. Easy to forget how gentle Carl can be. There are times when Carl seems to see more than all his journeymen put together. There was me readying myself for sterner stuff.

So was I, Carl says, but you don't seem up to it at present.

You not furious?

I am, Carl says, but Carl's fury can wait. Will we be okay?

We will. Make half the road today, hit Calais teatime tomorrow.

Traverse, Carl says and pauses. Traverse that particular nightmare as best any of us can.

Nightmare?

Carl says sometimes he thinks that I inhabit my own private universe parallel to everyone else's. Carl reminds me of the jungle. I say it's all up here and tap my temple. Dover, M2, M25, M1 diagonal across country, M6 from Birmingham. Volvo returned safely if somewhat tardily to our mutual friend.

Howard?

Mention of Howard makes Carl's demeanour freeze. Am I being a smartarse? Do I look like I'm being a smartarse? I can't possibly look like I am.

Truck's no use where Howard's gone, Carl says.

Carl rambles on about this referendum, the madness of it, how if it happens the whole landscape of continental haulage could change indefinitely and not for any good.

She was in here, Carl says out of the blue to retrieve my attention.

Who was?

Your companion, Carl says. Carl twitches air quotes, a fag unlit between two fingers of one hand. Carl enjoys catching me off guard like this. Earlier, Carl says.

Earlier? My voice has angered. Earlier when?

Shortly after nine, Carl says, if I had to put a number on it.

We were still on the road at nine, still ascending to here. Nothing surer. Just when I'm coming to terms with her being a figure of my imagination, my little figment of speech, Carls claims that he has seen her too.

And very nice she is.

That a fact?

That's a fact, Carl says, very nice indeed.

This is my punishment. Not only does Carl get to see my other side, so to speak, but Carl also gets to ogle her. I could murder Carl. I feel plenty capable of it. It'd be easy. I could excuse myself, request a sharpened cleaver from Brian, slice Carl's carotid artery from behind, leave Carl slumped in his own sanguine chutney and be gone before any help gets dialled.

I nod a simper to match Carl's simper. After all his commotion, Carl knows, Pat has no option but to take this lying down. And Carl gets to taunt me with the mirage of her still with us.

Now I can tell the lads, Carl says, that our Pat's been keeping a nicely spoken bird to himself. And a right sort into the bargain.

If you say so . . . I could throttle Carl. I want out of this. Whatever you're having yourself, Carlos.

Very nice indeed, Carl says. And a little lad in tow.

A?

Carl's chair shrieks away from the table. Carl has gone too far, come too near. Carl can see that. Carl rises warily to his feet. Am I okay? I am, I tell him, though I'm not sure I am. Carl asks again. I'm sure I'm okay? As sure as sure can. Carl will have his phone on and I'm to call immediately if there's any hassle with boarding the ferry. There won't be. Carl places a sheet of print in front of me. My travel details. Confirmation numbers. Etcetera. My phone vibrating next to them.

They left bags behind the counter, Carl says. Check with Brian if you don't believe me. They went rambling down the hill.

My phone goes again.

> Can you talk? A

I text my brother back.

> Need a little time.
> Let me call you.

Carl gestures towards it. I tell him who. Carl remembers the name. Art! I won't go near it until Carl withdraws. Carl sees that and salutes once more.

Go easy, Pat.

Paddy.

Come again?

My name. It's Paddy. Not Pat.

That's what Howard said, Carl says, Paddy not Pat. Was always too embarrassed to call you it, Carl says. Like calling you Abdul or something.

It's just my name.

My brother's mobile goes straight to voicemail when I call. And again. Carl speaks to the counter and waves from the platform and disappears. To what? To a white truck decorated with sky blue fairy lights powered off the lighter socket. To another me. I try my brother's office number. I was never Carl's first rogue trader, nor his last. Carl seeks us out, brings us to heel, leaves us to it. Will I meet Carl again? My brother's office answers first ring.

*

There was an age when I knew Art's staff enough to pass the time of day. First name terms. How respective offspring were faring and travel plans. But it has been so long since I rang his place of work, and staff turnover is such that I'm now just another in a line. The young woman at the other end asks what it's in connection with. It's personal. I can hear Dublin going about the business of a Monday morning an hour behind. And who can she say? His brother. When she resumes speaking, she sounds excitable, pretty skittish. She never knew that there was any. Could she take a name? His only brother. She asks me to hold.

I didn't go to the. That word again. The word the suits used in the hospital corridor. I can still scarcely bring myself to utter the word.

That part of the funeral where the body is taken to the church on the evening before the burial . . . I didn't go to that. The specific word for it remains lost, lodged within. I feel, occasionally, its sharp edges shift. Nor did I go to the burial or the afters generously hosted in my brother's house. I brought her back to our mother's place for a few days, locked all doors, immobilized all communication with the outside world.

I'm afraid he's on another line, the young woman says. Can you hold or should I get him to call you back?

I can hold.

Sure?

I'd like to hold for him.

We sat up all night in the dark. The night of the. Removal. We didn't speak to one another. Just gazed at the flames. It was like she was livid with her father for not going, for being instead

255

there beside her. Beside myself with sorrow I was. There was no way my girl was lying alone on any altar. I must have drifted off where I was. Next thing was the gullsong of high summer and the hearth cold and her tub chair vacated the other side of the mattress. I was inclined to panic. I found her above. She had gone up to my old room. She was out for the count under the eiderdown, Kitty's mink wrapped around, talking in her sleep.

I am, she was saying as if at one end of a long-distance line and another was refusing to believe. I really am!

She materialized late morning, eiderdown worn like a cloak over the mink. She resembled an extra from her favourite show. She asked me what time it was at. She meant the service in her honour. I said eleven o'clock. It was already a quarter to. She opened the mustard velvet drapes of the French windows in the living room and let in vivid sun and mumbled 'Feck this for a game of cowboys' and suggested a dip. Seriously? She said that by the time that we had been and back, the whole shebang would be done, dusted.

Leave them at it, she said.

We went barefoot in convoy through the dunes, like decades ago. We left our towels where dunes gave onto strand. The tide was miles out. We kept walking until it got waist deep and we waded in that. Years since, but she was still a powerful swimmer. At one point she went under and stayed longer than seemed humanly possible. I scanned clockwise three hundred and sixty degrees. Shore and coast north and sea pleating into eastern horizon and coast south and shore again. The shore seemed very far away. So far away that I couldn't make out our house. She broke the surface behind.

Boo!

The tide was turning fast. It was passing us by. I wanted to stay out there forever and never head back. She seemed to hear my wanting. That was a first. She heard me wanting to stay out there and wouldn't allow it. She insisted that I take her hand before it was too late, that I run with her before we were out of our depth. So I did. She offered her hand and I took it and we ran for the one life left between us.

You're some boy, my brother says in his Dublin office. Some buachaill altogether.

I am. Sorry.

The mystery buyer, he says. No need to apologize.

Okay.

Why did you say nothing?

I tell him the truth. That I was embarrassed. That I felt I owed him the money and that I wanted the house for reasons as yet beyond me. That I, more than anything, simply forgot.

Do you plan on moving back?

I haven't thought that far. I had all this cash sloshing around from the flat sale and Tír na nÓg seemed the best place to sink it.

All yours now, he says, we've gone through.

He says nothing after this. I say nothing too. As if not talking money leaves us nothing to talk about. Chalk and cheese we may be, we were nonetheless children together. Once in another world.

I know she didn't make it.

Kitty? he says.

I know Kitty didn't make it.

Is it only now that's hit home?

It is.

You poor fella.

I should say thank you. Thank you for being so nice to madam. Thank you for taking such care of madam when I was off the wall. I should say that. I should thank my little brother. Just as I am about to, to thank my brother for taking my lost daughter under his wing, as if realizing that I'm going to and embarrass us both, he says what we usually say by way of signing off.

Okay, he says.

Okay.

Okay so.

One thing.

Yes? he says once and then once again. Yes?

Was it you nicknamed me Fredo or was that madam?

The line muffles.

Fredo? he says.

I saw it in a text.

That was me, he says.

He sighs heavily.

All mine that one, he says. You're going back a bit.

I don't speak. I don't make it easy.

If it helps, he says, your daughter well and truly marked her godfather's card.

Is that so?

It is, he says. She told me not to be a knobhead and to show some respect for my big brother.

He laughs. I do too.

Ouch!

Yeah, ouch, my brother says after a fashion. A bit special that one.

She was.

Without her, he says, how will the pair of us know not to be knobheads?

I don't know.

Okay, my brother says again and with that is gone.

I sit then. How long is anyone's guess.

It was you Carl was speaking about. Just there. Carl was telling me that it was you who was here earlier. It was you who walked down with your son to the nearest source of life. When will you come back? Your bags are behind the counter. I could walk down to meet you. But we might miss one another, and besides I've grown accustomed to waiting.

How did you know where to find me? Carl's truck revs heavily and crunches loose tar and shifts gears and becomes silence. No texts for days, weeks possibly, was you getting nearer. I could feel you. I just didn't dare think. A couple of hours here or there will mean no difference now. She didn't make it. All this time I told myself she had. Soon you'll be here. Do you know she didn't make it? Either way, I'll tell you for the first time when you come.

ABOUT THE AUTHOR

Conor O'Callaghan is originally from Dundalk, and now divides his time between Dublin and the north of England. His critically acclaimed first novel, *Nothing on Earth*, was published by Doubleday Ireland in 2016.

THE MARA CROSSING

BY THE SAME AUTHOR

The Mara Crossing

Ruth Padel

For Jim and Mo
with very best wishes

[signature]

7/7/12

Chatto & Windus
LONDON

Published by Chatto & Windus 2012

2 4 6 8 10 9 7 5 3 1

First published in Great Britain in 2012 by
Chatto & Windus
Random House, 20 Vauxhall Bridge Road,
London SW1V 2SA
www.randomhouse.co.uk

Addresses for companies within The Random House Group Limited can be found at:
www.randomhouse.co.uk/offices.htm

The Random House Group Limited Reg. No. 954009

A CIP catalogue record for this book
is available from the British Library

ISBN 9780701185558

The Random House Group Limited supports The Forest Stewardship Council (FSC®), the
leading international forest certification organisation. Our books carrying the FSC label are
printed on FSC® certified paper. FSC is the only forest certification scheme endorsed by
the leading environmental organisations, including Greenpeace. Our paper procurement
policy can be found at www.randomhouse.co.uk/environment

Typeset by Palimpsest Book Production Limited, Falkirk, Stirlingshire
Design by Richard Marston
Printed and bound by
CPI Group (UK) Ltd, Croydon, CR0 4YY

For Pedro, Gisa, Bruno and Mia

Contents

Contents

Acknowledgements

This book, travel for it and time to write it, was made possible by an Individual Artist's Award from the Arts Council of England for which I am very grateful. Many warm thanks also to the Environment Institute and History Department of University College, London, for a Resident Writer's Fellowship, which enabled me to finish it. Enormous thanks to David Harsent for his editing of the poems, and to Ian Pindar for his copyediting.

I have discussed migration with many people for many years and am very grateful to them all for their responses, especially those who gave their time and expertise to comment on the prose. They include Phillip Birch, Tim Birkhead, Kathleen Burke, Gwen Burnyeat, Mark Cocker, Elaine Feinstein, Eva Hoffman, Kerin Hope, Aamer Hussein, Sanjay Iyer, Sushrut Jardav, Lauro Martines, Jeremy Mynott, Michael Oberts, Sigrid Padel, Arshia Sattar and Tom Schuller. Many thanks also to people who gave material which sparked things off, especially Peter Conradi, Ruth Fainlight, Caroline Moorehead, Elizabeth Nabarro, Felix Padel and Alexa Walker.

Thanks to Susie Symes for an inspiring introduction to the Museum of Immigration at 19 Princelet Street, to Mark Baldwin for an invitation to watch Ballet Rambert rehearse and talk to the dancers, to D. V. Girish of Bhadra Wildlife Conservation Trust for guidance in the forest over many years (also for the Rufous Turtle Dove), to Andrew Morley for genetics and Claudio Scazzocchio for Lessespian migration.

I should like to thank the Wellcome Trust for a commission

to write the text for *Music from the Genome,* Somerset House Resident Writer's Programme for an invitation to talk on Bruegel's *Landscape with Flight into Egypt* at the Courtauld Gallery, and the Kate O'Brien Conference, Limerick, for an invitation to give an address on the theme of 'outsiders', which helped me shape reflections on the key figure of John James Audubon.

Thanks also to editors who published some of these poems – in *Acumen; Arvon Poetry Competition Winners* 2006; *Barque Bernaque (Poems commissioned by Newcastle Centre for the Literary Arts to accompany 'The Cultural Life of Barnacles' Exhibition at the Great North Museum Newcastle,*2009); *Best British Poetry* 2011; the *Guardian; Hortus; interLitQ.org; London Review of Books; The New Humanist; New Statesman; New Welsh Review; The New Yorker; Poetry Review* and *The Wolf.* Also to Sonja Patel, editor of the anthology *Nature Tales: Encounters with British Wildlife* (2010) where some prose passages were first published. Earlier versions of three poems appeared in my previous collections *Angel* (Bloodaxe, 1993), *Fusewire* (Chatto, 1996) and *Voodoo Shop* (Chatto, 2002).

I can't thank my editors, Parisa Ebrahimi and Clara Farmer, enough for their advice and support. Parisa's fine judgement, patience, kindness, vision and clear head made sure that whatever trees we wandered among, we never lost sight of the wood.

The Mara Crossing

Ripples on New Grass

When all this is over, said the princess,
this bothersome growing up, I'll live with wild horses.
I want to race tumbleweed blowing down a canyon
in Wyoming, dip my muzzle in a mountain tarn.

I intend to learn the trails of Ishmael and Astarte
beyond blue ridges where no one can get me,
find a bird with a pearl inside, heavy as ten copper
                                                coins,
track the luminous red wind that brings thunder
and go where ripples on new grass shimmer
in a hidden valley only I shall know.

I want to see autumn swarms of monarch butterflies,
saffron, primrose, honey-brown, blur sapphire skies
on their way to the Gulf: a gold skein
over the face of Ocean, calling all migrants home.

Migration Made the World

You really feel the earth turn in September. The planet is sliding us into autumn. On the other side of the equator it must be sliding everyone into spring, but here every morning seems a little darker.

I come into the kitchen and see starlings round the bird-feeders outside. Dawn glows through the geisha fans of their wings as they try to eat and flutter at the same time. One of them does it by hanging upside down and sticking its tail over its head. They may live in London the whole year but they could have flown across the English Channel last night. Starlings are partial migrants – some migrate, some don't. Huge flocks arrive every autumn on England's east coast and radiate out to join other starlings across the country. In spring, hundreds of thousands go back to nest in Eastern Europe.

We were all wanderers once. We walked out of Africa looking for food, safety, water, shelter and territory. Travelling was where we began and *Homo viator*, man the pilgrim, life as pilgrimage, is deep-engrained in Western thought. Mediaeval Christianity said we were strangers in this world, searching for the spiritual homeland to which we originally belonged. We weren't meant to be here – we were put in a garden. But that went wrong and now we are wanderers between two worlds, wayfarers on the *via*, the 'way', of life.

Human beings are both fixed and wandering, settlers and nomads. Our history is the story of the nomad giving way to the settler but when people are unsettled they have to migrate. The point of migration, whether you are a starling or a human being, is to reach whatever helps you and your children live in a new place. Home and migration belong together, two sides of the same ancient coin. Home is something we make, then things change, either in ourselves or in the world, we lose home and have to go elsewhere.

The word 'migrate' covers many sorts of move. It comes from the Latin *migrare*, 'to move from one place to another', and is related to 'mutable' and the Greek *ameibein*, 'to change'. We use it for two types of journey. Both can be undertaken either by large groups or individuals on their own. The two have a lot in common, but there is a wide spectrum of activity between.

The type of migration we think of in relation to animals, though human migrant workers and commuters also do it, is a periodic and usually seasonal move and return between one place to another. I shall call it Go and Come Back. The other type, Go and Stay, is a permanent move to a new region and often takes the form of invasion and colonisation. It seems to be typically human but animals and plants do it too.

Only humans, however, go in for emigration (going permanently away from home) or immigration (coming to settle permanently in a new home). These words suggest a political boundary has been crossed. Another word to throw into the mix, sometimes used interchangeably with migration, is transmigration. It can mean moving from one place or one stage of life to another but has the extra dimension of reincarnation: the soul is moving to another body to be born again.

Underneath all this is the idea of travelling towards something you need and don't have. Migration is a process with two elements: the journey towards a new life and the settling into it. This book is about the journey.

⸻

There is a push and a pull factor to migration. The push may be escaping war or famine or a freezing winter. The pull is usually safety, warmth, food or work. But whichever is uppermost, whether the travel is cyclical like swallows in spring and autumn, or once in a lifetime, migration is about survival.

The push factor is both outer and inner. The external force compelling you to migrate may be geographical and climatic like an ice age or the arrival of a competing species. But there is an abstract way of putting these: you leave because of some loss, danger, threat or lack which triggers inner pressures that also have abstract names (though they are not experienced abstractly) like hunger, fear and hope. The great dream is of something better elsewhere. Hope of a new life is the positive force behind human migration. Hope and imagination – picturing that new life – are push and pull combined.

Seven years ago I watched the wildebeest migration from Kenya to Tanzania, whose last awful stage is the crossing of the Mara River. I wanted to hold migration up to the light from a lot of different angles and set the struggle of migration, the effort of getting there, in the context of biology and history. But after the poems were written the background seemed so complex and extraordinary that I wanted to set it out more openly too, in prose. Switching between one place and another is intrinsic to migration, so it seemed apt to go between poetry and prose, and there was a wonderful model for mixing them whose title was also appropriate for migration: *The New Life*.

The mediaeval *prosimetrum*, a literary genre which combined prose and poetry, followed sixth-century reflections on happiness by the philosopher Boethius. *De consolatione philosophiae,* written in a Roman jail before Boethius was executed by an Ostrogothic king, tells the story of his philosophical and spiritual self-discovery. Mediaeval readers loved Boethius; mediaeval writers copied his shape-shifting blend of philosophy and poetry. *Cosmographia* was an account of the creation of the universe by the twelfth-century poet-philosopher Bernard Silvestris. *The Fire of Love* was a mystic poem on Christ by a fourteenth-century Yorkshire hermit, Richard Rolle. A French form, the *chantefable* or 'song-story', mixed prose and poetry to tell stories of knighthood and courtly romance. But star of them all was Dante's *La Vita Nuova*.

La Vita Nuova changed European poetry. Dante was writing not out of traditional convention but fresh from life. The prose he wove round his poems was both storytelling and critical exegesis. He had already written the poems and was thinking back to explain the thoughts and feelings which went into them, events which provoked them and poetic techniques he used. The story of how he came to write the poems became part of the over-arching story: his love for Beatrice. In 1295, Dante was stepping closer to the reader in two revolutionary ways. He was writing his own experience, and doing it not in Latin but vernacular Italian, the language his readers spoke. 'I was afraid to enter it,' he says. 'I remained for several days desiring to write and afraid to begin.'

The story I had to tell was how migration shaped, and carries on re-shaping, the world. I wrote the poems, then added prose to set them in context. The prose interludes are not essays but introductions to each run of poems – as in a live reading poets introduce poems with a little information, so the audience knows something about them when they listen.

Like most people I have both migration and rootedness in my background. On my mother's side my family is middle-class professional England, doctors, teachers, potters and scientists. But my father's grandfather, Christian Padel, was born in a German community in Christiansfeld, a border area between Germany and Denmark constantly tugged between these two countries. The town was founded, and a pharmacist's garden was laid out there, in the late eighteenth century by Moravian Brethren, Protestant refugees to Silesia from Moravia in the late seventeenth century. Christian's grandfather Abraham, an apothecary born in Danzig, migrated there to manage the dispensary.

Young Christian went to England for a year or so when he was seven to stay with an uncle who taught music in Harrogate and York. At sixteen he went to Germany to study piano at the Leipzig Conservatoire with the Bohemian virtuoso Ignaz Moscheles, a pupil of Beethoven. In 1865 he travelled to London, and eventually took over his uncle's teaching in York, where he taught the composer George Butterworth and became soloist with the York Symphony Orchestra. When he retired he lived with his son, my grandfather, in Carlisle.

Somewhere, very young, I got the idea that the Padels were Wendish. The Wends or Sorbs are a group of Slavic tribes who have lived in eastern central Germany for over a thousand years, an area which stretches across the River Oder into modern Poland. They kept their language despite pressure to assimilate and persecution under the Third Reich.

As a child, I thought the Wends were nomadic. I pictured them as Gypsies: apothecaries wending their way with piebald ponies and violins through dark forests and open hills, while healing people and playing wild music.

In fact they are mainly farmers not nomads, and whether we really are Wends is not certain. The name Padel is not German, though there are many Padels in eastern Germany and my family's immediate roots are German: they spoke German, not

Danish, in Christiansfeld. But the country with by far the largest number of households called Padel is France, mostly northern France, and the Padels may well have been French Huguenots, which means another earlier migration, escaping Catholic persecution. My branch of Padels migrated from Schleswig, but with me, as with many people, talk of roots and 'Where are you from?' leads to questions, not answers.

<hr />

London is immigrant city. When the Romans got here in AD 43, they built a settlement on a crossing on the Thames. A hundred thousand indigenous people, the Iceni, burned it down, but the Romans crushed the Iceni and enlarged their trading post into a city. London's walls were built by foreign soldiers, mostly mercenaries from Africa and Spain. Nearly a thousand years later, the Normans invaded: French craftsmen and architects built the Tower of London and Westminster Abbey, the city's oldest landmarks. Like Byzantium, Rome, the Mughal Empire and America, London was created by migration.

<hr />

We all descend from primeval slime. No one knows how the first cell arrived on Earth, but once it did, whether it was created by a deep-sea biochemical accident or blown in from outer space like the aliens in John Wyndham's fantasy *The Kraken Wakes*, the cell changed everything.

The first type of cell was the prokaryote, a single cell enclosing a circular strand of DNA, which contains the genes. The second type, which makes up most of the life we see every day, plants and animals, was the eukaryotic cell. Its DNA is balled up in a nucleus, tight-packed like the inside of a laptop with different structures called organelles. Each type of organelle has a different function and is enclosed by a membrane.

This was a great improvement on the first design. The membranes, soft inner boundaries, demarcate the organelles and, as in a society, it is their relationships and teamwork which create what life needs – energy. The eukaryote is a house of many chambers and ushered in a new era of life.

For a cell to spread it has to multiply, to copy itself. It breaks apart its DNA so the genetic information can be copied. The prime mover in this is the nucleotide Adenosine triphosphate, the coiner of energy which presides over the whole court of the cell. It begins the drama of replication by snapping the molecule down its long axis. The twirls of the helix unwind into two caterpillar-like halves whose flailing legs are the vulnerable genetic code. Each strand of the parent chromosome acts as a template to create for each flailing leg a new complementary strand, generating a new partner.

So the genetic code is passed on. But the two strands do it differently. The lead strand gives out its code continuously. The other, the lagging strand, grows in the opposite direction, against movement to the replication fork where generation takes place. At the tiniest, most intimate level, it seems, contrariness is built into us. The enzymes that synthesise new DNA can only work in one direction along the parent molecule, so on the lagging strand new DNA is copied in instalments.

Both strands, however, split apart and successfully unite with new-generated partners, and this is the process which enables living cells to replicate and multiply across the earth. The spread of life depends on this soap opera of relationships, breaking bonds and creating new ones with a swift, enormous violence which is happening inside the cell all the time.

Recently, after the funeral of one of my uncles, I drove to a family gathering at his home in the Chiltern Hills. Near the house I saw a red kite close up. There was a flash of hooded amber eyes and then it swooped away. Its shadow crossed a sunlit field while the bird itself was soaring into blue sky. Suddenly, cells got muddled up in my mind with what they sound like – souls.

For millennia we have taken birds as an image of the soul. Death, we have told each other, is the soul doing what birds do, winging its way to a better place, possibly to return. In sorrow for my uncle, I thought of transmigration: souls migrating into new life, either into a new body or into heaven.

The bird, I thought, and the shadow of the bird. The cell and the soul. Those are the boundaries of migration.

First Cell

Born in a deep-sea vent, synthesised
by lightning in a reducing atmosphere
or carried here by meteorite, we're all
from somewhere else. Algae, first
self-replicating molecule on Earth,

pulls carbon from organic substrate,
performs the world's first magic,
photosynthesis of air to oxygen,
and creates copies of herself, uncountable
as starlings flocking or the pure gold bricks

Sheba sent to Solomon by mule.
Cell in the air, on the rocks. Song
hoping to be heard in a heart cut open.
Little Blue-Green, dreaming of pattern
and form. Tiny horseman of apocalypse.

Dance of the Prokaryotes

Archaea, spirochaete. Cyanobacteria
patterning the genes in a circular
chromosome, like the ring of hippos

dancing in pink tutus in *Fantasia*,
genetic code exposed
on the outside of their home.

Revelation

'A ladder,' the master whispered, 'of nucleic acid.'
This was the first we'd heard of it.
Rain nosed the glass, wind lashed the trees
outside. 'Four hydrogen-bonded nucleotides
locking on like mating damsel flies. But each
a different size, pulling the ladder's sides
into a twist, like serpents on the sign
outside a chemist who for old time's sake
gives lodging in his window to the alchemist's
glass jars.' He drew those twinned snakes
looping up the wand
of God-Who-Escorts-Our-Morphia-Laden-Dead
to forest mist and shadowlands where they belong
and brings them back in dreams.
'But one snake, the lagging strand,
is upside down.' A squeak of chalk.
The pavilion, I recall, was dark.
Rain pooled on the *mesua* floor.
'We're conflict from the start. One thread
runs easy, the other's fitful. Tickertape
on which genetic script, your soul's barcode,
emerges opposite.' What did we know?
We longed for a match, a cellphone, anything
that glowed. 'As in a mirror, messages
are written here and must be read
backwards.' We waited for the prayer

that never came. '*Otherwise* is built in.
Behold your molecule of heredity.
Two cosmic serpents, yes; but tail to head.'

Breaking the Bond

Cell summons her treasurer,
hoarder of energy, Adenosine
triphosphate, to break the welded rungs
and separate the partners
in their hydrogen-bond pavane.

Got to be done. Like snapping a bone
to reset it. Now helicase joins the party,
zooming through the knuckled spine
of nucleic acid, tickling the origin-buds
of replication. Don't laugh: she tugs apart

the annealed strands like spiral fronds
of honeysuckle whose soft stems,
sheltering the nest of robins
you watched hatch out last spring,
have grown together, hardening into wood

for years. Helicase spins that poor DNA
like a turbo. Splitting begins,
then copying . . . Replication forks appear
just where you'd say they never could
in the filofax of the nucleus. Its very heart.

Go *and* Stay

From the kitchen window I see five goldfinches, flakes of flying red and gold flitting through apple boughs above the feeders. They are waiting for the starlings to leave. They raised a family round here this summer: I have watched the chicks grow the scarlet on their faces.

We are lucky to have trees – and very lucky to have goldfinches – in London. London has a whale at the moment too: divers from Marine Life Rescue have seen one in the Thames. They think it is a minke. There are many minke off Scotland, especially around Mull. They must be moving south now for winter.

A cell makes protein, dismantles it and starts again. That is metabolism, which creates the energy cells need in order to respond to whatever is around them. The first metabolising cells emerged from water and set off into the unknown on the adventure of self-replication as if they had heard God say on the fifth day of creation, *Go forth and multiply*. This was the original migration – the spread of blue-green algae over the globe.

Social studies say human migrants are changed by the new home, the place to which they come, but also change that place. This is exactly what the first cells did to earth's atmosphere. They oxygenated it, earth changed and as a result, more complex life forms evolved and spread further.

Five hundred million years ago, proper land plants developed and spread away from the water. A hundred and thirty million years after that the first tree, *Archaeopteris*, developed out of them. It grew sixty to ninety feet high and was the first plant to have large spreading roots. *Archaeopteris* is extinct now but in the late Devonian era, about 370 million years ago, it spread across the world to create the life form which made possible our life on earth – the first forests.

Archaeopteris changed the chemistry of the soil and the atmosphere. Its roots dug in and its ferny canopy absorbed carbon dioxide. Smaller plants developed, taking more carbon dioxide out of the atmosphere while injecting oxygen in. Carbon dioxide levels sank, land temperatures dropped and animals could move over land without overheating because with less carbon dioxide, the ozone layer above earth grew and shielded them from ultraviolet radiation. Trees nourished life in water too, because decaying trunks and leaf litter fed the streams. Freshwater fish evolved. Safe from ultraviolet rays, in a milder climate, the new animals ate food provided by the plants or by each other. Grass evolved and new animals evolved to eat it.

Plant migration made earth a place where animals could breathe. Trees and plants are rooted, but their migration created the forests: their very existence is a result of movement. Cells migrate in the body but stay safely (otherwise we'd all be in trouble) inside it. Migration is part of the restless, constantly self-renewing nature of all life, in creative tension between the fixed and the wandering.

———

When the starlings fly off, the goldfinches flutter onto the nyger seeds and a blackbird shrills an alarm call from the ancient plum tree.

Our plums are damsons, unusually sweet this year, unusually thick on the bough. Once handled, they change colour for ever: the indigo sheen disappears and you see pink-violet beneath. The tree itself now is almost blue; the plums have pulled the branches low over the grass. My daughter is in London at the moment, working as an intern at a foundation that helps asylum-seekers. She collects the blue plums in a yellow bucket.

Trees seem such fixtures, but they were the first great land migrants. Like their ancestor *Archaeopteris*, modern trees spread over the planet but as the climate changed, ice appeared and trees migrated away from it. Where there was space, as in North America, trees migrated over mountains and crossed continents. Northern trees migrated south during the Pleistocene age (2,600,000 to 11,700 years ago), when the Laurentide Ice Sheet covered North America east of the Rockies from the Arctic down to where New York, St Louis and Kansas City are now. When the world warmed up again, tundra plants recolon-ised the newly bared soil; then northern trees came back on the fringe of the melting ice. Eighteen thousand years ago came spruce and northern pine; several thousand years afterwards came fir and birch.

But in Britain trees had nowhere to escape to and the last ice age wiped them out, except the strawberry tree in south Ireland. When the ice melted, thirty-three species migrated back to Britain from what is now mainland Europe. First the birch and Scots pine, lastly the hornbeam and beech. Then rising sea levels cut Britain off from Europe, the Channel ended tree migration and Britain was left with those thirty-three, now called our 'native' trees.

But what does 'native' mean? These were post-glacial migrants. The DNA of our most ancient oaks says they came from the Iberian peninsula. That makes the Royal Oak, emblem of England, an immigrant from Spain.

Our small garden is stuffed with plants. We have been here fifteen years; my daughter has grown up here as the garden grew shaggier and more jungly. But few of these plants are native. Rhododendrons came from the Himalayas. The damson, like the horse chestnut, came with the Romans – who clearly adored damsons: archaeologists find the stones when digging up Roman camps. The Romans discovered damsons a hundred years before they colonised Britain while conquering a much older civilisation, Syria. But though the damson was first culti-vated in Damascus, the oldest continuously inhabited city in the world, wild damsons go back much further. They evolved where the ancestors of apples began too, in south China.

The apple family, *Malus*, probably evolved about twelve million years ago in the mountain system known as Tien Shan, bordering Kazakhstan and Kyrgyzstan. As these mountains rose, the snow melt created subterranean caves and the bear population increased. Through millennia, munching and choosing, extending their territory, bears gradually converted the hawthorn berry into the apple, and the sloe into the damson. They also spread them. Fruit trees migrate by forced migration: the seeds travel in the intestines of animals who drop them, fertilised by dung, in alien soil.

When humans appeared, they spread fruit trees further. They found they could store apples through winter and carry them on journeys. The story of the apple is the story of interaction between plants, animals and people whose horses trod pips into the soil of forests and plains.

Inside all these bears, apples, horses and humans, other life forms were evolving and migrating with them. Four billion years ago some genes discovered they could spread by tricking other genes into replicating them. Parasites replicate their DNA with the help of – and at the expense of – someone else's. They existed long before land animals appeared; new ones evolved at every new stage of life's complexity. Flatworms made their way into crustaceans, then diversified into flukes and tapeworms.

Parasites drove evolution. When their hosts evolved ways of

protecting themselves, parasites adapted to evade the policing and the host had to adapt further to protect itself. The parasites which survived were those that spread into more and better places to live. Today parasites make up most life on earth and outnumber other living species by four to one. Diseases migrated with their hosts.

From a parasite's point of view, many symptoms of disease, like coughing, are the clever ways it has found to change our body's behaviour so that it, itself, may multiply and spread. They do this in thousands of different ways, like the open sores of syphilis, which seems to be a comparatively new disease. Syphilis has always been seen as the unwelcome immigrant, coming from somebody and somewhere else. France called it the Italian Disease, the Dutch the Spanish Disease, Russians called it the Polish Disease, Turks the Christian or Frank Disease, Tahiti the British Disease. It was spread mainly by sailors but no one knows where it began. Was it a New World disease brought to Europe by Colombus or were Hippocratic doctors already describing it in the fourth century BC? The first well-recorded European outbreak was in 1494 among French troops who may have caught it via Spanish mercenaries while besieging Naples. Then it rampaged across Europe. Before 1530 the Italians, Poles and Germans were already calling it the French Disease.

Malaria, though, is much older. As the Romans brought damsons to Britain so humans brought malaria out of Africa. China and ancient Egypt knew it 5,000 years ago, India 3,000 years ago, the Mediterranean 2,500 years ago. Human migration spread it to southern Europe, the Arabian peninsula, Asia, northern Europe. In the fifteenth century, trade and colonisation spread it to the New World and South East Asia through Europe but also via African slaves brought by Spanish colonisers.

Plasmodium, the parasite that causes malaria, is passed on by the female anopheline mosquito which needs blood to develop her eggs. (Only the females bite; males stick to glucose.) The parasite develops in her tiny gut, enters our blood through her saliva and is carried into the liver where it invades cells and multiplies. Then it returns to the blood, penetrates red cells and multiplies further, breaking down the red cells.

Today a million and a half people die from malaria every year. *Plasmodium*, like computer hackers, always tries to be ahead of the game: it is constantly developing immunity to chemicals we find to counter it. Every forty-five seconds, says an ad in my newspaper today, another child dies of malaria. Nature's forms do not demonstrate benevolence, said Darwin, divine or otherwise.

In Christianity, the Fall is the story of how something harmful got into the system from the start. One name for Satan is *alienus,* the stranger, the outsider. Parasites tell the same story: cells have smaller cells within them that flourish at their expense and accompany them everywhere. We, mosquitoes and *Plasmodium* evolved and spread together.

———

But though migration spreads disease, migration also defends us from it. Atoms migrate in a molecule, teeth migrate in our mouths and cells migrate in our bodies. They move by pushing protrusions out at their front and drawing in their trailing ends. Their migration is the Go-and-Stay type and happens for two reasons.

One is to create new life: cells migrate in a pregnant mother to form a foetus. The other is to defend us against harm. Cell migration is the basis of the immune system. Cells migrate to a site of infection or trauma, travelling towards wounds to attack invading bacteria.

Cells migrate, in other words, to heal, repair damage and create new life. This is not circulation, but the maintenance of our fabric.

'Cells are guided,' a cell biologist told me, 'by migration-promoting chemicals they detect in their environment. They find some attractive and like to go towards them, they find others repulsive and try to get away from them. If you supply the chemical with a needle and move your needle around, the cells chase it.'

'Why call it migrating?' I asked.

'To give an impression of purpose,' he said. 'The cells just seem to be trying to go somewhere. Purposefully.'

So, I wondered, is all motivation ultimately chemical? Maybe the answer is that all purpose has some chemical dimension, but – as with the different factors of push and pull behind human and animal migration – that doesn't mean there aren't others, too. Our own bodies show us that however many purposes there are behind migration, two are constant – to heal and to create new life.

Allele

The variant. Scripture from a chamber of errors.
The ghost who stalks the body like a shadow
in the mirror, invisible – just so –

as planktonic stars on pulsing gills of foam
that seem themselves an animal
in the wake of the midnight ferry.

The Other, who reveals where you'll go
next. The stranger who should be welcome
in your home, for *stranger* may also be *god*.

Cell Begins Her Travels

Cytoskeleton, little net
of peel and fibrous scaffolding
within the cytoplasm, protects
Cell's shape so Cell can move, repair
the wound, attack a virus, create
an embryo. Cell waves longhaired
flagella like the spray of spores on mould.
In a blitz of lamellipodia, Cell
sprouts her motile fronds. She, the queen bee,
will fibrillate each organelle
in turn. Her ruffling front slides on,
retracts, moves on again.
So Cell migrates
like an old soul bent on heaven.

Spinning the Plasma

Nurse presses the switch
on the Refletron Blood-measurer
Machine, vulnerable
to rotor fatigue, and squeezes
bead-berries from the tip
of this stringy boy's index finger.

He sits sweat-sheathed
on his mother's knee.
Nurse spins the plastic wheel
like prayer, like fortune, till
hay-colour liquid separates from dark
sediment in red cells.

They have been penetrated
by *Plasmodium falciparum*.
The parasite has multiplied,
breaking the red cells down
which spells fever, shivering,
fever again
until – in the uncertain mill

of evolution
all hardworking parasites pursue,
shape-shifting to hoodies and hackers

as attempts to outwit them change –
it's curtains. Yes. Their mass
obstructs blood vessels in his brain.

Flight of the Apple

(for Barrie Juniper)

Fly me beyond Taklamakan Desert
and the blossom trees of immortality
to heaven's mountain Tien Shan,
heaving itself into air above the snowline.
Melt pours down. Floods
carve an underworld of caves
and in move the bears, whose lazy sorcery
turns hawthorn bullets into quince
and apple. Because everyone, given time,
changes everyone else. It's a world on fire
and the horse falls in love, the wild red
long-maned horse of the Lascaux Cave

whose teeth and gut help this pip
on its adventure. Hooves
drive the apple core deep
in the soil of the steppe
and the Turkic corridor. Horse dung
and dung beetle spread invisible
orchards, wouldn't you know,
hidden in the heart of apple – to William Tell
protesting an unjust edict,
Newton dozing in a Cambridge garden,
to Eden, to Eve. So apples sprang
wherever we tamed the horse.

Go *and* Come Back

The mornings are dark now, it is late October, the clocks have gone back like the songbirds, leaves are falling and the kitchen radio is saying they have found that whale dead in the Thames near Dartford. He was a young male with a totally empty stomach. He probably starved to death. But he's not a minke, he's a humpback. Humpbacks are occasionally seen off the west coast of Scotland but it's amazing to have one in the Thames. He should have been making his way slowly from the Arctic to the tropics but like all young males he was curious. It could have been his first lone exploration and it went wrong. Migration can be very wasteful.

Animals travel in many different ways through different environments all the time and there seems to be no definition accepted by every zoologist that covers all their migrations. Some are classic there-and-back affairs like the humpbacks from Arctic to tropics, or monarch butterflies between Alaska and Mexico, which happen at a specific season or particular moment in the creature's life cycle. Others are journeys from which the adults never return, only the children.

Migrations are thousands of miles and take months; migrations are a few miles and take less than an hour. They are seasonal and daily, regular and once-in-a-lifetime. Some are predictable, some seem quite random. Some are done by a group, others by lone individuals. Some creatures make epic journeys just to feed their young, like the albatross which flies for hours out to sea to bring back food for its helpless, land-locked chick. The dispersing young of many species migrate away from their parents' territories to find their own. Some animals seem pure nomads, constantly shifting in response to food and weather. Kangaroos follow no pattern in ranging through the Australian bush – is that migration? There are daily migrations like human commutes, regular migrations and once-only journeys. Some are predictable as clockwork, others seem entirely random – or so fluid that the animals seem to be responding to the slightest shift in wind.

Even seasonal migrations happen for different reasons. Many go to escape winter weather but the yellow-lipped sea kraits of the South Pacific migrate to a safe place to shed their skin, always a vulnerable moment, and tens of thousands of shelduck leave Britain and northern Europe after breeding to moult in one place – the Waddensee, mudflats off the coast of north Germany.

Male sperm whales, Australian giant cuttlefish and diamond pythons migrate to mate, setting off on arduous journeys in search of a female. Others, like grey whales, green turtles and emperor penguins, migrate to lay eggs or give birth in safety.

Some creatures migrate to find an essential mineral. But mostly it is for food. Everyone wants the best for their children: parents need food to get the energy to find more food for the babies. Swifts come to Britain to raise families because in summer there are fewer birds competing for the high-flying insects they eat than in tropical Africa, and longer daylight hours to find them in. North American migrant birds who winter in Mexico raise their young in the northern forests of Canada for the same reason.

The tropics offer plentiful insects and seeds and it's always warm, but the duration of daylight never increases and there is not enough food for everyone. So migrants raise their young where there's the best chance of getting food, leave when it disappears and return when it comes back. Temperatures change with the seasons, plants bear fruit at different times and when food fails, animals go to where it is. In summer the Arctic has extraordinarily rich, concentrated insect life in the air and plankton in the sea: thousands of birds and marine creatures go there to eat and breed. But to survive there in winter they would have to change physically and compete with other life forms through months when there's practically no food at all. So, from whales to warblers, they evolved to migrate.

Bird migration is the heartbeat of the planet. Along ancient routes, nothing to do with human frontiers, millions of birds are weaving the world together all the time. They are migration's blueprint, reminding us that both earth and the life it sustains are constantly changing form and changing place. It is especially their migrations which have made birds, for us, an image of hope.

'Hopes are shy birds,' wrote John James Audubon in his journal in 1820, 'flying at a great distance.' Audubon had been fascinated by birds since he was young. He had just said goodbye to his beloved wife and children and was taking a boat down the Ohio river on the first leg of his journey to Britain, where he hoped to find someone to print and publish his bird paintings. There, giving a talk in Edinburgh on the birds of North America, he would inspire a sixteen-year-old medical student (called 'Bobby' by his family) who hated the course he was doing just as Audubon had once hated being a naval cadet.

Audubon and that reluctant medical student had a couple of things in common. Both had to cope with great loss when they were small and did it by turning to nature – to long solitary walks and birdwatching. Audubon chose birds (or they chose him) as a way to make sense of the world. His mother died when he was little. Charles Darwin's died when he was eight. 'Why does every gentleman not become an ornithologist?' Darwin wondered when he was ten. At Edinburgh, instead of attending operations and medical lectures, Darwin took bird-stuffing tutorials from a local taxidermist. Birds are an image of escape from where and what you are right now. 'Hope is the thing with feathers,' says Emily Dickinson, 'That perches in the soul.'

Audubon was born in 1785, twenty-four years before Darwin, on Haiti, then a French colony called Saint-Domingue whose sugar and indigo plantations, worked by African slaves, supplied two-thirds of France's overseas trade. He was the illegitimate child of a Creole chambermaid from Louisiana and a French naval officer who owned a plantation and sold it before the slave rebellions began in 1791. When his mother died, Audubon's father took him to France, formally adopted him and brought him up in Nantes through the turmoil of the French Revolution. He grew up roaming the woods, bringing home birds' eggs and nests to draw. His father encouraged him, pointing out birds' movements, their sense of danger, their seasonal comings and goings.

But his father also wanted his son to be a sailor like himself and sent him, aged twelve, to military school. Audubon hated it, failed his officer's qualifications and went back to exploring the woods. In 1803 his father procured him a false passport and to prevent him from being conscripted into Napoleon's army sent him to America, to a farm bought with the plantation money on Perkiomen Creek, Philadelphia.

Here, Audubon continued to study birds. One of his experiments was to tie strings to the legs of eastern phoebes and prove that they returned to the same nesting sites each year. This was the first known bird-banding experiment in America. It is no accident, perhaps, that the young man who proved that birds came back to their first homes was a double immigrant who had already lost two homes of his own. Birds leave but come back, like the dove to Noah. Birds are images of escape but also of return.

It was escape which drove Daedalus, the mythical sculptor and inventor imprisoned on the island of Crete, to imitate birds and make wings for himself and his son Icarus, who, on their migration, flew too near the sun and fell into the sea. And it was escape that gave a name, the Wild Geese, to thousands of Catholic Irishmen who left Ireland to serve King James in France when English Protestants had beaten his army.

Caged or free, birds say it all. 'Oh that I had wings like a dove,' says Psalm 55. 'I would fly away and be at rest.' 'A robin redbreast in a cage,' William Blake said at a time when people still did cage robins in Britain, 'puts all of Heaven in a rage.' In Dickens's *Bleak House*, the poignantly named Miss Flyte, unhinged by the delays of her lawsuit, keeps wild birds in cages which she will open when her case is heard. The list of their names, charting what she and others have lost because of these delays, begins with Hope, goes on with Joy and Youth and ends with the injustices she cannot fly from: Waste, Want, Ruin, Despair, Madness.

We compare ourselves with nature and see ourselves reflected in it. Migration seems to lie at the heart of the birds' mystery; we feel they are free, as we long to be free, to get away – and, if they want, to come back.

Through the ages we have believed that along with the freedom to fly, birds have special powers, special knowledge and a special language. In ancient Greece and Rome, augurs deciphered their flight and their calls. Birds were omens, birds were the gods' messengers. The canary down the mine whose death warns miners of gas, like the dove with a green twig which tells Noah the Flood is subsiding, belong with an ancient feeling that birds are sign-bearers and foretell the future. 'Take note when you hear the voice of the cranes,' says the Greek poet Hesiod in the seventh century BC. 'Every year they call from the clouds above. They give the signal for ploughing, they mark the season of rainy winter.' Birds go between two worlds, and between air and earth, so why not between us and the gods?

Mediaeval alchemists spoke of a mystical 'Language of Birds' which translated what was divine, therefore of the air, into the base earth of humanity. Birds speak to us of distance; as in a poem by Matsuo Bashō, written as he travelled to the wild interior of seventeenth-century Japan:

> The horse turns his head –
> from across the distant plain
> a cuckoo calling.

Birds are harbingers of change. Maybe dangerous change like a storm or a battle – Homer compares the sound of the advancing Trojan army to cries of migrating cranes – but often hopeful change, like spring. To those who stay home, the great thing migrants say is renewal. Ancient Greek children welcomed swallows as messengers of spring in their traditional 'swallow songs'. 'They've made it again,' says Ted Hughes of swifts in *Season Songs*, 'which means the globe's still working.'

In Bhutan, where black-necked cranes are vital characters in folksong and folklore, the magic moment is late October when these birds wing in from Ladakh and Tibet. They come to just two places. I visited one, a bleak yellow marsh called Phobjikha, while looking for Bhutan's tigers. It was late March, the cranes had just left and everyone was feeling desolate. In October the villagers and the whole country wait anxiously for them to come back. If they're late it may mean bad luck or a ferocious winter, so their arrival is a national event. In November, when they are safely back, thousands of people celebrate the black-necked crane Festival.

Bird migration has sometimes been a bit too mysterious to get our heads around. The Greeks and the Old Testament prophets took it for granted. 'The stork in the heaven knoweth her appointed times,' says Jeremiah, 'the turtle, the crane and the swallow observe the time of their coming.' But in the Middle Ages this knowledge disappeared, as if mediaeval man couldn't believe that birds crossed the oceans he found so dangerous. 'Migrate' was first used in English (or rather first recorded) of people. That was 1611; it was used in 1646 of animals and only in 1697 did it begin to be used of birds. Where did swallows go in winter? It was commonly agreed (maybe swallows taking wet mud to make their nests helped the idea along) that they hibernated at the bottom of rivers. Mediaeval drawings even show fishermen netting swallows along with their fish.

Even Dr Johnson, in the eighteenth century, believed this. Bird migration is one of the wonders of the world and the theories we have come up with to explain it show how extraordinary it is. Aristotle knew swallows went to Africa for winter. He also noticed that different birds used the same habitat at different times of year. He saw redstarts in summer, he says, where in winter he saw robins. Early translators of his work knew less about bird migration than he did and translated him wrong. In their versions, Aristotle seemed to be saying that redstarts changed to robins in the winter. Only in the eighteenth century did someone test this theory by keeping redstarts throughout the year.

Above my head come the ancient cries of geese on a journey. Their asymmetrical V slides across the white sky like the long black tick to a maths problem. This winter Britain will get about sixty species of autumn migrant from Scandinavia and northern Europe where their food is disappearing under ice. They are mainly large water birds, but also some of the thrush family, and others who winter here but nest in the southern hemisphere.

Since the Middle Ages we have uncovered various bird migrating secrets. We know where many go, partly from bird-ringing or bird-banding. You catch the bird gently, put a light band on its leg saying where and when you saw it, and if it's caught again somewhere else you have its route, or at least the two end points.

Radar helps, too. A flock of migrating songbirds shows up on radar as clusters of moving green dots. Radar was originally developed to track aircraft and was key to Britain's success in the Battle of Britain. Pilots saw mysterious moving objects that were not other aircraft and called them 'angels'. Later they realised their radar angels were migrating birds. After the war, scientists used radar to map migrations and discovered a complex global knitting pattern of flyways. We now know that nearly a fifth of the world's ten thousand bird species are long-distance migrants. In the southern hemisphere birds breed in the south and migrate north for winter, but because there is less land in the far south to support life, most bird migration happens in the Northern Hemisphere.

The geese above our garden breed in the north and go south for winter like many other species: millions of brilliantly coloured American warblers, for instance, or Europe's smallest seabird, the European storm petrel.

Petrels skim the waves, sipping planktonic food from the surface and seeming to pat the water with first one trailing foot then the other. Sailors called them *peterelles*, 'Little St Peters', after the Apostle who walked on water. They thought storm petrels were an omen of bad weather and called them the children of storm.

When autumn temperatures drop, storm petrels leave the cliff where they raise their single chick – say, on the rocky remote island of Little Skellig in Southern Ireland – and fly to South Africa. They return in April, a thirteen-thousand mile-round trip, arriving after sunset to avoid getting attacked by gulls. One was once ringed on Little Skellig, set free and caught again thirteen years later. The delighted birders gave her a new ring and let her loose. That bird, so small it would fit inside your hand, had flown between South Africa and Kerry at least twenty-six times.

Many birds follow coasts, mountain ranges and river valleys. This works well in North America where coasts, mountain chains and large rivers run mainly north to south and where the four great flyways are the Atlantic coast, the Mississippi, the centre of the country and up the Pacific. (For most birds that fly on into South America these routes merge into one over Panama.) But between Europe and Africa, and over Asia, things are more complicated because the big barriers, the Alps and Himalayas, run east-west. So does that other barrier, the Mediterranean Sea.

Large land birds like storks and eagles rise on thermals of warm air and have to cross a sea in one long glide, because thermals do not form over sea. They look for the same routes human migrants try to find: the shortest crossing like the Straits of Gibraltar, western link between Europe and Africa, or the Dardanelles, eastern link between Europe and Asia.

When my daughter finished university we went to Istanbul and Troy. One September afternoon we looked up from walls built when the city was still called Byzantium and saw storks flying overhead from the Danube Delta to Africa, as they have done before Byzantium and Troy were founded. In spring, the skies above Israel too fill with storks flying north from Africa to nest in Poland, France and Germany.

Sea birds, mainly smaller than storks and eagles, don't need to worry about falling into oceans and it is they that migrate furthest. Some migrate in long loops. Wilson's storm petrels fly figures of eight from Antarctic breeding grounds to sub-Arctic feeding grounds and back; sooty shearwaters fly a different figure of eight across the Pacific from New Zealand and back, a round trip of forty thousand miles; Matsudaira's storm petrel flies East-West between the Indian and Pacific Oceans. One record-breaking Manx shearwater is known to have clocked up five million miles in its fifty-something years. The little grey-mantled arctic tern flies from its nest at the North Pole to the South Pole and back, a round trip of 45,000 miles. It eats and sleeps on the wing. During that time it never touches land and hardly uses its feet at all. A young one, ringed as a chick on the Farne Islands off Britain's east coast, once reached Melbourne three months after it fledged – a maiden journey of 4,000 miles.

But migration is as various as physiology. Both in little countries like Britain and huge countries like India there are internal migrations in winter, when birds shift from the country to a city or from north to south. Some birds simply go up and down the same mountain all their life. Nepal's national bird, the beautiful monal pheasant, migrates vertically between 2,000 and 4,000 metres, down when snow is thick and up when it melts.

Behind all this activity are two physical facts, the spinning and the tilt of the earth. As the angled globe rotates, temperatures drop variably in different places so birds move towards food and warmth.

Nesting, which means breeding, is the key. Nesting seems the opposite of migration but is also its goal. These geese will go back north in spring to raise a new family while summer migrants like swifts and warblers come from the Mediterranean and Africa to do the same thing here.

Go-and-Come-Back migration evolved as animals and birds adapted to terrain that was difficult to live in for part of the year and even, for some species, part of the day. It is a response to changes in the surrounding world outside and its evolutionary point is survival.

Their journeys and routes, their reasons for migrating, the risks they face and strategies they come up with, are parables for human migration too. How could birds not be our symbol of hope?

Dunlin

Light bursts around the body... Moving on
to wetland beyond full moon, next
water-and-feed. Draw breath; ease
hot muscle-protein, catabolised
in every dwindling breast.

Then the V, and my wing pushes down
making upwash off the tip
which my neighbour taps
and gets his lift for free.
Energy, flock, energy is everything.

Windflow, moonshadow. We read
the ground below. The rocking dark
protects. Over desert, not to overheat,
we take rock cover through the day.
In air we keep in touch, calling.

Insects, estuary, rest. Take off again
like that torn carob leaf
floating from shallow to open sea
beyond the headland, poised between
its own reflection and the white-spun meridian.

Where Clavicle and Wishbone Fuse

Radar operators, picking up echoes from migrating birds
write 'Angels' in the logbook, because they come

unbidden. Their licking silhouettes belong
to the school of night, drawn on

for hours across the moon by a magnetism you might
if they were us, call faith, and they keep going

on a butterball of gold fat glowing
in the breast like a secret love

where clavicle and wishbone fuse.
Silk-gristle wings, so easily blown off-course

or bagged by hawks and guns
in blue-blush-ivory dawn

at crossing-points of continents: Bosphorus,
Camargue, Gibraltar. Triggered by high winds,

barometric pressure, a drop in temperature,
the dying of summer flies or autumn seed; and inner
                                          need.

Children of Storm

(for Jeremy Mynott)

This is Skellig Michael, off the coast
of Kerry, darksummer home
to guillemots, shearwaters
and the bad-luck good-luck guys –
St Peter's Birds, the outriders,
who lay their one and only egg
in a chink of wall
which they enter and leave at night.
Yes it's touch and go
for Mother Carey's Chickens
hunting microscopic prey
with dangling toes as if they walked
over whipped-and-peaking waves.
They gather in charcoal twilight
flashing silver question marks
under black-sickle wings
then take off for the Cape
from this millefeuille granite ledge
over creamy North Atlantic thunderheads
to Africa's cliffs of lemon cloisonné,
sand schist. It would make a dog think
to see the same five grams
of close-feather muscle
venting back to where they hatched –
black igloo churches

growing on black rock like its own flesh,
recorded in the Martyrology of Tallaght
and Annals of Innisfallen.
Come spring, the Priest's Stone
watches for them at sunset
against a shine-and-shadowboxing sea.

Swallows Hibernating at
the Bottom of a River

– and a fisherman pulls them out in his net
along with dancing tench, bream, barbel,

cleft wings trickling, marbled in January sun
by headwater freshets,

the coiled-wire leg bones
you'd never normally see

tucked in riparian mud
like prayers engraved on a rice grain.

Rift

I give you Lotan, heart of Arava Valley
in the Gulf of Aqaba. Turn your head
to the umber-maroon of Jordan's mountains.
Turn again and it's mountains of the Negev
where shell-rock glimmers white as halogen.
If you come this evening, as you surely will come,
what you'll get is the mulberry glow
of a holy sunset, plus six thousand white storks
gliding between Africa and Europe
on warm blue thermals of spring,
scudding out from the cloudrim like rain
over this wound in earth's crust, opened
in the underworld by a clash of tectonic
plates from Turkey to Mozambique.

The Boy from Haiti

(for Mark Cocker)

He's eighteen, escaping conscription,
abandoning France. On the open sea
here's Earth's rim like he's never seen it,
a blurred brush-line of purple on aquamarine.

'Sorrow. Deep melancholy. My affections
still with those I left behind. The world
seemed a great wilderness.' Haiti at three,
the forest at Nantes, and now this.

He can't remember leaving Saint Domingue.
Wherever he's been he's watched birds.
'I felt an intimacy with them, bordering
on frenzy.' He reads La Fontaine

and scatters ship's biscuit on deck.
A flock of migrating pipits falls
from the heavens like a shaft of winter sun.
'They came on board wearied. So hungry.'

The crew see a forest, a shore. . .
He knew it. Birds unlock
everything. An inlet, wide, deep and certain.
Cries of gulls above East River docks.

The Watcher

(for Tim Birkhead)

Midnight in the castle at Radolfzell.
I'm gazing at our pixellated map
     of the Dark Continent
and a luminous full stop: a radio transmitter
fitted in east Germany five months ago
by a Vogelwarte Research Station ringer
to the leg – before wing-feathers grew –
     of a juvenile white stork
now standing in scorched savannah.
The pulsar, monitored by satellite,
flashes at the frequency of my heart.

Outside in the castle orchard, low winter sun
throws shadows longer than the trees.
     Why am I here? To record.
And – oh yes – retrace that juvenile's first journey.
One mouse click and a red vine grows
over eastern Europe, Eilat and Sudan to Chad
tracing the flight of magnetite, lodged between
     white stork skull and white stork brain,
held to Earth's magnetic field over mountains, sea,
fumes from the cities, frontier guns,
a thousand no-man's-lands, a thousand wars.
Not one year old and it's on the double pilgrimage
white storks evolved to make. Click again.

Quest for the sacred. And if I
could track that one stork down
on its winter ground, maybe I'd know
what has become of life and me
and where to go. I'd pour libations, follow
the omen, set up sacrifice
to the god of wayfarers, even pay a call
on the seer who decodes
the flight of birds. I'd prophesy.

Finding the Way

It is a gold and blue November day. Sun speckles my daughter's blonde hair as she sweeps up dead leaves, geese are still coming over from Scandinavia and I am digging up a bush. A robin, who sees this garden as his (or her) territory, is watching. When I bed the root in new earth it hops down to investigate and we look at each other.

Robins are the essence of a British garden. But the mysteries they hold go right to the heart of migration.

———

Many birds return to the same cliff or nest as the previous year and only get lost when storms blow them off-course. Young birds with no parental guidance, such as ospreys, end up exactly where their species has always wintered without ever having seen the place or route. A baby cuckoo raised by non-migrating foster parents will never know its real parents, yet migrates south along the routes they use to join other cuckoos in wintering grounds of East Africa and South East Asia. It is not only direction they get right, but timing. In some species, mated pairs spend the winter apart and synchronise their return to reach the nesting site separately within the same few hours.

How do they do it? We who lose our way so easily without satnav marvel that birds reach the right place from so far away.

For both timing and navigation, birds use a whole range of tools, some we share and some we don't. Parental guidance is the most obvious. We can relate to that – we often start our own life-course by following parents. Migrants who have done it before are the best navigators. Geese, like swans and cranes, migrate in family units. There are parents up there guiding their young, taking turns to lead, teaching them to follow the route and recognise landmarks like rivers, coasts, mountains and cities so they form their own mental map.

Young birds must also learn to deal with high winds and storms. Geese can copy parents but ospreys do it alone, and satellite trackings have shown how much better older ospreys are at correcting for wind drift. Young ospreys learn without a tutor, on the job.

Birds also navigate by sound. Sound orientates, helps you know where you are, where you're going and who's going with you: they steer you by waves crashing on the coast, a city's hum, the rustle of a forest, each other's contact calls. Migrating birds don't sing, they need their breath to fly, but those who migrate in groups utter road cries, a sonic hand-holding – *I'm here, are you?* – which keeps them in touch about what's happening and where they're going. The film *Winged Migration* follows a group of geese across Central Europe. The camera flies beside them as their wing muscles beat and contract, and they call constantly to each other as the land rolls away beneath. Migration can be a noisy affair.

Birds steer by smell, too. It may be strange to think of a hard beak picking up scent, but birds have a fantastic sense of smell. They need it to find food. Sea, rivers, mountains, woods and cities, they smell them all.

But senses we share with them are only the beginning of their toolkit. Our senses are not the world, they are only filters set by the limits of human physiology. Birds have an inbuilt sun compass and respond to patterns of polarised light and barometric pressure. Those that fly from pole to pole allow for earth's rotation, and those that migrate at night – when the air is cooler, and dense like dark cream, with less risk of overheating or water loss over desert, less turbulence rising from earth like bad dreams to throw them off-course – are imprinted with a particular map of the stars and steer by a star compass.

Their combination of precise timing and direction is demonstrated by the phenomenon known as *Zugunruhe*, 'journey unease' or 'restlessness about the move'. If a migratory bird is restrained during the hours it would normally migrate, it flutters and agitates for as long as its journey would take, in the to-and-fro twitchery you see in swallows before they go as their bodies are first preparing and then impelling them to fly. If the journey would normally take twelve hours, *Zugunruhe* lasts as long as that. If the species does a five-day journey, *Zugunruhe* lasts five days.

Scientists study *Zugunruhe* in the Emlen Funnel, a cage

shaped like the collar you put on a dog's neck to stop it licking a wound. The bird flutters up in it and slips down again and again. There is an ink pad on the bottom, so on each attempt it leaves an inky trail which points in the precise direction their migration would take. If the lab has a planetarium-like night sky, scientists can change the star pattern and watch the bird change its angle of flutter. How long it tries depends on how many hours, days or months it would normally take to migrate.

Behind a lot of this is a bird's response to earth's magnetic field.

In 1961 a geologist called Heinz Lowenstam made a momentous discovery – that living organisms contained in their bodies the mineral magnetite. Up to this point, everyone assumed that magnetite existed only in inorganic materials. The Greeks called magnetic rock after Magnesia, in Asia Minor, where a lot of it was found. Its power to attract iron was supposedly discovered by the sixth-century BC philosopher Thales (although one myth says it was a shepherd called Magnes) and in English it was known as lodestone: the 'leading' stone. Pilots were lodesmen; the Pole Star which led you north was the lodestar. Until 1961 magnetic rock was a static, inorganic thing which paradoxically caused other inorganic things to move.

Lowenstam was born in 1912 in Upper Silesia, a mining district in south-east Germany which, when Lowenstam was seven, was given to Poland after the First World War. He grew up fascinated by stone, studied geology in Munich and went to Palestine to research the East Nazareth Mountains. He came back to Munich in 1936, a week after a new law had forbidden

Jews to receive doctorates. In 1937 he migrated to America where thirty years later he published a paper announcing that certain sea molluscs known for their homing ability had crystals of iron oxide in the tips of their teeth. Lowenstam suggested that these molluscs were bio-synthesising magnetite and found their way using a magnetic compass. Magnetism, he argued, must be a property of organic as well as inorganic things like stars and stones.

Geologists were sceptical, but in 1975 magnetite was discovered in another life form, magnetotactic bacteria, which swung into line along earth's magnetic field. Bio-mineralism was accepted as a new fact of life.

I love that Lowenstam was a migrant like Audubon. The country he was born into became another nation when he was seven. At thirty-five he emigrated to survive. One immigrant found birds returning to the same nest year after year, the other found that magnetism is a property of living beings.

Thanks to Lowenstam we now know that magnetite plays an important role in the behaviour of a whole range of life forms: from birds to bees, crocodiles, tuna, fungi, sea turtles, fruit flies, sharks and lobsters. The fossil record goes back at least two billion years. Magnetite operates in them as a membrane-bound bio-mineral, helping them navigate by sensitivity to earth's magnetic field.

The advantage of a magnetic compass in your brain, thorax or teeth is that you are not affected by cloud or changes in daylight hours. The disadvantage is that you can be thrown off-course by electric storms or sunspot activity. Birds are disorientated by electric disturbance and get lost; mass beachings of sperm whales suggest that sunspots disable their magnetic compass.

Some species have magnetite in their brain or skull; monarch butterflies have traces in their thorax; pigeons in their upper beak. Some birds who migrate at night have a special light-processing region of the brain called (rather like a new galaxy) Cluster N. If our robin migrates this autumn, Cluster N will let it read the earth's magnetic field through photoreceptor molecules connected to the eye. 'Usually the left,' one of my uncles told me. He is a neuroscientist who works on the brain and eye. 'No one knows why.'

Earth's magnetic field is doughnut-shaped. Its elliptic forcelines run between North and South Poles like bars around a squirrel-proof bird-feeder. It turns out most animals know what part of the earth's surface they are flying, crawling or swimming over, because they detect the changing angles.

But birds, who seem so free, are slaves to their genes. Their precise timings, and the direction they take, are the result of genetic programming: complex inner drives passed down in their DNA. Their bodies and brains order them where to go and when. Because the earth rotates, they might have to fly an extra hundred miles if they are five minutes late in setting out, so a punctilious schedule could make the difference between life and death.

———

Migration makes enormous physical demands and birds prepare for it like athletes before a race. Feathers and pectoral muscles are crucial and to get feathers in perfect condition many birds moult before they go.

Heart and breath are crucial, too. A bird's heart is six times bigger than ours in proportion to its weight, and their respiratory systems are even more dramatically different. Ours is 5 per cent of our volume; a bird's is twenty.

But fuel is the key – do you take it with you or find it on the way? How they manage their energy determines their options. Catabolism is the set of pathways that break down molecules into smaller units and release energy. Birds who store up fat before long non-stop flights gradually deplete it and then start catabolising their protein, which they lose variably – from digestive organs and, more dangerously, the all-important breast muscles.

Large birds are already near the limit their wings can bear so they have to stop and feed on the way, but many little birds take their fuel with them like camels. Those who fly four or five days non-stop cram in food beforehand to build up fat. Some search out the kind of hormonal boost athletes find in steroids. Semi-palmated sandpipers fly for three days and nights over open water from the Canadian Arctic to South America. Beforehand the cooler temperatures and shorter days of autumn trigger hormonal changes which make them switch to a high-fat diet. Their gut grows so they can eat more. En route they stop at the Bay of Fundy on Canada's eastern coast to gorge on mud shrimp loaded with Omega-3 fatty acids. Over two weeks their body mass doubles, their muscles use oxygen more efficiently – and off they fly to South America.

Birds that migrate in flocks help each other. In V-formation, the leader breaks up the wall of air, creating a swirl that helps the birds behind, then drops back to let another take over. Everyone flies in the upwash from the wingtip vortex of the bird ahead. V-formation saves crucial energy: birds fly 70 per cent further and often faster than they can alone.

Some birds migrate solo, usually because of diet. Hummingbirds feed off flowers. You can't queue up and wait for a flower to make more nectar so they go alone, though when many are on the move they often travel in parallel flyways like commuters on the motorway.

At the other end of the spectrum is the osprey with its six-foot wingspan. Ospreys eat fish, and fishing too is often most effective alone. They mate for life but spend the winter apart. Most British ospreys winter in West Africa (some from Eastern Europe go as far as South Africa), while male American ospreys who winter in Florida may fly north to Maine to wait for their mates. Of a pair which nests in Scotland, the male arrives from Africa, then the female comes in by her own route. When they go, they leave the chicks, who may never have caught a fish alone, to find their own way.

———

Some birds follow different routes out and back. One of the greatest animal feats of endurance and navigation is performed every year by the tiny blackpoll warblers. The distance each one flies in its life is the equivalent for us of ten return journeys to the moon but that's nothing compared to the dangers of their autumn migration.

In spring they leave the tropical forests and coffee plantations of Venezuela and Brazil where they winter and fly north over the Gulf of Mexico, up the Mississippi Valley, over the Great Plains to Canada and Alaska, where they build little cup nests in small fir trees. Everything about them is small except the risk they take going back.

When their three weeks of parenting are over, they eat to fuel their return. In a few days they double their body mass, storing fat and protein, swelling their gut. If you held one in your hand at this point and blew the feathers apart you'd see bubbles of fat held in by grey, stretched skin.

In September they head south-east over the Great Lakes, rest on the New England coast and divide. Some follow the east coast down to Florida and cross the Caribbean, others go to South Carolina and island-hop through the Bahamas and West Indies to South America. But some, the risk-takers, fly east over the Atlantic and pick up strong winds which hurl them south-west over the east Caribbean, non-stop day and night, eighty-eight hours to Venezuela. Four days over the sea at 16,000 feet. Why so high? Maybe to find the best tailwinds. Or maybe for cooler air, to stop their miniscule breast muscles overheating.

The reason it is so – well, if they were human we'd say brave or reckless – is tropical storms. Autumn in the Caribbean is peak hurricane season. They are swept into spiralling winds, towering clouds, torrential rain. Many crash exhausted in the sea, others become disoriented, are sucked into a depression, hurtle across the Atlantic and land in north-west Europe where they are lost to their species with no chance of making it back:

prevailing winds over the Atlantic blow east and they are only programmed to fly south.

Nature is prodigal, said Darwin. So much waste.

But migration is about survival and most blackpoll warblers make it. Every speck of fat burns off. But if they survive it's worth it because the hurricane route is shorter by 1,500 miles. They get a head start on establishing a feeding territory in the new home.

Another story of waste, risk and endurance shows how ancient the birds' flyways are. Bar-headed geese nest in Central Asia but winter on the other side of the Himalayas in Assam, north Burma and wetlands of Pakistan. They go early before autumn storms and try to do the thousand miles over the mountains in one day. They gather in a valley, check the air pressure, open their charcoal-tipped wings and up they go.

At fifty miles per hour they pick up tailwinds and double their speed. In those winds every millisecond is a fight. If a storm rises and a young one falls out the mother has to keep going. If forced to land on the near-vertical mountainside they sleep in the snow and try again. Some don't wake and the living will freeze too unless they go at once. There's nothing to eat or drink, it's now or never.

The oxygen a bird needs to keep flapping is twenty times what it needs at rest and up here the air has a quarter of the oxygen available at sea level. But their bodies are uniquely adapted to the altitude. Their haemoglobin absorbs oxygen faster than that of any other bird and their capillary veins penetrate unusually deep in to their muscle, so the oxygen reaches further and they get more from each breath. They are powerful flapping machines and their circulation keeps their wings so warm that the roof-air of the planet cannot stipple them with ice.

Why are they like this, able to fly over Everest? Because they and their route are older than the Himalayas. Over the millennia, as these rocks rose across their path, they adapted their physiology to the increasing altitude. Their destiny is written in their genes. They went where their DNA said and instead of finding a way around they adapted to the increasingly demanding conditions. And year after year they make it. In spring they do it again going back.

Genetic script-writing brings us back to our garden robin, who has not migrated, yet, and is pulling a worm out of earth where I planted the bush. Like starlings, European robins are partial migrants. In winter some leave for Spain, but not all. What makes some stay, some go?

Migration is an adaptive behaviour. It seems to be always on standby and can be triggered by changing conditions: climate change, for instance. Many birds today are altering their migration patterns in response to climate change. Birds are harbingers because they evolve quickly, at least small migrant birds do because their individual lives and species depend on it. Maybe that is what a bird is – always ready.

Does partial migration mean robins are free of the genetic programming which hurls a blackpoll warbler into the maw of a hurricane? No – it is just more complicated. Older robins don't usually migrate. The journey is tough and you have to be up to it, so it is partly age that decides. But mainly the divide is by gender. One sex goes, one stays.

We might expect the boys to go. *The Lotus and the Wind*, John Masters's novel about the Great Game of Anglo-Russian espionage in nineteenth-century Afghanistan, draws a conventional distinction between men – who need freedom, like the wind – and women, who need to be rooted.

Robins play it the other way round. British robins discovered wintering in Spain or Portugal are usually female. Females are smaller and more likely to freeze to death in British winters. Males stay and brave the temperatures. (Or, seen from another perspective, they are dominant over females, so the only way females can survive is to migrate.) For us they become the emblem of Christmas, the gallant little red spark in the blizzard. In reality they are hanging on to their feeding territory till spring.

Chaffinches do the same. The scientific name Linnaeus gave them was *Fringilla coelebs*. In northern Europe, where Linnaeus lived, it is the males you see in winter and *coelebs* is Latin for 'bachelor'.

———

Many birds go in for partial migration: it may have been a between-stage in every bird's evolution. Some began going; then some did, some didn't. Then they were all doing it, those who didn't died and migrating became an Evolutionarily Stable Strategy: an ESS, a key concept in Game Theory, a way of doing things that sees off any other strategy that comes along.

The robin's great game is partial migration but this is not freedom, nor choice as we know it. A robin's decision is as genetically controlled as a blackpoll warbler's. 'Deciding' is our shorthand for 'programmed by natural selection to behave like this'. Each robin will have its own genetic predisposition to go or stay in a given situation, depending on age, sex, how dominant or adventurous it is, and what's going on outside.

It is with this pseudo-choice of partial migration that the parallel with human beings turns awkward. Is there an innate personality divide that lets some of us uproot easily when faced with a threat, and others not?

Before living in this house and garden we had a flat. Our neighbour in the flat above told me that when she was sixteen in 1930s Berlin, she asked her Jewish parents if they should leave. No, they said. It will be OK. She got the last train out; her parents died.

Go or stay, how do you choose? Going may save you but migrating is a high-risk, high-cost solution. Different family members make different choices. Factors that may tip your fate are age, gender, physical fitness and that complicated, luck-of-the-draw thing, personality – which, for people as well as birds, may partly come down to your genes.

However risky the journey, the real struggle starts when you've made it. That's why blackpoll warblers take a short cut through hurricanes and why male robins risk freezing to death. Everything is geared to the battle for resources, not only with each other but with resident species.

This means competition, beak to beak, for the calories. If you film birds at a feeding table and play it back in slow motion you realise how fierce this battle is – as with human immigrants facing residents who resent competition for work, food and homes.

That word 'home' raises a whole spray of questions. What is home, for a bird? We talk about nesting instincts but a nest is not a bird's home. It is where it hatches from the egg and what it makes to lay its own eggs and rear its young. But though some birds return to last year's nest, a nest is only temporary. It is abandoned as soon as possible because for predators – a hungry magpie, for instance – a full nest is an advertisement and a canteen.

Does a bird even have a home? Swifts are Britain's briefest summer migrants. They come in May and are gone by the end of July. When not on a nest they are always in flight. Once a fledgling leaves the nest it will eat, mate and sleep on the wing. A friend of mine who worked in three different spheres once told me, 'I feel most myself when I'm going from one place to another – like a swift.'

Migration means spending your life not only in two different places but also en route. A swallow spends a quarter of its life migrating. Maybe the real home of a swallow or swift is the air; or even the journey, the trajectory.

Some commentators talk of going 'out' from a nesting ground to a winter feeding area and 'back' in spring, but what does this language mean? One bird book on my shelf summons the last ice age to explain the migration of the small northern wheatear. These small birds nest in tundra of the Arctic Circle on several different continents – north Asia, Greenland, Europe, North America. But in winter they all converge, from east, north and west like spokes coming in to the hub of the wheel, on one area of Africa. Why don't those who nest in north Asia fly to south Asia like thousands of other species, and those from North America migrate to South America like the black-poll warbler? Why these long east-west journeys, even over the North Pole?

'Let's admit,' says my bird book, 'this is at heart an African bird which goes north to breed in spring.'

At heart? What does that mean? In the last ice age, says my book, northern wheatears must have stayed in Africa or maybe done a short hop to southern Europe. As the ice left they went further afield (less competition for insects, longer daylight hours to find them) and then edged north. The more adventurous went west and east, but all were still programmed to return to Africa for winter.

But there's something upside-down in this picture. These birds winter in Africa, but does that mean this is where they're 'from'? A Baltimore oriole hatched in Maryland winters in South America: try telling the Baltimore Oriole baseball team their black-and-orange mascot is a South American bird.

Calling the northern wheatear 'African at heart' suggests a peculiarly human and maybe spiritual image: that 'heart' is the end of an outward journey. The tired soul at the end of its life yearns, the Church Fathers said, for its home with God: a mystic home, never yet seen.

People or birds, migrating is all about home. The quest for it, changing it, making it. But maybe where you 'come from' is not as important as who you are at any one moment. One self, one place is not the only model any more than is one self, one language. Just as human beings speak different languages, in different places, so some birds behave differently in different homes. In summer the rufous turtle dove lives in the Himalayas and behaves like a yard bird, foraging for food in villages and farms. In winter it migrates to the Western Ghats in South India where it hides away in deep forest.

Some people live in one home all their lives, but what about first- and second-generation immigrants like my great-grandfather and his children? Is 'home' where your parents came from? Or *their* parents? How far back is back? A friend of mine born in South India taught in Chicago for many years and then moved back to Bangalore. 'My Indian students in Chicago felt American,' she says. 'Their parents came to America when *they* were twenty. My students didn't know Hindi or Gujarati, they didn't feel India was home. They hated it when their parents insisted on going back. I thought it unfair of the parents to ask them to. What was "home" for them felt foreign to the kids.'

The literary theorist and scholar Edward Said was born in Jerusalem. He had an English first name, an Arabic surname, he grew up in Cairo and Lebanon and was Arab but also Christian and Palestinian; and eventually he held an American passport. In his memoir, *Out of Place*, he says he felt at home wherever he was at the time. The Lebanese writer Amin Maalouf grew up in Lebanon but moved to Paris and writes in French. In his memoir *Origins* and his essay *On Identity*, he says he has a different identity in Paris from the one he has when he returns to his native country. Language we use about birds throws up a lot of the questions we ask ourselves about identity, origins and home.

When You're on Your Own

1 Osprey

Goddess of rose-gold pearl behind black cloud,
look after the lonely speck in empty sky
coming in from Senegal to mist over the loch.
One thin cry and she's here too, his mate
from another Africa. May, June, gold-green July –

and she's gone. The male, too. The chick, their brood,
is alone with gravitational pull and evolution
as her guides. France, Spain, North Africa,
Senegal. Fishing demands the quick eye, strong
talon, a spiral on an unscrolled map – and solitude.

2 *Hummingbird*

Someone has flung rainbow pepper on the air.
The hummingbirds are migrating, each alone:

Blossomcrown, Coppery Thorntail
and Flame-Rumped Sapphire.

They are alone because diet is everything
and you can't queue up for a flower.

They're safe, they're small, most predators
won't see them and a flock would be a target.

They're fearless – they out-manoeuvre everyone
and fly like helicopters

sideways, back, upside down. Pure iridescence:
the dimming light

skimbles like oil film on each metallic green
millimetre of one Ruby-Throat

strimming four hundred and fifty miles
of the Gulf of Mexico

in a twenty-hour dash through the dark
till throat-feathers flash to the rising sun

a sudden spark of bloodroot, cinnabar,
vermilion, puccoon.

That Bird Migration Records the Movement of Earth's Crust

(For Jo)

Overheard at breakfast in the guest house:
'. . . Three millennia of mapping. Furrows
on moonlight and never mind plate tectonics,
how mountains rose in a crash of the lithosphere.
Let continents do their worst – they split,
they clash – but the birds' flight path
is what it always was. Every heartbeat,
every contracting muscle, is a chronicle.'

Bar-headed geese wait for the perfect wind
in an ochre marsh. All heads turn – each bill
in parallel, rouge compass to a crystal –
towards the cloud-hidden peak. They take off
in a rush. First buffet, and a young one falters . . .
drops . . . The mother checks, wingbeats fail
then pick up – she can't spare – no, cut
to the quick – can't spare a second, tossed

sinewy neck back, up and aslant, by djinns
of the mountain. Hurricane gales
force them down to rock and ice.
They sleep, till dawn breaks gold-lattice
through blackshadow cloud. One lifts, a head
out of snow, and now another,

to wind-howl and glare. They stare
at the glacier. Yes, they call. Yes – to try again.

Oxygen speeds like cocaine
through capillaries in deep muscle and here
they come over Everest, gliding down
as if cannonfire ice, the dive-disappear
of a chick she nearly gave her life for
back in Kyrgyzstan and the entire flock's
fall into avalanche were all an absurd
nightmare from which she woke.

Star of the Different Road Back

He's a Zen thinker, clearly: alert
but giving no answers. Opal freckles
on the scatter-breast of an oriental alley cat.
A black velvet cap. Black wing-bars,

sharp orange beak and a back
like rippled rock. Little grey, little grey,
it is spring and all of you
blackpoll warbler brigade

are leaving the dazzle-forests of Venezuela
for fir trees with lichen beards
in Canada. Come September,
you're over the ferocious Caribbean

in the luminous blue upper air
where the Greeks said gods lived
and it's hurricane season. Four days
of battering-ram clouds and slingshot rain

and then the knife-fight for territory?
This is what you flew so far for, and so hard.
A jacaranda pod, blood-
oxide, flowers in the scented dark.

Choice

Digging a bush up, pitching in
to damp earth, getting out
clutch-arms and fingertip veins

as easily broken as silk
I look into the mica eye
of a robin. This is what we say

we all want. The choice –
to go, to stay. But how does a robin
decide? How does anyone?

The Hostile Planet: Sky, Sea, Land

Journeys happen in the air around us all the time, from stars travelling through the night sky to swallows arriving in spring. 'The moon and sun are eternal travellers,' said Bashō. 'Even the years wander on. A lifetime adrift in a boat, or in old age leading a tired horse into the years – every day is a journey and the journey itself is home.'

The sky contains many more aerial migrants than birds. Some which we don't welcome, like locusts, and others who, like fruit bats, disperse seed. These are vital pollinators on which the planet depends, in the silent ecological services by which migration keeps the globe working.

Dragonflies migrate on all continents except Antarctica. North America has nine types of migrating dragonfly: nine arthropod Muses with lovely names like green darner and wandering glider. They fly to Canada in summer cloud-swarms, with tiny writing motions of their wings. The next generation comes back south in the autumn and kestrels migrate with the swarm, snacking on dragonfly along the way.

The longest-known insect journey over sea is from India to the Maldives: millions of globe skimmer and vagrant emperor dragonflies fly fourteen to eighteen thousand kilometres for twenty-four hours against prevailing winds, from South India to east and southern Africa, and back. They breed in temporary rainwater pools, follow the rains from India's monsoons to the short rains of East Africa, summer rains of southern Africa, the long rains of East Africa and back to India for the next monsoon. They eat smaller insects en route while cuckoos, nightjars and falcons follow, with dragonfly on the menu.

Moths, a food source for many creatures, play a key role in the ecosystem and some migrant moths – tiny ones like the diamond-back moth or the twelve-centimetre convolvulus hawkmoth – are important pollinators too. The hummingbird hawkmoth and silver Y come to Britain and Ireland every spring, breed here in summer then go back south to Europe and North Africa.

The Greek word *psyche* means 'soul' but also 'moth'.

Most butterflies live only a couple of weeks and never fly far from where they are born. Others live up to nine months and migrate in spring and autumn. Monarchs fly south to Mexico, eighty miles a day at nearly 10,000 feet for 2,000 miles. They arrive around the time of the Mexican Day of the Dead and are greeted as the souls of ancestors. In the spring they go back to northern America. Other migrating butterflies (butterflies and dragonflies get the best names) include the cloudless sulphur, question mark, fiery skipper and mourning cloak. No one knows where their southern migrations end: probably north Mexico, the Gulf Coast and parts of California.

The painted lady is another long-distance migrant to Britain and Ireland from the desert fringes of North Africa, the Middle East and central Asia, but comes variably. Some years you see masses in gardens and meadows, other years hardly any.

———

Snowdrops are struggling through the frozen earth. In midwinter you feel things will never change. All these hours of darkness! Even at the beginning of February it still feels dark as Christmas. My daughter now has an internship in Bogotá and she says on Skype that the light there is wonderful. But now, by February's end, even Britain is lighter. You know the world has been turning, even though you did not feel it.

Red admiral butterflies come to Britain from North Africa. They used to leave in September, reappear in May and stay for the summer. Now the climate has changed they are seen throughout the year. Before 1990 you'd never have spotted one on a February flower, but today I heard that Britain's Chief Executive of Butterfly Conservation has photographed a red admiral on a snowdrop.

———

The planet's largest migration happens in the sea every night and morning. It is a vertical migration – billions of jellyfish rise to the surface to feed and sink back down at dawn.

Marine migrants have specialised skills. In 1678, the Italian scientist Stefano Lorenzini noticed rows of dots on the underside of a shark's upper lip; we now know these are gel-filled electro-receptors which detect bands of magnetism in the sea floor. Shark brains are swimming computers, constantly processing data about wave and current patterns, changes in temperature, chemistry, salinity and the Coriolis effect created by the earth as it spins, so the shark can allow for the planet's rotation.

Humpback whales, the globe's farthest-travelling mammals, swim 8,500 kilometres to the equator from breeding grounds at either the North or South Pole, then back again in spring. The total opposite of a barnacle, yet many barnacles attach themselves to ships' hulls or migrating whales and so become long-distance migrants themselves.

But some marine migrations are Go and Stay rather than Go and Come Back. This is where the word 'colonisation' creeps into scientific description.

In 1869 the Suez Canal, built by Ferdinand de Lesseps, cut a channel between two quite different seas. Since then more than 500 marine species, algae, snails, sea slugs and fish, have invaded the Mediterranean from the Red Sea in what is known as Lessepsian migration. It is causing serious ecological problems from Israel to Andalusia. A snorkeller who visits south-west Crete every year told me he now sees in all its little bays the Bluespotted cornetfish (*Fistularia commersonii*) which he first laid eyes on where it evolved, in the coral reefs of the Indo-Pacific.

Salmon, like the rufous turtle dove, develop a different identity in the different places they migrate between. The change is in their bodies as well as behaviour. We are so used to salmon on a plate we forget how extraordinary their life cycle is.

They are spawned in a river. As they migrate down towards the sea they reverse the osmotic functioning of their kidneys and gills to cope with the salt. Then they spend years feeding at sea. Scientists find out where by analysing the chemical signatures trapped in their scales. The salmon change again when they return, years later, to the same river. They give up eating as they swim in from the Atlantic (or Pacific) to the throat of their own river (having survived porpoises, seals, nets, fishermen and weirs) and become 'leapers', straining upriver to reach the ancestral spawning-grounds inland where they all spawn and die. Just as eels born in the Sargasso Sea in the North Atlantic (a sea boundaried only by ocean currents) swim thousands of miles through the Mediterranean, for example, to Lake Ohrid in Macedonia, stay there for years, and then head back to the Caribbean to mate, spawn and die.

Lemmings are very small Arctic rodents, tiny stripy hamsters of black, chestnut and white with long soft hair like the runaway guinea pig in Beatrix Potter's *The Fairy Caravan*. They live in tundra and eat leaves and roots. In winter they burrow through snow and eat grass, which they have sensibly stored in advance. They are shy and solitary. One sixteenth-century geographer thought they fell out of the sky in storms and died when spring grass grew.

Normally they only meet to mate, but their populations fluctuate wildly and when there are too many they disperse en masse. While doing so they sometimes cross rivers, become waterlogged and drown, which gave rise to the myth that they migrate towards mass suicide. So small, so retiring – but responsible for such a potent fantasy, which in 1958 was re-inforced by a master myth-maker.

The 1958 Disney documentary *White Wilderness,* supposedly shot at the Arctic Ocean, won an Academy Award for Best Documentary Feature. Its lemming sequence was filmed at the Bow river in Alberta where no lemmings live, so the film crew brought lemmings from two provinces away in Manitoba and put them on a snow-covered turntable. With tight camera angles, they turned a few pet lemmings cantering on a turntable into a massed mob-gallop over icy tundra.

'Compulsion seizes each tiny rodent,' read the narrator. 'Carried along by unreasoning hysteria, each falls into step for a march that will take them to a strange destiny. They've become victims of an obsession. This is the last chance to turn back yet over they go, casting themselves out bodily into space.'

In fact, the lemmings were thrown into the water; the final shot was of drowning rodents. In 1983 a Canadian documentary exposed what had actually happened. But the myth of mass suicide goes on.

From elephants to emperor penguins, there are hundreds of different kinds of land migration. Crowned lemurs in the deciduous forests of northern Madagascar migrate for miles over eroded mountain limestone karst. European toads struggle several challenging miles over rough ground to find a mate. In upland Sumatra, herds of up to a hundred bearded pigs on their annual migration for food travel at night on paths they have used for centuries, then retreat into thickets to rest in the day and hide from tigers. In North America the reindeer or caribou migrate across lakes and mountains, travelling up to 3,000 miles a year to find food, avoid cold and escape biting insects.

These journeys bring into play the same senses used by birds like sensitivity to earth's magnetic field. Sea turtles approach a nesting beach downwind, drawn by the smell. Migrating bats and porpoises navigate by echolocation, sending out little pulses of sound to map the reflected echoes. Some animals use phonotaxis, the power to pinpoint where sound comes from. The croaks of female toads in a breeding pool drifts through the night air, enticing males to join them. Last year I stood by a shallow stream in the world's only king cobra reserve in the Western Ghats and tracked loud calls echoing through the midnight rainforest down to a half-inch froglet, swelling a pale throat the size of a young pea.

All migrations have their dangers. Underneath migrating birds, the worst risks are posed by the desert and the sea. Deserts mean overheating, especially for the all-important breast muscles. Some birds stop in the daytime to hide from sun under bushes and refuel. But with drought and overgrazing by starving cattle the deserts are growing; there are fewer shrubs and insects, and less shade.

Many predators evolved to live off migrants. Some follow the travellers, others lie in wait. Whales and zebra migrate with still-suckling babies, who are targetted by lions and killer whales. Europe's largest bat, the greater noctule, which lives in forests from Spain to Turkey, preys off night-migrant birds; sooty falcons time their breeding on Mediterranean cliffs to coincide with the songbirds' autumn migration. The weary birds pass below cliffs where young falcons are honing their hunting skills; adults hang in the air in line and pick off the travellers.

Migrants face, as they have faced for millennia, a hostile planet.

Nocturne

Sundown. I imagine my father,
ten years dead, examining the lilied deep,
a whole marine community
on the move while the planet sleeps.
Zooplankton rise
to graze on surface phytoplankton –
that smudge of green you hardly see
but it's been busy all day
processing the energy of Sun –
followed by a host of arrow worms,
sea butterflies, comb jellies, larvae.
Other tenants of the dark
rise with them. Protozoa, copepods
and krill, a ragtag army
preyed on by larger predators still –
the bioluminescence brigade:
lantern-fish glowing cold
catoptromantic rays,
three hundred species
of dense-packed cephalopods;
and hatchet-fish
following their own fixed upward gaze.

Now he sees torpedoes through the murk –
dolphin shapes and sharks,
oegopsida squid with hooks on their tentacles
and, giant of the deep, the slow,

filter-feeding, eighteen-foot megamouth:
shadows, fighting the task of life in the under-dark
alone. But leading this spout of moon-milk
are the jellyfish. You think of them,
don't you, as flotsam –
mammary and malign, drifting through waves
which toss them on the beach like mermaids.
But tonight they are the stars
flowering to surface in translucent
violet-rose: a million moons
of tangled crystal and tilted curlicues
of lace. A ghost flotilla
escaping when the manhole cover
is removed. Parachutes blowing the wrong way,
lenticular galaxies, floaters in the retina,
translucent udders with a whiplash trail
of lambent fern; a pageantry of lights.

This is the full mooch skyward,
bubbles of the soul, tendrils
of Old Man's Beard
peeling off from the unconscious
in pulp-and-tinsel-dribbles,
the book of the sea shredding as it unfolds.
The whole procession white as aluminium –
this suits my dad; he is, after all, a ghost –
or white as the sun when it slips
behind a cloud. A convoy
of wraith-buskers, creeping from the Tube

like rebellions of the night. All hail,
O jellyfish, you ripple-fringe
of poisoned toga, blip from the cauldron
of nightmare, the unnamed
that is always there under the surface
and what we were always afraid of.
We didn't know for sure but we suspected.
Then, at first light, the delicate descent begins
to a bed we only imagine – the floor
we never see, heaving crevices
and bubbled weed. The world is not all black
and all white. You are never safe.

The Ampullae of Lorenzini

Who doesn't long
for gel-filled pores
somewhere –
and under your top lip would do –

magneto-receptors, telling you
which geologic line
to follow
clean below Orion

over the East Nazareth Mountains
into some Gangetic Sea,
Cathay, Shangri-La or Eldorado
and along the seabed, home?

Barnacle's Love Song
to Humpback Whale

It's chaos out there, but my single eye
tells dark from light and nothing else
needs to be seen. There are no boundaries
or pattern, it's an anarchy I'm floating in
and I rely on cirri. My feathery appendages
reach into the water-column, froth it
like cappuccino, draw plankton into my shell.

I have no heart. But a series of muscles, salt
velvet origami, pump blood through my sinus
and oxygen comes through membrane
lining my carapace. I am always at home
upside down. Armoured in concentric rings
of lustrous plates, my gates of heaven,
I slide a shutter to keep out the world beyond.

What does connection matter? My ovaries
extend like angels' wings from my mantle
to jellied base; my testes run nape to thorax.
I have the longest penis, relative to body size,
in the world. When I was larva
being adrift was a blizzard of risk. Free,
before tying the knot, to probe potential surfaces.

You've only one shot: I hitched my wagon
to everything I'm not. Life on the move.

At the North Pole in summer, we gorge
on nutrients, he and I.
Through the radiator grill of his baleen
he takes in shoals of krill like whiskery paper clips.
We share the translucent zooplankton

welling like gladioli in three-mile plumes
off the arctic floor. While he puts on
ten tons of blubber, I decorate
his stratum corneum and epidermal layer.
When the temperature drops
we race for the equator. He flings
himself loose of the sea and we're in free fall.

Who hasn't seen us burst like a raga to the Sun –
a prayer in dancing turquoise –
and lob our tail-fluke down (he's laughing, look)
to smack the shawling foam? That's me up there
riding his leap, hub to his wheel of black air.
And we make music. Those world-class,
bourrées, gigues and habañeras are composed for me.

I ripple to his tunes like castanets
but my own songs are only for him:
my fifty-foot wanderer, my ocean troubadour,
my Ararat. I am his *petit point*
embroidery. From his ventral groove
and under-jaw, I console
his mammal heart, his loneliness.

In Praise of Eight Million Fruit Bats

Here's to eight million straw-coloured fruit bats
living cheek-by-mouse-jowl in colonies
at the edge of forest, on the fringe
of cities all through Africa; who converge
for November and December on the dark border

with Congo, one skid-scented corner
of Kasanka National Park, to gorge themselves on fruit
and then fly off, *syrop*-filled dancing particles
dizzy as customers at the bar of the Electric Ballroom:
heroes, jittering a boogaloo, strobing the skies like a
                                                    twister

to disperse manure, scat, soft serve, butt drool,
Gatling gun, jailbreak Havana omelette
and butt burrito, their little dingleberry brownies –
that's sixty per cent, to you and me, of seed
that pollinates all the rainforest in Africa.

The Miracle of the Fish-Counter
in Budgens

All face the same way, tear-proof painted enamel
laid out on crumbled ice like a racing shoal –
of, let's say, salmon. I see them migrating

from the wild Atlantic or Pacific
they've known for five years, maybe six,
back to the river where they hatched

to leap together in parallel, just like this,
hurling their silver-paper forms against the exact
current which swept them down when they were smolts

before their mystery began, that metamorphosis
from fresh to salt when their kidneys changed,
gills reversed the direction of their frantic pulse

and the adult fish shot into open sea. And now,
changing again, they eat no more, burning the energy
sea-stored in years of freedom, for the release

of spawning: to reproduce in turn the perfect
workmanship we pass, dreamwalking
through the supermarket's mazy hieroglyph,

all this crinkled glitter, each mirror-glazed button-eye
stamped on the ice like a mourning brooch
collecting the glare of the strip light.

Or eels, born in the shoreless sea, who journey
a thousand miles then thousands more
through the bruised Mediterranean
to Ohrid and Crni Drim, to live in lake-mud glue
like a man who has forgotten how to love,
then suddenly return

thousands of sea miles again
to the Caribbean. As if go home and breed,
go home and die were the norm.

Ethogram for a Painted Lady

I'm six and we are *keeping still.*
We're looking at shadow on grey stone
in the sunken garden
and an orange-black fan – two fans, really,
with dribbles of milk on each tip
and a bravura range of little eyespots –

looking back at us. I have never heard
of Morocco, or anything outside this strip
of Eden with its secret sundial
I thought only I knew,
but I will remember standing here
with my grandmother, watching

flying blossom of the meadow
sun itself. Maybe I'm there still,
I never left;
I've never heard of Morocco
where these guys stream in from
steering by polarised light into Europe

over the Straits of Gibraltar,
funnelling in on the shortest sea crossing
like eagles gliding from thermal to thermal
on the same route;
a million-thick cloud of half-inch souls
swarming to the fields of asphodel.

Blade Runners of Madagascar

Did I dream them up? Those lemurs on late-night TV
pelting for days, striped tails like silver-and-black
bananas held high; the babies leaping too
or missing their step and falling one side or the other,
furry limbs bouncing through four
thousand metres of drop, through turrets

of tropical forest, lianas wrestling them down
in true no-holds-barred kung fu to the jaws
of pythons below. It's a hurtle for miles
over limestone pinnacles, raw knife-edges
scraping the sky, in a race for a safe place –
the good place – to breed, feed and rest.

Road Closed to Save Mating Toads

Listen, children. If you're out late afternoon,
just before the first warm wet evening of spring,
you'll hear a rustle in leaves at the side of the road.
That'll be the male toads, crawling from
your gardens, from hedgerows and ditches,
back to the pond where they were tadpoles.
When they reach the water they begin to sing
and to this male-voice chorus, trilling away
like nobody's business, come the amber-eyed females

drawn from the silent woods by a fusion
of phonotaxis, trigonometry and hormones.
It's a life-and-death affair, this half-mile crawl
in straight lines, toes spread for good contact
with earth, struggling through rough grass, power
lines, slip roads and a motorway. When a female arrives
the males grab with warty tubercles
on their fingers, to get a tight amplexus. And the whole
joyous event tends to coincide with the rush hour.

Chemical

There were stories of mountain goats in Montana
climbing sheer cliffs for a lick of salt

and brocket deer wading in Amazon quicksand
pumping their front legs to stop sinking

and suck the rich mineral upwellings.
We flow to what we need, they said.

Elephants in Kenya march their young
through tunnels under Mount Elgon.

It's no stroll in the park, they said. Pitch dark
and the boulders are slippy and loose.

The elephants feel the slime-walls with their trunks,
play blind man's buff with the stalactites

and can't see a thing, but remember the treadings
from last year, from all years, steering

with giant foot-glands right to the core,
the great dead-end heart of salt rock

then going at it, gouging it out
with their tusks. Listen to them crunch,

crunch, crunch for their life.
The babies are bored,

they play with stones they cannot see
but remember this gash in their lives,

this every-year-a-bit-longer inward journey
under the mountain, into the dark.

There is Always a River

Today *seven* goldfinches on the feeders, the most I've ever seen: a charm of goldfinches. They form little flocks in winter but now, in March, they must have several nests close by. But we have to say goodbye to them. My daughter will be home in a couple of months, but then she'll go back to Colombia to work for a year or two and without her our beloved house and garden are too big. We've got to look for something smaller.

I should be house-hunting. Instead, I'm looking back to Africa where Britain's nightingales and swallows still are, where *Homo sapiens* and human migration began, and where I watched the climax of the three-month trek over the Masai Mara endured by wildebeest, zebra and Thomson's gazelles.

From a parked jeep on a riverbank in Kenya I saw a scene which summed up for me the unstoppable pull of migration. It was early morning, the air still cool. The sun had only just got up. Below was the Mara River, the end of the animals' journey. Nothing stirred – then three absurdly delicate Thomson's gazelles, a buck and two does, arrived. They stopped on a flat stretch of shore and stared at the shining water. The river drew them. They could hardly bear to glance away to check for lions.

I had come to Kenya to see one of the wonders of the world – a million and a half wildebeest, 300,000 Burchell's zebra (Plains zebra) and 50,000 of these gazelles, finishing their annual trek.

Words migrate too: 'trek' is Afrikaans, from Dutch *trekken*, 'to journey, to pull'. It means 'to travel or migrate by ox-wagon'. The *Groot Trek* began in 1835, when 10,000 Boers fed up with English rule left the Cape Colony and went north. These gazelles had trekked north too from Tanzania and the river was their last obstacle.

Everything was quiet. The fairy-like gazelles – our guide called them Tommies – tiptoed to the water's edge, flirted away and then came back, tails flicking side to side. There is a scent gland under their tail: wagging it sheds scent to spread alarm.

I watched the flicking tails and thought about rivers, the last barrier in so many stories of escape. I thought about magic objects you throw down behind, the mirror or handkerchief which turns into a river to block your pursuers. About the Red Sea parting to let through the Israelites following Moses away from Egypt and into the wilderness; and, four books of the Old Testament later, the Jordan River stopping its flow as the Israelites follow Joshua out of the wilderness. The priests carry the Ark of the Covenant into the water and the people follow through it safe and dry, over to the Promised Land.

Rivers are natural borders. Mexican immigrants to the United States are called wetbacks because they swim the Rio Grande to get there. Rivers are often sacred, too. Hermann Hesse's novel *Siddhartha* tells the story of the Buddha leaving home to learn the world. He crosses a river in a forest and years later he returns to become the ferryman on the same river, which represents life flowing on to its goal. In Hinduism, pilgrimage sites are crossing-places. The sacred place to which the pilgrims are journeying is the *tirtha*, which originally meant 'crossing-place' or 'ford' and now (whether the place you head for has a ford or not) means simply 'pilgrimage'; for pilgrimage itself is a crossing.

For the Ancient Greeks, the River Styx was the crossing from life to death and that morning in Kenya we could see death waiting for the gazelles in a silver ripple.

———

They had come from the Serengeti, following hundreds of thousands of zebra and even more wildebeest in the greatest migration of mammals on the planet.

In March or April the Serengeti grass dries up and herds of these three species begin drifting north, following the rain, occasionally cantering, often walking with bowed heads, following a pheremone trail laid by scent glands in the hooves of those ahead.

Large groups stay together like flocking birds. As with jelly-fish rising to the surface of the sea, scavengers and predators follow: lions, cheetah, hyena, jackal, wild dogs, insects, parasites and birds who perch on wildebeest backs to get out the ticks.

The wildebeest thrive because of their enormous numbers. They are stupid and helpless as individuals but successful as a herd because they do everything at the same time. Females drop their calves in the Serengeti all at once. Two-thirds of them survive simply because the waiting predators are glutted.

Darwin's principle again – nature is indifferent to the individual and frighteningly wasteful, but the species survives.

For lions and other predators, the long columns are a walking canteen. When they attack there is a stampede, calves get separated, kicked, disabled and then lost. I saw one lying on its side in burning sun, feebly twitching the hooves it was never going to stand on again. Even without predators, exhausted young zebras fade with hunger, heat and thirst. Clear pools turn to mud as they walk through, the sun bakes the mud into a shell and traps weak calves.

As they go, the wildebeest keep in touch with a sound like burping. *Erb. Erb* . . . it is a froggy moo, a million-strong conversation like that of migrating geese. In June and July they reach the Masai Mara, stop on the banks of the Mara and stare at fresh grass on the far side.

The crossing is not just one event. There is not one herd but dozens in different places all along the Mara. Groups of all three species kept arriving, congregating at different spots along the bank.

The day before, we had watched thousands of wildebeest mill round on the bank, kicking up dust clouds. They had burped their way from the Serengeti and now, weary after months of travel, faced the river. If they were human you'd have said they were plucking up courage. It wasn't deep. It would take three minutes to splash through to the grass they smelt. But they knew, whatever knowing meant inside those bearded heads, that there was danger.

There were hippos upriver, but hippos keep themselves to themselves. The Masai say hippos spend the day telling each other jokes on the riverbed and rise up at night to laugh at them. There were six different types of vulture, too, walking about on the bank among the herds, as tall as a calf's withers. The wildebeest ignored them but the reason they were here (as well as hundreds of tourists, waiting in jeeps along both banks like spectators at a Formula One meeting) lay hidden in the water, where the largest crocodiles in Africa awaited their summer banquet.

The stage was set. It was up to the wildebeest. Crowds of them built up on the bank, jostling from behind like a stadium audience. Sometimes a crossing begins when one animal is pushed off the bank by pressure of numbers. One male tip-toed down to the edge, snorted at the surface, swung round and cantered up the bank again. They jostled as he joined them, skipped and reformed their crowd, facing the river.

Another herd came up behind and suddenly another male leaped into the water, landed with a belly flop and thrashed towards the far bank. The water came just above his tummy. Clouds of fawn dust rose as hundreds plunged in after him. Calves went in over their shoulders, swimming. It was Follow My Leader, a distillation of programmed compulsion. Dust on the bank turned to mud, calves were trampled as the herd came pouring down.

Then the crocodiles moved in. As they pulled wildebeest under the water the vultures came to life. Perching on animals which had been alive beside them five minutes before – now carcasses sticking on boulders – they spread their huge wings to balance.

Cameras whirred.

The centre of the river became clogged with dead wildebeest. A pale-blue mountain wagtail flicked down to get food for her young. A weaver bird picked off ticks crawling away from the dying.

There were no zebra that day. Zebras are stronger and more intelligent: wildebeest often follow their lead. Zebras cross as they migrate, in family groups. A blow from a zebra hoof could disable a jaw, so experienced crocodiles wait for the wildebeest and take just the odd timid mare or foal which hangs back and gets isolated.

Most zebra make it. So do most wildebeest, because there are so many. But their crossing is pure carnage.

The gazelles come last. They, too, cross in small groups, but they are smaller, they have to swim. Only zebras are brainy enough to calculate entrance and exit from the river and these gazelles had picked a place where they could not possibly scramble out: the far bank was a sheer black cliff.

———

The male gazelle took his first step into the shallows, bounced in on impossibly cotton-thin legs, stopped and looked back and then gazed at the far side, a wall he could never conceivably climb. He was knee-deep. You could almost see a magnet on the other bank pulling.

This is it, I thought. The pull of the world. Migration in action. From higher up we could see an enormous crocodile drifting slowly towards him. Water refraction must have made it invisible to the gazelle. Gazelle brains and eyes did not evolve to wonder about water and what lies beneath. They evolved for the plains, to see a long way and keep alert to whatever lion might be hiding behind the next anthill.

He wheeled round, the does flitted and flinched – and all three ended up staring at the river again. Suddenly he started swimming. He was a clockwork gazelle doing a splashy butterfly. He was little and had chosen the deepest place to cross. The females watched, their faces filled with him, tiny hooves standing in the choppy waves he made, their reflections trembling beside the shore they were driven to leave. There was a slash of brown lightning, a split-second open jaw and their boy was gone.

Crocodiles pull prey under the water to drown it. There was barely a struggle. The two does looked at water-gleam resettling on the surface. They'd watched him go and now he wasn't there.

What compels them is the grass. They migrate for food and water in a continual cycle through the year. The three species act on the land like a giant lawnmower whose dung puts energy back in the soil, keeping the all-important grass stimulated with nutrients.

Most grass-eaters live in herds, balancing competition for resources against the advantages of being many: more eyes on the look-out for danger, more voices to give the alarm.

Those that make it over the Mara instantly begin to feed, like birds after a 6,000-mile migration. Grass is armoured against grazing teeth by hair-flakes of silicon, which wear down ivory teeth, but the tough teeth of zebra strip the top rough stems, the wildebeest go for the lower stalks and the latecomers, the little Tommies, nibble the lowest tenderest shoots which the others have laid bare.

Come October, however, the rains will trigger their return. They will all surge back through this hard-won river. Crocodiles cull hundreds – but hundreds of thousands get through and trek south to the grass plains of the Serengeti.

Why go back? Why another Mara crossing, another dangerous journey, when grass still surrounds them like bright fur?

They go because mammals need minerals. We look for gold, bauxite, iron and oil in the earth, but wildebeest, zebra and gazelles look for the phosphorus they find only in the Serengeti, in the soil of Ngorongoro. The Serengeti grass was just withered stalks when they left it behind nine months ago, but now they need it again, to absorb the phosphorus and bear their young in a cycle that never stops. Twice a year they are driven to cross, to face the crocodiles. All for a mineral, all for a phosphate.

Song of the Herbivores

Even grass defends itself. Hair-flakes of silicon
armour the blades, making the aerial culm
and its inflorescence a cutting edge
of gritty emerald, wearing all ivory down.

We open our dental roots so teeth can go on
growing. Alone on an open plain, in the whisper
of long grass, you're easy meat for wild dog,
hyena, lion, so let there always be somebody's head

raised up, always a rolling eye, an ear
cocked. Stamp, snort; shed alarm
through your scent-gland. Paw earth,
toss your head, drop dung and follow the herd

to the sweet brachiating seed-pod,
dry peeling kernel, stem-moult and mineral
rise in fresh sap, in the battle
to not get eaten, the battle to eat.

Zebra Go First

They've spent the wet season on Tanzania's soil
where phosphorus bleeds oil through grass-veins
in Serengeti. Now the rains fail, waterholes
shrink and dry, they start moving away.
Long columns trek to the river
and beyond. He is Moses, a stallion,

black pigment blazon
over homozygous white. For six miles behind
they hang heads in a dustcloud and follow.
He is energy, razor heels in sorrel dust,
yellow teeth bared on this stream of striped ponies
in their thirst, their great thirst, for the north.

Dream of the Zebra Foal

Head lower, then lower under a lenticular
dark cloud, he drags harlequin fetlocks
through the pimpling dust. Slower, then slower
through night ringed with eyes,
this soot and fester theatre of leopard
and caracal, watching him weaken. All he knows

is that he doesn't know, and is afraid
of moon-shadow where the great rocks part;
where heat detectors crowd
the auditorium of the midnight plains.
Predator cilia radar in on flesh
that does not know it glows, it draws.

Let's give him one dream-memory,
one zebra wish fulfilled
in a green wall of sugarcane.
And look, he's made it through
to the rose-bleach and blaze of dawn.
One more day nearer the water.

Wildebeest Calf

A red sun falls under tick-filled blond grass
through curves in dun stalks and the ear-outline
of a low-slung lion. Chestnut eyes are making a choice.
Bee-eaters leave the *croton* bush – a squawk
of crown plovers – then a scuffle, thud, gurgle.
A bellow; a cry cutting caramel skies.

Night. And the soft breath beside him, the horns
that kept away danger, have gone. *Bleat.*
Losing the herd, he lingers to morning.
No milk. *Bleat.* Calling for comfort.
Here comes a stallion's zebra-kick
stopping the cry that draws predators.

His front leg hangs from his knee.
Afternoon – and he's alone, first time
in his life, flat on earth,
ribs grazing the sky. Glistering flies.
He scrabbles; he waits in a daze
for vultures, jackals and dusk.

Vulture Optics

Raising chicks in the dry season,
spreading gloss wings to mantle
hot hungry fledglings, he guides
red gut-threads into ever-wide maws.

Through their clamour for more, he checks
from the cliff on herds he has followed
for weeks, alert for signs of weakening.
His wide-angle eye keeps shifting, as if he saw

all body-mass through the background swirl
of Thomas Bewick, focussing
on just this knee-buckle, flop-flurry
of a foal, and the mare's hanging head:

her black whiskers puzzling, her breath
stirring fur on a thin tummy heaving
where stripes fade to cream.
She's been all his shelter. Her jaw

shadows his face, now cheek to cheek
with the earth. The herds file past, seven miles
of smoke-yellow glare. She must follow or die.
The stallion snakes his thick neck;

teeth draw blood on her buttock
locking her back to the herd.
As she leaves, ants cluster
on moisture – nose mucus, eye membrane

and a fluttering lid – while vulture-wings
rattle. Now the curved beak
plunges, tasselling to shreds
the opened muscle. A foal, a living feast.

The Mara, Rising

Water slaps lolling tongues, cools the dry throats.
Stop, look around, look up and behind

then gulp, gulp, suck. Jigsaw muzzles
join their own reflection

in bombazine blistered with rain.
Above, the marbling rapids. Sand martins

and swallows in hollows of the bank.
Below, the largest crocodiles in Africa.

How Does a Zebra Decide?

Over the river are rains and the grass.
At his back the hot herds jostle.
They've come five hundred miles
for this rattle-flow over grey stone.
Striped faces stare at the rock.
He paws the beach-sludge, splashes; stops
at one flash-memory of slaughter.
He swings his head down, then up
with a knee-flex and crazing of bubbles.
The weak, the hesitant won't make it.
He plunges, a reel in the eddies,
a stagger in rust-colour mud –
and he's steady in a breast-high current.
Whirlpools of white mark the spot
where each fetlock enters the water.

Pregnant Gazelle

You're in your worst dream.
An hour to giving birth
and you've got to get over a river
piled with split bodies. She opts

for the rapids' sharp rocks
and struggles alone through the hiss-slap
of foam. She wasn't made for swimming.
She's used to the herd, not this roar

of cirrus spray, an under-whirl tug
to the waterfall, the sluice, the crocodiles.
But she makes it, she joins the hundreds
that got through. By the time she heaves

out of the river and drops her fawn,
zebra molars are stripping the serrate
leaf margins of new grass
and rough cauline outer layers

and ten thousand wildebeest
grazing lower axils, where each petiole
joins the stem, have exposed
the glabrous shoots, bracts, umbels,

the branching lobes, paired glumes
and tender root-scales
of spikelets she can eat. Her son
wags his black tail, a ticking pendulum

that'll only stop when life ends,
and starts to nurse. The world
stands over them. The trek
begins and ends. Begins again.

History's Push and Pull

'Look at that!' Two bright green parakeets zoom through the April fizz of white blossom, shrieking. The plumber stops servicing the boiler and we both stand marvelling at this flash of tropical palette.

Rose-ringed parakeets evolved in the tropics. They live from West Africa to India; I've seen them in the Western Ghats and Mumbai. But they began escaping from captivity in Britain and establishing flocks here in the 1970s and now feature on CDs of British garden birdsong. They have survived the snow and here they are in our own (though not ours for much longer) backyard. They dangle opposite each other like emerald shoulders of a translucent heart. The male has a beautiful pink necklet. The tits and goldfinches have vanished: there's only room for so many birds. Darwin, thinking of the ruthlessness of competition, compared nature to a yielding surface with 10,000 sharp wedges packed close together and driven inwards, sometimes one wedge, sometimes another, by incessant blows.

Ornithologists worry about the effect these parrots are having on our birds, both resident and migrant. Who do they compete with for food and nest holes: woodpeckers, starlings, nuthatches? If these stick around, our goldfinches won't get so much food and will raise fewer babies this year.

Human history, like that of the plants and animals, is a story of migration. But compared to the animals' slow subtle adaptations to the spin of the globe, our history is perhaps – as Vermeer suggests when he represents History as a maenad in his picture *The Art of Painting* – less balanced.

Some human beings live by Go-and-Come-Back migration. Herders move flocks to higher pasture for summer and to the valley in winter, up and down the mountain like Himalayan pheasants. Many Greeks who left for Australia generations ago return to the family island for three or four summer months. More generally, people go where the work is. Our morning and evening commuting in and out of cities across the globe mirrors the daily ascent and descent of jellyfish. Like birds following migrating wildebeest for insects, migrant workers travel wherever there are crops to be picked or roads to be built. Gabriel García Márquez's story 'Leaf Storm' describes the arrival at a small town in Caribbean Colombia, in 1909, of a foreign banana company followed by 'the chaff of a civil war' – men hoping for work carrying 'their single piece of baggage, a wooden trunk or bundle of clothing'. Specialised workers, stonemasons, glass-blowers, entertainers and musicians like my great-grandfather Christian, have always moved from town to town.

What we mainly do as a species, however, is Go and Stay. We spread out of Africa just as animals spread, in search of territory. The ancient sign for wagon, carved into crags across mountains and plains, tells archaeologists the ways we went. Young tigers disperse from parents to find territories of their own and avoid inbreeding: so do we. Plants spread and so do we. 'Diaspora' is a 'seeding across', and we have seeded every continent.

But with human beings, Go and Stay needs some redefining. Animal and plant migration is various. It may be done by individuals or groups, may take place once in a lifetime, seasonally or every day, but at its heart is a search for something that you can't get at home. Migration is going where the thing is which you need but don't have. There is a push and a pull. You are drawn to the other side of the river, to the grass, but are also escaping what's on this side: drought.

All this is true also of *Homo sapiens*, but with extra complexities. Human migration is about not only need but want. Our wants are more unpredictable than those of animals and plants, and there are two ways of taking that word. If you're *in* want, you don't have enough – your family will die if you don't migrate. If you've always lived off fish and there are no more fish – as today on the coasts of Somalia and Senegal – you send your young men to Europe to get money to feed the family.

But human beings want more than they physically need and their search for what is lacking at home is more varied and ambiguous than that of the animals. We want spiritual and educational sustenance, for instance. Folk 'long', according to Chaucer, to go on pilgrimage; ancient pilgrimage routes run all over Europe, the subcontinent and the Middle East. We also take seasonal group journeys as tourists for pleasure; and many of us go abroad to school.

Last night I asked an Australian friend who lives in England if she thought she was a migrant. No, she said. Why not? 'Because I didn't *have* to come.'

'You came to Europe,' said her English husband, 'because you wanted to go to university in Paris. That was something you couldn't do at home. You did have to come – there was something you needed. Besides me,' he added.

Unlike most other life forms, we want more territory and possessions than we need. A tiger does not want more territory than it needs but we, or some of us, do. This means that human migration is inextricably mixed with trade, invasion, conquest and empire. Some migrations are a spreading to get more; others are escape from foreign incursions.

Of all the pull-and-push factors behind migration, war is one of the greatest. The Second World War created 40 million refugees. While Napoleon invaded Spain, during the Peninsular War of 1808–14, Goya etched his sequence *The Disasters of War*. On two of the etchings (of refugees fleeing famine in Madrid) he wrote, 'I saw it', and 'And this too.' His painting *The Colossus* dates from the same time. The terrified refugees fleeing from a naked giant, who appears to be blindly roaming the Spanish countryside, sum up the push factor behind migration. If your house, city, country or temple is destroyed and something terrible has entered your landscape, all you can do is run.

—

Hope is the great pull – but there is usually a push factor behind it. Hopes are born, says John Berger, the great writer on migration, on the site of loss. Most stories we tell about past migrations, or more largely where human beings came from and how they spread, invoke a violent loss.

According to the Bible, human wandering began with the loss of Eden. Subsequently, Noah's sons spread out and populated different quarters of the globe, but only after the rest of humanity was wiped out. In Michaelangelo's painting of the Flood in the Sistine Chapel, the Ark floats safely away while refugees desperate to escape the rising waters climb trees on a mountaintop and cling to a capsizing hull.

In Greek myth, Europe began with a raped Lebanese princess. In the Bronze Age you'd have called her Phoenician: Europa descended from the Asian people who first navigated the Mediterranean and gave Greece its alphabet. Her father ruled a coastal city south of where Beirut now stands. Its name meant 'Rock' – *Sur* in Phoenician and *Tzor* in its sister language Hebrew. The Greeks called it Tyre. Myth said that Zeus, the king of the gods, disguised himself as a bull, kidnapped Europa and swam with her to Crete where he raped her and so founded the house of Minos. European culture, therefore, begins with a kidnap, a rape (which literally means a 'snatching') and a forced migration – like the forced migration of enslaved Africans which created African American culture.

The Trojan War was caused by a kidnap in the opposite direction when Helen, wife of a Greek prince, was carried east by a Trojan to Troy. The Greeks' war to get her back created the West's first great image of a fallen city. Troy, the beautiful walled city, is burned, its women are enslaved and Prince Aeneas sails to Italy, a refugee. He is blown off-course to North Africa but crosses to Sicily and then on to Italy, where he founds a new city and new civilisation – Rome.

Homer's *Odyssey*, icon of twentieth-century imagination, is a long homecoming and a painful reassertion of identity: the war veteran returns. But Virgil's *Aeneid* is a story for the twenty-first century: the displaced man who has seen his city burn and has lost one identity forever must make a new home and a new identity in an unknown land. Civilisation is the story of building but also of losing. Behind the arrival in a new land often stands catastrophe and destruction. London was a Roman *colonia*, a colony or 'settled land': the word comes from *colere*, 'to inhabit, to cultivate'. But the Romans used it to translate Greek *apoikia*, which also means a colony, but meant literally, 'being away from home'. For Aeneas, Rome itself was 'being away' from his burnt home.

———

The historical Greeks who colonised Asia Minor in the seventh century BC migrated for trade. Trade moved over deserts, mountains and seas – the Sahara, the Himalayas, the Mediterranean, the Indian Ocean – and migration follows. Religion follows, too. It was traders who brought Hinduism to Indonesia in the fifth century AD, Buddhism soon after and Islam from 1200 onward.

Christianity, however, was set up to spread from the start. 'Apostle' comes from Greek *apostellein*, 'to send out', and the Apostles spread Christianity through the Roman Empire. In 1095 this became a violent spreading: the First Crusade began centuries of war (mainly against Muslims, but also against Jews and Orthodox Christians) for Catholic control of the Holy Land.

People migrate to spread their own religion ('missionary' comes from the Latin *mittere*, 'to send') but also to escape other people's. In 1492 the Inquisition expelled the Jews from Spain (or forced them, and Spanish Muslims, to turn Catholic). In 1620 the Pilgrims boarding the *Mayflower* were escaping religious persecution: they wanted a place to worship as they pleased.

Trade and religion *can* move without war, but often arrive because of it. Before the Second World War, Coca-Cola was bottled in forty-four countries. After US troops landed in North Africa in 1943, General Eisenhower requested ten bottling plants there. At the end of the war the troops went home but Coca Cola stayed. Sixty-four new plants were shipped abroad during the war; by the 1960s the number of countries with bottling operations had doubled.

———

Did oak trees spread to England after the ice age, or colonise it? Shift the language and you shift the perspective. Even with algae and fish, that word 'colonise' entails pushing out what's been there before, like marine species from the Red Sea triumphing over Mediterranean fish. A successful human colony or settlement means turfing someone else out; or else killing them, enslaving them or taking them over. For residents, the advent of a new species or tribe means invasion; as the City of Sydney recently acknowledged when in its formal account of its history it changed the words 'European arrival' to 'European invasion'. 'In respect to the Aboriginal community,' said the Lord Mayor, 'it's very important.'

In histories of many other civilisations you find the words 'The X Invasions'. Han Tribes into ancient China, Dorians into ancient Greece, Mongols, Normans, Vikings, conquistadors, Pilgrim Fathers – they rode, sailed or walked into other lands and created a new culture on top of – and often at the expense of – something else. Unless there's been an ice age or a Great Flood, there's no clean slate.

⁂

Sixteenth- and seventeenth-century European migrations into new lands, and the trade routes which European powers developed in order to reach them, shaped the modern world. By the 1580s Spain controlled Mexico's two most valuable exports, silver and cochineal. Wealth was pouring into Spain from the West Indies and South America while Britain, Holland and Portugal were competing to send adventurers into other lands for gold, spices and timber, and to control the sea routes that led to them. Meanwhile, in the East, empires and trade networks rose and fell between and through India, China, Japan and South East Asia, creating new migrations.

Walter Raleigh dreamed of colonising America. He tried to

go in the early 1580s, but had to turn back. The expeditions he went on later (drawn by rumours of a City of Gold) were to South America. But between 1584 and 1590 he was the prime mover in the first colonial expeditions to North America. These are now known as the Roanoke Voyages, since their base was Roanoke Island within the Carolina Outer Banks.

In 1585 the expedition artist was John White, commissioned to 'draw to life' the inhabitants of the New World and their environment. He painted in watercolour (unusually – most painters preferred oil-based paint) and seventy-five of his water-colours survive, showing villages, harbours, crops, fish, wild birds and people: the sixteenth-century, south-eastern Algonquins who inhabited what is now North Carolina and South Virginia. One thing I love about White's portraits – women and children, husbands and wives – is their warm smiles. They seem easy and natural with the artist and each other.

But relations with the villagers, at first so friendly, deteriorated. Over the next five years, things were to go very wrong.

The first expedition returned with tobacco (which Raleigh popularised) and the potato, which Raleigh introduced to Ireland. Two years later Raleigh encouraged White to go back as Governor, leading a proper colony of settlers including White's daughter Eleanor and her husband Ananias Dare, whom she had just married at St Bride's Church in Fleet Street.

But their Portuguese pilot refused to take them on to Chesapeake Bay as arranged, and abandoned the settlers on Roanoke Island. Eleanor gave birth to a daughter, Virginia, but White himself had to return to England for supplies and couldn't get back to the island for three years: all boats were commissioned to fight the Spanish Armada. He returned on 18 August 1590, his granddaughter's third birthday. The settlers had gone, but the letters CRO were carved on a tree, possibly as a sign that they were safe, and had moved on to Croatoan Island.

This was the mystery of the 'lost colony', the earliest attempt at a permanent English settlement in America. No one knows if they survived. White retired sorrowfully to Raleigh's estates in Ireland where the English were meanwhile displacing other indigenous inhabitants.

In 1585 Queen Elizabeth knighted Raleigh for his help in 'putting down' a rebellion in Ireland. She also gave him estates in Munster. Further north in Ireland, the English were slower to take control. Before the 1590s Ulster was thickly forested with few towns or roads. Many people there lived by seasonal migration with their cattle. From 1594 several chieftains fought the English incursions, but in 1603 they had to surrender. In 1607 came the Flight of the Earls, when the chieftains left for the continent. The English began planning settlements. 'Settling' sounds calm but this was a violent, invasive colonisation, displacing the inhabitants, dispossessing them, driving them into marginal mountain land and replacing them with English-speaking Protestants. But many stayed to work for these new owners on land they had once owned: hence the patchwork of Protestant-Catholic settlements, and the enduring antagonism in Ulster.

This was just about the time that the word 'migrate' is first recorded in English, used of people. The settlers were told that the natives would be eradicated, but the woodkerne, men who had lost their lands and fought the English, hid in forests and carried on fighting until they were killed, deported, or accepted English-speaking rule.

At the Battle of the Boyne in 1690, William of Orange ensured Protestant English rule over the whole of Ireland. Thousands of Irish who had fought for Catholic King James left to serve him in France and became known, as we have seen, as 'The Wild Geese': the title of the Irish Brigade in foreign armies throughout Europe and South America, and today the name of the Irish cultural society in America; wild geese who never returned.

On the continent, Europe entered a new wave of religious conflict in 1567, when the Netherlands finally rose against Spanish rule. This was three years before Pieter Bruegel died. The run-up to the Eighty Years War, and Spanish persecution of Protestants, formed the background to his last decade of painting.

Bruegel's peasant scenes, his strange brand of social criticism and allegory which earned him the nickname 'Pier den Drol', Pieter the Droll, are landscape-free. Their point is people and their behaviour. But Bruegel had seen the Alps when he went to Italy as a young man, and when he painted religious and mythical stories he often set them in Alpine landscape which somehow claims more of our attention than the human drama it contains. In *Landscape with the Fall of Icarus* (1562) the lush Italianate scenery is the foreground while in the middle, very small, is the failed refugee. The son of a man trying to bring his child safely away from Crete, is drowning in the sea.

Bruegel also displaced on to older stories the cruelty he saw around him. In 1568, after war had begun, he painted *Massacre of the Innocents*, setting the story – women weeping over slaughtered babies, families begging in vain for their lives, soldiers breaking into homes – in his home town of Antwerp. Five years before, he had invoked Alpine scenery to paint what was happening while that massacre took place: Joseph leading Mary and child secretly away on a donkey. European artists had painted the *Flight into Egypt* since the eighth century: the holy asylum-seekers save their baby from persecution in an archetypal escape from a Colossus. The scene is the New Testament echoing the Old: one family seeking refuge in the country from which Moses led his whole persecuted people.

Many painters of this scene showed pagan idols slipping from their shrines as the child went by, and so did Bruegel. He set the scene high in summer mountains. Mary's eyes are turned down, Joseph has his back to us and the baby is hidden but the landscape tells us as much, or more, than the characters about all that this moment means. Behind and below are two shores, presumably the Holy Land and Egypt, facing each other. The towns from which the family has fled are blueish, as if under-water. The ones they are travelling towards are sunlit and clear. A falling tree and red flowers presage the Crucifixion; a white bird flies over the dark chasm ahead.

The painting is a small theatre of displacement, of the seen and the veiled, reminding us that asylum-seekers carry with them both a future and a past. Landscape, Bruegel lets us under-stand, is not only the context of our lives, the place where we enact life-changing moments, but also earth in active relation to the human. This is not the hostile planet faced by migrating birds but nature taking part in our history and in our own migrations.

The Wild One

(for Roy Foster)

She stands beside a death mask under a chandelier,
head turning from an unseen source of light.
She's holding a leather Thucydides
and a seventeenth-century trumpet
without piston, slide or valve
as if she doesn't know what to do with it
and might prefer a lute. On the map behind

South is torn from North, the West on top,
East nowhere. On the canvas, all that shows
are glaucous leaves of laurel for her hair.
The real picture, the one Vermeer never sold
even at his poorest, is himself – painting History
in disguise as a maenad. We might take her hand,
step her down from the frame,

dress her in jeans and a T-shirt, open those eyes.
She's not a scholar collating an archive
though she'll help if they're fair, nor a journalist
after a story, twisting what's said to make scandal,
sell. Though she's on their side too, if they mean well.
She's blood from the heart's right ventricle,
witness and balance, sift, record and judge.

Her name Clio comes from glory, telling
glorious things we did. But she's a wild one!
Look at her – making us feel out of depth
or guilty for not listening. Oh, she's foul play.
She's dust on a galactic nebula, nothing to do
with today. She'll spend centuries name-checked
and dismissed. *History's bunk*. But she's all there is.

Johannes Vermeer, The Art of Painting
(The Artist in his Studio) *(1666)*,
Kunsthistorisches Museum, Vienna

Homo ergaster *and the Red Horizon*

One move will betray us to predators
but in this pink haze, a mist so close
to the scorching ground it's almost solid,
are fingers chipping stone flakes

and something is splashing through streams
rising from a ridge where earthquake
has tilted the land, and Olduvai Gorge
has split into opposing cliffs.

There are five of them, look, silent as blown seed.
But they're being followed. All of them,
forerunners and pursuers, heading for the red
horizon, where cumulus burrs the soil

like dough of unleavened bread
which just might rise and ferment.
They're following the valley-bed
through the crewel-work of thorn on rock

past a gold flash of an estuary – ocean
seen for the first time – into the first new continent.
But we're stronger, we survive.
This is the winnowing, the winning out.

Stone strikes stone, shaping an axe
and a knife. Sparks fly into the night.
A soft gasp of fear, and surprise, fans the dark
isosceles bud of the first flame into life.

Riders from the East

Wheel. Axle. Chain. *These are the three sons*
of Noah. Of them was the earth o'erspread.
Breath of horses at night. I drink mare's milk
and eat foal flesh. I listen for hooves on the plain
and herd-swirl in cold starlight.

They went forth from Ur of the Chaldees –
artists of collapsible homes, learning to ride
in the Steppes: inventing the bit, inventing the rein.
Travelling was where we began. Yak, camel, boat . . .
Leaving on every trail the written sign for *wagon,*

adding a pebble to the cairns on the pack-path
towards the holy mountain; stringing bright flags
for the wind to carry our prayers
up over the misty pass and its guardians
to the realm of the Thunder Dragon.

Leaving Troy

You've given away your temple, Lord,
your altar-stone, dun flame of burning myrrh,
oil poured in long libations, soaking our turf,
smoke rising to your sky from incense-
sacrifices kindled by our grandfathers.
You've given away our holy mountain,
dipterocarp, deciduous, evergreen,
where wolf and panther pugmarks
print ivied ridge-trails, and cedars flush
in dawn's first light under snow.
You've betrayed all this
to our enemies, the Greeks.

I was on his boat. As we left, we saw
an old man – a fire-eater, deranged –
caper on the beach. The scorched hills
behind our charred walls
quivered through the dark part of his flame.
Our city was a scatter on the plain.
Old men and children
huddled round griddle-stones watching us go.
This was the shore where for ten years
they beached their carbony hulls
like a pod of orca, and sat by driftwood fires

like the thousand brightspeckle stars
of the Milky Way. This was the jetty

where they herded our women on board
at spear-point, and sailed away.

The prince couldn't take us all
and few, even now, would exchange
their wrecked home for this terrace
of salt in blue cellulite, green petals
dimpling on milk, a sheen like snow
cancelling its own shadow.
Me, I was OK up to Tenedos.
I'd gone there once with a girl, before
the enemy hid in the island's little bay
and we thought they'd gone.
It took a hard heart to leave
those inlets behind for the blazoned sea.

Light, scattered from a cereal packet.
Razzle like cameras at an audience of the Pope.
(Forgive me my clairvoyance.
Let's say I was a prophet, once.)

Then hammers of rain,
I remember, that first day. Our wake
was a greenish patina, a portal
to the undercounter world, gritty caverns
of nymphs, lamp eyes, blubbery warriors.
Jade on a flayed-steel prairie; fields of cream
on ocean-flesh soon dark in our first sunset.
No room for pity here: just red,

syncopated green. What lies ahead?
Charybdis, Scylla, Africa, civil war.
Take it or leave it, the bread we eat
was baked in the volcano of our city.

The Mission

(from Virgil, The Aeneid, *Book 4)*

Who could fool an obsessed lover? The woman ran
on absolute jitter anyway, even over little things,
and now was the first to realise they were leaving.

She trembled, break-steel rigid, furious. He and his boys
were fitting up the ships! She raged through the streets
like a maenad blooded by the god. 'Traitor! Did you
$$\text{think}$$

you'd slip off on the quiet? What about our love –
and the death I know I'll die here if you go?
Why scuttle across high seas in winter storms? If Troy

still stood, if you weren't flying into the unknown
to grab someone else's lands, would you rush headlong
into the waves? Is it me you're running from?

See these tears? There's nothing else left me, is there?
Think how we came together, the marriage we've begun.
If I've deserved anything, if any bit of me was dear

to you, give up this wild scheme and wild mood you're
$$\text{in.}$$
It's your fault my people and the Libyans hate me. Look
what I've earned for your sake – shame!

I called you *husband*. Now it's *guest* –
and you're leaving me to die? If only there'd been a child
to play in the palace courtyards and bring your face

                                                    back to me,

I wouldn't feel so used and so abandoned!'
He struggled not to meet her eyes.
He thought of the gods' warning. He tried

to quash all feeling in his heart. 'I can't deny
I owe you a million kindnesses. I won't forget.
I didn't plan to slip away in secret – don't think that!

But I didn't pretend to marry you, either.
That was never on the cards. If Fate had left me free
to follow what I love, I know where I'd be now –

rebuilding Troy, looking after my family.
I'd think of the defeated, the hell they went through
and put back Priam's roof. But I'm a refugee –

you know that – on a mission. God told me to take Italy
so Italy must be my country and my love. You're Asian
in a Libyan city: what's wrong with us Trojans

finding a place in the sun – in Europe? Don't we have a

                                                    right

to kingdom? Every night, as darkness wraps the earth
in shadow, and star-burn rises in black sky,

I see my father's ghost panicking, warning me
that by staying I defraud my own son of a future
in the west. But now the gods have sent, I swear,

a messenger. I saw him in plain daylight. The gods
have spoken! So, enough. Stop this hysterical
sobbing, torturing us both. I'm not going of my own
                                                free will.'

The Appointment

Flamingo silk. New ruff, the ivory ghost of a halter.
Chestnut curls, commas behind the ear. 'Taller,
by half a head, than my Lord Walsingham.'

His Devon-cream brogue, malt eyes. New cloak
mussed in her mud. The Queen leans forward,
a rosy envelope of civet, a cleavage whispering
                              seed-pearls.

Her own sleeve rubs that speck of dirt on his cheek.
Three thousand ornamental fruit baskets swing
in the smoke. 'It is our pleasure to have our servant
                              trained

some longer time in Ireland.' Stamp out
marks of the Irish. Their saffron smocks.
All carroughs, bards and rhymers. Desmonds

and O'Donnells grin on low spikes, an avenue
of heads to the war tent. Kerry timber sold
to the Canary Isles. Pregnant girls

hung by their own hair on city walls. Then plague,
crumpling gargoyles through Munster. 'They spoke
like ghosts crying out of their graves.'

Kywash (On John White's Lost Colony)

*'Master White, an excellent painter, carried very many
people into Virginia, there to inhabit.'*

Forgive me. Even cats dream. When wind fans these
Atlantic
mists apart, you, sir, may see wave-fleece breaking on
Irish rocks.
But I see snow geese on Croatoan Island, melon-vine
lacing the sandbars, dogwood leaning from wild gusts
the other side of this same ocean, yes, the very same,
and yaupon berries red like holly here at Yule.

I see us arrive at Wococon that first time. The marsh
grass
ruffling. Our first sight of them, fishing. A woman
seething meat in pots of earth, a child
moving logs under as they burned. I see myself
painting an old man smiling at me from his winter rug
and a mother with her child, at Pomeiooc.

Their sitting at meat: a husband and his wife,
smiling at me and at each other. I painted Secoton
village in its muffler of pumpkins and corn.
The Charnel House, where they preserve each
werowance.
There they lie for eternity, side by side, their flesh
removed, their skin replaced and stuffed with leather,

black topknots on their heads, watched over by their
                                                              idol,
mysterious Kywash. How do *we* keep those we have
                                                              lost?
At the summer feast, I painted their circle-dance,
intricacies of tattoo on shifting muscle. We dreamed
a fortune, too. Of course we did. We'd traded
one copper plate for fifty skins. They were welcoming,

they taught us how to live: to open clams dropped by
                                                              gulls,
pluck bayberries to make candles. Then the Governor's
silver cup went missing and we burned
the village of Aquascogoc. I came back to a lost place
in the temple: my dear wife had passed. But the child
                                                              was fine
and the man I chose for her was good. Amen to that.

The second time, we came with women – and one of
                                                              them
my girl. I watched her child grow inside her
through the three-month voyage. From the Sound,
we saw our ramparts down. Deer
grazed the vine on our roofless huts. We stumbled on
one broke-up skeleton – a man we'd left, but who?

My brave girl: first sight of this new world
and she was near her time. Then we lost a fellow
shot in the surf by an arrow. In punishment

I burned their village. I would to God
men could undo what they have done.
In August she bore her child, Virginia.

If I could hear her voice, I'd die a happy man.
But it was me they chose – they entreated me – to go
back for supplies. That was the only hour I saw her cry.
I touched her temple, soft as the baby's head,
and rowed out to the boat. Now look at me,
the father who came three years too late.

My third time, the water was boiling round the rocks.
I found the fort deserted, chests I'd hid dug up.
But no sign of distress. And the code we agreed
was part-carved on a tree. I tell this for her sake.
They journeyed on without me. This I know.
They're deep now, deep in the mainlan. Safe.

John White, Watercolours of America *(1585)*,
British Museum, London

Directions for the Plantation
of Ulster, 1610

'We go with thirteen squires. Richard Hare
of Suffolk, income fifty pounds per annum,
has the papers. You're a lucky man to get on the roll.
The softer Worcester lot prefer Armagh
and lay their orchards out like dreams of the Vale
of Evesham. We clear the land of rock
then break it, keeping caliver and musket primed
in the last furrow, against black trees.

We built turrets of local granite, throw up wattle
                                                    bothies
for our tenants, track the human wolves unto their lairs
and terminate. A pleasant sport – and fair prey falls
to the followers.' So wrote Thos Blennerhasset,
Norfolk squire, dedicating his pamphlet
to the youngest British prince
and smiling like one of his sponsored angels, carved
on lime-wood rafters in the village church back home.

The Colossus

A naked giant, fist raised, eyes closed,
cut off at the hips by the skyline, strides
across the land, buttocks swaddled
in black smoke. He's backdrop to our lives
and dwarfs the lot of us. We're incidental.
Wherever he's from, he's heading for beyond.
In the valley, villagers pour away.
You've never seen cows run like this
or riders fall. Only one thing stands still
among hurtling refugees. A donkey –

bemused or shocked; or bloody-minded
and just not going to budge. Maybe deaf
and it hasn't looked behind as the giant thuds,
flattening God knows what
beneath his feet, revving the blaze
of his torso, a swish of rage
out of any scale we knew about,
invisible loins feeding their own mad dream.
Will you kiss its hand? Where will it stop?
How did it stomp so easily into our home?

Francisco de Goya, The Colossus *(1808–12)*,
Museo del Prado, Madrid

Landscape with Flight into Egypt

Here we are in mountains, at a pass
between two shadows, before we descend
the black path. Against the gleam of an inlet
fretted with tow-coloured towns, a black tree

splinters and falls to an upside-down cross.
An idol slips out of a shrine and above the gulf
a hooded crow sits on a leafless stump.
Landscape is your life seen in distance, when you know

for just an interval of sunlight, how to join
time travelled with time still to go.
We have passed a red scatter of anemones
with no fore-memory of blood. Before us and behind

are cities, all that sweet clustering of 'civilised'.
In one, the massacre we're running from.
The other is asylum. I can't see your eyes
and you can't see mine, but a white bird flies

across this chasm we have to go down into.
It's us and the child. Home is the journey.
Home is the wild, with no one to share it,
no one to stand and gaze

at pale light falling on arches, alleyways
and ziggurats clenched in their own lives
like crowds dancing in a street outside
while the Lover, the wild Singer, dies.

Pieter Bruegel the Elder, Landscape with
Flight into Egypt *(1563), Courtauld
Gallery, London*

Strangers

In the nineteenth century a new country rose like a new moon for refugees from all over the world, a home for the homeless, celebrated in lines written by the Jewish-American poet Emma Lazarus in 1883 and inscribed below the Statue of Liberty:

> Give me your tired, your poor,
> Your huddled masses yearning to breathe free,
> The wretched refuse of your teeming shore.
> Send these, the homeless, tempest-tost to me.

Here was a nation created by migration. A society of immigrants, as John F. Kennedy called it long after: 'A nation of people with the fresh memory of old traditions, who dare to explore new frontiers.'

Immigration into America, and migration west within it to find new land, was happening long before the Statue of Liberty arrived. If one could have looked down from a satellite on Russia and

America in the middle of the nineteenth century you would have seen two streams of similar wagons crawling across the two huge continents in opposite directions.

The Russians making for the wild east of Siberia were escaping the feudal system of the Tsars, hoping for land and dreaming of fortunes to be made in mining and furs. The new Americans, inching west, were escaping poverty and likewise hoping for land, gold, fortune, work and a new and better life.

In 2003 in Siberia I met the descendants of native peoples whose land the Russian pioneers had taken in the 1860s. The grandmother of Olga, the woman who escorted us into the forest, had been born in one of those pioneer wagons. In an area set apart as a reservation and a museum for the tribes who once lived by fishing along the Amur River, Olga introduced us to the Nanai, whose land her forebears had taken.

Until Ellis Island was enlarged by landfill from the New York subway and a processing facility built, immigrants to America arrived at several different landing-points. When Ellis Island opened its doors to immigrants in January 1892, first through was a fifteen-year-old Irish girl. Twelve million followed. In the peak year, 1907, it was a million and a quarter.

For the indigenous tribes, one focus of resistance was the railroad. The 1962 film *How the West Was Won* follows four generations of an American family moving west from the 1830s. They are first attacked by Cheyenne Indians; then a railroad company violates a treaty by building on the territory of the Arapaho Indians, who retaliate by stampeding buffalo through the camp. The railroads opened the land to the settlers, they unified and connected, but whatever joins can also separate and the railroads became a symbol of loneliness. The blues of Robert Johnson (born in 1911 in Mississippi, when slavery had been abolished but its legacy remained) spoke for all railroad workers in the Delta, and his songs echoed among later African Americans leaving the South for Chicago:

> The train it left the station with two lights on behind.
> Well the blue light was my blues and the red light was
> > my mind.

Migration builds civilisation. But as civilisation grows, it also causes displacement and fragmentation. In Europe, the Industrial Revolution had winners and losers, creating massive emigration across frontiers and seas, and also inside each country. In America, one railroad theme was the way it took people away from those they loved. 'I was riding Number 9, heading south from Caroline,' sang Hank Williams, born in 1923, the frail son of a railroad worker. 'Left my gal and left my home. I heard that lonesome whistle blow.'

In the twentieth century emigration became the quintessential experience of our time, and a key self-image was the human being unhoused, like Beckett's tramp heroes or Brecht's Mother Courage. And one of the most famous twentieth-century American photographs was 'Migrant Mother'.

During the Great Depression the photographer Dorothea Lange was working for the Farm Security Administration in California. In March 1936 she came to a camp of migrant workers devastated because the crops they had come to pick had been destroyed by freezing rain. She took six photographs of Florence Thompson with her children in their canvas shelter, telling her these pictures would help people in other camps. Florence had left Oklahoma in 1926 for California. Her husband died, leaving her pregnant, and with five children to feed. With another partner and a growing family she joined the thousands of victims of the Depression streaming into California in old cars and trucks from the Midwest, Arkansas, Kansas, Texas and Oklahoma.

Lange gave the photos to the Resettlement Administration in Washington, which sent 20,000 pounds of food to migrant camps. (Migrant was the polite word; residents called them Okies.) But Lange also gave the photos to the Press. The *San Francisco News* published one of Florence which became known as 'Migrant Mother'. 'A migrant agricultural worker's family,' ran the caption. 'Seven hungry children.'

Long after, in the 1970s, Florence wrote to a local newspaper, 'I wish she hadn't taken my picture. I can't get a penny out of it. She didn't ask my name. She said she wouldn't sell the pictures. She said she'd send me a copy. She never did.' In 1983 Florence got cancer and had a stroke. Her children couldn't afford nursing care and gave her story to the *San Jose Mercury News*. The story and picture made national headlines. Two thousand letters, and $35,000 in crumpled bills, poured from all over the United States into a Migrant Mother Fund administered by the Hospice Caring Project of Santa Cruz County.

'The famous picture of your mother for years gave me great strength, pride and dignity because she exuded those qualities so,' wrote a woman from Santa Clara. 'Enclosed is a check for $10 to assist the woman whose face gave and still gives eloquent expression to the need our country has not met,' said a note from New York.

'None of us understood how deeply Mama's photo affected people,' said Florence's son. 'The photo had always been a bit of a curse. After those letters it gave us a sense of pride.'

But there's a twist here that touches on all questions of 'migration' and 'native', all the 'where-are-you-froms?' Florence, born Florence Leona Christie in 1903, was a full-blooded Cherokee. She was born in a tepee on an Indian reservation, descendant of the forced migrations known as the Trail of Tears. Her ancestors had come to Oklahoma a hundred years before, when the Indian Removal Act of 1830 forced Native Americans out of their southern homelands. The Choctaw had already gone, giving up their homeland by treaty. Their chief told the *Arkansas Gazette* the migration was a 'trail of tears and death'. The Seminole were shifted by force. Four years later the Cherokee followed: 4,000 out of 15,000 died from exposure and starvation on the way. By 1883, 46,000 Native Americans had been forced from their homes in the south-east states, leaving 25 million acres for European settlers.

Florence died aged eighty. Her tombstone reads: *Migrant Mother – a Legend of the Strength of American Motherhood*. By a stroke of the mad muse of history, a Cherokee woman whose family was displaced by white America became the icon of American motherhood.

Blossom is browning and fading on the grass. The parakeets have not stopped the goldfinches breeding. We see very busy goldfinches every day: there must be at least two nests near. And we have found a house we might move to, if we manage to sell this one. Everywhere I go, I keep thinking of what has to be dismantled, left behind and got rid of, such as furniture and books, to fit into a smaller house; and wondering what plants I can take. Migration means leaving things behind. It moves you into a disoriented world which doesn't add up in the way you are used to. You have to start putting things together in a new way.

Without a home, everything is fragments. In the twentieth century, the 'chaff' produced by war and violent economic changes blew through the inhabited continents in stories of migration even more varied and dangerous than those of animals and birds. But migration also creates songs. Music unifies. Orpheus drew together rocks, trees, animals and people; songs connect the disconnected. Italian migrant workers remembering the railway stations where they parted from their families, sailors singing shanties at sea, slaves singing spirituals in the Delta, the Irish and Scots in America – all these songs reach back to a lost home, uniting singer and listeners with a place and people left behind. From 'Loch Lomond' and 'Shenandoah' to Hank Williams's 'Lonesome Whistle', songs of exile are a vital part of the music of every diaspora.

The Greek word for exile is *xeniteia*. Monks of late antiquity, yearning for spiritual detachment from society and remembering Genesis 12:1, 'Get you out of your land, your kindred and your father's home unto a land that I will show you', used it to mean 'alienation'; a 'being foreign' at the spiritual level they desired. But to nineteenth- and twentieth-century Greeks, *xeniteia* meant *having* to be away. *Xeniteia* was exile and pain; it was a longing for home that could not be assuaged by getting there, because you'll have to leave again.

This Greek diaspora was made of many social layers, ship-owners, sailors, merchants, metalworkers. They went not only to America and Australia but western and eastern Europe, the Danube Delta, the subcontinent and the Levant – wherever there was cloth or metal to be worked and carried elsewhere by an expanding fleet of merchant ships. Meanwhile, many Greeks came to Greek cities for work, missing their island homes. For all of them, the great note in their songs was longing for a home the singer could not live in; estrangement, both from that home and from whatever new place he had come to. It was the same hurt, angry mix of love and alienation from what you love which powered Argentinian tango, Portuguese fado and the blues. This is what the Greeks associated with *xeniteia*, whose basic meaning is 'being strange'. It comes from the Ancient Greek *xenos*, 'stranger', from which we also get that word (which reminds us that *alienus* is a name for the devil) 'xenophobia'.

But in the earliest recorded Greek, *xenos* meant not only 'stranger' but 'guest-friend'. This was a pivotal relationship in an ancient culture which knew that when you were travelling you needed protection. A network of reciprocal 'guest friend-ship' spread across the archaic Greek world. *When you come, I will look after you. Make yourself home in my home.* Homeric hosts give their guests rich presents on departure.

The rules of generosity, hospitality and its obligations were often abused, of course. But they *were* the rules: *xenos* was the basis of the system underlying social relations.

Helping strangers was an obligation in ancient Judaism, too. If you look up the word 'foreigner' in the Bible, you find many exhortations to help the stranger. 'If any of your fellow Israelites become poor and are unable to support themselves,' orders Leviticus, 'help them as you would help a foreigner and stranger.' 'I was a father to the needy, I took up the case of the stranger,' says Job. 'No stranger had to spend the night in the street; my door was always open to the traveller.' 'Do not forget to show hospitality to strangers,' Paul reminds the Hebrews.

Despite the pogroms and anti-Semitism that were to scar Europe later, built into her most ancient language and also her most ancient faith is the obligation of generosity between host and guest, resident and migrant.

———

There are hundreds of diasporas all over the world, but as birds are the blueprint for migration so are the Jews for diaspora and exile.

In the seventeenth century BC, famine forced the Israelites to migrate to Egypt. In the thirteenth century, Moses led them out of Egypt, and after forty years of wandering Joshua led them in to the Promised Land. In 586 BC Jerusalem and the First

Temple were destroyed and the Jews were exiled to Babylon. Many came back fifty years later when the Persians overthrew Babylon, but in AD 70 the Romans destroyed the Second Temple and the Jews were scattered, and often persecuted, over the globe.

In March 1938, when Hitler entered Vienna, even the author of *Civilisation and Its Discontents* found himself at risk from persecution. Sigmund Freud was eighty-two and in constant pain from mouth cancer. He had lived and worked in the same flat since 1891 and was reluctant to leave. He hoped fame would protect him. But the Nazis kept his home under surveillance, fixed a swastika to the building, sent storm troopers to invade the flat and interrogated his daughter. When Freud was invited to England, friends advanced the money the Nazis demanded (they called it income tax) and secured him safe passage. With his wife, daughter and dog, Freud left for London. Five months later came Kristallnacht, the Night of Broken Glass and the beginning of Hitler's Final Solution. Ninety-five synagogues in the city were destroyed; fifteen hundred throughout Austria. Thirty thousand Jews were taken to concentration camps. His four sisters died in the camps.

People from other religions projected on to their own situations the plight of the Jews in Babylon, in bondage in Egypt, or in the wilderness.

When Protestantism was banned in France, French Huguenots fled to (among other places) the Cévennes. Pastors preached secretly on mountaintops and women carried portable altars hidden under their skirts. They called this period of the sixteenth and seventeenth centuries Le Désert, after the years the Jews spent in the wilderness. African American slaves in the southern states of nineteenth-century America identified with the Jews hoping under Joshua's leadership to reach the Promised Land. The Ohio River was Jordan – they sang of home, sweet Canaan, and the free country across the Jordan. *One more river, and that's the river of Jordan. One more river, there's one more river to cross.* In 1998 the Dalai Lama, before he was awarded the Nobel Peace Prize, asked Jewish leaders what their secret was. Tibetans, he said, admired the Jews because 'no matter how they are scattered through all corners of the earth, they maintained their sense of unity of the people'. How had they done this through 1,900 years of diaspora? The rabbis explained that in Jewish observance the centre of cultural and religious identity is the family home. This is what replaced the destroyed Temple. All over Europe, North Africa and Asia, lighting candles in the home on Friday night, saying prayers which bless domestic tasks and welcoming the Sabbath in under your own roof, countered the estrangement and displacement of exile.

Jewish exile and longing for the Promised Land also became a Christian image of spiritual alienation: of the longing to return (after the Fall) to a right relationship with God. In 1843 a British Christian who felt Palestine should be given to the Jewish people spoke of 'a land without a people for a people without a land', a phrase which ricocheted through Middle East politics and in the twentieth century was taken to express a mistaken Zionist belief that the land was empty of inhabitants before the settlers got there. And so, eventually, reversing one exile created another. The refugees became the new Colossus.

After modern Israel was founded, its first great fiction writer was Yizhar Smilansky, whose pen name was S. Yizhar. Yizhar's parents were Russian immigrants to Ottoman Palestine, where he was born in 1916. In his autobiographical novel *Preliminaries* he describes what it was like for his parents working this supposedly empty land. His father sees it in animal – but also Biblical – terms as 'a place of snakes and scorpions'. The baby nearly dies of stings because the father, ignorant of the indigenous fauna, leaves it on a wasp nest while he ploughs. Is this the promised land? Maybe, thinks the father, driving his son across the desert scrub to a doctor, 'it was a fundamental mistake. Maybe this land doesn't want us at all.' The mother sees it in human terms. 'Who knew about the Arabs where she came from? Nobody talked about them back in the Volhynian forest on the bank of the River Styr.'

In his novella *Kirbet Khizeh*, as controversial when it appeared in 1949 as it is today, yet still on the Israeli school curriculum, Yizhar drew on his experience as an intelligence officer from 1946 to 1948 to describe the clearance of Arab villages. Young Israeli soldiers capture a peaceful Arab village and load villagers into trucks at gunpoint. Aren't they allowed belongings or water? asks the driver. 'No,' he is told. 'Take them away from here, let them go to hell.' The soldiers ease their conscience by saying these people are 'like animals'. When the narrator voices moral qualms, the others say 'stop thinking so much'.

The parents of the Palestinian poet Mahmoud Darwish lived in a village called Birwe in the district of Akka (Acre, to the Crusaders) in Upper Galilee. When he was six, Israeli soldiers attacked his village. The family joined 900,000 other Palestinians fleeing the possibility of massacre and became refugees in Lebanon. When they returned 'illegally' to their village in 1949 it had been cleared of Arabs like Yizhar's fictional Kirbet Khizeh, rebuilt and colonised by Jews. Four hundred other villages suffered the same fate. The family settled in Galilee too late to count as Arab Israelis, so they were denied Israeli nationality. Unable to travel in their own country without Israeli permission, they now had a new identity as illegal 'infiltrators', 'present-absent aliens'. They were internal refugees.

No poet is a stranger to estrangement. Many write out of their relationship to home but this relationship changes through a working life and some write out of a sense of *not* belonging. In a poem called 'Exposure', written when he was migrating from conflicted Northern Ireland to the Republic of Ireland, Seamus Heaney uses the phrase 'inner émigré' for his relation to the land where he grew up. The poem portrays the poet leaving his troubled homeland as a 'woodkerne escaped from the massacre', and invokes two other poet exiles, Gerard Manley Hopkins and the Russian poet Osip Mandelstam.

For Hopkins, an English priest posted to Dublin, Ireland itself was exile. His sonnet 'To Seem a Stranger' voices his estrangement 'in Ireland . . . at a third/ Remove.' Mandelstam was sent into internal exile by Stalin in the 1930s. In 1938 he was again accused of anti-Soviet views and sentenced to Siberia, where he died. Heaney describes Mandelstam as a man who deliberately travelled light; for whom the prospect of exile 'was not altogether disabling'.

Elizabeth Bishop's aesthetic was inseparable from her travels away from home. Her collections are titled *North and South*, *Questions of Travel*, *Geography III* – just as those of the Greek poet George Seferis, through the Second World War, are *Log Book I, II* and *III*, as if his poems are notes from one voyage of exile.

The poet Ramsey Nasr was born in Rotterdam, but his father came from Salfit on the West Bank – where, in 1978, soldiers took away his fields and built Israel's largest settlement, Ariel. The town has 45,000 people. There is now a wall through it to protect the settlers against the land's original owners, like the Ulster settlers of 1611 protecting themselves against the woodkerne.

Thirty-three years later, as the Knesset passed the draft of a law directing Palestinians to pay the costs of demolishing their own homes, Israeli soldiers took over the land of a Palestinian man with heart disease. They prevented him from stepping on it, declared it a closed military area and pulled up his 300 olive trees.

'When you are displaced,' says another Palestinian poet, Mourid Barghouti, who, as a student in Egypt during the Six Days War suddenly became a permanent exile from his home town of Ramallah, 'every home you have is the home of others too.'

During the Israeli invasion of Lebanon in 2006 I was in Madrid. My daughter was working there and I took my mother to visit her. In the Prado, the first thing that hit us was Bruegel's *The Triumph of Death*, painted in 1562 (around the same time as

Landscape with the Fall of Icarus), while the Spanish persecution of Protestants was getting worse. Not until Goya painted *Disasters of War*, 250 years later, did European art depict war at this pitch. Pictures of Lebanon that night on TV struck the same chord.

Migrant Mother

They are Okies, pea-pickers brought to ground
by a skanky engine, crawling through the Land
of Promise like her grandma up the Trail of Tears
a hundred years before. In the lens, they're a study
in achromatic grey. *Yes, you may take my picture.*
Freeze-dust, an hour-after-hour glass, spun
by the Witch of the East and blown through
a workless morning in spiralling wind.

Just one freak frost. They're screwed,
the battered pea-vines say so. Those that can leave
have left. *Count yourself lucky if you find
rope for the canvas, a real floor
under your feet.* Seven hungry children.
Folk selling their tents for food.

The Letter Home

(for Gieve Patel)

You painted the Saturday queue
for a Letter Writer cross-legged on a shawl
in shadow of the unfinished flyover. *I have health,*
again and again. *I am sending the money home.*
But what is home? Where you began,
where a sister – with a husband whose salary is regular
but he resents you anyway, this indigent
who sees more of the world than he – has turned
your family against you while you are gone –
or where the journeys take you: where work is
when you sleep behind plastic, tacked
to urinous breeze block, and cook at the edge
of a five-lane you are helping to build
watched by ashy-necked crows who make their nests
out of sanitary towels from mounds of trash to the east?

We are breaking stone for the motorway.
I will come home when work is done.

Under the luminous fuzz that does for stars in this city
you look into the well, wondering where it went wrong,
what you could have done better. Look up.
The hurt sky is bandaged in cloud,
earth has reversed her magnetic field
and the Mumbai monsoon, blown sideways

like glycerine skirts, has calmed the grit
that gets everywhere into wetsilk paintable gleams
reminding us where it has come from, this element
we all desire and have to struggle with. Home.
The round white pebble with a blue-cut heart.
Whole geological dowries
of copper, hooded turquoise, amethyst.

Mumbai, July–November 2010

What You Told Me about Islands

(i.m. Kay Cicellis and Nikos Palaiologos)

1 The Two Flames

Let's say you found each other like repeating flames
in an antique mirror, trailing the memory
of two Greek ports in foreign lands
where you were born, and two islands
you fled back to when the devil began to dance
in mad *Evropi* and you learned the island song
of eternal *ritornelle:* one hotgold summer
when you find yourself, then rage to get away,
darkwinter alcohol, high winds to cut you off,
a closed-in grey horizon and a harbour
where all your debts and fantasies are known;
while beyond the mountain one small bay
waits on: never not dreamed of life-long
loved – and left. The soul's a wanderer and fugitive,
driven by decrees and laws of gods.

2 Blown Ruby

As if they were itinerant stained-glass makers
setting up camp outside a mediaeval town
at the edge of forest, or here in Athens by *Plinteria*
ti Merimna, even as we speak, or on the island

at the corner of Ayias Annas and Spiridonos,
they're lighting their transformation fires to conjure
                                                    glass
from wood and sand. Bellows. Three furnaces
for heating, cooling, melting. *Cristallo*, azurite,

blown ruby. They come, villagers would say,
they speak in foreign languages, and when they go
our windows are alive with coloured light.
By the fire at night you'd hear their stories

of other worlds they brought to life in glass.
Slow campfire melting. Tools, barter, trade.
Sun scatters, uneven as heartbreak,
through imperfections in everything they made.

You transform *us* we'd say, in welcome.
They will not come again. Close your eyes.
A branch is being broken
and the soot-bruised earth is warm.

Athens 2005

The Music of Home

(for Nikos Daskalakis)

Arriving at Ellis Island, I watch the glass alps of
                                        Manhattan soar
above one-storey buildings
that must have looked terrifying when they were the
                                        only ones
as you came over the rainbow from Europe in 1854 . . .
Yes, soar, and take off from the emerald of Battery Park
like vagrant emperor dragonflies beginning their long
migrate across the Indian Ocean. Arriving at Ellis Island
(hoisted on landfill from bowels of the New York
                                        subway
from a knoll once private to fishermen and gulls),
I head for treasures donated by families
whose great-great-grandparents manhandled them
all of three thousand miles. 'She took all she could
                                        carry,'
fathers reminded children in a thousand languages.

How about we go there Niko, someday? You'd get up
from your apartment in Heraklion where your daughter
is at music college and where, before you were so ill, I
                                        heard her sing
under the old walls which used, as I recall, to shelter a
                                        bar
hollowed out from Saracen stones

where we'd swig home-stilled raki and dance on
                                        sawdust
while an old man sang the *Erotokritos*
and played spoons on his knee. The moat is cleaned up
                                    now,
paved and re-hewn for family recreation.
Yes, arriving at Ellis Island, you and I,
we'd begin with a Finnish copper coffee pot,
a panel of embroidered silk from China, a mould
for rice crackers (Japan), a Turkish towel from Palestine,

a brass noodle-cutter from Austro-Hungary like two
linked raincoloured spurs, and a carved coconut
from Guyana. But then we'd light on the Armenian 'oud
and Hungarian zither, the horsehair bow from Korea,
the Irish tambourine and finally the little Cretan lyra
carved from a single plank, complete with its bow
of hawk bells like the lyra Thanassis Skordalos played
for his first recording, 1946, with Giannis
Markogiannakis on lute. And we'd remind each other
how we used to work all day in the burning sun
then dance all night. How Kostas, aged seventy,
showed us the steps of Pentozali but we could never
keep up with the flicker of his neat black shoes.

And we'd laugh, that dancing and singing to lyra
mattered more in the dark, on Ariadne's shore,
than anything on earth. Arriving alone today
at Ellis Island I think of the years you worked

the boats. Your letters came rarely because your hand,
you said after, was never steady. One ship
anchored you a year off Egypt, a national scandal
hushed up, two hundred Greek cement vessels
dead in one enormous harbour –
no one had paid anyone, it was a combat zone
for dodgy insurance companies with you
in the middle, you never got your wages
and had to pawn your underpants to get repatriated –

but one velvet night you heard Cretan music
over the water and next day you dived
into that swamp of sewage, sharks and garbage thrown
from a thousand ships, as into an avenue
of green silk, to find the one guy
in this madhouse playing the music of home.

Music from the Deep

(for Nicholas de Lange)

Clio? I met her in the synagogue of the Mellah
behind the gun of the Moroccan security guard
who asked for our ID. East and west
changed place up there among the headscarves
of the women's quarters, looking down
on pews of men with *tefillin*
strapped to their foreheads and biceps.

Hearing the Book of Esther read at Purim,
in Hebrew, was like listening online
to music from a deep-sea crustal plate.
She introduced me, your Clio, to the system
of imaginaries – like checking the atomic weight
of a syllable under a microscope
or embracing algebra as the science of pure time.

The Two-handled Jug

A stork is flying low
above an acre of graves
wrapped in pink dust

and protected by pink walls
on which the storks nest.
This is the Jewish cemetery

Marrakesh. Scimitar wings
of the swallows, blue
calligraphy on blue. Plague tombs

of the fifteenth century.
Husbands, children, wives:
and bronze epigraphs

in French, Arabic, Hebrew.
Wearing a *yarmulkah* lent
by the caretaker, you decode

the names. I join you at the exit
where you wash your hands
in a cracked marble basin.

From a copper jug
you pour water, glass blossom,
through my fingers too.

The Freud Museum

It's 1938. Here's moss on red brick
at Nutley Terrace and an old man displaced,
just not too late, by swastikas on the portico
in Vienna. His daughter has been caretaking
their flight. The trunks hold a red-topped desk,
T'ang camel, phials of Etruscan glass
dug up from tombs, a print of the Pharoahs
at Abu Simbel and a red-lozenge Persian rug.
What is an object?
Shards from a lost world, gone to ground
then brought to light. *And home?* A sleeping child.
A nick-of-time railway pass. A letting-go
of neighbourhood gone wild.
Breath on the mirror. A dog, a garden. Found.

Freud Museum, London, 2011

Entry of the Sabbath

Only half-heard, the autumn
smoke of a viola blows
through the orchestra.

Far off, a blackbird
calls from that ancient temple
in the hazel grove.

Friday. Sunset.
A man lights two candles, alone,
and under his breath

intones a prayer
for love never possessed
too deep to say aloud.

Godfearing

We listened for the ringing of a bell
and catnapped between electric muezzin calls.
One of us got a photo of a mirage on the asphalt
over Ur – the very spot, they said, where Abraham

set out into the Talmud, into the Qu'ran
and then into small Saxon churches
and the sixty-foot Bleeding Heart, dripping neon
in Tennessee. They've named a war

after a racehorse and sent us to the desert
to interview a pilot
in chocolate-chip uniform. A brave boy
briefed to avoid mosques and never gloat.

How did he feel, making the first score
when he turned another plane
to a comet-hair fireball? With a man
like himself in there, who had a family, like him?

The difference, he guesses, *is the country*
you come from. On the right side. Godfearing.

London, 1990

Pieter the Funny One

Paint us, they said, the world as it is. No more
of your children's games and peasant weddings.
He painted *Procession to Calvary*, Saul
blasted by glory on the way to Damascus.

At home, now, transposing Holy Land to his own
familiar yellows, he did *Adoration of the Kings*
in snow. He was good at snow. Go on
they said. He did *Flight into Egypt*,

a *Census at Bethlehem*, branchy veins
down a red hound's legs.
Not one was satisfied. He made smoke
like dry ice lift over a bust chandelier

in rubble just that shade of dun
we see night after night on TV
in a totally annihilated village.
There are bodies in there you can't see,

he said. Forty disabled kids
with their mothers. And a Beirut reporter.
That's more like it, they said. We want
the world we live in. He painted *Slaughter*

of the Innocents (putting them, too, in snow)
and three hundred thousand refugees
in a red-and-black landscape.
Not hell, but it could have been.

From a plasma screen
he painted a boy of twelve,
his mouth that open-mouth mask
of Tragedy, plastered crimson

head to toe, standing over
his mother's living torso;
her arms taken off by bomb-blast
on the way to Damascus.

He conjured the home of the Caliphs
in flames like orange lilies – thrown
by an emperor whose religion
was founded on mercy –

and a game-show host from Nebraska
upset the President of Iraq didn't get
that Israel had a right to defend itself.
(By now the boy's mother had died.)

He started a new thing, skeletons
knifing a king,
another side-saddle on a grey horse
in the shafts of a broke-wheeled caboose

laden with bodies; a lone corpse
floating, swelled belly upwards,
downriver, dogs gnawing the face
of a toddler: plus three-headed Cerberus,

one head searching for fleas, one head
asleep, the third keeping watch
on a black bird making its nest
in red jasmine. They praised

the painstaking draughtsmanship
in his torn men dying on wheels,
failed rebels stuck on poles
in a cassis-coloured sky

and black plumes on a high thin horizon
from cities on fire: including
I may say Nazareth. And Bethlehem
where the emperor's pin-up,

a.k.a. the Prince of Peace, was born.
He said that's what I've seen. Yes,
they said, that's what we wanted.
The Triumph of Death.

Madrid, 2006

Sphinxes on Thames

An obelisk set in Egyptian sands, 1460 BC,
winched vertical beside this khaki river
and inscribed with names of volunteers
who died in barge-boat *Cleopatra*, towing
a granite rocket through the Bay of Biscay.
Michael Burns, James Gardiner, William Patan,
Joseph Benton, William Askin.
Why yearn for the faraway monument
from someone else's home? A riddle
for Pharaoh Thotmes III – and these two
cat-calm Victorian lookalikes
on the bank, one shrapnel-pocked
by London's first air raid and both dreaming,
dreaming of Giza.

               What we've done comes back to us.
Lies told upriver in a Parliament; a war declared;
Michael Burns sent east again. The faraway
ignites in London. What moves
on four legs in the morning, two at noon
and three with the gathering twilight? At Victoria
bus routes are blocked for bomb alerts.
Gas canisters and cellphones wait in cars
outside a nightclub. A burning jeep
crashes the airport door while doctors,
trained in Bangalore, lay bombs
in the nearby hospital carpark. Scan

every city, jittery along its arteries.
Violence returns to violence
and the answer to the riddle, always, Man.

London–Glasgow, 2007

The Broken Mirror

A man met a lemming on a mountain path.

'What I've always wanted to ask,' he said, 'is why when you migrate, you all jump off a cliff into the sea.'

'What *I've* always wanted to know,' said the lemming, 'is why you don't.'

It's late May, my daughter is back from Bogotá, we have cleared out the garden shed and attic, got rid of a thousand books, and moved. I've spent the last month taking cardboard boxes to the dump, but yesterday we went to a ceremony in Keats House. They were planting a new plum tree in the spot where one stood in May 1819, when the house belonged to Charles Brown. The previous December, when the brother of his friend John Keats died, Brown had invited the 23-year-old poet to stay with him in Hampstead. Keats had arrived in shock and grief; now he had become fascinated by the song of a nightingale nesting in the garden. One morning, Brown said:

he took his chair from the breakfast-table to the grass-plot under a plum-tree, where he sat for two or three hours. When he came into the house, I perceived he had some scraps of paper in his hand, and these he was quietly thrusting behind the books. On inquiry, I found those scraps, four or five in number, contained his poetic feelings on the song of our nightingale.

Brown said it was he who rescued those scraps of paper, that he helped Keats put them together and 'Ode to a Nightingale' was born.

You can rescue a masterpiece, you can plant a new plum tree, but you won't catch nightingales nesting around here any more. Since 1994 they have declined in Britain by 60 per cent. They winter south of the Sahara and we have made the air they fly through and the land they fly over far more dangerous and inhospitable.

In the last five years there has been a drastic fall in the numbers of long-distance migrant birds coming to Britain. The lesser spotted woodpecker has declined by 59 per cent: tree pipits and spotted flycatchers by 70 per cent, cuckoos by 37 per cent since 1995. In 2007, scientists recorded 16 million swifts flying from Africa to Britain. Sixteen million exhausting journeys sounds a lot, but the numbers are nothing compared to what they used to be: swifts have gone down 40 per cent since 1994.

Every twenty minutes another animal or plant disappears. Ever since we discovered fire we have been changing the earth as it was formed in the late Devonian era by the first tree,

Archaeopteris. Since 1945 our population has more than doubled. Using up more of the planet we share with animals, driving them to extinction faster than new species can evolve, we live today in the midst of a great dying. The habitats in which animals have evolved to exist disappear as we expand and industrialise more of the globe. In Flatford Mill in Norfolk the summer air was thick with swallows twenty years ago. This year there's one nest. 'Not enough insects,' a birdwatcher told me. 'We've been too successful in eliminating insects. There's simply not enough for the swallows to eat.'

A few years ago, in the Natural History Museum's Old Store Room, I wandered through chill corridors of staring animal heads, past carefully made glass eyes fitted into the heads of deer which no longer exist.

A village called Al-Qurnah stands today where the Tigris and Euphrates flow together to make a river known as Shatt al-Arab. This river flows on into the Persian Gulf but is drying up now, polluted by human activity.

Many say this was the original site of the Garden of Eden. The villagers of Al-Qurnah identify one tree on the bank as the Tree of Life.

We are the Colossus now.

———

Migrant birds are particularly at risk from the way we have changed and are changing the planet, for they have to negotiate so many different habitats and we are altering them all. Birds adapt quickly to change because their lives and species depend on it and today, with the changing climate, many have already altered their patterns of migration. With rising temperatures in spring and summer, some long-distance migrants have shifted their breeding ranges north. But this lengthens their spring journey and as the Sahara creeps south their autumn journey will lengthen, too. So fewer of them make it and their numbers thin. Thousands of other birds are also sliced up by wind farms just as geese stopping for a rest are trapped in oily rivers.

Other migrating species are affected too. Indian elephants are hit by trains running across their migration corridors; global warming is changing the places and food sources on which marine as well as aerial migrants depend. The Arctic is no longer the place to which thousands of creatures evolved to go in summer. Naturalists live with the nightmare that one year the migrants won't show up at all.

We are like but also unlike the nature which surrounds us. Animals use magnetite to respond to earth's magnetic field; we don't. Scientists recently found magnetite in human brain tissue, but don't know what it's doing there. It may be doing nothing and is merely a by-product of the way our tissues handle molecules of iron.

But we have words instead. We give 'directions'; we tell each other where to go.

The Aboriginal people in Australia migrated there from Asia around 30,000 years ago. Across this new land they followed songlines, which they believed were dreamed by a creator-spirit singing the plants, rocks, waterholes and land-marks into existence. There were song-paths across the sky, too. Songlines were verbal maps, threading the desert and the heavens with words.

Imagination and words are not a substitute for magnetite. Stories are a kind of mapping but are not navigation. Still, poems, songs, histories and geographies help us share with each other the way to go. We find stones that point north; we invent technologies; we have creativity and a sense of the past.

Compared to a storm petrel, however, returning to the same chink of Irish cliff from Africa year after year, it's easy to feel that's not enough. Our relationship with nature is ambivalent, and it's changing. We feel we have a right to control it, but we also like to use it as a mirror, something to think with about ourselves. Strong as an oak, free as a bird. But as the planet changes, the mirror is cracking. We can't use water and snow as images of purity now the seas are full of particles of our plastic, and layers of the carbon we loose into the air are embedded like tree rings under the North Pole.

———

The moon, too, is our ancient mirror. One way of looking at the moon is wish-fulfilment: it is the place to start again and do what we haven't been able to do on earth. The first recorded fantasy of a trip to the moon was written in the second century AD by the Syrian-Greek writer Lucian. Even then, this idea involved colonisation rights. Lucian described a boat navigating the Straits of Gibraltar suddenly lifted up by a waterspout. The voyagers land on the moon and get caught up in an interplanetary war: the kings of the moon and sun are fighting over colonising Venus.

Thirteen hundred years later, in *Orlando Furioso*, written by the Italian poet Ariosto between 1516 and 1532, an English knight flies to the moon on Elijah's chariot. Orlando has gone mad because the girl he loves has eloped with someone else. The English knight will bring back his wits, because on the moon you find everything you've lost on earth.

The German mathematician Johannes Kepler wanted a vivid way of demonstrating that you did not have to put earth at the centre of the universe. He published his first major work, *The Cosmographic Mystery*, in 1596, but even before, as a student, he'd begun a book on lunar astronomy, eventually published after he died as *The Dream*. It is an extraordinary piece of writing which includes an imaginary trip to the moon but also fleshes out in mathematical detail how space would look from the moon.

Wanting more – more resources than the planet has, a place where we can see from a different angle, find what we've lost on earth or get what we never had – is wanting the moon. If we've used up treasure here, let's move on to the next world. If we've fouled up this nest, fly to a new one. This lunar beauty . . . Finding in a new place what you've lost in the old is the dream of every migrant.

We destroy, but we also reclaim. The Mesopotamian marshes of southern Iraq were once the world's third largest wetland, a floodplain where the Euphrates and Tigris rivers divided into a network of tributaries meandering and pulsing south to the Arabian sea. For birds travelling from Central Africa to northern

Europe or Asia and back, these marshes were a vital stopover and refuelling site. Saddam Hussein drained them, turning the huge, once-teeming delta of reed beds into a dry, salt-encrusted desert. But now local people and Iraqi conservationists have restored the marshes. The reed beds are buzzing and twittering with life again. In Eden, at least, the harbingers are back.

Lodestone

I am Magnes the shepherd who found a pebble
stuck to a nail in his boot and discovered the mineral
Attract. I am Heinz Lowenstam, geologist from Silesia
who identified magnetite in tooth caps
of a homing mollusc. I am magnetotactic bacteria
knitted with crystals which orient to earth's
magnetic field. I am also your garden robin
who reads geomagnetic lines the way you scan
a newspaper, navigating folded thunderclouds at night
by neural pathways of Cluster N wired to my left eye
from light-processing regions of the brain.

I am the photoreceptor protein which draws young
monarch butterflies hatched on a month-long
journey to the same old Mexican forest their ancestors
                                                    knew.
I am salamander, spiny lobster, bee, crocodile and whale
and also that flock of cranes passing silently over the
                                                    moon.
I am fish, mammal, fungi and bird. I am two billion
                                                    years
of life-forms steering by the minerals of which I am
                                                    made
and molecular feel for the pull of the earth.
What about us, poor wanderers with no inner compass?
You inscribe the globe. You map, you have words,
you foresee your death. Isn't that enough?

Gun

Case-toughened breech inlaid with two pair
platinum lines. Steel tang lock
engraved with heads of hounds enclosed in foliage.
A scrolling serpent and a figured walnut stock.

Steel barrel, bolt escutcheons, chequered grip,
etched mount, back-action locks. Grip safety-catch
behind the trigger-guard. A cut-down butt,
steel ramrod-pipe plus brass-tipped ramrod.

Rainproof pan, shell finial, butt-cap. Rotation,
recoil. Look, a twin bore and extended magazine.
Piston. Stress, slide, hammer, pivot, bolt.
Noble. Rod. Device. Cartridge. The axial groove.

Assemble. Washer. Transverse tongue.
Cheek-gauge and shoulder-gauge. Thumb-hole,
hinge, flange and firing pin. Cylinder.
Double action, yes. Screw-bracket. Nut.

The annular chamber. The alarm call. Target
and observation post. The running of the deer.
A glazing eye. Scut and whisker. Trophy.
Tinder. Tender. Final. Finial. Disappeared.

End of the Line

I am standing at the end of the District Line
beyond Putney Bridge in the Old Store
of the Natural History Museum, a forest
of glass eyes, beside giraffe heads mounted on necks
like gingham lilies, each a different length.
The ears fan out for danger like gold leaves
from what had been a stereo of coclia and brain

checking for lion in the gullies.
The highest head, monsieur, is male
watching over his herd from the back
just where Myall's *Rules for Flower Arrangement
in the Drawing-Room* advise to slot the focal stem.
Behind him, a Hoolock gibbon's shrunken head
and brown eyes under his sad white tiara

and a wild ass of the Bible. Antelope brows
on mahogany shields, thousands of each species
inscribed with the place and the date
of a hunt. This is the underworld library of death
but you'd never guess. Anyone would take
this warehouse in a side road for a factory,
not the stilly realm where Persephone sits enthroned

and Nature ticks the extinction boxes one by one;
Hades arrived at by airlock and a puddle –
a slot for the hoist which levers giant auroch

or other large latecomers to their last bolt-hole –
whose greenwater sump-breath wells
into carefully calibrated air
like a rumour of greed in the human soul.

Sea Catch

What luck! A harbour
seal, *phoca vitalina,*
albino. Unique.

Whiskers lifted, look,
a face on him of gentle
curiosity.

Shot 1903.
The left eye socket empty
and the other eye

veiny crimson glass
like a rosy marble lost
in wet meadow grass.

The Mirror of Nature

Svalbard. Crack of a bubble, caught
ten thousand years in ice and now released.
Water has eaten the island's underhang.
At the glacier's core, carbon archives
have been identified, sooty bindweed
like the black line of Brünnich's guillemots –
the thick-billed murre, recorded as far off
as California – now zipping up
the quick gold of an Arctic horizon.

Eden, they say, as they always have.
All this is Creation, made for us to enjoy.
What can we do with a mind
that told itself jaw-cracking lies
then patted itself on the back? That knew
it was a bit of a bastard, but richer for the devil
in it; always so sure it was washable-clean
and could be redeemed by worldwater – so pure,
so green – and by *religio*, meaning 'a tie'?

But no tie endures. Milk-gothic spires
slide into the sea. Feather whips of zooplankton –
the dinoflagellates, eukaryotic protists
and foraminifera in the kingdom of protozoa
on whom we all depend – drift-ride to shore
on sparking waves plated, floe by floe,

with particles of plastic.
Tidewater glaciers unleaven
like loaves deliquescing back into dough.

Rabbit on the Moon

Fly to the moon as dusk comes on
and you'll see twelve celestial signs light up

like the *tapetum lucidum* of a stag
crossing the lane at night, looking at you

in the beam of your headlight.
Whose light is whose? There they are, twin

animal eyes into which you fling your dreams
when this world of men and all they ask

becomes too difficult. New light, here I come:
pour everything you are in here and start again

like the god who hurled a rabbit
at the inner segment of the moon.

See yourself up there, only visible when she's full.
Pure, beautiful, a door cut into time . . .

Remember the Spanish friar, shipped
to the New World, who spent seventy years

on Aztec grammar, Aztec lives,
Aztec myths, marriages and syntax

set down in Náhuatl, the dying language
of just one beloved tribe.

The Camden Telescope-Making Class

(In honour of Maggie Aderin-Pocock)

I'm leaving this sessile globe behind
to look for something better. A floating astronaut
steps from the glazed cover of a library book

and talks to me. Let me polish with satin cloths
my catadioptric reflector, home-grown
refraction and reflection which combine

in a field of view that's aberration-free.
I shall point it at the sky, and greet from afar
the *deus absconditus* himself. I plan to chart

the secret life of a mirror, chemical reactions
in each gas ring of Saturn, the objective dunes
of starlight a billion and a half years old,

the meteor's polychrome heart
in falling threads of albumen and gold
and every one of Jupiter's blue moons.

Letter to a Portuguese Cosmologist

'The Universe has no doors and no edges. There is
nothing stopping us from seeing what is going on in
any direction except the cosmological horizon.'
　　　　　　– Pedro Ferreira, *The State of the Universe*

You talk of Gödel, Pedro, truths that can't be proved,
and the surface-of-last-scatter origins of light.
You pit tokens of dark matter, shrinking us, against
a mysterious safety pushing everything further apart,
but don't know how to answer where you're from.
You look for things that do not shine,

a mathematics of connectedness
in what the rest of us see
as spotted lacquer. Then add in Africa
where both your grandfathers were born. Shanty-

　　　　　　　　　　　　　　　　towns,
streetcorner Kwaito music, glottal grammar
of too-quick-to-follow Xhosa chat shows,

acacia tines on sulphurous horizons
and surnames you recognise from Portugal
on fading turquoise petrol-station signs.
We don't know, you say, *how the first stars*
were born. If the universe wraps round itself
we should see tapestries of repeating lights,

distant copies of ourselves, our galaxy
and neighbours as they were in the past.
I'm at the kitchen table, night flaunting
her dark energy, and the moon above my head.
All that pushing apart! We close our prayers
on open numbers, *three, five, seven, nine,*

most inward when most looking out.
We come home to ourselves, following
a silver-paper trail among elliptic nebulae,
light-paths and strings of misalignment,
rough space that's never empty
and the hot dense core of stars.

Advertisement: The Lunar Registry

'This clear-view folder engraved with your own name
on a hundred per cent Cotton Ledger stock
with certificate borders elegantly lithographed
gives latitude, longitude and the Claims
Register number of your ownership. It contains
the sample deed for your acre of the Moon
and your membership in Lunar Republic,
official Website of the Moon. The future of the Moon
sitting up there in her mushroom lustre,
innocent as a newborn, is in your hands:
settlement, tourism development, industrial land.

Is that you listening to Frank Sinatra
on your birthday all alone? *Fly Me to the Moon!*
Virgin Galactic are planning a Space Hotel.
They land, or they will, with a heat-free
feathering system, kind on the environment
and safe safe safe. It's all arranged.
If you already own the hottest property on earth
the only better view is outer space.
What have you to lose? A million dollars
to the Moon and back, only five times
the chartered flight from Chennai to Dubai!

You also get mining rights. Prospecting for Helium 3,
the fusion-reactor fuel, rarer on earth than platinum,
must be high on every list of things to do

on the Moon. Space tourism's here to stay.
Only a fool would pass up the Sea of Tranquillity
with Tom Cruise and George Bush Senior
next plot along. Fancy a château by scenic Sea of Cold
on our roses-and-cream peninsula? How about
the Lunar Alps? There's so much to choose from.
Take my favourite, the Bay of Rainbows,
or the Edeny, dark-fruit-magnificent Lake of Dreams.'

Sharing Space

How far can you go? What does Fate
hold now by way of soothsaying?
The night before 9/11

a million Swainson's thrushes
must have flown
over the towers. Their road songs

have been recorded other years
on just that date
in the skies above Manhattan.

Farming the Wind

White cutlass on a space march to nowhere.
Knives hidden in cloud – slicing thorax,
breast-muscle, wings and liver
of osprey, plover, peregrine –
creating this spectral litter
of dead and dying biological masterpieces.

O birds who weave worlds together,
how nothing in your fossil footprint
prepared you for this. We are Odysseus' men
opening a skin bag expecting treasure
and getting blown to shipwreck
by all the winds of heaven.

If only the birds, said King Solomon, possessed
our rituals for detecting the presence of Belial
like burning a black cat's afterbirth
and sprinkling the ashes in your eye.
If only birds could see the wind atlas
we consult as we position our turbine.

The Marshes of Eden

(for Gwen at twenty-five)

We carry loss with us, as if we'd had a share
in when the world was new – some Garden
we don't know but must be the Home we left.

We dreamed of whispering wetgrass, the Everglades
beyond the freeway-turn for Disney World
where we saw through a glass-bottomed boat

one manatee afloat; quite possibly asleep.
You were eight, a small girl
laughing in a pedigree Keeshond T-shirt

and a tangle-cloud of wild-silk old-gold hair.
Heart like a wheel . . . The world turns
and I'm bartering in Bombay

for your birthday present,
the Goddess of Security,
and dreaming of Al-Qurna triangle

where the River Shatt al-Arab is born
and Tigris joins Euphrates, where Eden began
and backwaters melt from the mountains of Iran

to glimmer among reclaimed wetlands:
the ancient stopover
for sacred ibis, marbled teal.

Children of Storm

The new garden is an empty yard paved in pink and yellow stone. We've cut down leylandii taking all the light and there are no trees. I've seen a wren once, and two goldfinches. But it's July, birds will be finding food elsewhere. We'll have to wait till we plant trees, grass and bushes. My daughter has fitted her stuff into her tiny new room and left for work in Colombia, and there's a lot to do to turn this into a home. But we love it; these back gardens now seem normal.

But they're not normal – not in the age of migration with billions of people moving unhoused across the globe.

Thousands of migrations are smooth and happy, but this book is about the crossing, the journey. A million new immigrants enter the United States legally every year but thousands come in illegally, especially from and through Mexico. Cubans often arrive via Isla Mujeres, a small island off the Yucatan coast which they reach on home-made craft. In south Mexico, migrants from Guatemala, Honduras and El Salvador arrive in Tabasco and Chiapas. It is a dangerous border: corrupt police and immigration agents exploit them. Three Mexican National Migration Institute Officers were recently caught on video chasing a Honduran migrant with a machete into the Usumacinta River that borders Guatemala. They watched her struggle with the current until local villagers rescued her.

Mexico's northern border is even more dangerous. Barricading it, to keep illegal migrants and drug traffickers out of the United States, involves three operations called *Gatekeeper* in California, *Safeguard* in Arizona, and in Texas *Hold-the-Line*. The border is a patchwork of walls and cameras; supporters of the 'Border Fence Project' want a double fence along all 1,952 miles. Opponents say the fence destroys animal habitats and stops animals migrating or reaching water. They also say it doesn't work. Anyone with wire-cutters can get through the fence, and migrants also detour through the Sonoran Desert and Baboquivari Mountains.

The Mexican government has condemned the fence. So has the Governor of Texas (who wants better support for legal migration, instead) and the Mayor of Laredo, a town of 236,000 inhabitants on the river's north bank. 'These people are sustaining our economy by 40 per cent,' the Mayor says, 'and I'm gonna close the door on them and put up a wall? You don't *do* that!'

Thousands die trying to cross. Many drown in the Rio Grande, others die from heatstroke and dehydration in the desert, or in road accidents while chased by Border Patrol. As vulnerable as migrating birds, they are also shot by Border Patrol, vigilantes and the people-smugglers, there called 'coyotes'.

Casa del Migrante in Tijuana provides temporary lodging to people trying to cross. One worker there, describing in a podcast why they keep trying, says, 'Three months trying to cross and cross, even losing their lives, is better than go back. They borrowed money. They can't go back.'

This scenario is so familiar there is now an iPhone game about driving illegal migrants into the United States. In *Smuggle Truck* you dodge bullets from the drug mafia and border guards, tilt your pickup to catch babies bouncing out at the back as your cargo gives birth, and get them to the border where 'The Star-Spangled Banner' strikes up and you get a green card – and your score.

The Australian government uses a similar game to try and change attitudes to immigration. *Kick A Migrant* begins with immigrants huddled like lemmings on an Australian cliff: you see how far back into the sea you can kick them. But when your migrant splashes down, your inbox scolds you. 'That one came with a business degree! He's a Scout leader now, he gives jobs to Australians and owns a convenience store. Net loss to the economy of your kick – five hundred thousand a year.'

That sea drowns many real migrants. The detention centre on Christmas Island, 2,600 kilometres north-west of Perth, currently overflowing with people from Afghanistan and Sri Lanka, holds migrants while their claims for refugee status are assessed. In December 2010 the islanders watched helpless from a cliff as asylum-seekers – men, women and children in a boat from Indonesia – drowned or were battered to death on the rocks.

Since 2005 a European Agency based in Warsaw called Frontex has co-ordinated patrol boats and border guards controlling illegal immigration into the European Union. Many come west into Greece, from Afghanistan, Pakistan and Bangladesh, either by land from Turkey or in boats to the islands. Many others come from Africa. The independent, US-based Migration Policy Institute believes there are 8 million illegal African immigrants in the European Union. From West Africa they often go to the Cape Verde Islands, or the Canary Islands, where between twelve and thirty thousand arrive every year. They are too weak to walk or stand. When a boat approaches, the harbour fills with tents, hospital beds, police, sirens, wheelchairs and helicopters. Fishermen find bodies caught in nets. Lining the harbour, among the pleasure boats, are piles of bright-painted wooden fishing boats in which a hundred people have sat for many days. These are a health hazard and are cleaned, before being crushed, by men with protective clothing. Sometimes dead bodies are found in them.

Outside the Senegalese capital Daka is the poor suburb of Thiaroye. It was once a fishing village, but the villagers' traditional fishing can't compete with overfishing by huge European trawlers. This is the launch pad for thousands of young West Africans trying to reach the Canary Islands.

When the *passeurs* (traffickers) come through, hundreds of young men sign up, desperate to get to Europe. Women whose sons have already died in that attempt try to argue them out of it. Meanwhile, families from other rural areas club together to pay the *passeurs* to send their boys across the Sahara and out from Libya in little boats. In March 2009, 400 drowned in one night. They were packed into three small fishing boats and had come from Lagos, Accra, Addis Ababa, Nairobi, Yaounde, Banjul. From Egypt, Somalia, Ghana, Nigeria, Tunisia, Algeria, Morocco, Gambia and Cameroon but also from Bangladesh, Syria and Pakistan. They were hoping, said one of the few survivors, now in prison in Libya, for 'a better life'.

It has always been tough being a Mediterranean island. Through the centuries the islands have been invaded by Crusaders, Saracens, Venetians, the Templar Knights and the Ottomans, and now it is especially on islands that detention centres multiply. Like Aeneas sailing from North Africa to Sicily and then Italy, migrants leave Libya in these tiny frail boats (making them is an industry now) and go north. They land up in Crete, Sicily, Lampedusa or Sardinia and hope like Aeneas to reach Italy eventually. Or else they go to Spain.

Like long-winged birds who can only glide over sea, they try to find the shortest sea crossing. They often follow exactly the same south-north and east-west journeys as migrant birds (who also depend on the islands to stop over, rest and refuel). If you superimposed human and avian journeys on a world map, many lines would become one. Over the Strait of Gibraltar, over the Bosphorus or coming up from South America to North, human migrants face the same hostile planet as the birds: desert and sea, mountain and storm – and predators.

They are often blown off-course to Malta, needing medical help, screening, food and a place to sleep. They don't want to be there and the Maltese don't want them, but EU rules say asylum-seekers must make their claim in the first EU country they enter. Maltese ministers say their whole island is now a detention centre.

The EU agency Frontex helps the Maltese patrol their waters with helicopters and speedboats, but cannot turn back ships in international waters. If they see migrants turn up in distress they have to rescue them.

'We give them food, water, blankets, fuel, maps, things like that, and say, the best thing for you is to turn round and go back where you come from, because there is no future for you to enter that country,' said the Director of Frontex in 2007.

'Our fishermen feel overwhelmed,' says the commander of the Maltese maritime squadron. 'Their boats are built for six. Suddenly thirty migrants are trying to get in, too, and the boat turns over.'

A robin, once he's won his territory, fiercely defends it against other robins, often to the death. So do we. In every country, earlier immigrants resent new ones and try to keep them out. From the beginning of mass migrations to America in the 1880s, there were calls for restrictions and immigration laws. The Chinese Exclusion Act, Alien Contract Labor Law, Quota Laws, National Origins Act.

Twenty years ago, when my daughter was small, I lived in Greece. Albanian immigrants were then a new phenomenon. The same Albanians are now the naturalised fathers of children persecuting Pakistani and Somali immigrants – to keep Greece, they say, for the Greeks.

The Sangatte refugee camp opened in 1999 half a mile from the Channel Tunnel. It closed in 2002. Between 2004 and 2009 the number of illegal immigrants detected trying to enter Britain from France and Belgium trebled. Hundreds of Tunisians sleep rough today in the woods outside Paris. They have crossed desert and sea, realised their dream and want work. But there are 24 million Europeans out of work too. Now they want to go home.

In the UK a new Border Agency was created in 2008. Its parent agency is the Home Office and its job is 'to protect the UK border'. Many of its employees work at checkpoints at Calais, whose Chamber of Trade spends £12 million a year securing the port area, and blames Britain's immigration system for thousands of people on their land trying to climb into lorries and trains for the UK.

UK tabloids keep a tally of capture. Thirteen Afghans and two Iranians in a Hungarian-registered lorry of light bulbs; two Vietnamese in a load of nappies; four Afghans in a lorry of champagne; three Afghans, one Palestinian and an Iraqi in a shipment of bananas; ten people in a truck of sofas bound for Wrexham; eight in a truck of mozzarella cheese for Newmarket; twelve Afghans hiding in a thirty-two-foot Christmas tree; eighteen in a lorry of Spanish lettuces; a sixteen-year-old Vietnamese girl curled up with a white stuffed rabbit and surrounded by electrical wiring in sweltering conditions, squeezed behind the dashboard of a car. Three Afghans were found in a truck of Sainsbury's toilet rolls driving from the Czech Republic to Northfleet in Kent. 'Bidding', said the *Sun*, 'for a soft life in Britain.'

Recently a German truck driver drove off the ferry at Dover and heard singing in the back of his lorry. He drove to a police station and police arrested twelve men: four from Iran, four from Afghanistan, four from Iraq. Six were under sixteen. They had been singing to celebrate arriving in Britain.

Asylum means 'the place which can't be plundered' and was a sacred concept in archaic Greece. At an altar, you were safe. You were a recognised suppliant, you had crossed into sacred space and anyone who violated your asylum was accursed. But the first reliably dated event in the history of Athens, a hundred or so years before democracy began, was the betrayal of asylum.

In 632 BC an Athenian nobleman named Cylon attempted a coup d'état at Athens. He captured the Acropolis, but was besieged there and sought asylum in the Temple of Athena. He escaped, but the rulers persuaded his less fortunate supporters to leave asylum and stand trial. They promised to spare their lives, but the suppliants were rightly wary and tied a rope to the goddess's statue as they came out in order to maintain contact with asylum. The rope broke, or was cut, the rulers claimed the goddess had repudiated her suppliants and the suppliants were stoned to death. But the rulers had violated the law against killing suppliants so their clan was cursed. This curse was still significant 200 years later in the democracy, and was used politically against their descendants. Asylum was a political issue before democracy began and has remained so ever since.

Today, supporters of an Open Borders policy in the UK call for the abolition of border controls, because they create worse suffering and human rights abuses; they believe the free movement of peoples should be recognised as a universal human right. But the UK is a small island, too.

In the last ten years a stamp saying LOC – for Lack of Credibility – has appeared on files as a reason to refuse asylum. One small mistake in any part of your statement is a reason to disbelieve all your testimony. Applicants are held in detention centres while a decision is made either to let them stay or to deport them to the country they came from.

The UK has thirteen detention centres, formally rebranded in 2002 as Immigration Removal Centres. Some of these are run by private companies contracted by the Government. They are for people seeking asylum, or people thought to be illegal immigrants. Asylum-seekers are put in them when they arrive and held while they wait for their case to be decided, or wait to be deported if it is refused. The conditions of these centres have been criticised by the UK Inspector of Prisons. A report by the Medical Foundation for the Care of Victims of Torture and Medical Justice speaks of 'systematic abuse' within them; of hunger strikes, riots, suicides; complaints of rape, assault, intimidation and lack of information about basic rights.

People will do anything to keep out of them. In 2004 twenty-three Chinese migrant workers died in the mudflats of Morecambe Bay. Nick Broomfield's film *Ghosts* (2006) recreated their story. Having paid snakehead gangs to smuggle them on a year-long journey across Asia and Europe, they were put to work by gangmasters. The *Aeneid* ends with indigenous Italians making war on the Trojan refugees, and the Chinese immigrants were beaten up by British rivals who took their cockle-sacks. So they picked cockles at night, stuck in the mud as the tide came in, and drowned.

Migration is a lottery. Thousands of migrating animals and people die. Conditions in the new place are often very hard. For humans there are further psychological costs. A friend of mine, a psychiatrist for the homeless, was called out recently in the night because one of his patients, a Muonyjang from South Sudan, suddenly had to be hospitalised.

Several years after coming to Britain this man and his mother were reunited with his elder brother. All three escaped massacre in South Sudan when the boys were eight and five. To give the family more chance of surviving they decided to split up. The elder was recruited as a child soldier. He saw and did unspeakable things but eventually escaped, was rescued in Ethiopia by the UN, and is now a successful businessman.

The mother went with the younger son to Egypt; they reached Britain, he grew up and went to a British university, but suddenly broke down and ended up homeless on the London streets.

Migration may bring new life. But the loss of home and the traumas you endure, the reason you have to flee in the first place, may take its toll long afterwards.

Turn the crystal of 'migration' and you get 'home'. In Britain it is the Home Office which deals with immigration and detention – and also with deportation. In the 1990s, the Home Office began what medical agencies call outsourcing abuse, hiring private companies – called escort agencies or security solutions firms – to accompany refused asylum-seekers back to their countries of origin by force.

This is a new industry. Reports on it by charities have found multiple abuses. Escorts are on hourly pay, have a financial incentive (no bonus unless they return their deportee to his country of origin), a record of criminal assault is no bar to employment and their actions are not open to public scrutiny.

In 2010 at Heathrow three escorts from the security solutions firm G4S boarded a plane for Luanda with an Angolan man, Jimmy Mubenga. Passengers heard Mubenga shouting that he didn't want to leave his wife and children, that he couldn't breathe. His last words were, 'They're trying to kill me.' The aircraft returned to the terminal; Jimmy Mubenga was pronounced dead in hospital. Escorts are allowed to use control techniques approved by the Prison Service but pushing a deportee's head between his legs is forbidden. Death from it is called positional asphyxia.

These three escorts are currently suspended and under investigation for manslaughter. One recently posted a photo on his Facebook page showing two south Asian men sitting on an aeroplane, one of whom has his seatbelt across his shoulder as in a car. Comments of this escort's Facebook friends laugh at the seatbelt mistake, mock the men as 'depos' and say they should be in handcuffs shouting 'kill me now'.

This new legal industry of 'security solutions' and escort agencies mirrors the illegal one of people-smuggling. Two lots of money made out of people who have none. Trapped between criminals and governments like wildebeest between crocodiles and lions, migrants are big business, except to themselves.

Migration is essential to life on earth. Cells dismantle their structure and start again, or migrate to form new embryos. Life-forms migrate constantly, our species is *homo viator*, our civilization began with migration. 'Asylum-seekers' implies a 'they' who want something from 'us' and ignores what immigrants give. As the Mayor of Laredo says, migrations sustain society. But because of our expanding population, and what we are doing to the earth, migration is at unprecedented levels. People emigrate from desperate need. Like blackpoll warblers in hurricanes, they suffer terrible losses. Reaching countries in recession with rising unemployment, many find no work, merely hostility. British readers of a 2009 newspaper article on Gambian families of migrants drowned in boats off Libya commented online, 'The UK's not a dumping ground for illegal immigrants!' 'They're like burglars breaking into your home demanding food.' 'If they want a better life they should stay in their country and improve matters there.' The religious requirement behind Western religions is sympathy. *Help the poor as you would a stranger, for you were a stranger too.* What hope is there, in a world where nations are closing the portcullis?

Mara in Latin means 'bitter'. In North European folklore, Mara is a nightmare demon of horror and death. Buddhist Mara is a demon of illusion: once the Vedic demon of drought, he now spreads terror through deception, threatening us by obscuring truth. He tempted the Buddha too, who touched the earth and realized enlightenment so that Mara disappeared. The Proto-Indo-European root *mer*, 'to die', and Sanskrit *mara*, 'obstacle, death', stand behind these Maras, but by phonetic accident they resemble the Masai name for the river at the end of the wildebeest's journey. Since I witnessed what happens at that river, 'Mara' has come to me to represent bitter losses, struggle, barriers and obstacles, but also the triumph of survival. Like the wildebeest, migrants cross over to create new cultural life.

Hope, that word which powers migration, lies in staying open to what is happening. In not looking away, questioning those who operate the portcullis, exposing and resisting cruelty in implementing government policies, paying attention to the developed world's responsibility for displacements (fished-out seas, corporate over-use of resources which uproots people and destroys their land), keeping sympathy with other people's stories, seeing their experience as part of our own. Some readers of that newspaper did reply to those comments. 'It is only by the Grace of God,' said one, 'that you are not one of these unfortunates. You are an accident of birth, as they are.' Hope springs from that faculty which other animals don't seem to need but *homo viator* needs more than ever today. Compassion – and beyond that, empathy.

The Desert and the Sea

'I might not survive. I knew this. The only way
is risk your life. In Eritrea you're never free;
if I want to go to another city I must pay.
In Europe I go anywhere I like.

My first time, I was with a hundred families.
Big boats came after us. After five days at sea
we were back in Libya, in prison. Children
and pregnant women, all in prison.

I tried again. Out of one hundred, twenty-five
may get to Italy. You will not know. Some die
in the sea, some end in prison and some die
in the desert where you don't die quick.

Is it worth the risk? I cannot say yes
or no. It depends how your soul
buckles under the burden
of months – no, years – of *almost*.'

Ghost Ship

You have to get out. But this is how you imagine
you might go, when you wake at night afraid
of moving on, from Gambia or Guinea Bissau,

and hear the redslick in your temple beat
like waves around the ghost ship
discovered off Ragged Point, Barbados.

A six-foot yacht, adrift. No name, no flag
and a phantom crew, eleven young men
in green, red, orange, blue,

mummified in salt of their own sweat.
You can't shake out of your head
that airline ticket from Senegal, the note

in a dead boy's pocket – *Excuse me, this is the end,
sorry to my family in Bassada* – saying how the skipper
disappeared before they left Cape Verde;

how he could have jumped like his friend;
when they were towed; and how one night
the rope was slashed by a machete.

Orestiada

(for Kerin Hope)

Any weakening in Fortress Europe
will show in ripples of the icy Hebros
still carrying a memory
of the floating head of Orpheus.
Twenty years ago, the novelty
was Immigrant Market at Theseion:

Albanians, squatting on unravelled
plastic tartan, offering cut-price replicas
of everything under the sun.
You invested, Kerin, in a present
for your god-daughter: a cochineal
post-Soviet My Little Pony.

In Athens today, you see *No Mosques*
and *This is Greece* sprayed over the square
as Albanian vigilantes chase the Afghans out.
People-traffickers from Troy
throw their customers in the Hebros
and asphyxiate stowaways in trucks

but they keep coming, over a forest frontier
of landmines and razor wire,
carrying toddlers and plastic bags

to hide behind a furniture factory
in suburbs of Orestiada, the city named
for the boy who knifed his mother and went mad.

Wetbacks

(for Issam Kourbaj)

'Mexicans cross a river, Cubans cross a fucking ocean!!
Cubans are the wetbacks, not Mexicans.'
                    – Blogger at Urban Dictionary.com

We're sitting on paint-splashed stools in your studio
sipping wine. You talk of Damascus, show me your

                                        design
for postboxes floating in air. 'How about those

                                        chairs, Issam?'
'Ah Cuba! Ruth, the beach was dark with them.

A sea of broken chairs! They lash them together
and push off. After seeing that, I found chairs
in skips, and throw-outs from the restaurant downstairs,
to make a Migrant Monument in their honour.'

You pile up legs of beech and deal. When the chips
are down, this is all we need: a stack
of splintered wood. Like José Luis, fridge
repair-man from Havana, who took five days

to make it to Isla Mujeres,
Mexico, spread-eagled on inner tubes
bound to a chair-back powered by
a *put-put* used for irrigating fields.

Maltese Fishing Boat and Broken Net

They set off in a Phoenician fishing smack
with the Eye of Horus kohl-outlined –
the pupil turned in as if squinting –
on a double-ended hull.

High bows of ochre, red and green
swoop waves now indigo,
now khaki, transverse and longitudinal,
which will mean a bit of a swell.
She's built to take six men, with nets
for amber jack, stone bass, white bream.

Here's a *cayuco* – the kind one sees limping in
to Tenerife, where migrants are trucked
to La Esperanza Detention Centre
while the boat is sterilised and crushed –

so low in the water a hundred pairs of hands,
up to the elbows, are batting the waves.
Where's Frontex Patrol? She's broadside –
now she's turtle. They're clinging on, slipping,
pushing. Most can't swim. But some
splash over, grab the net, pull us down . . .

Cut the rope! What would *you* do?
We lose our catch but we get home.

A hundred are drowning –
why should we six die too?

The Place without a Door

Listen. There are dragons under cities
and monsters in white spaces on sea maps.
Sangatte is Gap-in-Sand. When we were there
we knew it was The Place Without a Door –
that commune on the coast of France
facing water which the English
call English Channel. A border
for which many men, and women, too,
have died. Mark the spot in my brother's heart
where he built a cardboard shrine
for our wasteland jungle. Check the wall
where someone graffed, *Nous voulons de l'air
pour nos enfants*. The cement octagons
where we hid at night to rush the axle
of Spanish lorries. The bridge where my brother
jumped that train into the tunnel.

Immigration Counter and
the Gates of Ivory

They're flying back to Canada, after summer in
           Mumbai.
'Think they're still awake now, Grandpa and Granny?'
Wails fill the cabin as lights go down
and we're in the Moonlight World of the Small
           Mammal
House at the Zoo. Her face is a fire-lit mask
as she settles their blankets and the rest of us try
looking this night in its indigo eye, pleated
like inner petals of a gentian. We doze
while in the Mumbai suburb where, let's suppose,
she grew up, her parents still flick through the photos.
Home was festivals, the kitchen, the shrine of a front
           room.
But that's over now, with the grandchildren abroad.

Light glimmers through the thicket of the aisle.
Roll on seven hours, we're in Passport Control
with a flight from Abuja. The family in transit from
           Mumbai
have papers fresh as snow
but here's an old guy from Nigeria, alone
with a string bag. Behind the officer in blue,
turning every page of my passport,
a kiosk of Travelex World Wide Money glows
like Santa's Magic Cave.

Then I'm through,
the Mumbai lot too. But for the old man
she's called a colleague. They winnow

his papers like a rice harvest. No Travelex for him.
A man may dream his wife returns, or he returns
to her, but dreams are shadow-customers. They flit
from the underworld through two doors – one horn,
one ivory. If your dreams pick
ivory, the ancestors are amusing themselves
I'm afraid, floating illusion upward to the living.
Dreams that arrive through horn come true
but how do you know? At the Styx
of the UK Border, a gentian blossom
is forcibly removed. We progress to Luggage Claim.
Indigo petals fade, curl and close on nothing.

The Apple Orchard in Ghosts

That moment in the film
when there's no more work in the fields

and the leather-collared bull-man
gangmaster shifts them to an orchard

harvesting its last fruit
before the Worcester Pearmains

and Red Falstaffs are torn up for ever.
Suddenly it's the 'People Will Say We're in Love' scene,

all trees, wicker baskets and sunlight,
from *Oklahoma*

and England is no longer grey mud
beyond the greasy windows of the minibus

but green – yes, and real people,
gentle and sad themselves,

in a misty kitchen
offering what passes for tea.

The Prayer Labyrinth

She went looking for her daughter. How many
visit Hades and live? Your only hope
is the long labyrinth of Visa Application
interviews with a volunteer from a charity
but you're not allowed to meet her.
You've been caught: by a knock on the door
at dawn, or hiding in a truck of toilet tissue
or just getting stuck in a turnstile.

You're on Dead Island: a Detention Centre.
The Russian refugees who leaped from the fifteenth
                                  floor
of a Glasgow tower block to the Red Road
Springburn – Serge, Tatiana and their son
who, when immigration officers
were at the door, tied themselves together
before they jumped – knew what was coming.

Anyway you're here. Evidence of cigarette
burns all over your body has been dismissed
by the latest technology. You're dragged
from your room, denied medication
or a voice. You can't see your children,
they're behind bars somewhere else.
You go on hunger strike. You're locked
in a corridor for three days without water

then handcuffed through the biopsy
on your right breast. You've no choice
but to pray; and to walk the never-ending path
of meditation on *not yet*. Your nightmare
was home-grown: you're seeking sanctuary.
They say you don't belong. They give you
a broken finger, a punctured lung.

Purple Ink

She has waited three years for this. Too ashamed
to even half-tell the young woman in spectacles
tapping a purple biro on a desk

exactly what the soldiers did to her, each versatile
in his turn, she gets wrong *Date your mother was born*
and sees a stamp the colour of desert night descend on
her file.

Carpet Karaoke

New life forms are entering the world:
government agencies, like young dragons
on a moonlit beach, in a transitional period
of operation. Let's imagine you're standing
at Gatwick Airport in the Year of Our Lord
2008 and a Secretary is launching the UK
Border Agency to be a shadow to the Home Office.

Now let's suppose you slip out of the House
of Lords onto Cornish granite, and hammer
on the Great West Door of Westminster Abbey,
yearning to sing the Office of Compline.
Rays stream in through Gothic stone, lighting up
the eleven-circuit labyrinth embedded in the floor,
and the filigree rosette at its heart
signifying compassion and enlightenment

while shadows multiply under home floorboards
and Securicor blends with G4S
whose motto is *Securing Your World* –
yes, the escort agency, silent as the Chinese word
for secrecy, where a criminal record for assault
is no barrier as security escort; providing solutions
to the problem of not enough world to go round

in the shape of escorts trained in pain compliance
who have taken a shine to one particular technique
and compare notes on it on Facebook. Ride the 24
to the end of the line, studying case histories
from the Medical Justice Network, and you find
the word 'breathing' twined through them all
like flowers through a kelim.
They hand-and-leg-cuff their deportee,

double him up on the seat, three or four
to one, and push his head between his legs.
Think iron grinding ice, think don't-want-to-look.
'They fist-squeezed his testicles, kicked in
his ribs and his stomach.' He cried, they say,
they always say, for help. But fighting for breath
he can only shout at the floor.

Dancers with Bruised Knees

(for Mark Baldwin, Siobhan Davies and the
dancers of the Rambert Dance Company)

A rainy day in Chiswick. They are working on
The Art of Touch, dropping out now and then
to rewind bandages on ankles, stick a plaster
on a toe, do leg-warms at the barre.

Mark, born in Fiji, has invited me to watch
rehearsal. They're all from somewhere else.
'It's hard for them to come. It takes four
months to get a visa and never certain.
You're not allowed to bring dancers from abroad.'

Bodies hurtle over space, their calloused feet
accurate to music of glass and steel
by Domenico Scarlatti. Pieter, Gemma, Eryck,
Dane; Estela from Spain; Miguel

from Cuba – following Acosta, star
of *No Way Home*. They're here, they've made it.
Kirill from Latvia, Vanessa from Singapore.
Show foreigners hospitality, says the Bible,
for many have entertained an angel unaware.

They're wiping sweat, checking feet for scars
and strain. *Diagonal – long hop – ker dum! –*

and kneel. Stefano from Italy. 'Loosen your arms!'
Home is a white bird over the chasm.

Help the poor, say the verses. *Treat them fair
just as you would a stranger, for you were a stranger*
                                        too.
'No matter where you're from,' the dancers say,
'you need the choreography. You have to know
exactly where you're going on the floor.'

I sit in the corner on a plastic chair.
Their steps, repeated over and over – the same
but different in each body – are a meeting-ground, a
                                        prayer.
When they touch the floor

or touch each other, how do they pitch their body
and not get in their partner's way?
I was a foreigner and you welcomed me.
I see the world, the air, hang like a curtain
and swing apart for a single swan.

Where your feet are is all the home there is.
We dab the stage for certainty, we strangers
on the earth, the way an Indian dancer
touches the ground with her hand before coming on.

The Wanderings of Psyche

We migrate not only on the road but in the mind – and, we like to think, in the psyche. Escape literature, armchair travel and fantasy express our migrant souls. It's an attractive notion. Yeats's phrase 'pilgrim soul' was even taken as the title of an episode in the Eighties revival of the American TV suspense and science fiction series *The Twilight Zone*.

We also want to migrate after death. Migration is the great let's-get-out-of-here hope for our body, and we have always dreamed of our souls carrying it off too. Egyptians gave the dying soul equipment for the journey; many more modern religions treat dying as 'migration' to another body, another life or land. A better land, glimmering beyond this one like sky behind branches of a tree.

Hinduism says souls migrate from one life to another and each life is a pause in the cycle. After every life you are born again. *Shakuntala*, a Sanskrit play from the first millennium BC, tells the story of a king who has been cursed to forget his beloved. One day he hears a woman singing outside his window and feels a strange pang, as if reminded of something he loved in another life. The song, he says, seems 'to cling like a fragrance to my migrant soul'.

The Orphics believed the soul was on a perpetual journey to new reincarnations. Gold leaves found in Greek graves of the fourth-century BC were inscribed with instructions for the dying soul. Plato ended the *Republic* with a man who came back to life and said he had seen souls choosing their next life, then flying away like stars to be born again. 'Beautiful is the struggle,' says the dying Socrates at the end of Plato's *Phaedo*, referring to his belief in the transmigration of the soul, 'and the hope is great.'

'The Aspiration', a penitential poem by the seventeenth-century poet John Norris, speaks of getting out of the body up to heaven, and early Christianity took the myth of Psyche and Eros (or Cupid) as an allegory for the soul's search for God.

This story migrated into European folktale, but was written up first in Latin by a migrant of the second century AD in the satirical novel *The Golden Ass*.

Apuleius may have been a Berber. He was born in a Roman colony in what is now Algeria and went to Athens to study, then travelled to Italy, Asia Minor and Egypt. In *The Golden Ass* he tells the story of Cupid and Psyche. Cupid forbade Psyche, he says, to see his face. He visited her only at night and Psyche's sisters said that he must be a monster – she should check. So Psyche did and realised that her lover was the god of Desire. But her oil lamp dripped on his shoulder and Cupid woke, caught her looking and flew away. Psyche set off to find him and her hazardous journey culminated in a trip to the

Underworld to fetch a box of beauty for Cupid's mother, Venus. Opening this to take a little for herself, Psyche was overpowered by sleep. Cupid came to help and repacked the sleep in its box; then Jupiter made Psyche immortal and the pair, reunited, now live among the gods.

Christianity saw this story as an allegory of the soul in its search for divine love, which like Psyche we lose through our own fault. God forgives us as Cupid forgave Psyche. United with God, we find our divine home. Our *psyche* migrates to heaven.

While physical displacement is the main push factor in migration, psychological displacement is the motive force in imagination and creativity. Plato assumed a parallel between body, soul and society, or the body politic: they are metaphors for each other. In the *Republic*, damage and healing in one is an image for damage and healing in the others.

Freud described the ego as a 'frontier-creature' which polices the borderlands of identity and mediates between the world and the unconscious. The personality, he suggested, is formed partly by psychological 'displacement'. As we grow, and respond to what happens around us, we deal with painful feelings like anxiety, grief or anger by constructing defences against them. Displacement, that word which echoes also through explanations of migration, is one such psychological defence. We 'displace' our disturbing feelings into areas where they feel less threatening. By withdrawing from a trauma, the mind reroutes feelings about it on to something else and so transforms these feelings.

We go on doing this throughout our lives: we all displace unpleasant emotions into areas where they don't feel so destructive and may even be creative. But psychologists say that painters, theoretical scientists, philosophers, poets and mystics make particular use of withdrawal and displacement.

If you displace pain you escape it, not by denying it or distorting reality but by migrating to a different (and with any luck creative) perspective. You're not misunderstanding or denying the world, you know the massacre has happened, but you're making something of it. Goya paints *The Disasters of War*.

Seamus Heaney's phrase 'inner émigré' reminds us that artists have always had complicated relationships to exile, both outer and inner. The fifteenth-century Aztec prince Nezahualcoyotl became an inner émigré as a teenager, when a rival kingdom conquered his city of Texcoco. He fled into exile twice, but eventually got his city back. He brought it law, art, scholarship and aqueducts, made it the pre-Hispanic Athens of the Western World and went down in history as a warrior, architect and philosopher-king – but most of all as a poet, whose psyche was formed in exile.

Matisse was an inner émigré in a different sense. According to his biographer, a tension between the making of astonishing visible beauty and crippling anxiety (which is well-documented but was often invisible) marked his life as well as his work. Matisse 'the anxious, the madly anxious', a friend described him. His biographer conjures up a life marked by desperation, self-doubt, and a pain which required art to be a force of calm.

He said art should be about art, not life; a refuge from reality, 'devoid of troubling or depressing subject matter, like an armchair which provides relaxation from fatigue.'

But Matisse was not denying the reality around him. At forty-five he volunteered for service in the First World War, though was rejected because of his age. He was seventy when the Nazis entered France and although he had a visa for Brazil he refused to leave. 'I would have felt like a deserter,' he wrote to his son. Both his wife, from whom he divorced painfully in 1939, and his daughter Marguerite were active in the Resistance. Afterwards he was very shocked to hear that Marguerite had been imprisoned and tortured (she escaped from a cattle car that stalled on its way to a prison camp). But during the war, he withdrew to Villa Le Rêve, a house on the Côte d'Azur. He was diagnosed with cancer in 1941 and had to have surgery. He became isolated, shielding his art fiercely from politics. Long before, he had watched Renoir, very near death, painting with a brush strapped to his bandaged hand. 'I have never seen a man so happy,' said Matisse, 'and I promised myself then that when my time came, I would not be a coward either.'

Materials were hard to get in the war and Matisse turned to a new technique: the paper cut-outs which he called 'painting with scissors'. Afterwards, in 1947, he published *Jazz*, an artist's book of these cut-outs. Later, near death himself, he fastened bits of charcoal to a fishing-pole and drew faces of his grandchildren, whom he adored, on the blank ceiling above his bed.

We displace pain by transforming its presence in our lives into pattern. 'After great pain,' says Emily Dickinson, 'a formal feeling comes'. But such displacement also happens in the middle of trauma. Picasso, Matisse's friend and rival, painted *Guernica* in 1937 immediately after hearing that the most ancient centre of the Basque Country had been bombed in the Spanish Civil War. And it was in the 1560s, at the start of the Eighty Years War, that Bruegel painted *The Massacre of the Innocents* and *The Triumph of Death*.

The British space scientist Maggie Aderin-Pocock became a different sort of inner émigré. She was a second-generation immigrant: her parents came from Nigeria and her father saw Britain as his homeland. But the move and the marriage did not work, the parents separated and the little girl went to thirteen different schools. From the age of three, she turned to the moon. 'Outer space saw me through,' she has explained. She watched *Star Trek*. She fell in love with an astronaut on the cover of a library book. She was diagnosed with dyslexia, and her teachers said she must take up nursing, but at fifteen she saved to buy a telescope from Argos. It didn't work, so she made her own; she went on to study science, maths and astronomy at Imperial College.

Wonderful determination, but also powerful displacement. Hope, curiosity and intensity projected outwards – not in a flight to unreality or to fantasy, which would have denied the real pain of her life, but to the hard work and patterning of science, maths and astronomy, where hurt was irrelevant.

W. H. Auden's elegy for Freud portrays him as wanting us to be 'enthusiastic over the night' – the unconscious, presumably

– because of 'the sense of wonder it alone has to offer'. Around Freud, the poem sees 'fauna of the night': unconscious feelings, 'dumb creatures' who are also 'exiles', longing for 'the future that lives in our power'. It is a hopeful vision, of the unconscious as the source of imagination and transformation. The power to move our lives, the poem suggests (or suggests that Freud suggested), lies inside us invisible, dumb and estranged. If we encourage it we shift our alienated feelings into the light; we give them a new life, a 'future'.

This is the dream of every artist as well as every migrant. Tennyson said that ever since he was young he had thrilled to the phrase 'far far away'. This phrase and feeling are encapsulated in the song 'Over the Rainbow', sung by Judy Garland in *The Wizard of Oz* (1939) before the screen explodes into colour. The melody begins with an octave leap. Its first two notes ('some-where') are a musical migration like an uprooting of the self. Salman Rushdie calls it an anthem for all migrants; for anyone searching for where 'the dreams you dare to dream come true'.

At the film's end, the ruby slippers carry Dorothy home while she murmurs 'there's no place like home'. But then she discovers that the people at home were also her friends in Oz. 'So Oz finally became home,' says Rushdie. 'The imagined world became the actual world.' There is indeed, the film suggests, a place 'like' home. It is the place we create in our imagination.

Fantasy is not the same as imagination. Fantasy escapes reality by denying it. Imagination transforms it, lifting us from our current life to a colour-filled place which doesn't exist but might if we can make it. And so, like Psyche, we end up with a new life. Or, like Dorothy, we get our old home back but see it with new eyes.

The poet Jalāl ad-Dīn Muhammad Balkhī, or Rumi, was born in Balkh, one of the oldest cities in the world. The Arabs called it Umm Al-Belaad, Mother of Cities; the Greeks called it Bactra. It is now in northern Afghanistan. Rumi was born there in 1207, but his family left when he was a boy, in the face of Mongol invasions. They migrated to Konya, which is now in Turkey and was then the capital of the Sultanate of Rum. Rumi, often called Maulana, the Learned One, became the leading religious scholar in Konya's dervish community.

Dar is Persian for 'door'. Just as an open door is at the heart of the Christian icon of the Transformation, so a *dervish* transforms by opening doors. What opened the door for Rumi's poems was his friendship and mystic conversation with Shams of Tabriz, a wandering dervish. Then Shams disappeared, probably because Rumi's students became jealous. Shams was found in Damascus and brought back, but one December night he was called to the back door and vanished forever. He was probably murdered. In his grief, Rumi began writing poems. The spring of his poetry was loss and the mystery of recovery. As the bonds in the DNA molecule are broken so that the proteins can replicate the genetic code, and as cells migrate in the body to heal or to generate an embryo, so in the mind the drive to re-find and re-place what has been lost is the driving force behind both creativity and migration.

A shabby Georgian house in Spitalfields, in London's East End, is a monument to the imagination and hope behind migration.

Nineteen Princelet Street is an unrestored house built in 1719 for Huguenot silkweavers escaping Catholic persecution in France. In the nineteenth century it was inhabited by Irish immigrants escaping famine, and then by Jews escaping pogroms in Eastern Europe. In 1869, the Jews made a synagogue there. New immigrants from Poland formed in it a United Friends Friendly Society to help incoming immigrants. In the twentieth century, Bengalis lived in the area around it, and later on Somalis. It is now Britain's first Museum of Immigration. Artists working with immigrant children from local schools have created in it a permanent exhibition, *Suitcases and Sanctuary*. As on Ellis Island, this commemorates successive waves of immigrants, but does so through the eyes of the East End's current children.

This modest place embodies Britain over the centuries as a place of sanctuary and new life. It tells the story of a house, a parish and a city whose walls, as we know, were built by immigrants. Very quietly, it shows how multicultural Britain – and every modern, multilayered society – was made, just as the world was made, by migration.

The Wood Where Birds Die
for Christ and Rise Again

William Wey, sir, from Devon, on pilgrimage
to Jerusalem, between two worlds like a wind
off the desert. Make sure you carry candles,
cooking tools, a lantern – and a chamber pot
in case you are too sick to go on deck.

A chandler in Venice, by St Marks, will sell you
a feather bed for three ducats and buy it back
for one and a half, if you return. Look where I retrace
my steps, on this map whose green itineraries curl
like knotweed. A pack-path pinpoints recurrent miracles

like that Saracen story of songbirds in a certain wood
who die every Passion Sunday and come back to life
on Easter Day. Here is the river which bubbles
at Epiphany, between the singing of one vesper
and the next; and here you pass into a twilight zone,

the Palace of Loss where Hope began. The world
is not what you see. This is the seat of the soul
where inner and outer meet. You reach gold
pomegranates hanging in the mist; moon-milk
in a mountain cave; wild thyme; a scallop shell.

Only Here on Earth

'Earth is the region of the fleeting moment.
Will I have to go, like the flowers that perish?
Will nothing remain, not even my songs?
Is it only here on earth we come to know
our faces?' So wrote the teenage prince

exiled to Huexotzinco. Boughs of the pecan
tree, flash of a flycatcher's wing,
indigo wool in grey spice of a Tepanec rug.
Smoke rises over Mount Atloyan like foxing
on a mirror. Distant melodies – clay flute

and ocarina; and that tricksy pass
from cello to viola in the first-time bar
of the minuet. There's no other world.
Feather gloves lie in a patch of sun
on parquet floor. The perfect moment

comes to us in its own time:
planting bulbs for spring, hearing the purr
of a stranger's orange press
or laying the table, hunting four-
tined forks in the chaos of a cutlery drawer.

Matisse Writes a Postcard after the War

He's old. He's ill. He takes black ink
and watercolour to the patio
to sketch the only wine glass on his table.

The coiled thick stem; the little row
of blobs below the bowl –
a seed-pearl choker for a very slender throat –

and a candy smudge of thinning pink
within. This need to know the worst
but hope to hold . . . Beside the pale-rose tint

of water drying in grey circlets
and the eyelash line where he sketched
the hollow bulb, he writes *6th May*

1947. This is the glass in which I drink
the fresh and perfumed wine of Alsace.
À ta santé. Tous les jours que tu n'es pas là.

Prayer on an Orphic Gold Leaf

Don't be afraid. On your way you'll pass the rivers
Mnemosyne and Lethe. Don't drink the water –
you don't need any longer to remember or forget.
You're a lily closing on its stamen, the zendrum
of a heart in tremolo. You may hear music. Whip-rays
of light converge by the bed on a Book of Psalms
left by your last visitor. You are glass, annealing
to that celestial temperature where molecules
rearrange all inner stress to perfect surface tension
in a new, fused, tough material. In the distance
you'll see one pine-tree, needle-leaves
clumped in three balls on a trunk like black bone
twisted in wind. You'll know
you are making, and coming, home.

Open Door: *after Rumi*

(for Nikos Stavroulakis)

What is not exile? Beginning is flight.
(The end is free flow of breath.)

I am inside your looking, I wait to be light.
(Rustle of water, of wind.) Cling
to the surface. Hold to the depths
as tired eyes look forward to sleep.

Why should I seek? (Rusty cliffs glow
in the lake. Tremble of aquamarine.
White mosque silhouette on the peak.)
A hand closes and opens like wings.

You are where I am. Let go
what you thought you had lost.
Praise those who wake early in grief.

Time to Fly

You go because you heard a cuckoo call. You go
                                        because
you've met someone, you made a vow, there are no
                                        more
grasshoppers. You go because the cold is coming, spring
is coming, soldiers are coming. Plague, flood, an ice age,
a new religion, a new idea. You go because the world
                                        rotates,
because the world is changing and you've lost the key.
You go because you have the kingdom of heaven in
                                        your heart
and the kingdom of hell has taken over someone else's
                                        heart.

You go because you have magnetite in your brain,
                                        thorax, tips
of your teeth. Because the grass is green
over the hill and there's gold, or more likely bauxite,
inside the hill. You go because your mother is dying
and only you can bring her the apples of the Hesperides.
You go because you need work.

You go because the astrologers say so – the sea
is calling – your best friend bought a motorbike
in America last year. You go because the streets are paved
with gold and besides, your father went when he was
                                        your age.

You go because you have seventeen children and the
                                    Lord will provide,
because your sixteen brothers have parcelled up the land
and there's none left for you. You go because the waters
                                    are rising,
an ice sheet is melting, the rivers are dry,

there are no more fish in the sea. You go because God
has given you a sign – you had a dream – the potatoes
                                    are blighted
because it is too hot, too cold, you are on a quest for
                                    knowledge
and knowledge is always beyond. You go because it's
                                    destiny,
because Pharoah won't let you light candles on Friday at
                                    sundown.
Because you are looking for

an enchanted lake, the meaning of life, a tall tree to nest in.
You go because travel is holy, because your body
is wired to go, you'd have a quite different body and
                                    different brain
if you were the sort of bird that stayed. You go
because you can't pay the rent, creditors lie in wait for
                                    your children
after school. You go because Pharoah has hogged
the oil, electricity and paraffin so all you have on your
                                    table
are candles, when you can get them.

You go because there's nothing left to hope for;
because there's everything to hope for and all life is risk.

You go because someone put the evil eye on you
and barometric pressure is dropping. You go because
                                        you can't cope
with your gift – other people can't cope with your gift –
you have no gift and the barbarians are after you.

You go because the barbarians are gone, Herod
has turned off the Internet and mobile phones, the modem
is useless and the eagles are coming. You go because the
                                        eagles
have died off with the vultures and the ancestors are
                                        angry
there's no one to clean the bones. You go in peace. You
                                        go in war.
Someone has offered you a job. You go because the dog
                                        is going too.
Because the Grand Vizier sent paramilitaries to your
                                        home last night,
you have to go quick and leave the dog behind.

You go because you've eaten the dog and that's it,
                                        there's nothing else.
You go because you've given up and might as well.
                                        Because your love
is dead – because she laughed at you. You go because
                                        she's coming with you:

it will be a big adventure and you'll live happily ever

after.

You go in hope, in faith, in haste; in high spirits,
deep sorrow, deep snow, deep shit and without question.

You pause halfway to stoke up on Omega-3 and horse

shoe crabs.

You go for phosphorus, myrtle-berries, salt. You go for oil
and pepper. You go because it was your father's dying

wish.

You go from pole to pole, you go because you can,
you sleep and mate on the wing.
You go because you need a place to shed your skin
in safety. You go with a thousand questions but you are

growing up,

growing old, moving on. Say goodbye to the might-

have-beens –

you can't step into the same river twice.
You go because hope, need and escape
are names for the same god. You go
because life is sweet, life is cheap, life is flux
and you can't take it with you. You go because you're

alive,

because you're dying, maybe dead already. You go

because you must.